Sky of Ashes,
Sea of Flames

Sky of Ashes, Sea of Flames

Kimberleigh Caitlin

INNER CIRCLE

Copyright © 1987 by Kim Ostrom Bush

This edition first published in
Great Britain in 1988 by
Inner Circle Books Limited of London
by arrangement with
The Berkley Publishing Group, New York, NY 10016

British Library Cataloguing in Publication Data

Caitlin, Kimberleigh
    Sky of ashes, sea of flames.
    I. Title
    813'.54[F]   PS3553.A394/

    ISBN 1-85018-073-3

Printed and bound in Great Britain by
Biddles Ltd, Guildford and King's Lynn

With love –
To my Father, for picking daisies and
stargazing . . .
And to Mom, who never stopped
believing

One

Meaghan O'Leary pressed her face against the rough bark of a storm-struck oak tree, gasping for breath. Her copper-bright hair fell in a silken tangle to her waist, its tumbled curls snarling on the splintered wood as she fought to banish the nightmare from her mind. It had tormented her nights for weeks, now it haunted her daylight hours as well. Her father drowning in a tempest-tossed sea, his body, blotched by disease, being hoisted over a ship's twisted rail into the murky water. Ma waiting in the tiny thatched cottage for a letter that would never come.

"No! It's only a dream," she said aloud, taking a tight rein on her emotions. "Da's alive. He's fine. He hasn't even left Wicklow yet." The words were like a spur goading her on. "I have to see him . . . reach him before he sails."

Pushing herself away from the tree, she stumbled up yet another sweep of hill. Her lungs were bursting beneath the pale gold of her bodice, and blood trickled from a gash in one bare foot, but she felt no pain except the clutching misery in her heart. Never in all her nineteen years had she felt so alone.

The Wicklow hills swam in an undulating ocean of green before her deep brown eyes, their rich swells studded with crystal lakes and tumbling streams, as she struggled to focus on the meadows spilling beneath her. Where was he? This father who had borne her on his shoulders, taught her to ride, to read and cipher though the neighbors shook their heads in disapproval at her hoyden ways.

It was then that she saw him, a stooped figure in a gray shirt. He sat on a stone, binding the flapping sole of his boot together with a strip of rag, whistling the hauntingly sweet *Eileen Aroon*. It was a sound etched in Meaghan's most treasured memories.

"Da?"

Matthew O'Leary's head jerked up, joy and disbelief lighting his face. "Meggie . . . Meggie darlin'." Tears ran down the crevasses carved in his visage from worry and toil as he enfolded his only daughter in a crushing embrace.

"You didn't even say goodbye," Meaghan whispered, burying her face in her father's shirt. "I ran all the way home from the market, but Ma said you'd already gone." She fought to keep her words from sounding like a child's accusation, but they caught, ragged-edged in her throat.

Matthew stroked her cheek with a work-rough hand. "I thought to meet ye on the road. By the time I knew I'd missed ye, it was too late to turn back. Oh, Meggie, it tore the heart out of me to leave Ireland without one last look at yer bright face."

The hurt and betrayal Meaghan had felt since she had arrived home that morning to find her father gone, melted under his loving gaze.

"I wanted to give these to you." She drew a pair of thick woolen socks out of her pocket. Stitches, dropped and retrieved by her awkward needles made little bridges across the creamy whiteness. She picked at one. "I was up most of last night to finish them. They'll keep your feet at least a little warmer until you can earn enough to get your boots fixed."

Her father took them, testing the texture between his fingers. His eyes misted. "This yarn is away too fine to make an old man socks," he said slowly. "Feels more like a shawl should be— pretty, soft with posies woven through . . ."

A tiny stab of loss stung Meaghan's eyelids, as she saw the wool as it had been, a web of beauty, her father's gift on her sixteenth birthday. She brushed it away. "You should've heard Tom grumble about the rushlight. I scarcely breathed, waiting for you to push open the loft door to hush us like you did when we were small."

"It's that used to the lad's grousing I am that I noticed it not at all." Matthew shook his head ruefully. "But if I had, I would have stopped ye. A woman grown needs a pretty, to wash the flour dust from her hands and from her heart. I know, little one, what this gift cost ye. These socks, they'll warm more than my feet in the days ahead."

Gruffly, he cleared his throat. "I have something for ye, too. I was meanin' to give it to ye sooner, but what with yer ma sick, and always about . . ." Meaghan watched as her father bent down to wrestle with the knot securing the bundle of possessions he was taking to America. "Here," he said. "This will tide ye over till I can get some money to ye." He rose, cradling a honey-brown fiddle in his arms. "Take it to the gombeen-men an' get what ye can for it. Tell 'em it's been in the hands of an O'Leary for a hundred years, an' it sings like the angels in heaven."

Meaghan bit her lip to keep from crying. "No, Da," she choked out. "Not your fiddle. It would break your heart." She didn't add that it would break her own as well.

"I wanted it to be yers, ye know. It belongs with ye, though ye've never played a note. Ye'll have to carry it here, now," he touched his fist to his heart. "But I know ye already do."

"Ma . . . does she know?"

"Nay. The music was her life an' her joy. The only thing that made her smile. Ye mustn't tell her, Meggie. She mustn't know I pawned the fiddle away."

"I won't tell her, Da," Meaghan whispered, a tear trickling down her cheek. "I promise."

"Now then, hush, darlin'," Matthew soothed, laying the fiddle in Meaghan's arms. "Don't cry. 'Tis naught but an old fiddle. We'll have a fine one in America. A fine one."

Meaghan choked back the sobs, clinging to the fiddle and her father, to the last vestiges of childhood past.

At last her father set her firmly away from him, his dark eyes probing hers. "Enough. It's trustin' ye I am to be strong. Ye'll take care of them for me? Yer ma, Tom, Brady? I love 'em so, Meggie."

Meaghan nodded, the strings of the fiddle biting into her hand as she clenched her fingers around the instrument's neck.

"Tom's a fury, I know, but he's a good heart under it all. Don't let him do somethin' foolish. God, don't let him rot in some bloody English jail." He went on, not wanting an answer, boring into her with the desperation in his eyes. "And the baby . . . just love 'im, child. If anything should happen to yer ma . . ." Eyelids, wrinkled from hours in the sun, closed as if this pain ran too deep even for Meaghan to see.

"She's better, Da. Getting stronger every day. You have to believe she's going to get well." It was a lie. They both knew it.

Without the vegetables and nourishing meats Bridget O'Leary needed to gain her strength, without hope of obtaining any more, her family was becoming ever more desperate. Three months past they had butchered the cow. It had proved a deadly gamble, for there was no more cheese, no milk, no butter to sell. And the help from England that all had thought surely must come had been as lasting and ephemeral as the mists over the moors.

"Dear God, I don't want to leave her now!" The anguish in her father's voice cut Meaghan as he wrenched her face up to meet his gaze. "America's our only hope. If I stay we'll all die!"

"I know, Da. I know." For two years the potatoes had rotted in the pits, slimy, black, their stench hanging like a pall of death over the land. The harvest of 1846 had been a disaster the likes of which Ireland had never seen, the winter after a horror of empty cook pots, emptier stomachs. And now a whole nation was starving to death, but nobody gave a damn.

"Ye have to promise me, Meaghan, that ye'll keep the family together till I can send money from America. Swear to me on all that is holy."

"I swear, Da. When next you see us we'll be waving from a ship's deck. Won't Tom love to go to sea?" But instead of the smile she had hoped for in reminding her father of the thirteen-year-old's outrageous cajolings to accompany him on the voyage, an even greater sadness creased his brow.

"Damn the times that put the yoke of a man on a child's shoulders and tears families to bits and pieces scattered to the wind."

Meaghan put her hand in his. "I'll take care of them for you, Da. You always said I was strong as Saint Catherine on the wheel. We'll be together soon."

She heard the baying of distant hounds, felt a sudden rush of tension shoot through her father as her fingers were crushed painfully in his grasp. His face was hard as granite, a murderous fury raging in his eyes. "Da . . . what . . ."

"Damn them! May God cast the cursed bastards to the devil!"

Startled, afraid of the sudden change in him, Meaghan followed his gaze to where three horsemen leapt a stone fence, a symphony of color and grace. Even from a distance, the opulence of their riding habits, the rich velvet jackets and immaculate breeches, marked them as the conquerors, the wealthy, the English. As they skimmed across the heath, Meaghan stared at her father's face. Hatred had mingled with very real fear, a fear that seemed to explode when her father's eyes fell on her.

He pulled her behind him, as if to shield her from some unknown danger. "I'm takin' ye home," he growled, snatching up his bundle and taking her roughly by the arm. "Be quick now."

Her eyes widened. "You have to catch the ship. I don't understand . . ."

"The ship can damn well wait! I have to get ye safe, child."

"I ran all this way alone. There's naught to fear."

"Only the spawn of the devil himself. Radcliffe, Meggie. That be his lordship. Colin Radcliffe."

Meaghan's mouth fell open in astonishment. So that was Colin Radcliffe, their ruthless landlord. He had returned from England after three years' absence. Why? To bleed from his tenants rent they could not pay?

She stared with all the fascination of a field mouse at the talons of an eagle, as the black-haired rider reined in his mount. Revulsion crawled up Meaghan's spine as she felt his eyes rake her. He spun the massive black stallion in a tight circle, reaching out his hand toward her to grasp the air, as if to pluck her like a stem of grass, then rode, laughing, after the others.

Whispered tales flooded back to her, tales of her distant cousin, pretty Maeve O'Donal, who had paraded around in silks for months, riding in fine carriages, then suddenly hidden in the loft of her father's cottage, belly bulging with Radcliffe's bastard. She had died in childbirth, and still her unearthly screams plagued Meaghan's dreams. Brave, fiery Sioban O'Brian, who had spit in his lordship's face, only to find her family's cottage leveled, and her brother, Michael, dead. Radcliffe's treachery had driven her over the brink of insanity. She had thrown herself into a well and drowned.

Meaghan shivered. She would have taken Da's scythe to Radcliffe if he had touched one of her own. He was no god, no devil. Or was he?

"Meggie, on with ye now." Her father pushed her along, holding her elbow. "We'll take the—"

"Da, stop. You can't come with me." She pulled away. "If you miss the *Irish Rose* you'll have to wait weeks, maybe months to book passage on another vessel. Even then it might be too late to make the crossing, what with the threat of winter gales bottling up the harbors. We have scarce enough to make it through the winter now. If you wait . . ."

Death. The word hung, unspoken between them. Horror on the open road. There was no money to buy spring's seeds, no livestock to sell, no way to raise the fare to keep Radcliffe's rentmongers at bay. Eviction. Death. The sentence was the same.

"Meaghan, ye know nothin' of a man like Colin Radcliffe. Ye don't—"

"I won't need to know anything about him, for I'll not so much as see his boots. They're on a hunt, and it's not likely the poor fox's path will cross mine. If I do hear them coming, I'll take to the fields. You taught me every bush and stone on the way. They'll not find me."

Matthew O'Leary raked his fingers through his hair. "It'd be just like ye to chase the fox yerself an' hide it in the folds of yer skirt, or give the lord of the manor the sharp side o' yer tongue for worryin' the beastie."

"My soul to God, I'll do nothing foolish, Da. They're probably to the next county by now. I'll be all right." The curve of her chin jutted stubbornly.

Matthew touched it with the tip of his finger. "Sure and ye will. It's pityin' Lord Radcliffe, I am, if he makes the mistake of tanglin' with ye." The attempt to lighten his voice failed, as his forehead puckered with anxiety. "Take the far road. Ye'll have to stop at the gombeen-man's to sell the fiddle. Then follow the stream home."

"I will."

Holding her at arm's length, her father looked deep into her eyes. "Ye make my heart proud, Meaghan O'Leary. I'll be thankin' God every step of my journey that he let me look upon yer face." He clutched her to him, stroking her fiery hair.

"I love you, Da," she whispered.

"And I ye, child. And I ye."

The tears she had willed to stay hidden surged to the surface. She was frightened now, suddenly and terribly alone. Her father cupped her chin, his eyes radiating infinite strength, infinite love. "Hush, now, little one," he murmured. "Let the last thing I see of all I love in Ireland be yer face. Smiling."

She never knew if he looked back. The sun's glare blinded her to all but his silhouette as he shouldered his burden and trudged up the hill. Meaghan prayed that he had looked at her one last time, prayed as she stood in the middle of the road. She waited there an eternity, lips curved into a trembling smile, until at last his mournful whistle faded into stillness.

"The kettle's next! I swear it is!" Grace MacFadden vowed, her green eyes blazing as she hurled her wooden spoon at Sean O'Fallon's head. He dodged, one sun-bronzed hand shooting out to catch the missile as it whizzed past his ear. His laughter filled the room. Deep brown, tinged with gold, his unruly hair tumbled across his forehead, capturing the rays of the afternoon sun as they slanted through the window. He wheeled, grinning broadly at the lanky woman who could only be beautiful to loving eyes.

"You lift anything heavier than a teacup and I'll have Liam lock you in your room until your lying in," he warned her. "You'd better start obeying doctor's orders, Grace MacFadden. I'm used to getting my way."

"Humph! As though a man born could make me do what I don't have a mind to!" Grace grumbled, running a peeling, red hand over her swollen belly. "All this blather about me havin' a babe! Much good *ye'll* do me if ye die of the scurvy afore it's born!" She yanked a chair from beneath the sturdy table and banged its legs onto the hard-packed floor.

"Sit ye down an' eat ye surly whelp or I promise ye I'll—"

Sean's eyes, crystal blue as a mountain stream, sparkled with merriment as he warded off her threat, raising his hands palms up in surrender, his smile all the more wrenchingly beautiful because of its rarity. "All right, all right!" he said. "Far be it from me to argue with a MacFadden! I'll take the bread and cheese you offered and eat it as I walk. *I will!*" Sean answered her snort of disbelief. "But you humor me as well. Liam and Annie will be back soon. You should lie down a bit and rest."

"Aye, and I should meet Queen Victoria, too, but it's not likely I'll do so," Grace muttered, splitting a loaf of hot bread with her knife.

"She'd like you, I'd wager. Victoria, I mean," Sean said, taking a chunk of the crust and sinking even white teeth into it.

"Like me! I'd give that Englishwoman the cut o' my cloth, I would! An' she'd not be pleased with its fitting!" Grace pressed the bread and a hunk of cheese into his hand. He slipped them into his pocket. Grace glared. "It'll do ye no good in there, Sean

O'Fallon. Ye'll forget it an' it'll be food for the mice."

"Grace, how could you even suggest I—"

"It's four years now I been sewin' the buttons on yer trappin's an' ye have yet to bring me a coat with empty pockets. Ye'll not eat it, I know. But I've done my best to keep yer soul in yer body."

"You've done that more than once, haven't you?" The sudden ache in Sean's heart crept around the edges of his voice. Grace looked away, but he knew without seeing that there was a troubled light in her usually tranquil eyes.

Sean cupped his hand, dipping it into the wooden bowl filled with spring blossoms Grace's little daughter had picked that morning. They floated free, droplets of water glistening on their jewel-hued petals. He held one up. It clung to his fingers.

"You think of her . . . still," Grace said softly.

Sean walked to the window, trying to shut away the face her words had conjured in his mind. Bracing his arms on either side of the window frame, he stood, lost in silence. Muscles rippled, stiffened, beneath the thin chambray of his shirt. "It doesn't matter *now* does it?" he said bitterly.

"Sean, what happened was Alanna's doin', not yers. Ye have to quit blamin' yerself. Yer a man at the dawn of life, an' ye've love in yer heart that would make any woman want ye. It's been three years, lad."

"No. It's been a lifetime." Harsh, unyielding, the lines deepening at the sides of his mouth, he stared past her into nothing. "And it's going to be even longer."

"Don't do this to yerself." Grace caught his hands, forcing him to look at her. "We love ye, me an' Liam, like ye were born our own blood. It's wastin' yer life ye are, grievin' for somethin' ye can never have."

He pulled his hands away from her, pacing to the other side of the room, then turned, his face hardened again into its accustomed bitter mask. "Give up, Grace. Let be. What could I offer a woman except pain?" He grabbed his coat, slinging it over his shoulder in an air of dismissal, but Grace would not be dissuaded.

"Ye could offer her what ye give every one of the poor souls ye treat. Strength an' courage an' gentleness."

"Gentleness?" Sean sneered, the word a mockery. He strode to the door, pausing in the rectangle of meadow that it framed, feet spaced apart as though awaiting a heavy blow. "Do you ever think about her, Grace?"

He could hear the shifting of bare feet on the floor, the ticking of the clock on the mantel.

"Aye. I think of Alanna DuBois."

"And when you do, do you remember the day you dragged me half-dead from the carriage circle in front of Radbury Manor?" Her silence was his answer. "You should have left me there."

"Sean." Grace reached out to comfort him, but he was already gone—fleeing from memories he could never escape.

Fifty shades of green were blended on the palette of the moors but Sean drew no pleasure from their beauty. Even the sun seemed to mock him, burning with a brilliance that made last night's storm seem like a dream.

Alanna. God, why did she still haunt him, torment him? Beautiful, spoiled Alanna with her childlike caprices, her temper, her full, pouting mouth begging to be kissed. The woman he had loved. The woman he had killed.

He clenched his teeth, pushing himself with long, hard strides up the steepest part of the embankment, welcoming the burning in the muscles of his hard thighs.

He had been shaken from sleep by a frantic girl who had run thirteen miles from an outlying farm long before the first birds welcomed dawn, then ridden at breakneck speed across the countryside to set the girl's father's broken leg. A nasty fracture made worse by the threat of infection, because the exposed bone had dug into the mud beneath the wagon wheel that had crushed it. He had left the horse, tied in the family's byre, so that if the man's condition worsened the girl could reach him in all haste.

All haste. He closed his eyes, remembering the feel of the horse surging between his legs, the branches tearing at skin and clothes, the feel of Colin Radcliffe's fist slamming into his face again and again as five burly men held him pinioned against the manor house wall.

How many times did he have to finger the memory like rosary beads, in some kind of litany of pain and guilt? His eyes narrowed as he forced the thoughts away, fighting to rebuild the wall he had constructed around his inner self to keep such ghosts at bay.

It served no purpose to dredge up the past, to think of what might have been. Alanna was dead. He could never tell her the truth ... tell her he ... *love*. Sean grimaced. A twisting, bitter thing, it had destroyed them both.

Sean grasped a tree branch, the coarse bark worried by some beast and left to hang, dying, raw, white wood. Alanna ... she had all but driven him mad.

A sudden animal instinct sent Sean lunging to safety as the earth beneath him buckled, baring a frame of slender saplings roofed with twigs and sod.

"No ... wet ..." He heard the words, muffled, indistinct, as though blurred by a tongue parched and swollen from thirst. "... my babe ..."

A cloying dread trickled ice through Sean's veins. He had seen them before, scalps, dens, warrens, dug into the ground for the homeless to die in when their own cottages had been leveled by unfeeling landlords and their bodies had been made skeletal by blight. But a babe. He shuddered. To find a babe in one of these muddy holes ...

He vaulted into the ditch, his lean hand jarring one of the saplings jabbed into its top. Debris rained down on the tattered forms beneath it. The babe made no sound.

His dread deepening, Sean peered into the dim interior of the makeshift shelter. Mud clung in heavy brown globs to sticks, their ends splintered like the branch he had held but a moment before. The gentle warmth of the sun had no home here, not seeping in to ward off the chill, as though death had already claimed it.

Sean's mouth set in a grim line as he edged forward, crouching his long body into a seemingly impossible compactness beneath the steady roof. Drops of water still clinging to the rich loam dropped and ran down his neck under his collar. He arched his head back, blotting the wetness with his shirt.

The moans came clearer now, as his fingertips brushed a body that was at once fire and ice. "Help me ... please ..."

Sean felt the words clutch him, as though each faint syllable dug into his flesh. "I will," he said. "Hush now." With the greatest of care he eased his arms under swollen knee joints and narrow shoulders. Protecting the shivering form from the muddy floor with his body, he slid her out into the sunshine.

It was as if the rains themselves had washed all the color from the hair that clung in a damp web to the hollow cheeks of the girl who now rested against his chest. She was no more than fifteen, he was certain. And damn, she was cold. Sean felt the raging fever burning through the thin muslin chemise that stuck in transparent wetness to breasts no larger than buds.

Stripped to this torn garment? God, what could have possessed her? It was then that he saw it, clasped in arms scarcely more than skin-covered bones, a tiny rag-wrapped bundle. Threadbare, the girl's brown woolen dress skirt wound about it, so tightly that not an inch of flesh showed beneath its folds. Yet Sean knew in a gut-churning instant what it held. "Couldn't keep her dry...rain always rain..." Huge, glassy with fever, the girl's eyes pleaded with him from bruised circles.

"You've done all that you could," Sean said, wrapping his coat around her quaking body. "I'll take care of you now."

"She's so cold..." Her eyes found his again.

"I know," Sean said softly.

"Make her warm again. Please make her warm..."

Sean's jaw tightened as he slid his fingers beneath the sodden cloth, peeling a corner away from the still form.

"Sleep, babe, good babe..." The girl crooned, trailing her fingertips over sparse blond hair. Sean fought not to recoil as the stench singed the insides of his nostrils. God. Dear God.

With infinite gentleness, Sean smoothed the rag back in place, his arms tightening around her. "It's going to be all right," he murmured.

"Danny...he promised he'd come back for us...said he'd walk all Ireland if he had to, to find work...but he didn't come home...He didn't...I had to look for him...find him..." Her voice broke. "Danny...have you seen Danny?"

Sean closed his eyes. How many men like Danny had he seen straggling across the country in hopes of work, only to end up huddled, weak, dying in poorhouses so crowded and full of disease they were little more than a resting place before the grave. Or worse still, left as nameless corpses, their bodies stacked like cordwood by the side of the road, families never hearing, never knowing. He looked down at the girl he held.

Her wasted face was crumpled and gray. Tears oozed weakly from the corners of her eyes. "Couldn't feed her...my baby... clawed at my breast..." Threading his hand through her hair, Sean pressed her into the curve of his shoulder. He swayed, trying to quiet her with the rhythm of his body.

"I took good care of her...she was cold, hungry...my skirt

...it wasn't warm enough. She kept crying...looking at me with Danny's eyes...I had to wrap her tighter, don't you see. To keep her warm...I had to."

"Hush, now, hush." Sean heard his voice from somewhere outside himself as the truth, stark, pathetic, tore at him.

"She's all we have...Danny and me..." Her fingers caressed the skirt-shrouded child. "He says...she's going to wear silks...someday..."

Sean raked his dark hair back from his forehead, disregarding the strange wetness he felt on his palm. "She'll be beautiful," he said. Carefully he slid his hand underneath the tattered covering wound about the baby. Already a cold wet oval marked where the child had been. His coat was little enough warmth for the ailing girl without becoming wet as well.

The instant his hands made to lift the child, the girl's grip tightened convulsively, her eyes clouding with distrust.

"It's all right," Sean soothed, his voice low and gentle. "I'm just going to lay her down for a little."

"No!" The girl's eyes darted from Sean to the baby. "Make her warm *here*. I have to hold her. I promised I'd keep her with me." Her bloodless lips quivered.

"She'll be right beside you, lass. You can reach out your hand and touch her."

"You...you'll take her away! You won't give her back to me!"

"I won't hurt the baby. I swear to God."

A new wave of tremors tortured the girl's slight form. Sean's brows met in a harsh line. He wouldn't let her die out here, like an animal, though she'd been forced by a world of cruel and greedy fools to live like one. The girl collapsed against him, exhausted by the fit of trembling. "There now, rest," Sean said. "The babe will be right here."

He had scarcely had time to ease the child onto the grass before the girl sprang to awareness, her face that of a wild thing.

"You promised! You promised you wouldn't take her!" She shrieked, clawing for the bundle. "Danny, help me! Danny!" Sean caught her to him as she tried to escape his grasp, but she fought like one possessed.

Great sobs shook her wasted body while she struggled against him. "Give her to me!" she screamed, tearing at his hands. "Give me back my baby!"

Still Sean held her, oblivious to the nails raking his skin, the small fists flailing. "Damn." He gritted his teeth against the agony in her cries. "Oh, damn how I wish I could." Blue, icy with hatred, his eyes burned a path to the sky where the sun blazed on merciless and unyielding as the God who could still make him feel.

A slender spike pierced deep into Meaghan's palm, tearing from its mooring on the coarse bark of the gnarled blackthorn tree. She winced, biting back a cry of pain, and fought to gain a foothold as she renewed her grip on the fiddle and struggled up, up into the tree's sheltering branches.

Fool! She had been such a fool, ignoring her father's warning to hasten home, dreading the lost look on her mother's face, Tom's glowering. And now . . .

Her heart hammered in her breast, matching in rhythm the pounding of fast approaching hooves. Radcliffe.

She tore her skirt loose from thorns that seemed alive, pulling her downward, cutting off her escape. The cloth gave, with what was to her ears a deafening sound. Like a gold banner the scrap of fabric swayed on its thorn staff.

She paused, anchoring herself with her elbow, the other hand reaching toward it in a futile gesture. There was no time.

With one last, desperate glance at the thing that could betray her, she levered herself onto the topmost limb, praying it would support her.

Meaghan peered down through the leaves at the crazy quilt patches of ground beneath her, freezing like a cat in a snare as the sleek midnight coat of Colin Radcliffe's stallion blotted out the heather.

Her fingers tightened on the branch they held, as she marked the soft clops of the hooves as they fell. Close, he was so close she could drop a spiney twig into the gap between his starched collar and his neck. And he, from his massive horse, could reach up and . . .

White-hot shards of pain shot up her arm from the spike imbedded in her flesh as her hands clenched about the branch. Seconds, only seconds, and he would be past.

Sudden, savage, the oath sent Meaghan's heart leaping into her throat, choking her with a solid lump of fear.

"Damn you! Damn you, Pinkerton!" The tall, black-haired

rider yanked back cruelly on his stallion's reins, halting him directly beneath her perch. Radcliffe. His voice was as malevolent as the man who owned it. She steeled herself, waiting for his hand to close about her ankle, waiting for his weight to drag her down. She wouldn't let him see she was afraid . . . She wouldn't.

"I tell you, Pinkerton, she's nearby. I know she is," Radcliffe snarled. "That wench didn't crawl out of some wine bottle. A cask of Alicio's finest couldn't make me imagine such a body, and hair . . . red as the sins I intend to commit with her!"

"Bah! There was no one but that broken down old soddie, Col," another voice countered. "He was hot for your blood all right, but not between the sheets!"

"Scum, riffraff," Radcliffe growled. "He'll not be so arrogant when he finds out what I have in store for the girl!"

"I tell you, Col, there *was* no girl. Even if there was, if she's anything to that old man we saw she's probably scrawny as a half-starved hound. I like my women soft underneath me, with flesh enough to pinch if they set up a cry."

"And even if they don't, eh?" the third horseman taunted, jabbing the other with his crop.

"There were no bones poking out on this tempting morsel, I can assure you," Radcliffe sneered. "And the blight, well, it has its advantages. A woman will do most anything to keep the souls of her loved ones in their bodies. That soddie had a hungry look about him for all his glaring. If the girl is any kin to him, she'll crawl to me on her belly begging for my leavings."

"More likely she'll slice *your* belly open, Col. But if she's half as delectable as you insist, she might be worth the risk. As long as she didn't slip and sever any, shall we say, vital parts."

Meaghan felt her stomach churn. Her . . . they were looking for her. She remembered her father's fear, the way he had pulled her behind him as Radcliffe stripped her with his eyes. She bit her lip. In all her life she had known only the indulgent smiles of her father, Ma's head shaking in resigned disapproval, Tom's temper with its clean, hot blaze. Never fear. Never this cruelty, cold and deliberate.

Would she surrender to a man like Colin Radcliffe in ransom for the lives of her mother and brothers? Was she strong enough *to* do it? Was she strong enough *not* to?

She jerked aside, barely stifling a scream as something

swooped past her face, screeching in a cacophony of angry sound.

Her breath caught in horror as she felt the neck of the fiddle start to slip from her grasp. She clutched at it, catching it by the carved spiral scroll. The shining wood rasped across the twisting maze of thorns, the hollow sound echoing again and again in Meaghan's ears.

Meaghan couldn't move, couldn't breathe as Radcliffe's face angled up. Thin as a knife blade, his nose cleaved his face; his lips, dark red, slashed beneath it.

Meaghan's own jaw set in defiant courage. He would see her. And when he did there would be naught but disdain for his kind in her eyes.

At that instant, the bird renewed its agitated cries, brushing in flight a cup of twigs in the blackthorn's lowest branch. Three speckled eggs nestled in its lining of soft grass and feathers. The creature darted again, drawing Radcliffe's gaze.

"Damned noise!" Radcliffe snarled. His quirt lashed out at the bird, narrowly missing. Soulless eyes fastened on the nest. The quirt flashed out again, sending the eggs and their shelter scattering to the ground.

The bird screeched, her wings beating helplessly as Radcliffe raked his stallion's already scored shoulder with the leather-wrapped rod. The beast snorted, its huge hooves cutting the turf, crushing what remained of the nest into the earth, as it tried to escape the pain.

Meaghan stared, dazed, as Colin Radcliffe threw back his head and laughed. "Well, you fools," he said. "I'll not get between that wench's legs by spending the afternoon under this tree. I swear, I'm that hot for her I'd take her if she was the Blessed Virgin herself!"

The thunder of the horsemen retreating gave Meaghan no ease of mind. She stared at the distraught linnet, still skittering around the remains of her nest. The bird had saved her.

Slowly, carefully, she made her way down the tree. A myriad of tiny scratches stung her legs and arms, and half of Ma's patch box wouldn't repair the damage to her dress. But only the damage to the fiddle mattered. Long streaks of white were gouged out of the instrument's belly, the gleaming of the varnish only accentuating the scars.

Meaghan blinked back the tears. She wouldn't sell it. She wouldn't let a man like Colin Radcliffe rob her of this last, tangible link to a happier, safer time. When she brought Ma and Tom and Brady to America, the fiddle would be in her hand. Her chin lifted in determination. She would hold it up over the ship's twisted rail, and Da would make it sing.

The fiddle jarred her hand. Spikes of pain stabbed her. Gingerly, she ran her fingers over her palm. The thorn's end was circled in a ring of blood. She pushed down with the nails of her thumb and finger, gripping the slippery base of the thorn.

"Christ and his saints, don't let me swear now!" She muttered the curse her father had always used to tease her mother, then pulled the thorn free. Pain pulsed up her arm with each drop of blood that welled from the wound.

Meaghan closed her eyes. It needed to be cleaned, that much she knew. Ma had always been adamant about keeping injuries pure. On cuts she smoothed a scraping of the mold she nurtured in a jar by the chimney corner, and bound it onto the wound with a clean strip of rag. Meaghan smiled weakly at the thought of her mother, even now in the midst of the great famine hoarding her bit of bread to "feed" to that jar.

How she had railed at Da when he had insisted that since the jar felt no hunger pangs, it could very well do without a meal. Meaghan fingered the frayed edge of one of the tears in her dress, even the ghost of her smile vanishing.

What would Ma say to her, late as she was, her hand cut, her dress torn to ruins from climbing a tree? Should she tell her about the three men, about Radcliffe, his threats? No. Better that Ma think her careless, thoughtless, than to add yet another burden to her thin shoulders. Tears pricked Meaghan's eyes. If only it didn't hurt so much to know how easily Ma would accept a tale of selfish indulgence.

If only Da could be home to tug on her coppery curls, and smile that secret smile of his that understood all, forgave all.

Meaghan blinked back the tears that stung her eyes. Da wasn't home, wasn't ever coming back to the only home she could remember. The tiny cottage with its slope-roofed loft, her mattress tucked under the eaves, Ma's Saint Bridget's cross woven of clean gold straw; it was as if they already were lost to her, bundled in the pack slung over Da's shoulder.

She looked out over the rim of the valley. She had to get

home, regardless of the confrontation with her mother that was sure to come. Radcliffe and his cohorts had ridden west, the direction she should be traveling as well. She would have to go south, then double back when she reached the ruins of St. Michael's. It was not the way Da had sent her, being less familiar, yet the path she would take would be safer. There were places to hide, silent and still.

Shadows stretched across the heather like arms welcoming night. No matter how she hurried now, it would be late when she reached the cottage, well past dark. Pushing ahead, Meaghan walked with quick strides. She was not afraid of the dark or the night things creeping, only of the man who might be there, lurking, beneath its velvet cloak.

Meaghan laid the fiddle in a nest of grass, and knelt beside the hidden stream, letting the crystal waters burble over her injured hand. For two hours she had kept pace, traveling quickly, stealthily, seeing no one. Yet instead of serving to calm her, the unnatural silence tightened the coil of unease in her chest with each step. Something was not right. She could feel the danger as though it were a cat's paw toying before the kill.

Radcliffe had told the men he wanted her. How badly? She was no beauty in the current sense of the word, that much she knew. Her cheeks glowed with a rosy hue that never faded to an "interesting pallor," and her features were far too animated to play the languishing maiden.

If he failed in his current search would Radcliffe forget about her and turn his lust to another? Or would he hunt her down ruthlessly as he had Sioban O'Brian? It was certain that if he did discover the tiny thatched cottage, barren of all but hope, he would think no more of crushing the O'Learys than he had of smashing the linnet's nest.

Da's words flooded back to her, Radcliffe's savagery bringing to her a new understanding of the fear that had been in his face. "Ye have to think with yer head, colleen, instead of yer heart," Da had warned the night before he left, the light of the peat fire casting shadows across his craggy countenance. "There's such a way ye have of plungin' in first an' thinkin' after. Lovin' isn't enough. It won't keep ye all alive. Ye must be more than brave, now, Meggie. Ye must be wise."

Wise. Meaghan gave her reflection a rueful smile. Her tip-tilted eyes, a warm spicy brown, gave her face a pixyish look. Her nose was sprinkled with cinnamon freckles, her full lips were indented in the corners as though from constant smiling. All gave a picture of a child who loved mischief more than mending, running wild in the fields more than sharing girlish confidences behind the nunnery.

She had been labeled a good many things in her lifetime by Father Loughlin and the sisters at St. Colmcille's, but wise had never been one of them.

Piercing, terrifying, the keening cry shattered her reverie. The hair on Meaghan's scalp prickled, a chill racing down her spine, as she leapt to her feet.

"My baby . . . give me back my baby . . ." Meaghan fought the urge to cover her ears with her hands. Terror, there was ungodly terror in the woman's screams, terror of a depth that Meaghan knew, even now, she had never experienced.

Her senses were taut as a bowstring, tingling, jumping as she raced to the brink of the hill. She should run, run away, as far as her feet could carry her. Why, then, was she cresting the hill, peering down the embankment?

She paused but a heartbeat to take in the scene across the ribbon of road.

Dark hair, features shadowed in the sunset, shoulders broad beneath a white shirt, a man battled to contain a half-naked woman who looked more dead than alive. Radcliffe! Fury welled up in Meaghan, sweeping from her mind all vows to her father. He stole their land, their crops, their lives, and still he demanded more, not even allowing death to be unsullied by his touch.

Pain knifed deep into her hand as she gripped the end of a thick branch, twisting it from a nearby tree. She was beyond feeling it now, beyond caring.

"No more," Meaghan swore, tears scalding her cheeks. "No more."

She gave no thought to her father's warnings, nor to the family waiting at the cottage in the valley.

Primitive and tearing, the woman's shrieks closed like claws about Meaghan. She plunged, downward, into the ditch.

Two

Afterward, Meaghan would always remember hands. Hands, greenish, grotesquely swollen, clinging to a bit of rag that trailed from the babe's swaddling. Hands, sinewy and bronzed, manacling fragile wrists. Her own hands hurtling the makeshift club down toward the man's dark head.

He turned, his strongly chiseled features incredulous just an instant, as he tried to avoid the blow. Wood gashed flesh, the sensation horrible as it coursed up Meaghan's arm. The man pitched forward, a rush of crimson bloodying his hand as he swiped at his temple. He sprawled across the woman's slight form and lay, unmoving. Relief and a heady exultation swept over Meaghan. At last she had been able to strike back for the blows Colin Radcliffe had dealt her family.

She grasped a limp arm to drag him off the girl. "Swine!" she muttered. "English sw—"

The curse died on her lips as a leg shot out, sweeping her feet from under her. Air exploded from her lungs as she struck the earth.

Instantly, the stranger was upon her, one heavily muscled thigh flung across her.

She had a moment to take in the stunning realization that this was not Colin Radcliffe. A moment, too, to know it mattered not who he was, only that he was stealing the child and raping the babe's pathetic mother.

Raping her . . . She felt the heat of his skin against her, his breath . . . terror.

A savage oath ripped from his mouth as she slammed her knee up, narrowly missing his groin, and she knew the desperation of a trapped animal.

"You're only making it worse! Damn you!" He bore his weight down, giving no quarter. "Lie still!"

In impotent fury, she bucked her hips up, trying to loosen his hold on her, but even as she did so, she knew her struggle was futile.

Lean and hard, the body crushing hers was honed to perfection. Granite bulges of calves and thighs trapped her legs. The planes of his stomach flattened the soft swell of her own.

Tears of frustration stung her eyes. Unwanted sensations sparked under her skin, tiny flares that snapped like brush fires. Her heart surged beneath the flatly corded muscles of his chest, his skin burning through her bodice to brand the rosy crests beneath.

Revulsion gripped her, for this man and all he stood for, for the betrayal of her own body.

She sank her teeth deep into the flesh of his shoulder, the small white points cutting through the chambray of his shirt to leave a ring of crimson stains.

"Sweet Christ!" He jerked away at the unexpected pain.

Meaghan pressed the slight advantage, twisting from beneath him.

"You little fool!" He caught her wrists, fingers tightening until needles shot through her hands.

Cerulean fire blazed from the depths of his eyes, inflaming the most intimate parts of her. He disgusted her. . .

Helpless, a hardened lump in her throat, she searched for a word, any word, bad enough to call him. "You bastard!" she spat. "You filthy bastard!" It was a curse, pure venom, but in no way was she prepared for his reaction.

Bitterness eclipsed the man's eyes, bitterness and pain that shocked Meaghan in their intensity before they were shuttered away.

His jaw, hard before, seemed cast in stone. "You'll have to find a new epithet to wound me with, my hell-cat," he grated. "That label lost its claws long ago. The name bastard was mine since the day I was born."

A coolness in the air chilled her as he rolled away. She sensed her words had reached deep inside him, scraping an old, still-festering wound. She had to fight the crazy impulse to comfort him.

"You rape the dying!" she flung out, astonished that she felt compelled to justify her attack. "You use her babe to threaten—"

"I'm a doctor."

Meaghan felt as if she'd been kicked in the stomach. She pushed herself up from the turf. "The English are uncommon good liars. How do I know it's the truth you tell? How—"

"My name is Sean O'Fallon. Half English. And no one has more of a right to hate Victoria's lapdogs than I." His upper lip curled sardonically. "Would you care to examine the name tooled in my medical pouch?"

"But the screaming . . ."

"She's delirious with fever."

"Fever?" Meaghan froze.

"Typhus. Black fever. Road fever. Go ahead," Sean sneered, as though he read her thoughts. "Run. You've not touched her."

Winter had finally faded, but still Meaghan heard the whispered stories of cottages in the west peopled by the dead, families unshriven, unburied. Now fever had come to Wicklow . . .

"Easy, isn't it," he goaded, "to face danger in a blaze of anger, weapons flying? More difficult to risk your body rotting with disease." He seemed to be watching for something in her face, finding it, she was sure, in the flicker of fear she could not wholly conceal.

She scrambled to her feet, unable to tear her eyes from the woman who now lay curled around her baby.

"We can't . . . can't leave her here. There must be somewhere we can take her."

"And where would you suggest? Colin Radcliffe's manor house?" His hands settled on his lean hips, as he stared out across the heath. The clean lines of his face were the work of a master, etched by life, bitterness carved therein.

Meaghan looked down at the crooning woman, then looked back at Sean O'Fallon. "We'll take her to my house. My ma just had a babe. She could wet nurse—"

"Perfect. Just perfect. Then I'd have a house full of fever victims instead of only one." He started to rake back his hair, cursing savagely as he collided instead with the still bleeding gash in his temple.

"I didn't think . . ." Meaghan said in a small voice. Her father had depended on her, yet in the space of a few hours she had brought Radcliffe on her scent and the threat of deadly illness to her loved ones.

"No. You didn't think. Are you even capable of the process?" His eyes bored into her. "Let me return in kind the 'compliment' you paid me earlier by saying that the poor souls who have the misfortune of relying on your good sense have my sincerest sympathy—be they husband, parents, or, God forbid, children."

Had he been an expert marksman, he could not have delivered the thrust to cause more pain. She swung her hand at his face, wanting desperately to slap away his derisive sneer, but he caught it easily, hauling her against him. "Hoping your hand will accomplish what the club did not?"

Her eyes blurred with tears she vowed she would not shed. "I couldn't leave her there. Anymore than you could leave her."

The arms that had crushed her grew gentle. "Don't," he said.

"Don't? Don't what? Don't cry? Don't feel? Aye, it's not convenient, not safe! Ask them, ask the fat merchants drooling on their bellies, the English eating their hot buttered scones! My mother, ask my mother, who says it's better strangers should die than us." Tears started then, burning her cheeks, burning her spirit.

Sean lifted his hand, unable to stop it from tracing the subtle beauty, the courage in the face turned up to him. His fingertips whispered of their own volition over the pliant warmth of her lips. Their ripeness trembled beneath his touch, striking through him like an arrow's shaft. He wanted to back away. Couldn't. "I'm sorry. I had no right. I don't even know your name."

"Meaghan. Meaghan O'Leary."

She leaned against him, the silken cascade of her hair washing over him like liquid flame wherever it brushed his skin, searing him more surely than the blaze he had likened it to. Searing him with remembered pain. Alanna. He had not felt in his blood this soul-piercing sweetness, since the morning before he had found Alanna in bed with . . .

"Damn!" Sean tore himself away from the trembling girl, bitterness twisting his face, as he quelled the swift, unwelcome flare of desire, furious with himself, with her that he could even so briefly have felt it at all. "I've no time to waste playing nursemaid to a whining child."

Scarlet stained the cheeks that had flushed so delicately at his touch. Yet despite the hurt and confusion in her rosewood eyes, there was steel in her voice, a steel that matched his own. "You can be sure, Doctor O'Fallon, that I need no help from a—" She stopped, following his stricken gaze.

"No! Oh, sweet Christ, no!" He shoved Meaghan out of his way, running the steps it took to get to the sick woman's side. He pressed his hand to the side of her throat, searching for even a flutter of life. It was gone. He had let her die, let her die without even a hand to hold on this godforsaken hill. She had died while he had lain atop Meaghan, felt her stir desire in him, desire to tame the wood-witch that taunted him from her eyes.

"Sean . . ."

Savagely, he knocked away the hand Meaghan had laid on his shoulder. He wheeled to face her. Even in anger he was stung by her beauty, the true grief he could read in her face. That this woman he didn't even know could touch him so, breach his defenses, incensed him.

"See what your fit of temper has gained?" he snarled. "She could have had the dignity of dying in a warm bed, hot broth to ease the emptiness of her stomach, food she's not had in God knows how long. But no, I had to deal instead with a spoiled brat, who bashes me on the head and then cries when she discovers she's not the savior of the hills."

"I never thought . . . I didn't mean . . . I . . ." Meaghan twisted her hands in her skirts, needing to hold something, anything, to keep from being swept away by the fierce light of those implacable blue eyes.

"You want to help this woman? Fine. Then leave. Turn around and walk to wherever the hell it was you were going before we had the devil's own luck to catch your eye."

He had beaten her, though he'd not raised a hand against her. Her whole body ached with the pain of his condemnation. She sank onto the grass beside the woman and child. "The baby," she said, "at least let me give it a chance. I'll take good care of it."

"The babe is dead."

"You can't be sure of that. Just because the mother had fever doesn't mean . . ." She raised the child, as if to shelter it from Sean's words, her soul screaming to deny what he said was true.

"Meaghan, no."

She heard her own misery reflected in his voice, as he grabbed her arm to stop her. But she shook it off, tearing back the swaddling.

Horror crystallized in her face. Mummified bits of skin curled back from the flesh beneath the babe's tiny lips, blackened and rotting. Links of tarnished chain, mended with string, circled its neck, a disc of tin in the center. A medal, kin to the one she had given little Brady at his christening two months ago.

" 'Saint Jude,' " Sean read, as he covered the little face. " 'Patron of the hopeless.' Meaghan . . ."

She felt as if she were strangling, the image of the babe branding itself in her mind. Like a macabre puzzle, the child's features shifted, the blond threads of hair washing red, the eyes, forever closed, opening to stare at her, the deep gray of her brother's.

Blindly, she stumbled to her feet.

"Meaghan . . ."

She jumped away from the hand raised to detain her. She was born the child of a land rife with mysteries, omens—fears she had laughed at, used to her advantage in childhood pranks. They haunted her now.

The child . . . She couldn't shut away the image of its face. Saint Jude, patron of the hopeless. The irony jeered at her. She didn't know when she started running, running from the mocking vision, running from Sean, who was calling her name. But she clutched her skirts and plunged on, neither knowing nor caring where she ran, as long as it was away from the searing horror of the hollow, away from the bitter cerulean eyes of Sean O'Fallon.

Sean seized the twisted limb that served as the scalp's last remaining support and jerked it out from under the teetering roof. It caved in, sod tearing free to shroud the woman and child who had lain, hours before, beneath its meager shelter.

There had been no keening, no whiskey running free, only the wool of his coat shielding their faces from the earth as it fell, and a prayer that their Danny lay dead somewhere as well, safe from the agony of finding his wife and child swallowed up by the gaping maw of a country clutched in the grip of death.

Swallowed up like the copper-haired beauty who had fled, sobbing, driven by the jolting sight of the dead babe, by his own cruel words—words he had wielded like weapons to banish his feelings of guilt and the desire that even now mocked him.

She had seemed so small when he had held her, pinioned beneath him, her struggles pitiful, yet her eyes spit fire and her spirit . . .

Sean brushed the dirt from his hands. Damn, she could have been killed. To a man unfettered by his past the promise of soft flesh, the firm breasts thrusting upward, the tangle of hair so wild it begged a man to tame it with his hands, could well have proved temptation too great to resist. And yet, even sensing the danger, to her body if not to her soul, she had tried to strike him down in defense of a woman she had never seen before.

Sean pressed his fingers to his eyes. She had plunged, reckless, into danger today. How much more likely would Meaghan be to do so now, running, heedlessly, his diatribe ringing in her ears?

No. The girl was no concern of his. Why, then, did her innocence bewitch him, her courage inflame him? What was it about this Meaghan that made him lash out in ways he knew would surely hurt her?

Damn. A score of times he had ignored Grace MacFadden's angry glare as he had none too subtly disentangled himself from the wiles of women seeking to ensnare him. Never had he felt remorse, their clinging hands and limpid eyes stirring in him nothing but distaste. To his bed he had taken only those women who demanded nothing of him but the sating of their lust and his own.

Now the look of helplessness that had shadowed Meaghan's face gave him no peace. Something more than the woman's death and the babe's had driven her to run. He sensed it, with the instinct for gauging another's fears he had gained in the hundred boxing saloons and fair rings where he had battled for the purses that had financed his training as a doctor.

For all her show of bravado Meaghan had been afraid. Of what? One corner of Sean's mouth lifted at the absurdity of the question. Half of Ireland was afraid. The rest were fools.

The girl was nothing to him. Nothing. By now she was probably safe within the walls of her cottage, berating her hapless husband for some imagined slight. Damn. Why did that picture seem so unlikely? Why did he wonder at all?

Exhausted, Meaghan slowed her pace at last, rubbing the traces of tears from her cheeks. Her chest ached, and her bare feet were bruised from the sharp-edged stones that had bitten into them in her flight from the hollow. Yet in all the time she had run, she had not been able to escape the mindless terror that had engulfed her as she stared at the face of the child.

How she had retrieved the fiddle from its place beside the stream, she couldn't remember, being only grateful, now, for its familiar weight within her hand.

She had thought herself invincible, thought her father able to stem the tide of any maelstrom that threatened to sweep them all away. How childish her beliefs now seemed, cast in sharp relief against the tragedy she had witnessed.

Home. She wanted only to reach home, to listen to her mother's voice scolding her, to coax from Brady a toothless grin. If only she could see them, touch them, maybe then she could wipe away the horror of this day.

But would she ever be able to chase from her memory the dark bronzed visage of Sean O'Fallon? The bitter lines of his face, the quicksilver flashes of pain and fury? The hard heat of him crushing her until she couldn't breathe, couldn't think?

She hugged her arms against her breasts. The chill of evening crept beneath her skirts and prickled her legs. The sun was setting, its colors spilling across the sky as though a mischievous child had tumbled his mother's dye pots upon it.

It seemed a thousand years since she had watched her father walk away. Where was Da now? Under a friendly roof or settling himself for the night in the shelter of a tree?

A distant rumbling made her search the sky for clouds heavy with rain. "I hope he's safe . . . dry . . ." she whispered aloud. No threatening gray smudge marred the golden-red expanse, no jagged streaks of light had cleaved the sky. The source of the sound hammered not from the sky, but from the strip of road behind her.

Hooves. A sudden fear shot through her as she wheeled. She had forgotten—dear God, how could she have forgotten . . .

Like raging demons the horsemen crested the hill, the menacing figure of Colin Radcliffe in the lead. Low over the neck of his stallion he bent, lashing the beast with his quirt.

"Run, damn you!" he screamed, gouging his spurs into blood-soaked flanks. The stallion shot forward, eyes wild, flecks of white spattering Radcliffe's breeches from its lathered body. Meaghan's eyes widened, locking with soulless black. "She's here! By God, it's the wench!"

Colin Radcliffe's lips twisted into a satanic, triumphant leer. He reined the crazed beast toward her at a dead run.

For the ghost of a second Meaghan stared, frozen in disbelief. "Mother of God," she gasped. Desperately, she dashed for the side of the road, the fiddle clutched in her hand. Terror choked her. The frightened scream of the horse split the air through a maze of thundering hooves and thickly muscled legs. She crashed to the .ground, the neck of the instrument slammed from her grasp. She groped for it, her stomach wrenching as horse and rider plunged to the ground inches from where she lay.

Pain slashed through her as the horse's flailing hoof cut into her breast. She clutched the bloody gash, blackness threatening to engulf her.

"Radcliffe, you crazy devil! Are you all right, Col?" Evanson's voice grated against the release unconsciousness offered as the other horses fell back on their haunches, bits sawing into their mouths.

A hand tangled in Meaghan's hair, jerking her upward. She stumbled, her feet unable to obey her mind's commands.

"Look at her, Pinkerton, Evanson." Radcliffe gloated. "Tell me that this fox was not worth the chase."

"I'd hound her to hell and back," Evanson leered. "She could slice any part of my body she touched, and I swear that with those hands upon it I would feel nothing of pain."

"Pain can have its pleasures, as Pinkerton here is so fond of reminding us. But this wench, she will be soft and hot as a harlot when I bed her. You'll serve me well, won't you, my pretty," Radcliffe wrenched her face up to his. "Oh, how you'll serve your lord and master."

Fiery anger blazed life into Meaghan's wobbling limbs. "You swine!" she spat, tearing away from him. "The earth will crumble before the likes of you will be my lord and master!"

Slowly, slowly, Colin Radcliffe circled her, tapping his hand with his quirt. His eyes crawled along the contours of her body, lingering on the swell of her breast, its creamy skin peeking through the rent in her bodice.

"Stranger things have happened," he said, reaching out a hand to touch her cheek. She jerked back, but his fingers tightened cruelly on her chin. "Oh, no, my elusive little beauty. You'll not escape me again." His whiskey-tinged breath was hot on her face, his mouth slack with lust. "You have much to learn before we part. Ah, don't be afraid," his thumb raked down across her lips. "My specialty is breaking spirited little mares like you to the harness. And you . . . you will be well worth the trouble."

Sharply, Meaghan wheeled her head, sinking her teeth into his bruising palm. With a yelp of pain, he released her, stumbling back. "Bitch!" His hand flashed out, cracking into her face. Her mouth filled with blood as she reeled against Evanson's horse. "Filthy Irish bitch!"

"If you can't handle her, Col . . ." She felt the other man grab at her. Stifling a sob, Meaghan stumbled away from him, not seeing the leg Radcliffe extended. The heel of his hand slammed between her shoulder blades.

Stones scoured skin from her chin and elbows, the dirt of the road clinging to the blood, sticky on her breast.

"I'll break you, by God, or I'll see you dead!" Radcliffe snarled.

"Kill me, then. I'd rather die than let you touch me!" She rolled to face him.

"And the old man? Would you rather he die, too?"

"No! Da's gone! You'd never find him!" She couldn't tear her eyes from Radcliffe's face, dangerous, corrupt, yet fascinating, like the head of a viper.

"Never underestimate my power. I would think nothing of ridding my land of the scum that infects it. Refuse me, and I swear I'll hunt your family down like vermin."

"I have no other family!" Meaghan lied in desperation. Laughter, cruel and mocking, terrified her.

His fingers closed on the tear in her bodice, ripping it back to expose one full white globe. Wet lips revealed small white teeth as he drew a handkerchief from his pocket, and dampened it with his spittle. He rammed the linen square against the jagged cut that curved from the base of her throat.

"Pinkerton, do you hear? She has no family, she says. Is that why you're trembling, or is it desire at my nearness?"

Meaghan writhed, trying to get away from the hand that held her, the feel of its skin as repulsive to her as the belly of a snake. She was the trapped animal, driven by the terror of knowing that in all of Wicklow there was no place to hide from this man.

Her hand knocked something smooth and hard, which

twanged as it slid across the ground. The fiddle skidded over the jagged stones, its fragile wooden shell miraculously undamaged in the fracas.

She grabbed for it, the only constant thing in a world gone mad. Radcliffe tore it from her grasp, lips curling in sick amusement as Meaghan's eyes flooded with tears. She scrambled to her feet.

"No! No, don't! Don't take it!" Pleas she would never have uttered for her own safety she now cried unashamed.

"You want this, my little dove?" Radcliffe's voice was silky with venom as he held the fiddle just out of reach. "Shall I give it to you? Shall I put it in your hand or shall I crush it as I am going to crush you?"

"Please . . . It's my father's . . . It's all I have . . ."

"Father? But you have no family, remember?" Caressingly, Radcliffe ran his fingertips over the honey-colored wood. The taunting cruelty of a dungeon master plying his tortures lit his eyes. "Beg. Ah, yes, plead with me. I'll have you begging often, my love." He forced her chin upward with his thumb, running his nail down the slender column of her throat. "Begging for my favors. Begging for my bed."

"Just . . . just give Da's fiddle back to me." Hot shame choked Meaghan, bile filling her throat, but she did not flinch away.

"Not quite so anxious to sink those sharp little teeth of yours into me now, are you my she-devil? See, Pinkerton, how simple it is to tame these Irish whores to your hand?" He caught up a skein of Meaghan's hair, wrapping its length around his wrist. "But it doesn't do to indulge them. They get to thinking that they're people. That they matter. You don't matter, do you, wench? Not to me. Not to anyone."

Only a narrowing of his eyes betrayed his intent. Desperately, Meaghan threw her weight against his arm, trying to deflect it from its path. Her hair tore at the roots, yanking back brutally as he hurled the fiddle at the trunk of the tree.

The sickening crack of splitting wood cleaved the air. Strings screamed as they flew from their anchor, echoing the sound of the woman in the hollow, the screaming denial in Meaghan's own throat.

She flew at Colin Radcliffe, nails raking bloody gashes in his face, gouging at his mocking smile. He laughed, pinning her arms behind her, wrenching them upward until the bones threatened to burst from their sockets.

She spat into the leering face, sobs of helplessness racking her body. "Damn you to hell!" she cried. "God damn all of you bloody English to hell!"

"Hell? Ah, my sweet, my angel-love. You don't even know the meaning of the word. Yet."

"But you, you'll teach her, will you? Like you taught me? Like you taught Alanna?" Meaghan knew the voice, hard and cold, with the first syllable uttered, long before the tall bronzed figure stepped from the shadow of the tree.

"Who the hell—" Pinkerton blustered.

"No . . . it can't be . . ." Radcliffe breathed, not even turning to see the intruder, a chilling blend of hatred and anticipation on his face. "O'Fallon. Sean O'Fallon."

"How touching you remember me, your *lordship*." Deadly menace twisted Sean's finely carved features. "Now take your God damned hands off of *my wife*."

Three

"Wife?" Radcliffe's mouth was ugly as he wheeled to face Sean, one arm clamped around the girl. *"You've taken a wife?"*

In that bitter, frozen instant, time seemed to shatter for Sean O'Fallon, hurtling him through a thousand blade-edged memories to the day he had last seen Colin Radcliffe with a woman in his arms. The leering horsemen faded away, the grass became pools of deep green velvet cast by a careless hand on the rich carpets of Cottage Gael.

Violet skirts were clutched before nakedness, black tresses tumbled from ribbons, lips, swollen from Radcliffe's kisses, trembled, pleaded, sobbed... *No, Sean! Stop! You'll kill him!* Alanna.

Kill Radcliffe? God, how he had wanted to! Seeing his hands on her, knowing he had taken her... A shudder iced through him. No, he hadn't killed Colin Radcliffe that day, and because of that Alanna had died...

"Lost in fond memories?" Radcliffe jeered. "It's been a long time, O'Fallon."

Sean's fist knotted as Meaghan's chin raised, a curtain of hair falling back from her cheeks. Her face was pale as her bared breast, a drop of blood at the corner of her lips giving them their only color. The spirit that had challenged him earlier was nearly broken, ravaged by a despair that was stamped as clearly on her features as the scarlet print of Radcliffe's hand.

Rage ripped through Sean, rage that had nothing to do with himself or the woman he had loved.

"You son of a—" He lunged for Radcliffe, but the Englishman

twisted, bringing Meaghan between them, one large hand on her throat. Sean froze.

"Son of a bitch? My, my, Sean, we mustn't cast aspersions on one's birth! Why, your charming little *wife* here might be offended, considering what she married." A predatory gleam lit Radcliffe's eyes. "Of course, there are those women who would rather be a nobleman's *whore* than a *whoreson's* bride."

The screech of laughter Radcliffe's taunt brought from Pinkerton rasped across Sean's wire-taut nerves. They were poised there, the other two, like scavengers over carrion, eyes eager in their fleshy pockets, waiting . . .

Muscles strained beneath the white of Sean's shirt as he battled to chain his temper. He was outmanned three to one. Radcliffe wanted him to strike, to do something foolish. He had to keep a clear head, look for an opening. He had to think about *her*. Meaghan. For Radcliffe there would be another time.

"Find one of those women who slaver over your title like bitches in heat," Sean bit out. "It only serves to sicken Meaghan the more."

"Do I sicken you?" Radcliffe captured a strand of glowing copper that trailed down her neck. "You sicken me, wench. Sicken me with a lust that drives me—"

"Please . . ." Meaghan sobbed. "Just let me go."

"Ah, you don't want to go with *him*. I can give you anything you desire, my red-haired beauty. Jewels, silks—bastards like your husband." His hand forced her back into his body, her breast thrusting from between the ragged edges of her bodice. "It was three days before your husband was to be wed that I sampled Alanna's charms. I'm but a trifle later now."

Meaghan's tiny animal cry as Radcliffe's fingers closed mockingly on her rose-tipped breast snapped the thin veneer of Sean's control.

He launched himself at Radcliffe, ripping Meaghan from his grasp, flinging her out of the way at the same instant his fist flashed out to burst the Englishman's lip. Radcliffe fell, sprawling backwards as Sean's fist found its mark again.

"Get him!" Radcliffe snarled at his cohorts, wiping his mouth with the backs of his fingers. "Get the—"

"That's right! Come down here and bloody yourselves so his *lordship* doesn't have to get dirt on his hands!" Sean's eyes flashed challenge.

"Of all the impertinent—" Pinkerton sputtered.

"Still not fighting men, eh, Radcliffe?" Sean cut in. "Only defenseless women. Show your friends, Radcliffe. Show them what a coward you really are!"

Sean sensed a silence, a waiting in the other men.

"Hold!" The two in their saddles stilled as Radcliffe growled, "He's mine! O'Fallon's mine!"

Grit from the road swirled in a blinding veil from Radcliffe's hand as he flung it into Sean's eyes. In the second it took Sean to wipe it away, Radcliffe sprang to his feet, driving his knee into the pit of Sean's stomach.

The explosion of pain sent lust for the kill surging through Sean, as though three years had never passed; as though his agonized denial of Alanna's death was fresh and new; as though again it were just he and Radcliffe on the cobbled circle outside the gray stone manor house.

With a feral snarl he flew at Radcliffe. His knuckles bruised and bloodied Radcliffe's mouth as the Englishman fell back beneath his onslaught. "Don't try, Radcliffe!" Sean growled. "You couldn't hide in hell."

"Stop! Please!" Sean shook off the hand, urgent on his arm.

"Stop! It's all right!" The arc of his fist grazed creamy skin as the girl leapt between him and the battered face of Colin Radcliffe. Eyes . . . he had seen eyes like that before, desperate, imploring. Not golden brown, but amethyst, with something lurking in their depths that jabbed through him like the thrust of a pike.

"They'll kill you." Soft, so soft were the words Sean wasn't certain he had heard them as she pressed her hand on the flat of his chest. Her full lips trembled; her silky lashes were heavy with tears. Sean fought the urge to hold her, the sudden, overwhelming need to put his body between her and anything that threatened the innocence of those black-fringed eyes. The feel of that hand, trusting, warm, seemed to suck the hatred from him, leaving only the need to see her safe. He touched her face.

"How poignant." Radcliffe sneered. "The beast tamed by the lamb." He was standing now, if somewhat unsteadily, blood smearing his cravat, the velvet of his coat layered with dirt. He pressed his hand to his bleeding lip. "Amazing, isn't it, O'Fallon? How your women always leap to my defense? Could it be that they know a *man* when they *feel* one?"

Meaghan caught Sean's fist as it hardened against her cheek, terrified of the resurgent fury she sensed in him. His lips were a grim, white line, his eyes ablaze as they flicked from Evanson and Pinkerton, tense and alert on their horses, to Radcliffe, then back to her.

An odd smile crooked the corner of Sean's mouth. "My wife has a penchant for rescuing whipped curs," he said. There was a tenderness in his voice that, despite the danger, flowed to the tips of Meaghan's fingers.

"Then we will give her a beaten dog." Radcliffe's eyes glittered. "Or a dead one. It matters not to me if it takes one man or twenty to obliterate that insolent smile of yours. As long as it's gone. I've been looking forward to this, O'Fallon. For a long, long time."

"You want my blood?" Sean challenged. "Take it if you can. But leave Meaghan out of this. Let her go."

"I'm not leaving you!"

"You'll do as you're told," Sean said harshly. His lips curled as he goaded Radcliffe. "It took five of Wilde's thugs to drag me off you three years ago. My odds are better now."

"Bastard scum!"

"Aye. Bastard. But a bastard who can drench your face in your liegeman's blood. I'll be your damned diversion for the day. Let her go."

Radcliffe brushed the dust from his sleeve. "I think not, Sean. To cheat your lovely bride out of the sight of you whimpering in the dirt?"

Meaghan felt Sean's fingers tighten around her wrist.

"Did you ever tell her the truth about how Alanna died? No, I vow not. Not a pretty tale with which to bed a woman." Radcliffe's eyes flicked from Sean's face, raw with pain, to Meaghan's bewildered one. "By his own hand Sean admitted he killed her," Radcliffe smirked. "By his own hand. But I'll save you from Alanna's fate, my pretty one. And you . . . you'll pay me well."

"You touch her and I'll—"

"You'll do nothing, O'Fallon. You'll be dead. Pinkerton, Evanson, catch hold of this blackguard's arms. It's time our Sean-o learned to grovel before his betters."

Sean's nostrils flared, a carnivore scenting danger as he judged the time it would take Radcliffe's cohorts to reach him, gauged the distance from where Meaghan stood to the safety of the trees. Damn, she *had* to run, he thought desperately, remembering the stubborn set of her chin when she had refused to desert him earlier. She had to. He'd push her, then dive for Radcliffe and hope he could dispose of him before the others closed in.

Sean clenched his teeth. He'd show these English cowards the meaning of the word courage.

At that instant Pinkerton's foot left the stirrup.

"Run!" Sean cried. His hands crashed into Meaghan, catapulting her across the narrow hump in the center of the road. She stumbled, catching herself with one hand, her eyes holding his for the space of a heartbeat. "Go, Meg!"

Fear drowned Sean, choking him as gold lights flashed from rosewood depths. She had to know. Damn her, he had to stay and fight. Her only chance was to leave him to the whims of chance and the power of his fists. "Damn you, run!"

Meaghan righted herself, scooping up her skirts in her hands, her hair wild round a face tortured with indecision as Pinkerton's leg swung over his sorrel's rump. "No!" She screamed, defiant of Sean, of them all. In a flurry of slender ankles and worn petticoats, Meaghan flew at the terrified horses, screeching in a banshee's wail, flapping her billowing skirts beneath their noses.

Wild-eyed, Radcliffe's already skittish stallion reared, a rippling tower of muscle, pawing the air with its great hooves, their deadly cutting edges slicing a path to the turf bare inches from Meaghan's head. Its black haunches bashed into Evanson's mount, its heavy shoulders crushing Pinkerton's booted legs against his horse's flank in its terror.

Evanson lunged for the reins of the frenzied stallion, off balance as his own mount shied. His groan as he smashed to the ground was swallowed up by the thunder of hoofbeats as Radcliffe's stallion bolted across the heath. Pinkerton struggled to regain his seat on the sorrel, his plump legs flailing as his mount shot after its stablemate.

"Meaghan!" She glanced up at Sean's sharp cry to see Radcliffe crumpled on the ground, nose bleeding from a blow she had not seen, Sean's thighs clamped around Evanson's mare. His arm curved, a hook to scoop her up in front of him, but she dodged it, grabbing instead the muscled length above his elbow to swing lightly onto the horse's rump. Her skirts hiked up over her legs as she fit her body to the taut curves of Sean's, arms clasped about his narrow waist.

His head turned, a strange mixture of amazement, amusement, and irritation sparkling in his eyes. He smiled. "It seems my wife has tired of your company," he drawled to Radcliffe as the Englishman tried yet again to gain his feet. Sean bowed with mock courtliness. "Another time, your lordship."

Black eyes oozed hatred. "To be sure, O'Fallon." They coursed down Meaghan's body. "To be sure."

Four

Meaghan clung to the lean hips of Sean O'Fallon, too shaken by the vengeful lust in Radcliffe's eyes and the loss of the fiddle to feel joy at riding again after so long. The man in front of her was silent, his natural grace on horseback in sharp contrast to the stiff play of muscles under her hands.

Heat from his body singed the delicate skin on the insides of Meaghan's arms as he reined the winded mare into a hidden glen. A tumbling ribbon of water burbled over stones glistening with the fireshine of the dying day. Peace gilded the tiny valley, sanctified it, holding it somehow apart from a world that no longer held safe harbor.

Sean reined the horse to a stop, letting it have but a sip of the chill, clear water before he pulled it away. In a single lithe movement, he swung one lean leg over the slope of neck, sliding down the roan's sleek shoulder to the ground.

Glowering from beneath thick, dark brows, he reached up, hauling Meaghan off the horse, his hands hot and hard around her ribs. The tips of her breasts grazed the bronzed plane of his chest, half bared by his torn shirt. He flinched, and Meaghan felt her knees tremble.

"What you did back there was stupid," he blazed, the corners of his sensual lips pinched with scarcely suppressed rage. "Inexcusably stupid. That little attempt at heroics could very well have gained you something even worse than a night in Colin Radcliffe's bed! Do you have any idea of the kind of filth whose face you were grinding in the mud? Do you have any idea how far he will go to avenge himself, now that you made him look like a fool before his friends?"

"And if I had run?" Meaghan flung back. "You would be dead by now, or the space of a whisper to it! I suppose you'd rather I'd left you there!" She strained her body away from him, trying to free herself from Sean's grasp. His fingers tightened like the twin irons of a vise.

"I've survived worse beatings than the three of them were likely to deal me." His breath flooded her face, his anger pulled at her, a swirling eddy that threatened to engulf her in its fearsome current. "And you can *damn well bet* I would rather you'd left me there than risked what would have happened to you had Radcliffe turned chance in his favor. You were playing with the devil, little girl. Laughing at hell."

"Don't tell me about hell! I bloody well don't need your defining it for me! Radcliffe has taken everything I had! My ma's health, my father, the only thing Da had to leave us when he sailed for America!" Sobs caught in Meaghan's throat at the image of honey-brown wood splintered in the dirt. "I don't need your railing at me, *Doctor* O'Fallon! I don't need you pawing me! And I *'damn well'* don't need your protection!"

"Don't you?" Sean snorted. "You seemed glad enough to have it when Radcliffe started smashing things."

Pain. Meaghan felt it slice up from her toes in a churning, twisting path as the ruin of her father's beloved fiddle tortured her mind. Her fist balled, struck at the ridge of Sean's cheek.

Sean caught it, holding it on his own beard-roughened skin. His eyes pierced her, incredibly blue, suddenly gentle. "It was yours," he said, understanding dawning in his face. "The violin Radcliffe smashed was yours."

Tears streamed down Meaghan's cheeks, shattering her, breaking her as surely as the fiddle had been. Sean drew her against him, cradling her head in one large hand, the other stroking wispy curls from her face, tracing her tears.

"I . . . It was my Da's . . . the only thing he had . . . He had to leave . . . wanted me to sell it . . ."

"When I saw you before, at the scalp—"

"I left it by the stream . . . thought you were Radcliffe. He'd threatened me . . . I heard him and hid. I thought you were Radcliffe . . ."

Meaghan sobbed brokenly into the security of the arms that held her. She felt the surprisingly soft texture of Sean's lips against her cheek. He slid them to her temple, her eyelids. His hands cupped her face, thumbs gliding over her mouth before he tilted her chin up. He swallowed, and Meaghan felt him tremble.

"I didn't know. I'm sorry." His mouth hesitated above hers, a kiss more of breaths than of bodies. Sean's head dipped down. Warm and moist, his lips closed on hers, soothing her, comforting her. Slowly, slowly they changed, hardened, opened.

Tight into his tall frame he pulled her, flames licking her from the hot cavern of his mouth, from his hands holding her, from his heart crashing wildly against his ribs, where the nakedness of her breast was crushed.

She felt him, felt the rich silk of sable hair tangling around her fingers. His breath caught in his throat as his tongue searched out her mouth. She grew dizzy with velvet roughness, sleek wetness.

"No!" Sean's fingers dug deep into the flesh of Meaghan's arms, shoving her back from him, his body snapping like a whip cracking. Her eyes flew open, heavy-lidded still from the sensations pulsing through her veins. "We can't do this," he groaned. "I can't do this."

"I—what—" Her hand slid down beneath his open collar. She didn't have the will to pull it away.

"Damn it, Meaghan, do you want me to finish what Radcliffe began? You're a beautiful woman and it's been too damned long since I had—" He wheeled, raking his hair back from his face with fingers that seemed at once to want to caress her and strike her.

Meaghan pulled the edges of her bodice over her breast, painfully aware of its nakedness, how she had pressed it like a wanton into the hair-roughened chest of this man but a moment before. Two tags of the cloth hung longer than the rest. She knotted them over pale swell, coral tip, with shaking fingers. Hot shame spilled color to her cheeks. She turned away.

"Meg..." Her name sounded sweet, right from his lips, tinged with a kind of loneliness, regret. One finger hooked gently under her chin, forcing her to look at him, then eased up to rest in the soft hollow beneath her lower lip.

"I didn't mean for that to happen. You were upset... so beautiful, innocent." Tears trembled on her lashes. He wiped them away. "I don't want to hurt you . . ."

"Hurt me?" she choked. "I only threw myself at you until you finally had to pry me away!"

"The only one I 'pryed away' was *myself!* There are so many things you don't know about me . . ."

"You don't need to explain. You won't have to trouble yourself further with me, Doctor O'Fallon—"

"You're no trouble," he said gently. "And my name is Sean."

She closed her eyes, wanting nothing more, now, than to escape the burden of his kindness. "I'll get home on my own from here. We must be nigh the boundaries of Radcliffe land."

"Radcliffe land? Colin Radcliffe is your *landlord?"*

Meaghan nodded, looking up to find Sean's face incredulous, his mouth tight above the crest of his square jaw. "And just how long do you think it will take him to find you? *A tenant on his own manor?"*

"I'll go into hiding. Maybe . . . maybe he'll forget me." Meaghan swallowed hard, her own worst fears put into words.

"Hardly!" Sean snorted. "After our little scene in the road Radcliffe will be snarling after you like a hound on a bone."

"You told him I was your wife . . ." Her voice tripped over the last word.

"If anything, the thought of you being linked to me will heighten the spice of his chase! How, Meaghan, will you explain living apart from your supposed husband? I'm not a man who would tolerate my wife living off somewhere, separate from me. Colin Radcliffe knows that! Anyone who knows me at all knows that!"

"What do you want me to say or do? *I'm* not the one who claimed we were wed—" Stricken, she pressed her knuckles to her lips. "I'm sorry . . . I know you only tried to help. I didn't mean to sound . . ."

"Ungrateful?" Sean arched his head back, staring up at the sky. "Why, in the name of God, should you be grateful to me? You're trapped. Trapped in a lie that will be impossible to keep Radcliffe from discovering." He rubbed his eyes with his fingertips. "My lie."

"You did what you thought best at the time—you did all that you could."

The words he had said to the fever-ridden woman little more

than an hour ago haunted him. *All that you could* . . . It hadn't been enough to save the woman's baby. Would it be enough for this girl with her spun copper hair, the fire in her eyes?

He fought back the gut-wrenching need to kiss her, knowing that to touch her again was to take her, to take her would be to destroy her. There was no room in him for love, for the pain it would bring. And she needed love, this Meaghan, this wood-witch. It shone out from the sensitive curve of her lips, from her eyes, too wide, her heart, too open. Striding the few steps to the horse, who cropped at tufts of grass, Sean lifted its reins.

"We'll ride to Cottage Gael first, before I take you home."

"Cottage Gael?"

He mounted, swiveled at the waist, offering his hand.

"My home. I think I can find something there for you to . . ." Her fingers slipped into his, so small, yet callused and strong. He didn't finish the sentence as she swung up behind him, her slender, supple legs meshing with his.

Her arms slid around him and she leaned her cheek against his back like a weary child. Child? She was no child. He felt the awakening in her, the promise. It lay against his body, a sweet, heavy weight.

She sighed, the flutter of air, warm from her mouth whispering through his shirt. Sean's hands clenched the reins.

He was taking her with him for but a breath of time, time to cover her with something more than rags . . . time to free the tenuous hold she had gained on his heart.

But not long enough, God, no, never long enough to discover the agonizing secrets locked within his soul.

"Hold on, lass. We're here."

Disoriented, Meaghan raised her head from its warm nest, her hair tangling across her sleep-clouded face. Needles from heaven had pricked holes in the night's velvet curtain, the points of the stars seeming to bite through her petticoat as well, to jab life into her benumbed limbs. A large hand burrowed between her fingers, loosening her hold on what had been her pillow.

Afraid. She knew she had been afraid, with the same kind of bottomless terror she had felt the day she had fallen through the MacDonough's stable rafters. But why? Of what . . .

"Awake?" The form in front of her slid off what she now

dimly realized was a horse's back. The rich tones of a voice reached through the haze. "I almost lost you riding up that last hill."

Moonglow outlined features, devastatingly handsome, already too disarmingly familiar. The events of the afternoon flooded back to her. "I feel like I bumped down that hill on my backside," she said, kneading a hip muscle. Her bruised cheek stung.

Sean grinned. "It's a wonder my ribs aren't cracked, the way you held onto me." Silence fell between them at his words. But she was too tired even to blush as he lifted her from the horse.

Shadowed arches scalloped the darker supports of what looked to be a veranda, a large black rectangle blocking out one section of its rail. Above, three peaks of roof crowned its majestic silhouette.

Meaghan watched Sean run his hand down the roan's white blaze. "Just let me slip this bridle off and you can find your way home," he said, fingers working the leather straps through the buckles. "Minus these reins that could trip you, but not much worse for the ride."

Free, the mare nuzzled his chest, rubbing her nose where the bridle had chafed. Sean gave her a gentle slap on the shoulder. She tossed her head and trotted off into the darkness.

"Are you all right?" Sean grasped her elbow, leading her up three wide stone steps. The backs of his fingers imprinted on the side of her breast. Meaghan felt the blood rush through her body. His hand tightened then pulled away.

He hunkered down for a moment to examine the rectangular board on the veranda. By the silver light of the moon, Meaghan could make out a squiggly line of light paint slicing darkness, tiny painted squares of every shade scattered haphazardly along pale, winding lines.

Sean twirled a slate pencil attached to the board's corner by a string. The muscles of his thighs bulged beneath his black breeches as he straightened, smiling at her. "No emergencies while I was gone."

"How can you tell?"

"A map. A good number of my patients can't read or write. Since I don't keep any servants, there is no one to take a message. Each one of these squares is a cottage." He tapped a light-colored box. "When anyone wants me, they draw an X on their square. I circle the places I'm to visit, and draw lines, connecting them in the order I'll be there. Down here in the corner I slip a peg in the section signifying morning, afternoon, or night. That way they know what time I started. It's simple to find me."

"Simple?" Meaghan asked, dubiously. "It looks anything *but* simple!"

"Even the smallest children can remember their square. We make a game of it. They get so good at remembering, they keep me in short supply of peppermint drops."

His arm curved under hers again, guiding her across the veranda, to a carved wood door. He opened it and led her inside.

"How did you think of it?" Meaghan looked over her shoulder, unwilling to let go of this idea that was at once brilliant and childishly simple.

She felt, rather than saw, his mouth harden. "I did it in a fit of total frustration. One day, I almost had to amputate a girl's arm because so much time had passed between the actual injury and the time I arrived. Her father didn't know how to write, and he ran all over the countryside looking for me. I must have gotten home minutes after he left. By the time he came back here, it was nearly too late."

There was a shuffling sound and a clinking of glass as he fumbled for something in the inky darkness. A match flared to life, illuminating Sean's hand in a wash of orange and gold. He touched the wavering flame to the wick of a lamp sitting on a small stand to his left, then settled its crystal globe into place.

Large frames lined the walls of the arched entry, portraits of a type Meaghan had never seen before. A dirt-spattered waif proudly displayed a mud pie; three village girls, shy in Sunday hair ribbons, whispered behind a battered cart; an old woman, her face still shaded with the beauty of her youth, was frozen by the artist in a swirl of dancing abandon that made Meaghan feel burdened and tired.

Sean followed her gaze to the paintings. "By one of my patients. I keep him supplied with canvas, he pays for my doctoring with these. His work is as good, if not better, than anything I saw at the Louvre, or in England."

The sound of Sean's boot heels on the wooden floor echoed through the hall as they made their way past several propped-open doors and up a flight of stairs. And suddenly in the flickering of the lamplight, Meaghan felt how very alone she was with this man.

With one broad shoulder, Sean nudged open the first door at the head of the stairs. The room focused in a golden glow. Shelves, stacked to capacity, with the tools of his profession sectioned off the longest wall. A narrow cot stood, blocking a door in one corner, a blue plaid blanket thrown carelessly across its foot.

The bed was rumpled, and Meaghan had a flashing image of Sean's bronzed body sprawled upon the white of the sheets, his hair tousled across the pillow, lashes resting on his cheeks in the peacefulness of slumber. Her own face pinkening, she looked away.

Her troubled gaze fastened on an elegant fireplace carved with wood and marble. From it the aroma of meat curled in a tantalizing web around Meaghan's nose. It had been so long since she had smelled this richness, let alone tasted it.

"I'll have a bowl of stew in your hands before you can lift a spoon," he said, depositing the lamp on a rough hewn table. Meaghan swallowed convulsively, her stomach clamoring for food. She'd not eaten since last night's meager portion of stirabout, the last meal the O'Learys had shared together before Da left home.

They had walked in from the twilight, Da and Ma, her shrunken arm linked through his elbow, Da's face more drawn than the sickly one of her mother, Tom trailing in his father's wake, trying not to cry.

The walks had become a grim ritual, Da insisting he needed his Bridget to see the land's beauty, dead certain that the scent of the wildflowers and the touch of the breeze would kiss the light back into her smile. But each walk was a little shorter, each evening she tired a bit sooner. Each night infant Brady screamed his indignation more, butting his tiny forehead against Ma's shrinking breasts.

Meaghan had turned to the kettle she was tending, heartsick as she scraped the last rime of porridge from its black bottom, dividing it equally between only three wooden bowls.

"And what of ye, Meaghan Mary?" Da had asked, eyeing the table set with three spoons.

She had circled around, skirts swirling, the bowls balanced in her hand. "I ate my bit while you were walking. Brady's been in such a blather all day, I thought I might wrap him up and walk over to Widow MacDonough's. She's not seen him since he sprouted this tooth, and that way you can eat what little there is in peace."

The bowls had clunked down on the table, her shawl but a finger's breadth from her reach, when Da's brawny hand had stayed her. "And were ye after eatin' from the kettle, colleen?" he said softly.

"I . . . no, of course not, I . . ."

"We all clean our bowls, we do. But I've yet to see one this well scrubbed without a thimbleful of water to the house." Meaghan felt her face burn as he pointed to the empty water pail, Tom's neglected chore.

Da's eyes had glowed gently, through the harsh sound of her mother's angry scolding, as he took the fourth bowl from the shelf and spooned his own stirabout into it.

The porridge had stuck in Meaghan's throat with tears she hadn't wanted him to see. Meaghan swallowed again, eyes tear-washed with the memory as she stared at the kettle bubbling over Sean O'Fallon's grate.

The warm roughness of Sean's palm on her cheek shook her from her daze. He stared at her, assessing the planes of her face. Meaghan pulled away, held by pride, knowing the O'Learys' lack of food was all too evident in the skin pulled over her delicate cheekbones.

"How long has it been since you've had a decent meal?" His hand stroked up, only the edge of his little finger skimming to the hair that curled at her temple.

Meaghan flushed. Silent.

"How long?"

"I was fit to be bursting last night," she lied, her chin jutting stubbornly.

"Not by the feel of you. And not from what you've told me. Tell me, Meaghan. How desperate does a father have to be to desert his child in a famine-stricken land?"

Meaghan jerked away from his touch, livid. "He didn't desert us! He had to go!"

"Why? To be off for high adventure? Because he couldn't bear your headstrong ways? Why?"

"Because we were—" Meaghan stopped, glaring defiantly.

"Starving?" Sean demanded.

"Hungry." She stalked to the shelves, pretending to examine shiny metal instruments, varicolored bottles, a myriad of sizes and shapes. Her finger tapped the ridge of leather binding one of the thick books that bowed the wood beneath.

Sean came to stand behind her, the firelight enveloping her in the wings of his shadow. "How many are there 'hungry' in your family?"

"It's none of your concern. I can take care of them. I don't need your pity." Meaghan felt Sean's hand reach out to touch her. She whisked from beneath it, blazing with the fierce pride of her father.

"I'm not offering you pity." His voice was deep, husky in his throat.

A tremor went through Meaghan, her heart pounding as Sean's eyes swept her body. She swallowed, aware of her hair cascading about her shoulders, aware, too, of Ma's oft-repeated warning that *hair a-hangin' down is temptin' sure as offerin' a man apples from Eden.*

Meaghan pulled the heavy length back, bundling it into a loose knot at the nape of her neck as if taming the curling strands could protect her from the crackling desire in Sean's face. The pins that had remained tangled in its silky mass, when it had tumbled down hours ago, now seemed to leap from her fingers as she struggled to anchor the knot.

He picked one up from where it lay on the woven rug, deftly catching a loop of copper spilling over her shoulder. "I'm not offering you pity," he repeated, his fingers brushing the fine hair in the hollow at the back of her neck. Meaghan felt the caress trail like fingertips down her spine. "I'm offering you stew."

Her eyes darted up, captured by azure lights twinkling beneath Sean's dark lashes. His mouth curved into a smile so disarming it sent shivers coursing through her body, his face alight with an understanding so deep it terrified her. The smile faded. "Damn, I'd forgotten."

Meaghan's hand flew to her bodice as his gaze dropped to the bloodstained homespun, which made a lump where she had tied the edges across her breast. "You can't . . . it's fine . . . I . . ."

"I'm a doctor, remember?" He lifted a ladle from a hook beside the fireplace, dipping into the rich brown gravy, scooping out chunks of meat, golden carrots, and turnips, spooning them into a deep china bowl.

"Eat first. I'll get things ready," he told her, setting the bowl and a spoon on the table, one hand splayed on the oaken surface. "Take all you want. Grace always sends more than I can eat."

Even the agitation prickling Meaghan's stomach at the thought of Sean's impending examination could not keep her mouth from watering. It was all that she could do to keep from slurping up the stew like Patrick O'Riley at a whiskey barrel.

She slipped into the chair, grabbing with dismay at the hastily pinned chignon as it tumbled from its confines, washing over Sean's long, strong fingers in waves like old wine.

For what seemed an eternity, they both stared at it—hard sinews, spun silk—woman . . . man.

"I have to get something belowstairs," Sean rasped, pulling his hand away. He strode to the door, hesitating, as though he wanted desperately to say something, eyes straying to the sliver of white flesh she could not wholly conceal.

The thin layer of gold-colored fabric seemed to melt beneath his gaze. Something flickered in his eyes, something that made her want to run, something that made her want to stay. It terrified her, the stark emotion she saw crossing his rugged face.

"I won't hurt you," he said, the words more a vow than a comfort.

And then he was gone. Meaghan stared at the door he had shut in his wake, her hands trembling as she braided her hair into a glossy rope down her back. She picked up her spoon, filling it with the steamy richness. But suddenly the stew had lost its savor.

Sean gripped the carved wood banister, white-knuckled and damned aroused. There was nothing he needed to collect outside his office chamber except the shredded remnants of his self-control, something that had been in definite short supply since Meaghan O'Leary had smashed her way into his life. She cut to the core of him. He could feel the bite of her in the proud lift of her delicate chin, in her courage, in the feel of her body branded into his lean, hard frame.

He could hear his defenses snapping around him like twigs in a gale, touching that part of him buried deep, that was raw and bleeding from a hundred scars laid open again at the brush of her hand. He was scared. Damned scared.

For the first time in the five years since he had become a

doctor, his palms were sweating at the thought of touching a wound. No, at the thought of touching a woman. Wrong as it might be, Sean knew it to be true. He wanted to touch Meaghan, not with the detachment of his profession, but as a man touches a woman.

And she would let him. God, yes, she would let him, baring her breast to him, trusting him with that blind innocence dusted across her as lightly and beguilingly as the sprinkling of freckles across her nose. And once he felt her breast beneath his hands . . .

"Damn it, O'Fallon, you're doing it to yourself!" he muttered, gritting his teeth. But his mind went on, relentlessly, searing his loins with images of his mouth on her breast, his body braced above her . . . No!

He wheeled, flinging open the door. Its handle banged against the inner wall crashing the silence into a hundred scattered pieces. Meaghan jumped, her eyes wide and face pale; the silver spoon clattered into the empty bowl.

"I'm cleaning that laceration now before it putrefies," he growled, yanking down rolls of bandages from a basket on a shelf, tossing them onto the table. "Then you're going home. For God's sake, *somebody* must be worried about you." Scissors jangled onto the wood. Clean water sloshed into a basin, a spotless cloth floating in it.

"Unfasten your bodice and any other frippery you have on underneath it," he ordered, his voice harsh even to his own ears. "Fold them back until the injury and the area around it are bare."

Her hand fluttered to her breast, slender fingers hesitating on the tiny round buttons at her throat. That single act of uncertainty was more seductive to Sean O'Fallon than anything he had experienced with a score of faceless women well versed in the arts of love. He banged the basin onto the table, water splashing over its rim. His eyes narrowed with what he prayed would pass for impatience.

"I'm a doctor, Meaghan. If I was going to rape you, I certainly wouldn't have bothered to bring you here."

She shot him a glare, fumbling the first button through its hole. He could see rosiness flushing her cheeks. "I'm not exactly used to . . . to doing this . . ."

"I am," he said. But he wasn't. Not like this, not watching her fingers baring the hollow of her throat, the palm-wide plane just above where her breasts rose in firm, ripe mounds. The curve of white swelled from between the edges of cloth as they fell open, a teasing crescent of darker flesh peeking from its shadows.

Sean grabbed the rag in the basin, wishing to blazes he could twist the desire he had for this girl from his body as easily as he wrung the excess water from the cloth. "Get it over with, O'Fallon," he upbraided himself silently. "Just get it over with and get her the hell out of here."

With one hand he pulled her, chair and all, back from the table, then sank down on one knee, his line of vision as level as possible to the cut which scribed a wide arc from collarbone to mid-sternum. One of her arms was crossed over the naked mound of her breast, her fingers chafing the fabric of her collar between them.

"Is it giving you any pain?" He reached up, loosening her grip on the small upstanding ridge of material. Her hands were like ice.

"A little."

The words faltered for all her bravado. Sean squeezed her fingers, holding them long seconds before he laid them gently on the top of the table.

He forced a smile to put her at ease. "I'll have you know, that spot of black you have your hand on almost started a war that would have made Drogheda seem like Sunday Mass."

Her eyes darted up to his, then flashed down to a mark as large as the bottom of a milk pail burned into the golden wood. "My great grandda, Donal O'Fallon, made that table as a wedding present for Fianna, his bride, just before Cromwell's Puritan army leveled most of Ireland."

Sean dabbed at the top of the cut. The side of his hand brushed smooth skin rising and falling with her breath. It was firm, warm with a heat that sluiced down his arm, resting heavily between his thighs. The tip-tilted crest beckoned him.

Sweat beaded Sean's upper lip. His voice stumbled as he went on. "When they were forced to take to the caves, Fianna insisted that she'd take the table with her, or she'd not set foot outside her door. Cromwell and the English be damned. A group of them, mostly Donal and Fianna's kin, set up housekeeping in a cave in Donegal, living off the land, stealing lead from the rooftops of castle ruins, melting it for bullets to fill the guns they stole from stray Englishmen they killed."

His hand eased down slowly, slowly. He felt her shiver

through the tips of his fingers, her eyes half closed as if he were loving her. His mouth went dry.

"The . . . the mark . . . how did it get . . ." she quavered.

Damn, he could scarcely breathe let alone talk. "Donal was . . . molding bullets. An English soldier surprised them . . . swung his sword . . ."

"Sword?" She echoed the word, but she wasn't hearing him, wasn't feeling, he could see it. Her lips fell open.

"The sword . . . swung it at Fianna. There was a dipperful of molten lead. Donal threw it on the . . . the soldier . . . it . . . some splashed across the . . . table . . . She never quite forgave him . . ." Sean looked up at Meaghan, child-woman unfurling petals of innocence, unknowing, exposing for him the deep gold center of her need . . . her need to be taken, to unite with a man. "We pass it . . . from generation to generation," Sean rasped. "Father to son."

Hard, hot, he felt the bulge in his groin tighten with his words to a physical pain. A tiny gasp wisped from Meaghan's mouth to his hands as they brushed an answering hardness in her rose-tipped breast.

"Christ!" he hissed, his jaw clenching and unclenching with mind-shattering need.

Her finger touched his cheek, smooth to the sensuous roughness of a day's growth of stubble. Sean groaned, taking it into his mouth, easing it out between the gentle sharpness of his teeth. He ran her palm over his face, smelling the fragrance of her, guiding her hand over the clean sharp lines of his jaw, his lips, the muscled column of his neck.

His whole body trembled as he brushed her parted lips, with his own. "Meaghan . . ."

The tip of her tongue touched the corner of his mouth as she tried to wet her lips. "Meaghan!" His mouth slanted across hers, harsh, demanding what she promised with her eyes, with her body.

His hand took in the fullness of her naked breast, his thumb skimming the taut nipple until it begged for his mouth. "Meaghan . . . I have to . . . I can't . . ."

She arched back, and he tasted of her, her hard nipple and soft breast, her sweetness and warmth, his tongue and teeth teaching her the hunger of his sex.

Her whimper drove him like a white-hot brand, her hands

caressing his mouth as he suckled. "Sean . . . it's so . . . good . . . I never . . ."

Was it her broken words? Her fingernails, bitten to the quick like a child's on the hand that stirred him past reason? Or was it the fleeting thought of the last time he had allowed himself to feel this searing need, and how much it had cost him? He never knew.

With a savage oath he tore himself from her, slamming the basin from the table in rage and frustration. He couldn't have her. He wanted her. God, how he wanted her!

"Sean . . . What . . ."

"Don't! Don't talk. Don't move. What in the hell did you think you were doing? What the hell do you know about me? About any man? How far, Meaghan? Just how far were you willing to let me go?"

His words swept over Meaghan like the spray from the ocean in winter, icy and angry. It was as if she were fighting to claw her way to the surface, only to be shoved back under by the fury in Sean's rigid stance. "I wasn't . . ." she choked. "I didn't mean to . . ."

"Didn't mean to what? Here I am, thinking you're some kind of virginal innocent and you all but beg me to make love to you! What the hell did you expect! Damn, what the hell did I expect?"

"I am . . . I mean I didn't . . ." She fumbled with the pieces of her bodice, trying vainly to cover herself. Tears stung her eyes, shame and hurt warring inside of her. She had acted like a harlot, the way she had held him . . . urged him . . . He had touched her where no man ever had. Why had she let him? Why in God's name had she wanted him to?

He swept up a bandage roll and jammed it into her hand. "Here. The cut's not deep and shouldn't flaw the beauty you were offering up to me like some kind of sacrificial lamb. Keep this. If it starts to bleed again wrap it with this." He glared down at where the fingers of her other hand clutched her bodice. Meaghan flinched away from that searing gaze, hunching her shoulders together, trying to hide that part of her still aroused from his lips.

"Damn!" Pain and anger clashed in Sean's face as if he could still see what lay beneath the homespun. He stormed across the room to where the door stood, half hidden by his bed. Viciously he kicked the cot out of the way, slamming it into the shelves. Meaghan cringed as glass and metal teetered and toppled. Sean didn't spare them even a glance.

He flung the door open, disappearing into the dark room, stalking back out before the chinking of bottles and instruments had stilled. Meaghan froze. His face was chalky pale, lavender silk and creamy lace dripped from his arms, motes of dust sprinkling to the floor from their folds. A chill ran through her. He thrust the bundle of silk into her arms. "Dress yourself. I'm taking you home."

"Home . . ."

"Yes, *home*," Sean sneered. "In the *gig*. Or were you planning to stay the night and share my bed?"

Meaghan's hands clenched the froth of lavender. "No." She saw his eyes rake her lips and throat, then flash away.

"Damn you!" he grated. "Damn *all* of you!"

He spun on his heel, the muscles of his shoulders standing out in taut ridges against his shirt as he strode out into the hallway. The retreat of his footsteps echoed into the room. A door slammed.

Fingers numb, Meaghan pulled her sleeves down her arms, letting her ruined dress slide down the thin bell of her petticoat before she stepped out of it. She folded the dress, placing the square of gold cloth on the table. Slipping the cool silk over her head, she let the lavender gown billow around her, a cascade of ribbons and lace. She paused for a moment, somehow uneasy as she smoothed the deeply cut neckline up over her breasts, holding it there with her arms.

It had the same aloof elegance as the house, a coldness, an essence of . . . what was it? Evil? Never in her life had she touched anything so beautiful, yet even though she ran her fingers over the silky smooth interior of the dress, it seemed to scrape across her skin.

A soft whoosh, like a whisper, breathed from the hidden room. It beckoned her, challenged her. Her hand trembled as her fingers closed around the lamp. She raised it, drawn to the chunk of blackness outlined by the door frame as if by some unseen thread.

Her hand flew to her throat as she stepped into the musty-smelling room, the dress falling from her hand unheeded, a puddle of lavender on the lavish Oriental carpet. Light from the lamp glittered on pendants of crystal, shooting rainbows from a chandelier to the corners of the room. Intricate carvings spiraled the massive posts of a mahogany bedstead, its deep velvet curtains draped back by heavy gold cord.

A swath of violet coverlet was twisted from the bed, its flounce snared between the footboard and the bedpost. Twin embroidered chairs, their legs splintered, lay tangled with an overturned wash stand; shards of a broken china pitcher and bowl were strewn across the floor. Dark stains marked the wallpaper, where water must have splashed. Water or...

A rustle to her right made her heart leap in her throat. She spun, pulse racing like a hawk-swept bird as a taffeta gown crumpled from the open wardrobe to the floor.

Shaken, she set the lamp on the dusty top of a dressing table, trying vainly to calm herself. It was then that she saw it, a wisp of airy lawn, ivory with age. It peeked from the folds of the coverlet like a well-kept secret. It drew her like Sean had, like the room. She leaned down, touching the cloth where it lay. Sheer fabric, satin ribbons, caught on her work-roughened fingers. It was a nightgown twined with bands of lavender, seams caught with gold threads. She smoothed the bodice, carrying it to the glow of the lamp. Letters leapt out at her, embroidered in stitches like blossoms: A.D. S.O.

"Sean," Meaghan breathed. "Alanna DuBois and Sean O'Fallon." Radcliffe's words flooded back to her. *Sean killed her, by his own hand ... by his own hand ...* The hidden door, the shattered china, the stains ...

Had Sean killed Alanna? *Murdered* her? Here? In this room? Meaghan shivered. Could those hands, so strong, so bronzed, that had stroked her, coaxed from her sensations she would never have believed possible, be the hands of a *murderer?*

Fear iced through her. If it were true, if Sean O'Fallon had slain the woman he was to have married, what would he do to a lone tenant girl? A girl with no father to protect her? A girl whose family had no idea where she was? A girl who had stumbled upon his dark secret ... Her heart threatening to choke her, Meaghan wheeled to run. She froze in a silent scream.

Legs spraddled wide, face twisted in a mask of rage, Sean O'Fallon stood, blocking her only escape, an unholy light blazing in his cerulean eyes.

Five

Meaghan clutched the nightgown against the meager shield of her own worn chemise, her knees threatening to betray her. "I heard a noise," she stammered, falling back a step. "I thought—"

"It's cursedly obvious what you *thought*," Sean spat, closing the space she had gained between them with deadly measured strides. "The lamb who strays feels the bite of the wolf. Tell me. Do you feel the fangs snapping shut about your throat?"

"I was changing into the dress. There was a noise. You left the door open."

"Forgive me. I've never before had the need to lock doors inside my own house. You can be sure I won't make the same mistake again."

"No. You'll lock everything up tight. Block everything out of your life like this room and what happened—" She stopped, horrified at what she had almost blurted out, terrified of the menace in Sean's visage as his lips curled in a cruel mockery of his smile.

"What happened? Enlighten me. What am I blocking out? What happened here, Meaghan? In this room?"

"I . . . I don't know . . . I . . ."

"Come, now. Surely you must have some idea, some flight of fancy that has changed you from blushing maid to frightened child."

His words were a challenge, as though he were gauging her desperation with a kind of tortured amusement. She met it defiantly. "I'm no child! And I'll be damned if I'll tremble before any man!"

"You're wrong. So wrong. Shall I teach you what it is to

quake with an agony so devastating that it leaves no part of you untouched?" He trailed his finger down the white line of her naked arm, the very lightness of its callused tip upon her razing her like the lash of a whip. "Save yourself. Tell me what you managed to deduce about this room. Its contents. Me."

"Don't." She tried to escape him, but he shifted his weight, anticipating her attempt, crooking one knee with an effortless grace that sent her banging into the ridge of his thigh. The momentum forced her to slide down his muscled length, her palms flattening on the crisp mat of hair that spanned his chest.

She heard his bitter laugh as he tangled his fingers through the end of her braid. "Strange," he said. "You didn't object to me touching you before. What's wrong now, Meaghan? Can you smell the blood on my hands?" With taut deliberation he worked loose the copper tresses, holding her off balance, her hips crushed against him.

"Stop, Sean . . . don't . . ." She clawed at his fingers, raking red gouges into them, which he seemed not to notice at all.

His hand moved down, grasping the gold-stitched nightgown, catching as he did so the top of her chemise. The backs of his fingers burned into her flesh as she stared into his startled eyes. With a tiny cry she wrenched free. The aged lawn gave with a sickening sound, the fragile cloth covering her breasts rending as well, as her back hit the coldness of the wall, pinning her between Sean and the spindle-legged dressing table. He crushed the embroidered bodice in his fist.

"Shall I tell you what happened?" he demanded, his voice tortured. "What truths Radcliffe hinted at? What lies? This was hers. Alanna's. It fell around her body like mist, made her eyes a shade of violet that defied the hearts of every flower in Ireland to match it in its beauty. Her hair . . . polished like ebony . . ." He stopped, jaw clenched, eyes burning. "But she didn't die in this night rail. Didn't die in this room. She died by her own hand three days after I found her here, in this bed, with Colin Radcliffe."

"Radcliffe?" Meaghan whispered. "And you left it, all of this . . . all of her things?"

"The night I found her making love to him I shut out her very existence until . . . I wouldn't listen to her. She begged me to . . ." He closed his eyes, a jagged pulse beating in his cheek. "Radcliffe had forced her with some threat against me. When I

wouldn't forgive her she . . . Damn, didn't she know I'd rather
have died myself than see her with *him!*" He raked his hair back
from his forehead, eyes glinting diamond hard as their blue light
fell upon Meaghan.

"So now you know. I killed Alanna as surely as if I had
shoved her from the tower window myself. You can herald it to
the world. Sean O'Fallon is a murderer." His mouth twisted.
"That is, of course, if I decide to let you live."

Groping desperately, Meaghan's fingers closed on the lip of a
brass bowl that stood on the dressing table, ready to strike Sean
with it if he made a move toward her, but the torment on his
sharply chiseled features stayed her. He grasped her wrist, loosening her hold, bringing her hand up between their bodies.

"God," he rasped, reaching out to cup her face with hopeless
pain. "Meaghan . . . Do you really believe I could hurt you?" He
crushed her against him, lips bruising hers, fingers twining in her
coppery hair. "Damn, I can't stop myself . . ."

He slid her tattered chemise down the slope of her shoulders,
kissing every bit of the soft skin he bared, tasting her, taunting
her with expert strokes of his hard rough tongue. His palm caressed her breast, her nipple hardening in a peak of desire that
cried out for him as his hand slid down her ribs, the warm, wet
magic of his mouth skimming the path it charted.

Meaghan traced the ridgelike muscles of his back, the raised
arc of a scar that slashed down his left side to his flat belly, a
deadly reminder of the reckless danger in him. Danger that fueled
the raging emotions he set loose in her, that made her want to
touch . . . tame . . .

Fastenings tugged free, impatience blazing in his eyes, he slid
her petticoat down her legs to fall in a circlet about her feet. His
bronzed hands lingered on the silky curve of her hips, slipping
beneath the waistband of her pantaloons, gliding in ever widening circles on the yielding softness of her buttocks.

A moan escaped her lips. She arched back, offering her
breasts, offering anything he asked. Asked? No. Demanded.
With an answering groan, he raised his head. Like velvet fire his
tongue swept over her, plunging into her mouth as he jammed the
soft swell of her stomach against the iron-hard proof of his need.
The feel of it, so large, combined with what little she knew of the
act of mating, struck panic through her.

"No . . . Please . . ."

"God, don't stop me . . ." He said into her mouth, his fingers digging into her flesh. "You want me. I can feel it. Damn it, tell me you don't want me!"

"You don't want me!" she flung back at him, eyes swimming with tears. He would only be thinking of Alanna, wishing she were Alanna . . .

His mouth strung kisses from her mouth to her ear, his breath whiffling the curls at her temple. "I've wanted you from the moment I saw you on that hillside," he murmured. "All fight and fire, that ridiculous stick in your hand. I wanted to feel you naked beneath me, needing me. I wanted . . ." His teeth bit her earlobe. She cried out at the gentle-sharp pain, a throbbing sensation mounting deep in her secret places. He crushed her to him, heart racing, breath rasping, his long fingers plying her body with savage sweetness. "God, Meaghan! Please!"

Her body ached for him, with a liquid sweetness that drizzled down her like melting honey. She pressed her hips more closely against him wanting . . . something . . . Cool, delicate, the wisp of Alanna's nightgown, cast unnoticed on the floor, drifted over Meaghan's bare foot. With its texture came fear . . . fear of what this man could do to her. Not to her body, but to her soul.

"I can't . . ." She cried, her tears wetting his lips. "I'm afraid . . ."

"I'll make it good for you. Let me."

It was as if she were caught in the pull of the tide; she couldn't stop him, couldn't stop herself. She did want him, wanted to feel what strained beneath the breeches that clung to his thighs like a second skin, wanted him to take her breast into his mouth, wanted to delve the secrets of his body. To have him teach her the mysteries that lay between a man and a woman.

"Sean . . ." He bent low to catch her whisper. She hesitated, and even his breathing seemed to stop. "Sean, make love to me." His lips crashed down on hers as he swept her into the cradle of his arms, stripping back the satin sheet that covered the top of the bed. The cloth beneath it was free of the dust that coated the rest of the room, the bed itself scented by a small pillow stuffed with herbs and petals from the blossoms of summers ago. It lay tucked among heavenly soft lace-edged mounds that were piled along the carved headboard.

His lips never leaving hers, Sean laid her on the feather tick, easing her pantaloons down her slender legs, his fingertips lingering over well-turned calves, delicate ankles, small feet that seemed to her suddenly dirty and travel stained. He dipped his head, kissing the thin line of blood marking the gash in her foot she had all but forgotten. Her toes curled as heat flowed up her leg, nestling in that part of her no man had ever touched.

She tried to pull away. His grip tightened, and she went still. He placed her foot gently on the bed.

Straightening, he shrugged the shirt from his shoulders, baring a chest like rippling mahogany. A wedge of curly black hairs tapered down to his navel, its narrowed point disappearing into the waistband of his breeches. Meaghan wanted to touch it, to see if it was truly the spun silk it seemed. The brazen thought sent blood rushing to her cheeks.

He jammed the heel of his boot into the wooden V of a bootjack that lay by the side of the bed, not even glancing at it, as though he had made the same motion a hundred times in this room. The polished leather thunked to the floor. He kicked it out of the way, stripping off the boot's mate. His hands jerked at the japanned iron buttons that fastened his fly, freeing them at last, sliding the breeches down his narrow hips, divesting himself of his white tied drawers as well.

Meaghan drank in the beauty of his nakedness. His body was carved with the rugged power of cliffs upon the sea, honed to perfect smoothness, lean hardness, his head held proudly like a pagan prince.

Fleeting thoughts of Father Loughlin's railings about the wages of mortal sin, of Ma waiting, worrying about her at the cottage, of Sean's great love for Alanna DuBois vanished as his eyes captured hers.

The bedropes creaked beneath his weight. Meaghan turned to him, shame and fear gone as he pulled her to his chest, his warm mouth hungering.

His tongue struck deep into her mouth, fingers tangling in the mass of glistening copper that draped her breasts like a satin veil. She met his every swirl, learning the taste of male passion, the crevices and caverns of the mouth that seemed to suck from her the very essence of her being.

He tore himself away, burying his face in the lee of her

shoulder, taking her throat in tiny nips. She threw her head back, arching into his caress as he made his way down the firm swell of her breast, loving its peak with the strokes of a master.

"Beautiful..." he groaned. "Soft...smooth...Touch me, Meaghan. God, I need you to touch me." She quivered beneath him, fists balled on his fevered skin, unable to move as his fingertips trailed down her belly. He explored the valley of her waist, the small circle of her navel, and lower. His breath hissed between his teeth.

Burnished fingers grazed dewy curls, seeking the sleek wetness of her woman's folds. He parted her carefully, gliding his callused tips over her in a practiced rhythm that spiraled through her with an ecstasy akin to pain. He eased a finger in, filling her, then drawing out. He kept this rhythm up, never stopping his sweet, sweet torture.

She closed her eyes, writhing against him, caught in a tempest that seemed to whirl her into a million glittering stars. She clung to his voice, thick with passion, guiding her, urging her. "Open your eyes, Meg. See what I do to you. Let me. Let me take you..."

As she hurtled toward the summit, he bent his dark head, his tongue flicking over what his fingers had left. Her hands clenched in his hair, but the will to push him away had vanished. She arched against the pillows, head thrashing, white hot sparks of passion searing through her veins.

He poised himself above her, his sex thrusting against the softness of her belly, hands nearly spanning the slim curves of her hips. "So small...don't want to hurt you..." he rasped, easing a muscled leg between her thighs. "Always pain the first time. Don't want to hurt..."

He drove deep, her cry of pain like a fiery stake in his heart as her delicate membranes tore. His lips slanted across hers as if to draw the pain from her, shaking with the will it cost him to hold his body still, accustoming her to the feel of him inside her. A tear trickled from the corner of her spice-brown eyes; eyes that had brimmed with ecstasy now clouded.

"The pain's over, Meg," he ground out, every word an agony. "Now there's only loving..." Loving...God, it had never been like this with any of the women who had shared his body and his bed. His desire was something clawing inside him. He could hold back no longer. With smooth thrusts he set himself against her, deep and hard.

Her fingers clenched in the taut flesh of his back, the steely roundness of his haunches, her nails cutting his skin. Awkward at first, she bucked her hips against him, whimpering deep in her throat. He caught her with his hands, teaching her the ebb and flow of mating, feeling her silken softness begin to move against him in ways that drove him near to madness.

She cried out his name, rapture twisting her body beneath him, lips open as tremor after tremor shook her. On the brink of a climax more shattering than he had ever known, he devoured the sight of what he was doing to her, woman born. He buried his sex deep as fires surged through him, raging rivers, crashing and thundering until there was nothing in the world but the frenzied ecstasy of their joining.

A primal roar exploded from his lips as his seed spilled inside her, a terrifying yielding of body and soul. He crushed her to him, her skin still damp with his sweat, the wonder of their mating suffusing her face with agonizing beauty.

He had taken a virgin this night and made her a woman. A woman to whom he could give nothing, not even the empty shell he had become. And now? He rolled away from her, flinging his wrist up to cover his eyes.

Long minutes passed laden with silence.

"Sean?" Her voice wisped over his skin like the edge of a moth's wing. "It was . . . when you touched me . . ."

"I know." The warm skin of her arm pressed against the side of his ribs as she pushed herself up on an elbow. Hair, silken and scented, fell over the flat muscles of his chest.

"I want . . . to touch you now," she whispered, trembling against him. *"There.* I want to . . ." Sean drew his breath in sharply as she leaned over him, brushing his lips with the ripe fullness of her own. Her fingers, hesitant and shy, moved down the length of his chest, tracing the line of curling hairs that divided his flat stomach until they widened again, thickened around that part of him which deemed him a man.

He grabbed her wrist fiercely, forcing her to take his hardness in her hand. "Damn you, Meaghan," he hissed, bearing her down into the sheets, rolling his lean body atop her. "Damn you! You've bewitched me . . . bewitched . . ."

Need raged within him, a stormy torrent in his loins. His

tongue lingered over belly and breast, then mated wildly with her own in the hot sweetness of her yielding mouth. "Damn, I can't love you!" His words wrenched from his very soul, but she didn't hear him. She arched to meet his thrust with a cry of joy. And he took her, savagely, knowing that the harsh light of morning would destroy her. The harsh light of morning and the cruel words he would say to her then.

Cold terror drenched Meaghan's body as she stretched her arm out over the mist-shrouded water toward Da's unearthly screams. The dream again. It clawed at her, tore at her. Waves, stygian black, crashed over Da's head as his hand clutched at hers. She felt his fingers slipping, held only by the silver chain of Brady's holy medal, its links mended with string.

"Meggie!" Da choked, "Meggie, help me!" Desperately, she fought to regain her hold, but something held her captive, banding her in heavy warmth. It was Lord Colin Radcliffe, his eyes empty pits, laughing . . . laughing . . .

His arms cut into her breasts and thighs. Teeth gleaming in a bestial snarl, he yanked her hand from Da's. The chain snapped. "No!" Meaghan tried to scream, as a huge swell sucked her father into blackness, but no sound could squeeze through her strangling throat. She bit, clawed at the arms that bound her, forcing her back onto the splintered boards of the ghost ship's deck. But they were Sean's arms now, naked, a strange vulnerability chasing the bitterness from his eyes as he bent his head to taste of her . . .

Meaghan started awake, her heart slamming in her temples as beard-stubbled skin rasped against her. The ship and its horror faded away, until only the face of Sean O'Fallon remained, wrapped in slumber on the pillow beside her.

What had happened between them was real. The night flooded back to her—each stroke of his fingers, each touch of his mouth on her body. She could feel the dull ache in her woman's place, a slight, sticky sensation of blood upon her thighs, the stain of her lost virginity.

She had never even seen the sensual curves of Sean O'Fallon's mouth before yesterday's dawn tinted the sky. But now that mouth knew her body as well as she herself did. A shiver ran down her spine. Tales of hellfire and sin she had gathered as a child around St. Colmcille's had fled at this man's touch. Why?

Willful and headstrong she'd always been, Father Loughlin's imprecations ringing in her ears. But this was no childish prank, no fit of temper for Da to tweak her curls and forget. It had been wrong to give herself to Sean O'Fallon. Her gaze swept the curve of sooty lashes that fanned his cheeks, filling with images of the blue they shielded, dark with passion. Her fingertip trailed over his eyelids, the feel of him beautiful as it had been last night. No. Lying with Sean, making love, how could it be wrong?

He groaned, cradling her closer as she shifted away, strong arms encircling her, one long leg flung across her thighs.

"Don't leave me." His voice was raw, hurting, as he buried his face in her breast, rekindling fires of the night before. Bronzed fingers tangled in her hair as if somehow to hold her, and she felt again the rush of magic from his hands. His fist clenched deep in the silky skein. "God, don't go . . . I love you . . . Alanna . . ."

Meaghan's anguished gasp jolted Sean into awareness, his eyes, sleep clouded, struggling to focus on the woman he now pinioned to the bed. "Meaghan." The word fell like a stone between them as he stared down into her tormented face. "Oh, my God."

"Let go of me."

"No, I'm—"

"Let go of me!" She tried to jerk away, but his fingers dug into her shoulders.

"Meaghan, listen to me, damn it—"

Her fist lashed out, but his broad shoulder blocked the blow, her knuckles glancing off his jaw. He caught her face between his palms, forcing her to look at him.

"I never meant to hurt you," he said softly. "I loved Alanna and—Christ, I didn't try to hide it—"

"I heard all this, Sean, *before* you bedded me. I don't need to . . . hear it after . . ."

"Meg . . ."

"It was as much my fault as it was yours," her voice cracked as his lips neared her cheek. "Don't." She held up her hand in a plea for him to stop. His breath feathered, warm across her skin. His mouth set in a grim line. He drew back.

"Meaghan, what happened between us—"

"Don't!" She winced at the bittersweet memory of last night's wonder. "Sean, I just . . . want . . . to *go.*"

He eased away from her, releasing his hold slowly, reluctantly, a hundred half-formed words rising to his lips, dying there. There was nothing he could say to ease the pain that he had caused her, nothing he could do to rid himself of his own tortured guilt.

She rolled out of bed, her back to him, trying to hide the tears that glistened in her eyes, as she clung to what scrap of pride was left to her. She would not cry in front of him now. Not now. Taking the lavender gown, she tugged it over her head, fingers fumbling with the buttons up the back.

She heard his bare feet pad across the floor, felt his fingertips brush her spine. "Let me help . . ."

"Help what, I'd like to know, an' it after eight o'clock?"

Meaghan grasped the bedpost, face scarlet as a strange voice rasped through the half-open door. "Ye lay abed until breakfast is nigh burned an'—" The door swung open. Troll-like, a woman stood frozen in the door frame, her face pinched with worry scarce concealed by her bantering tone. Her eyes swept Sean's startled ones, and the lines etched in her face wilted a little, as though she had expected something frightening, almost horrible to be lurking behind the door, and found instead something familiar, something safe. But the relief in the keen eyes changed to astonishment as the woman's gaze shifted to Meaghan. The too-wide mouth fell open. Her hands clutched her pregnant belly as if to keep herself from toppling over.

Had it not all been so horrible, Meaghan would have laughed herself sick at the sight of Sean scrambling like a schoolboy to catch a length of sheet around his naked hips, a flush staining his cheekbones as he moved to shield her. "Grace, it's not—"

"Oh, and isn't it, now?" Green eyes darted from Meaghan to Sean, a twinkle of merriment lighting the homely face.

"Damn it, Grace, she's not some—"

Even lacking censure, the knowing look in those jade eyes as they scanned the unfastened dress and the tangle of hair around her shoulders, stabbed Meaghan with burning shame. She yanked free of Sean's hands, running for the door.

"For God's sake, Meaghan, don't—"

She heard him clumping down the stairs behind her, saw a flash of sheet tangle around his ankles. He cursed savagely as he fell, the palms of his hands slamming into the veranda rail, the sheet torn away. He pushed himself up, something haunting in his cry. "Meaghan!"

She looked back, just once, to where he stood, his body gleaming naked in the sun. A sob choked her throat as she lost herself in the open arms of the heather.

Six

Lord Colin Radcliffe rolled the squat crystal stem of the goblet between his thumb and forefinger, glowering through the leaded glass window. The lands of Radbury Manor spread beneath him, a queen's petticoat. Wide stretched pastures spangled with sheep and cattle, while beyond the wretched tenant farms patched the verdant green like soiled laundry.

Like starved rats, the tenants crawled through their existence, struggling to hold a patch of ground on which to grow the potatoes that were their only food, fighting to keep the clay-walled holes that were their homes.

They were laughable and powerless, hatred contorting their faces as they paid their rent of grain and livestock, watching it carted away to fill English bellies while in the throes of famine their own children starved.

Had she sprung from one of these filthy hovels, O'Fallon's woman? Her beauty secreted away behind whitewashed walls, hidden from sight like a prized gem?

Her gown had been made from the coarsest of cloths, but her skin had the texture of silk. He had merely wanted to use her, a diversion to while away his boredom in this infernal land, but now . . .

He threw back his head in a short, sharp laugh. Sean O'Fallon's *wife* . . . To take the woman of the stiff-necked O'Fallon and throw her back to him, her spirit broken and bleeding, to shatter that fierce pride that made the Irish bastard seem prince to Radcliffe's peasant . . .

Radcliffe wheeled, jerking on the bell pull, tossing the goblet onto a tray beside a half-empty decanter as a wide-eyed maid skittered into the room.

"Yer lordship?" She bobbed a curtsy, and Radcliffe could see her catch the inside of her lip with her teeth.

"I want Trevor Wilde, girl," Radcliffe snapped, brushing his hand on his kerseymere trousers. "Get him. He should be out in the stables."

The girl pressed shaky fingers to her mouth. Her round chin quivered. "Begging yer pardon, yer lordship, but, oh, sir, I daren't leave the house! It's almost time for the mistress to be risin' an' she vowed to send me on my way if ever I was late again. She said to tell ye I'm *her* maid, an' if ye have need of one ye'd best be hirin' a one of yer own."

The mouse of a girl rushed on, her whole body trembling as she pressed her fist to her heart. "Beggin' yer pardon, I'd never presume to speak so, yer lordship, but she told me to say those very words and she gets in such a temper that—"

"Incompetent fool!" Radcliffe exploded. *"Send* for Wilde, you stupid girl! Send MacDonough, or Larkin! Anybody! But get Wilde in here post haste or you'll think your mistress's temper's a priest's blessing compared with my own!"

Her face white, the girl fled through the door, crashing head-long into the bandy-legged form who stood, one fist raised to knock on the heavy wood panel. Radcliffe watched as the man grabbed her arms, setting her on her feet with a wide grin.

"By the sword, colleen, there's no beastie after you. Slow yourself down before you cause the death of some unsuspecting innocent in your way!" He gave her lace cap a playful tug.

"I . . . I'm sorry, Connor," the girl gasped, casting a glance over her shoulder at Radcliffe as she retreated down the hall.

"Well?" Radcliffe glared at the barrel-chested man. "What the devil is it?"

Connor MacDonough swept the battered hat off his head, shaking his wild orange mane into some quick semblance of order. "If I'm disturbing you, excuse me, your lordship," he said. "I thought I'd best come up from the stables to tell you myself that Lucifer is fit as a soldier. The limp was naught but a bit of strain in the one foreleg. Rubbed him down with liniment and wrapped it up."

"Good, MacDonough."

"Must've had quite a chase yesterday for that horse to take such a fall."

"Chase . . . Yes, quite a chase." Radcliffe's mind filled with visions of tumbled hair, firm breasts.

"Did you catch the poor devil?"

"What?" Radcliffe started.

"The fox you were after. Did you catch it?"

"No. We got separated from the others. But I *will* catch it. *I will.*"

"It's a fine hunter you are, sir. I've no doubt the beastie's days are numbered. If you're out again today, I'd advise you to take one of the other mounts. Old Luce needs a bit of a rest before he'll be up to his oats."

"I'll not need a horse to catch this quarry," Radcliffe sneered, "but twice as much cunning for twice as much pleasure. Tell me, do you know a winsome lass of, say, nineteen years, with hair like new copper and eyes the color of rosewood?"

Fear shot across MacDonough's features, then vanished. He braced his feet apart on the floor with the easy air of a natural horseman, but the line of his smile was taut. "Why do you ask?"

"She was walking on the road about six miles from Doctor O'Fallon's yesterday. Lucifer near trampled her. Her dress was spoiled. I seek to make . . . restitution." Radcliffe reached his hand across his chest to draw coin from his waistcoat pocket, rubbing the gold together between his fingers.

Connor's green eyes flicked to the glittering pieces. Slowly Radcliffe reached out, dropping them into the cap Connor held. MacDonough stared a long time at the coins, dimmed now inside the wool pouch. He looked up. "Nineteen, you say?"

Radcliffe felt a surge of triumph. A smirk creased his face. "Near that." He slipped another coin from his fingers.

"Pretty?"

"A wench ripe for bedding."

MacDonough's face paled beneath its ruddy burn. His warm eyes hardened. He tipped the hat, dumping the money into his rein-scarred palm. "No, my lord," he said, placing the coins on the edge of the massive desk. "I know of no red-haired colleen with the least claim to beauty."

Radcliffe's hand slammed down on the big one of the groom, pinning it to the mahogany surface. "I want that girl, MacDonough," he grated. "And I *will have her*. You tell her that. You tell her that for me."

The groom's level gaze bored into Radcliffe, thick with distaste, as he pulled from his grasp. He didn't wait to be dismissed, but settled his cap on his head and strode from the room.

Seething, Radcliffe paced to the decanter, righting the goblet, and sloshing amber liquid into its bowl. He knew, the prideful scum. Connor MacDonough knew the woman he was seeking, of that he was certain. What did she mean to him, O'Fallon's wife, that he would refuse gold, risk his master's ire?

But was he MacDonough's master? Was anyone? Known throughout Ireland as a wizard with horseflesh, Connor was the best of a rare breed. This was no unskilled soddie with no other place to turn. Connor MacDonough could name his wage. Why he had never gone to England . . .

A wash of warm liquid ran over Radcliffe's fingers, as the goblet tilted absently in his hand. With an oath he set the wet glass on the desk top, wiping at the spill with his handkerchief. If MacDonough knew the girl, someone else on the manor was sure to know her as well. Someone not adverse to tainted coin.

Yes, he had defeated O'Fallon before . . . He moved to the corner of the room where the curio cabinet's vine-patterned sides climbed toward the ceiling. Carefully he turned the tiny key in its lock and swung open the glass door.

From the top shelf Radcliffe lifted a delicate china figure. Black hair was painted, framing rosy china cheeks. Waves of a flowered lavender gown drifted in frozen ripples from its minute waist to its tiny violet slippers.

He turned it in his hands, remembering the day he had commissioned it to be done, a day of triumph greater than any other he'd ever known. The likeness had been a gift for the woman he loved. Loved? Possessed. Desired, yes. But loved? Radcliffe snorted at the thought.

Love was for fools like Sean O'Fallon, castrating them, leaving them half a man. He looked into the violet eyes of the china figure. Cold, pitiless violet eyes. He'd captured her exactly, the artist. Each feature a fragile iceberg, evil lurking beneath its surface to ensnare the unwary.

Alanna. O'Fallon had loved her, had been ready to die for her, yet how little he had understood her, the real Alanna, the woman secreted away beneath a veil of fraudulent gentility and treacherous smiles.

Had the fiery beauty on the road vanquished the specter that had haunted O'Fallon for so long? What was her power? Her secret? Soon, very soon, Radcliffe vowed, he would discover her mysteries for himself.

At the clatter of hooves in the courtyard Colin replaced the figure in the cabinet, and strode back to the window. The horse, Trevor Wilde's mammoth gray, was already riderless. Wilde's hulking frame darkened the doorway momentarily.

"News from England," he offered, tossing a bundle of letters onto the desk. "Important. Your grandfather." Porcine features took on a cunning bent as he surveyed Radcliffe with beady eyes, all pretense of formality gone. "I got the message you wanted to see me. What is it?"

Radcliffe slid into a leather chair, his hands forming a steeple in front of his face. "A woman."

Licking thick lips, Wilde heaved his wide buttocks onto the ledge of the desk. "This much ado for a woman? Tell me what you want me to do? See to the Red Room? Wine? Baths? Scented candles? Wooing doxies is not exactly my area of expertise."

He did not pause for an answer, but slipped the top trouser button from its hole, and heaved a sigh of relief as he scratched at the reddened skin of his straining belly. "Who is the fortunate wench this time?"

"Woman, Trev. Sean O'Fallon's woman."

Wilde's face went ashen. He slid down from the desk, one meaty fist knocking Radcliffe's goblet to the floor. It lay unheeded, brandy pooling on the carpet. "O'Fallon? Are you mad? He came within a whore's breath of killing you last time. If my men and I hadn't found you he damn well would have."

"And if you hadn't stopped me, I would have seen O'Fallon dead that day and saved myself the inconvenience of dealing with him now."

Wilde's pitted face grew red. "He'd outmanned every one of us. From the beating he took he should have died anyway."

"But he didn't, did he? He lived to take a wife. And I want her, Trev. The devil take the cost." Radcliffe rose, walking to the stand on which the decanter rested. Reaching beneath it he secured two fresh glasses, and poured the liquor into each.

"O'Fallon claims she is his wife, so start your search at Cottage Gael," he said, "but be subtle, my friend. O'Fallon is no *man's* fool." He turned, offering a goblet to Wilde. "I don't give a tinker's damn what you do to that Irish bastard, but the girl must not elude us."

Wilde's stubby fingers closed around the stem, apprehension etched on his low forehead.

Radcliffe lifted his glass, a derisive smirk twisting his mouth. "To love, Trev," he said, raising its rim to his lips.

"To love, my lord." Wilde drained the goblet in a single gulp, but he did not share Radcliffe's levity. He swiped his hand across his mouth as he started for the door. "I was told the letter was of utmost importance." Wilde gestured to the fat sealed envelope on the desk, then refastened his trousers. "Best not anger the old badger more, Rad. I say that as a friend."

Radcliffe picked up the missive, running his thumb over the heavy burgundy seal. "I want her, Trev."

"Damn it, Col, you want every woman in skirts."

"It's different this time."

"Because she's *beautiful?*" Sarcasm laced Wilde's words.

"Because she's O'Fallon's."

"Read the letter."

"I will."

"And answer it, Colin, for God's sake!"

The slam of the door and the slit of pen knife through paper mingled as Colin Radcliffe tore the letter from its covering and stared down at the crest of the Duke of Radbury. "Beloved Grandpapa," he sneered.

Black eyes scanned the bold hand scrawled across the page, and Radcliffe could almost see the craggy coldness of his grandfather's face. His hands clenched on the paper, white-knuckled as he read:

... acted a damned buffoon in Cannes ... flaunting that black-haired witch like a whoremonger ... be wiser throwing the empire I built to the pigs ...

Dark blood rose in Radcliffe's face, as he crushed the edges of the paper and read on.

Checked with Strathmore and found you've not deigned to dispatch the problem in Wicklow. Do you think this a God-cursed game of catch-skirt?

With a snarl, Radcliffe balled the missive in his fist, flinging it into the fire. The wax seal of the envelope sputtered and smoked, running down the flaming page in great gobs.

Problem! Damn his grandfather's all-consuming problem! Finding information about some tenant woman dead twenty years, reporting back to that sly weasel Strathmore like a damned lackey! Any hireling could do that! They were bastards, both of them!

His face twisted in an ugly sneer. Let the old man make his threats! As if the all mighty Duke of Radbury would soil his "holy" family honor by admitting to the world his only heir was less than perfect!

Letters, ravings—he'd listened to his grandfather's private snarlings since he'd been a child. It was but a day's annoyance. He would not let it ruin his pleasure. He had more delectable game to catch now, brandied with the taste of challenge. O'Fallon. To match wits with O'Fallon again, to defeat him . . .

He paced to the curio cabinet again, staring through the glass pane at the china likeness. His smile faded. Unbidden, thoughts of fury glimmering from piercing blue eyes preyed upon his mind. Twice in his life he had looked into those eyes and seen his death reflected in their depths—the night O'Fallon had discovered him making love to Alanna and yesterday on the road.

There was scarcely the click of the latch to tell him he was no longer alone; there was merely a web, misty and silken, that seemed to wind through the room. He turned to face her, a delicate butterfly of a woman poised just inside the door. A haze of white illusion iced the rose tarlatan of her gown, black eyebrows arched like wings over startlingly beautiful eyes. One brow raised, her face, only then, lost perfect symmetry.

"And what, pray tell, are you brewing in that evil mind of yours, Colin Radcliffe?" The tones were strangely discordant, like the dented crown of a silver bell.

A smile came easily to his mouth. "Merely admiring the beauty of glass until the beauty of flesh arrived to eclipse it entirely, as you always do."

He turned, crossing the room to brush his lips across the carnelianed curve of her cheekbone.

"You are a liar." A cunning smile tipped the corner of her icy lips.

"Am I?" His finger reached out, trailing to the fire opal that clasped the top of her bodice. The heavy ring curling at his knuckle caught the edge of one of the half-furled gold leaves curving around the stone. He pulled his ring free, the brooch's soft metal giving just a little.

"You are a vicious scoundrel," the woman whispered throatily. "But that is the key to your charm."

Radcliffe's fingers plied tiny jet buttons, laying them open to see a froth of ribbon-decked lawn. He looked to the open window casing, the open door, leering as he slipped the ribbons of her chemisette. "As it is to your own," he said, baring her breast. "As it is to your own, my Alanna."

Seven

Meaghan tugged helplessly at the tiny edged lace that sliced across the swells of her breasts, tears stinging her eyes as the delicate trim ripped from the bodice. The rising tops of the mounds threatened to burst from the cloth, the sliver of fair skin barely visible above the binding, violet bodice, contrasting sharply with the wind-seared curves painfully exposed by the decolletage.

Heavy folds of billowing silk wilted around her legs with each step she took, catching under her bare feet, tangling on thorn-starred shrubs.

Her whole body felt raw, as if Sean had branded each place he had touched with his lips, leaving their imprints blazing on her skin for the whole world to see. She pressed her hands to her cheeks. Was her guilt emblazoned so on her face?

She had been taken by a man in his bed, gone there willingly, wanting him, a man she knew not at all. And any naive thoughts of being swept from reason by impassioned love had been shattered with one word uttered in the unguarded honesty of sleep.

Meaghan felt a fist crushing her heart. Sean hadn't wanted *her*. He had made love to a chimera, closing those eyes that had pierced her to her soul, imagining the face of another woman.

The fever in him, the fight as he'd tried not to touch her, the hopelessness when no longer could he still his hands had all been because of Alanna, the woman he *loved*. He had trembled, even as he had caressed Meaghan with such knowing care, and when his body had pierced her own the cry from his lips had been a tortured mingling of both ecstasy and despair.

He had vowed he wouldn't hurt her. But it did hurt. God, it did!

Miserable, Meaghan crested the rise that gentled into the valley and stared down at the tiny cottage nestled in its bowl. It seemed a lifetime ago that she had slammed out the weathered gray door, childish in her determination to see her father before he sailed, still somehow certain he wouldn't really go.

Her hand fumbled again with the torn lace at her breast as she unconsciously tried to hide the bareness. She felt her face flame. What would Ma say when she returned home, clad in rich silk, having been gone through the night? How much of the truth would be stamped upon her face? How much of it could she truly hide?

If Ma guessed what had happened... Meaghan's fingernails bit into her palms. She couldn't lay herself open to one of her mother's tirades. Not now. What had happened between her and Sean was still too fresh, too cuttingly painful.

Swallowing hard, she raised the trailing hem of her skirt. She had to face her mother sometime. Better it be now. Taking a deep breath, Meaghan picked her way down the hill.

The path to the door, bordered with whitewashed stones, had been worn smooth by O'Learys for a hundred years. Skipping children, friends sobbing for their dead, loved ones seeking the song of Da's fiddle to give them peace—all had come down its winding ribbon. How empty it seemed now.

Meaghan paused at the door, laying her hand on it, as if to draw strength from its familiar roughness. Beyond, the cottage was strangely still. Steeling herself, Meaghan pushed open the door.

Smoke from the peat fire curled on the hearth. The cradle near it lay empty, stripped of its thin gray blanket; her mother's shawl, too, was gone from its place by the door.

Meaghan's eyes darted about the room, searching for some sign of where they could be. An accident? Visiting? Ma had not had the will to leave the cottage without Da for weeks.

Hand over hand, Meaghan scaled the ladder to the loft room, suddenly unaware of the clinging skirt, or the dread of her mother's railings.

Tom's bed had scarce been slept in. The covering nested deep in the hollow of the straw tick as though he had flung himself upon it in exhaustion, too tired even to turn back the quilt.

A sudden noise sent Meaghan rushing to the window beneath the slanting roof's peak. Trudging toward the cottage were two figures. The lanky form of Tom, with his twitchy, restless gait, and Ma, her arms weighted with Brady, her face tight with worry.

Meaghan caught her lip between her teeth, suddenly certain of where they had been: searching somewhere for her. She wheeled, but was stopped short, one violet flounce snagging on the corner of the wooden chest at the foot of her bed. Freeing it, she tore at the fastenings at the back of the gown, stripping it from her tender shoulders, and yanking a dress of her own from the peg above her bed.

The floorboards in the room beneath her creaked as she jerked the buttons on the fawn-colored dress through their holes. Only then did she realize she'd not taken time to even grab her pantaloons and petticoat from where they had lain on the carpet at Cottage Gael.

"Ma? Tom?" Dragging a comb hastily through her thick locks, she tossed it onto her pillow and leaned out over the loft opening. The faces that angled up at her were tired beyond belief, showing shifting emotions like tempests in the sea—joy, disbelief, anger.

Brady squalled as he was dumped unceremoniously into his cradle by arms that seemed no longer able to support his slight weight. Tom's mouth gaped open. "Meaghan . . . it's all right ye are, all right . . ." Ma repeated, as though she could barely believe it was true. The shawl fell from her shoulders. "Where in the name of the saints were ye, lass? We searched all morning, and last night until neither of us could stand."

"I . . . I'm sorry you were worried, Ma." Meaghan descended the ladder, her face beneath its gilding of sun suddenly very pale.

"Worried? That's the small of it, and ye gone the night through!"

"I . . ." her voice stumbled. "I stayed with Da last night."

"See? I told you he would let *her* stay!" Tom accused, freckles blotching his face red. "But when *I* asked—"

"Matthew let ye stay with him, knowing I'd be crazed with worry? Knowing we'd be searching?" Meaghan's mother cut in, her lips tightening.

"No. It was my doing. I followed him until it would have been dark before I arrived home. Da . . ." The lie scraped across Meaghan like nails across a slate. She fell silent.

"Da," Bridget O'Leary repeated, lines carving deep between

her brows as temper eclipsed thankfulness. "Always Da, catering to yer whims, encouraging yer selfishness. And I don't suppose the both of ye could spare a thought for yer brother and me, here alone, worried."

"It was my fault. I'm sorry. You're right to be angry."

"Right, am I? Tell that to Tom who begged to go with yer father for days before he left, but instead had to chase halfway across Wicklow after his sneaking, selfish sister!"

"Da was afraid Tom would try to board the ship, or do something rash."

"But Matthew didn't need to be worried about ye, did he? Not his precious Meaghan, so perfect, never at fault." Ma's gray eyes narrowed, and Meaghan felt as if she could see through the mists to all that had transpired the night before. "No, no." An edge cut into her voice. "Ye never do anything foolish!"

Meaghan blanched, slow tears forming in her eyes. She had known it would be like this, dreaded this, and yet in a way, did she deserve any less? "Da's always seen my faults," she said dully. "It's just that he understood them." Until now, she added silently to herself. She walked to the cradle, lifting the squirming Brady, burying her face in his little pieced dress to blot out the memory of Sean and Colin Radcliffe. No. This was one escapade even Da would never countenance.

"Da'd never have had to go if you'd got married!" Tom's lower lip stuck out in belligerence. "Connor would have helped and—"

Meaghan gritted her teeth. "Connor is married to someone else, Tom. Someone who loves him as he deserves to be loved."

"Aye, and Da is somewhere out on the ocean."

It was as if that thought wiped to insignificance the resentment and anger stifling the room. The three of them stared at each other, then looked away in the suffocating silence.

The sharp rap on the door made Meaghan jump. Tom bolted across the room and flung it wide. "Connor!" He gave an elated cry as the big groom reached out to ruffle his hair.

"How you farin', Tommy-boy? Ma Bridget?"

Connor MacDonough stepped into the room amid the excited flurry of Tom and Ma's greetings. He gave all the expected answers, about his young wife Mary and their new baby, but his green eyes sought Meaghan's, anxious, uncertain. Meaghan felt her heart plunge to her toes. It was not merely chance or friendship that had brought Connor to the cottage this day. She forced a smile.

"Connor," she said. "It's been a long time."

"Hello, Maggie." He took the cap from his head, rolling its small stiff brim between his fingers.

He had loved her since they were both in short skirts, running half naked in the sun. He had left offerings of white rhododendrons at her doorstep, and wee baby birds that had fallen from their nests. On her fifteenth birthday he had asked her to marry him, seen the anguish in her eyes, then stepped quietly out of her life forever.

"I was wonderin' if you'd care to go for a ride."

Tom's whoop was cut short by Connor's hand on his shoulder. "Not this time, Tommy-boy. This time I'm asking your sister."

"Not her," Tom wailed.

Meaghan felt an uncomfortable squirming in her stomach. "I don't think Mary—"

"It's not like that. Please." She felt the urgency in his tone.

"Ma?" A lift of her voice made the word a question. She looked at her mother. Her thin face had softened with Connor MacDonough's entrance, only the barest traces of her anger shadowing her brow. Meaghan felt a stab of pain. Ma had always delighted in him, the rough and tumble boy, who had been her daughter's partner in mischief, loving in him all the qualities she had disdained in Meaghan. He had been like her son until Meaghan had turned the gangly young horseman away.

"Go on with ye." Bridget slipped Brady from Meaghan's arms as Connor leaned to brush the gaunt cheek with a kiss.

His lips split in a preoccupied smile as he settled the cap back onto his head. "You come soon and see my little one."

"Now that ye've found yer way back, don't be a stranger."

"I won't. And Tom, I'll take you riding soon. You have my word. The fastest horse I can 'borrow' from his lordship's stable." Tom's scowl lightened a little.

Connor braced his arm on the door, and Meaghan slipped beneath it onto the path. Rather than swinging up on the big blood bay gelding tied to the post, Connor unlooped its reins, draped them over his shoulder, and began to walk slowly away from the cottage.

He stopped beside a gray stone that had served as their pirate ship in the child-dreamed days when Meaghan had played Pirate

Queen of Connaught to Connor's The O'Neill.

Connor gestured to its slightly sloping top. She sank down. "Lord Radcliffe offered me a goodly bit of gold this noon," he said quietly, "and not a piece of it anything to do with the stables." He paused. Meaghan looked away. "His lordship wants me to find a copper-haired lass, a beauty, with eyes of a color I know in my heart."

Meaghan's face flushed crimson and she bent to touch a curling blade of grass.

"Dear God, Maggie, how did you fall under his eye?"

"I was on my way home from saying good-bye to Da. Lord Radcliffe saw me on the road and . . ."

"And what, lass?"

She closed her eyes against the pictures of what had followed, but still she could see the unruly darkness of Sean's hair, the planes of his cheekbones, the lightness of his smile.

She heard Connor swallow. "In all the years I have known you, you've never been fearful to meet my gaze. Nay, not even the day you told me you didn't love me. Tell me. Did he do anything? Did he touch you?" Connor raised her chin to look into her eyes.

His touch was so different from that of the sun-browned hands that had caressed her beneath the lavender coverlet. His fingers were cool, with no demand in their roughened ends.

Sean had touched her just so once, tipping her face up to drown in the blue fire of his eyes. But then there had been little gentleness, only a torrent of emotions crashing over her with the force of the sea. Did he touch her? Oh, God! She bit her lip to keep from crying out. Connor's face went gray, his green eyes deadly.

"I'll kill him. I'll kill him with my own hands."

"No, Connor. It wasn't Lord Radcliffe. I mean . . . I am the girl he's searching for, but he didn't touch me. He didn't." She held Connor's clenched fist, detaining him.

"Who then?"

"No one."

"Meaghan, it's me. Old Connor, who knows you better than the fields we ran in. Out with it, lass, for I'll not stir a step 'til I have the whole of it."

"It was another man," Meaghan whispered, the hurt she had suffered lessening a little for being able to speak of it out loud.

"Sean O'Fallon. But it was as much my doing as it was his own."

Connor's jaw hardened. "He hurt you?"

Meaghan stared out over the hills toward Cottage Gael. Tears blurred the green swells, then ran unchecked down the slopes of her cheeks as she told the whole tale.

When the sobs seemed to choke her, Connor drew her into the curve of his shoulder, knowing the bittersweet pain of holding the woman he loved in his arms as she cried for another man, a man who, from all appearances, had used her badly, then cast her aside with no more thought than if she'd been a common trollop.

"Of all the idiot schemes—claiming you were his *wife!* Does he think Colin Radcliffe has no knowing of what is about on his own manor?" Connor gritted when she had finished. "O'Fallon will have to help, that's all there is to it. He's the one who thought up this ingenious ploy. Well, now, he can damn well get you out of it."

"No, Connor. I'll not have you breathing a word of this to Sean. I'd rather take my chances with Radcliffe than . . ." her shoulders drooped, "force myself on a man who doesn't want me."

"This is no game of seek and dare, Meaghan! Wilde, Radcliffe's hound, rode out before I did. He's got a pocket full of coins and a story of Radcliffe's goodness that would make my mother's heart bleed. And what in God's name have you got to bargain with? A sickly mother and a brother with more brass than brain! Lass, it won't be taking him long to find you."

"I'll brave this on my own. I have to. Promise me."

"Come stay with Mary and me then. They'll not dare to touch you under my protection. Bring Tom, your ma, Brady. Mary would be glad of the company—she's so lonely, losin' her folks and all." Connor grasped Meaghan's shoulders, and the look he gave her was almost a plea for understanding. "That's why I married her, Maggie. You didn't want me, and she was so young and alone. You'll never want for anything, neither will your family, as long as there's a horse for me to care for in Ireland."

Meaghan put her hand on his arm, a tired smile tilting her lips. "That wouldn't be fair to any of us. Not to Mary. Not to yourself. You've got a wonderful wife, Connor, and she loves you. You love her too, more than you know. I'll not drag you both down into this abyss with me." Meaghan rose, shaking the bits of grass from the hem of her skirt.

"Maggie," he started to protest.

"No, Connor. I'll stay out of Radcliffe's way as best I can, and trust to my wits to keep me safe. Sean, well, I'll take the dress back to him and leave him in peace. That is what he wants, and what I need."

"You can't just go traipsing about with Wilde on the prowl. If they believe you are this O'Fallon's wife, the first place they'll look is the bastard's house."

Meaghan cringed at the epithet, knowing Connor had flung it out in anger, wondering how many times Sean had endured hearing it; the stark pain that had been in his hooded eyes echoed through her. Her mouth set in stubbornness.

"You needn't stick your lip out at me, lass. It will gain you no ground. If you're bound to go I'll be taking you to O'Fallon's astride Tanist here."

"Connor—"

"Now. Get the cursed dress and tell Ma Bridget we'll be going to see Mary. She doesn't know any of this, your ma I mean?"

"No."

Connor retrieved the gelding's reins. "I'm thinking you should tell her, about Radcliffe anyway. She should know."

"No. There is nothing she could do. She thinks I just stayed with Da, the spoiled and thoughtless daughter." Connor met the edge of bitterness in her voice.

"She loves you, Meaghan."

"Loves me and loathes me and can't decide which." Meaghan said as she hurried into the house. Ma had lain down on the big bed, visible through the opening of the door between the rooms. Transparent lids covered her eyes, so fragile they were mapped with tiny blue veins. Meaghan stood a moment, watching her. Exhaustion etched deep in lines by her mother's mouth, caused, no doubt, by the search for her. If she only *could* have told her mother the truth, confessed to her, sought comfort. But there had never been that easy acceptance between them. Meaghan quietly shut the door.

Tom, too, lay asleep in the loft. His fists curled into his straw tick. His muscles twitched as if they could not be still.

Meaghan opened the chest, quickly donning new undergarments before wrapping the silk in an old gray shawl and knotting its ends. She passed it to Connor as she returned outside.

"I thank you, really," she said as Connor clasped her waist and swung her onto the horse. "It would have been long before I could slip away to take this back. I . . . I'll be glad to have it done."

Connor handed her the bundle and slid his boot tip into the stirrup. "He's a fool, Meaghan," he said, his eyes resting but a moment upon her lips. "O'Fallon's a fool."

He mounted, the easy gait of the horse lulling them to silence. Connor's body was close as Sean's had been, but there was no rushing of the blood in her veins, no flush of heat, only a droop in Connor's shoulders that had not been there when Tom had flung wide the door. It hurt to see it, and she wished with all her heart for the simpler days of minnows nibbling on bare toes, of buttered fadge and friendship.

The horse skittered to the side as Meaghan's skirt billowed in the breeze.

"Easy there, Tanist," Connor soothed, slipping his boots from the stirrups to stretch his bandied legs. "You must be mindin' your manners, for we're taking a lady for a trot." Meaghan warmed to the familiar lilt in his voice. He was trying to lift her spirits as he had so many times before, taunting her to be daring and spirited.

"Now, if Meaghan were a man," Connor continued his banter with the horse, "why then we could step out right bright and chipper. But being that Meaghan is only a poor *lady*—"

The teasing brought a smile, and lightning fast, Meaghan whipped the hat from Connor's head and brought it down on Tanist's rump. The horse shot out, full speed, Connor cursing and laughing as he clutched the pommel of the saddle.

Meaghan clung to the horse with her legs, whooping like a child while Connor struggled to regain the stirrups and control the horse.

From the corner of her eye, she glimpsed gray upon the hill, but as she turned her head to look the rustling of a rabbit in a gorse sent the horse leaping to the right. Meaghan felt the bundle slipping from her, felt herself tumbling from the thoroughbred's high back. She hit the ground with a thud, the air driven from her lungs.

She looked up to see Connor grinning at her from the horse's back. "Too tame for you, was it?" he called, holding out his hand.

Her laughter came out in gasps as she pushed herself up and

examined the scrape on her elbow. "Don't start with me, Connor MacDonough!"

"Some things never change." He shook his head ruefully. "Ma Bridget will blister my britches for bringing you home all skinned up again."

Meaghan picked up the bundle and grabbed hold of Connor's hand, swinging up behind him. "And I might help her," she threatened.

She stared for a moment at a distant rise, as Connor jogged the horse into a trot. It was empty. Too empty. She remembered the flash of gray she had seen, the silhouette of . . . something.

She shivered and looked away as thoughts of seeing Sean again chased away her brighter mood. She did not see the form again as it eased over the crest of the hill. She did not feel the probing eyes, or hear the swish of the straight-edged razor as the burly man drew its blade across his meaty arm.

Sean slammed the copy of *Lancet* shut and hurled it across the table, its slick pages scattering a dozen envelopes of powdered medicines to the carpeted floor. He pressed his fingers to his burning eyes. Damn! He'd been poring over the same two pages for an hour, and not one of the words had penetrated the haze that clouded his mind.

His hand fell away from his face, his gaze shifting again to the delicate china bowl Meaghan had used the night before, cleaned by Grace but left upon the table in a departure from her usual orderliness, to remind him of . . . Damn Grace, anyway! The knowing grin on her face when he'd at last mounted the stairs had eaten at his gut.

"I'm no monk, Grace," he'd bitten out, furious that he had felt compelled to justify himself at all. "You know there have been women."

"Aye, bloodthirsty wenches clingin' to ye after yer bouts in the ring, hands eager for the sweat of ye, lustin', and ye taking what they gave so free-like, living for the next crack of yer fist into flesh. And Alanna, suckin' the life out of ye, all smilin' an' pretty. Pretty like the devil."

"That was all a long time ago."

"Ye think it's not printed on my mind, the last time ye raised yer fists? Aye, and I'll never forget it, or the look of ye when I broke into the ring. You caught me, Sean, to keep me from goin' to him, and your hands still smeared with blood. Ye had sadness in yer eyes, deep down. I saw it there, when the others saw only ice. I saw it in yer face again this day."

"She was no one."

"No one, but ye take her into the room ye'd not let a soul into for three long years, layin' with her till ye know full well I'd be about. No one, but ye chase after her like a lovelorn colt, stumblin' on the stairs naked as God made ye. That girl was no doxy to bed and forget. And ye know it well, Sean." She had clunked the bowl onto the table before him. "Aye, better even than me."

She had gone through the rest of the light chores Sean would still allow her to do, whistling tunelessly, pausing often to throw him a smug grin and nod her head with the arrogant certainty of the sage, until finally he had exploded. "Go home! I'm sure you can't wait to be blabbing the whole thing to Liam!"

"Aye, he'll be pleased, sure," Grace had agreed, waddling over to where Sean sat. She gave his dark head a pat, as if he were a sulking child. Her brow arched, her eyes sparkling, as he stiffened. "Ye know," she leaned close beside him, her voice a conspiratorial whisper, "ye would have caught her if ye'd cast away the sheet!"

His laugh had an empty ring. Caught her? Christ, he didn't even know why he'd been *chasing* her! To apologize for stealing her virginity? He wasn't sorry, damn it! He had taunted her, knowing deep down what he was awakening, no matter how hard he had fought against it. But Meaghan, she had taunted him, too, all unknowingly, with her soft lips, her courage.

He had wanted her like something clawing inside him. Yet making love to her had offered no release but had only tightened the grip she held in the pit of his taut belly. If she had stayed, what would he have said? Could he ever have made her understand why he had to block her from his mind and how deeply she threatened him, touching not only his body but something much deeper?

A thud of something hitting the ground outside the house sent Sean bolting from the table, the bowl clinking upon its hard surface as he rushed to the open window. A huddled man staggered up from the dirt, weaving toward the veranda steps, slipping off their ledges. Bloodstained cloth swathed him from wrist to elbow, ends of white muslin trailing from where it was clumsily knotted.

Sean grabbed freshly washed bandages, bounding down the stairs three at a time to fling open the door. He wedged his shoulder under the figure slumped on the ground. "Good God, man, what happened?"

". . . Riding . . . fell . . . a stone . . ."

Sean whipped a length of cloth around the upper arm, twisting it in a tourniquet. There seemed to be so much blood smeared across the man's skin . . . so much . . . No wonder the poor wretch could scarcely raise his head.

Sean struggled to untie the knot, tied surprisingly tight for someone so injured. Sean's progress was hindered all the more by the man's fingers clutching at it.

The cloth fell free, dropping onto the step. Sean's eyes narrowed as they swept the bloodstained flesh. A thin line scribed across the fish-belly-white underside of the arm. So shallow was the cut that the bleeding had well near stopped. Finger marks were printed in the drying blood. Finger marks as if someone had squeezed . . .

A beefy hand closed over the wound as the man stumbled toward the door. ". . . Faint . . . inside . . . have to . . ."

The suddenly familiar voice was a slap in the face. Sean clenched his fist, sprawling the man aginst the rail. "Wilde!"

"O'Fallon, you have to help me . . . bleeding so bad . . ."

"Quit the dramatics, you son of a bitch! No bruise? No swelling? There's not a stone in Ireland that would make a laceration that clean! What in the hell are you doing here? The truth, Wilde. Save me the trouble of beating it out of you."

"I think it would be obvious." Wilde's beady eyes mocked Sean. "I'm bleeding like a butchered sow."

"You should have cut yourself deeper. I might have enjoyed giving you stitches." Sean thrust a bandage into Wilde's hand, shoving him toward his horse. "I know why you're slinking around here, Wilde, and I'll only tell you once. Stay away."

"I don't think so, O'Fallon. She piques my interest, this hot-blooded wench you're thrusting into. My interest and Col's . . ." Wilde licked his slack lips, hitching up his pants with a lascivious grin. "Work hard, Sean, to keep this one in your bed. You'll have to."

"What happens in my bedroom is none of your concern," Sean's eyes flashed warning, "or your master's. *My wife*, Wilde. Mine. I guard what is my own."

Wilde wound the strip of white around his arm, chortling. "If that's so you're doing a damned poor job of it! Of course, what I saw, well, it's none of *my concern,* especially since we both know you're quite *used* to sharing your women ... But with Lord Radcliffe's *groom?* Ah, Sean, if you can't satisfy your wife's lust you could at least give her to someone of station."

"I'd feed her to the swine before I'd let her touch your high lord's coat sleeve." The corner of Sean's mouth quirked, but there was no mirth in it, only danger.

"Oh, she touched more than MacDonough's coat sleeve, I'd wager," Wilde said. "She touched the fastenings of his pantaloons and what's hidden inside them. You should have seen her, Sean-o, rolling in the grass like a whore with a man whose wife lies weak from childbed." He turned to his mount, but a steel-taloned grip stayed him.

"What's your game, Wilde? Driving for a fit of jealous rage? Do you really think I'd believe a scum like you?" Eyes glinted like ice on a gun barrel. Despite his words, Sean saw her in his mind, Meaghan with another man, her hair tumbling in a red-gold river to pool upon another broad chest, her fingers closing with such delicate sweetness upon ... Damn! A muscle in Sean's jaw knotted. She bore no ties to him. Why should he care if she took a hundred lovers? He released his hold on Wilde and wiped his hand upon his pant leg as if Wilde had tainted it. "You lie."

"Nay, O'Fallon. She lies. With you. With MacDonough. With Radcliffe. Then when he tires of her mayhap with me."

Sean's mouth twisted as he plunged his fist into Wilde's belly. Wilde crumpled to his knees. Sean turned toward the house, hand on the rail as he mounted the steps, but with a sudden rush, Wilde was upon him. A crushing blow smashed into the side of Sean's head. Blood streamed down his cheek as the cut on his temple burst open, but he spun around, unfazed, pummeling Wilde with grim pleasure.

Neither man saw the thoroughbred dash into the yard or the white-faced girl vault from its high back.

"Stop it, Sean!" Meaghan screamed. "For God's sake, Connor, make him stop!" She caught Sean's fist as he drew back to deal yet another blow. With brutal force he severed her hold on him, whirling to confront her. His hand dug deep into the flesh of her arm.

"Meg ..."

"Take your hands off her." Rein-hardened fingers clamped on Sean's wrist.

Sean wheeled, the face of the red-haired groom striking him like a blow. His cerulean eyes flashed back to Meaghan, lips curling in a snarl. "I'll treat my *wife* any way I see fit."

"Aye, and Sean knows well how to treat a woman," Wilde sneered, his eyes narrowing with the glint of a swordsman driving his blade through gapped armor. "A woman who is a *whore* like his mother was."

Sean tore free from Connor's grasp, driving his body into Wilde's stomach, his fist connecting solidly with Wilde's bulbous nose. There was a sickening crunch of cartilage breaking, a gush of blood, rage unchained as Sean's fists hammered into him again and again.

Connor grabbed Sean, but Sean wrenched from his hold, doubling over. His hands rested on bent knees, breath rasping in his lungs as he seemed to battle for control.

"Get him out of here," Sean grated.

Connor worked his arm around Wilde's back, heaving the man to his feet. He turned, hoisting Wilde onto the gray. Wilde steadied himself with his hands on the pommel. His face was swelling and purple. "Just remember what I said, Sean. The truth is often . . . very clear to see." Wilde's beady eyes fastened on Meaghan's dress, lingering until Sean's gaze swept over it as well. Sean paled.

"Get out, Wilde!"

Puffy lips curled back from Wilde's teeth in a leer. "I'm going, Sean. But I'll be back. When Rad told me of his . . . fascination . . . I thought he was insane. But now . . ." his fingers brushed his broken nose, "I am more eager than he." Wilde raised the reins, and the gray started away.

The three stood in silence, watching the horse grow smaller in the distance. As it drew out of earshot, Sean wheeled to face Meaghan, his nostrils flaring in distaste, his temple still bleeding. "Now, you get the hell out of my sight."

"You cold bastard!" The step Connor took toward Sean was stayed by Meaghan's hand. Sean's gaze flicked down to where her fingers clutched MacDonough's sleeve. His harsh laugh grated.

"You'd know about bastards, wouldn't you, MacDonough?" he snarled. "Your wife with a babe still at breast, and you can't wait for her to heal before you father one by Meg."

"What the hell—"

"She's good, isn't she? Meaghan, I mean. That virginal innocence that tears a man's heart out, but so hot in bed—"

The tears of humiliation that burned Meaghan made Connor's
blow swim before her eyes. Sean's head snapped back, but he
didn't raise his fist.

His eyes seemed to sear through her, and had she not known it
impossible, she would have sworn there was agony in him as he
spun on the heel of his boot and stalked into Cottage Gael.

Connor bent down, scooping up the bundle that had fallen in
the fracas, throwing it onto the veranda step. He reached out a
hand to smooth away Meaghan's tears. "We've done what we
came for. I'll be taking you home."

"No." Meaghan peered at the corner of a frame, the globe of
the lamp showing through the door Sean had left ajar. "You go
on."

"Meaghan—"

"I have to talk to him, Connor."

"If I don't get back to the stables—"

"Go on. Wilde is no threat to me right now. It's early yet.
Just . . . just stop and tell Ma I'll be home soon."

"Maggie," Connor brushed the hair from her eyes, "if you
have need of me—"

"I know, Connor. I know where to find you." She watched
Connor mount the thoroughbred, reining it toward the meadow.
He looked back at her once. She waved, trying to tilt her mouth
in a smile to reassure him. Her hands gripped tight the knot of the
bundle, lifting it as she climbed the stone steps and went into the
door.

All was as it had been the night before, except that the lamp
chimney, soot smeared when she had left, had been polished to a
crystalline gleam and replaced upon the wooden stand.

"I thought I was rid of you when you ran out this morning."
Sean's sharp-edged voice startled her. He stood at the head of the
staircase, a handkerchief pressed to his temple. Cynical acceptance lined his face, and aversion, as if she were somehow
soiled. She put her hand to her breast. "You should have gone
with MacDonough."

"I came to return the dress you lent me."

"I meant for you to keep it. You knew that."

"Keep it? And where, pray tell, would I wear it? It's worth more than three harvests from our land."

"You could wear it for your lovers."

"My what?"

Sean dropped the handkerchief, and descended the stairs, each step toward her a silky menace. "Your lovers. MacDonough... the others... Wilde told me he saw you rolling in the field with MacDonough like a—" He reached out, yanking free a wispy blossom tangled in her hair, crushing it in his fist. "By God, for once it seems Wilde was telling the truth. You play the innocent like a master, Meaghan. I'm certain the skill will prove quite... profitable."

Meaghan stared at him, aghast, the burning of her cheeks no match for the anger raging through her. "How dare you—"

"Oh, I dare," Sean cut her off. "I'd dare much with you." His hand reached out, fingers grazing her breast. She jerked away.

"It's a little late to play the blushing virgin, Meg. Especially with the results of your morning's passion emblazoned on your skirt."

Meaghan's eyes widened. She looked down at the fawn-colored frieze. The corners of her mouth jumped, uncertain whether to match Sean's fury or laugh aloud. She ran a finger over the deep green stains, the results of her fall from Tanist's back. "Passion?" she echoed, dropping the bundle to the floor. A spark lit her dark eyes. "No. I'll not deny it."

His face went white. He raised his hand as if to either strike her or ward off her words.

"Passion has everything to do with these stains upon my dress, passion and friendship. The friendship that brought Connor to help me. The passion that made me fool enough to fall into your bed, the idiocy that had me so nervous about returning this dress that I fell from a horse when I've been riding since before I could walk."

"What?" Sean grabbed her shoulder as she wheeled to leave, spinning her to face him.

"I stained my dress when I fell off the horse," Meaghan flung at him. "I rolled in the meadow, I'll vow. Rolled and rolled until I crashed into a gorse bush!"

"I've heard the lies of a woman before. Save your pretty tales for the children."

"Pretty tales of love and a gallant Irishman?" she challenged.

"I was a maid when I came to your bed. I asked nothing of you, no promises, no honeyed words. There was always Alanna between us. I knew that. But what I felt with you was..." Pride choked the words. She broke away from him, leaning her cheek against the cool papered wall. "Dear God, Sean. Do you really think I hold myself so cheaply that I'd go to Connor's arms before your bed was cold?"

She felt his hand against her hair, but flinched away. "When I came to you it was foolish, mayhap, and most certainly without thought for the morrow, but you, above all, should know I had never been with a man before..."

His fingers slipped beneath the mass of her hair, gently tracing the hollow at the base of her skull. "Meg..."

She tried to pull from him, but his hand tightened, his body so close she could feel its heat. "You've made your feelings about me quite clear," she said. "Leave it at that."

"I can't, Meg. Wilde... he knows you now. It's only a matter of time before they pounce. You can't fight them alone." Sean raised her chin, cupping her face in his hands. There was the slightest tremor in his voice, then it was gone. "They'll find you, destroy your family if you try to resist."

Meaghan shut her eyes, the bittersweet pain of Sean's skin against hers far greater than the fear his words conjured.

Seconds passed, and she could feel his eyes move over her face. She shivered. "Stay with me." His voice was husky in his throat, heady with the warmth of his breath.

Meaghan's laugh had a hollow sound. She backed away, but he caught her against the wall, his hips pressed tight against hers.

"I mean it, Meg." She opened her eyes to the blinding intensity of his own. His lips brushed hers, once, twice. "Stay with me, here at Cottage Gael," he cajoled softly. "Stay, Meg... as my wife."

Eight

It was as if Meaghan were plunging down a precipice, falling into fathlomless blue depths. *"Marry you?"* she echoed the words.

"Would it be so terrible?" Sean ran his thumb gently over her lower lip, his face unreadable.

"Why? Why would you even consider... You barely know me... you... you don't love me..."

"Don't bait me, Meaghan." There was an edge to his voice, and she flushed in the realization that he knew her words were as much question as statement. "You know I don't love you."

She dropped her eyes to the wedge of bronzed skin bared where his silken shirt lay open at the collar, amazed at how much the words hurt, hating that part of her that had dared hope... hope what? She didn't love him either...

His tone grew gentle. "Meaghan, if I told you that I loved you, or that I could ever hope to love you, it would be a lie. We'd know it. Both of us. Though I'll not give you my heart, I'll give you my name. You'll be safe here, out of the reach of Radcliffe's treachery. I'll take care of you... your family..."

"How generous." She felt Sean stiffen. "No, I mean it. To take to wife a woman you feel nothing for..." She knew she was seeking... seeking something from him. There was understanding in his eyes, and regret.

Strong and warm, his hand stroked the line of her throat, down to her frieze-covered shoulder. "Our marriage will be no hardship for me, Meg. I'll never love you, but I'll never love anyone else. Since the moment you ran away this morning I've

90

been struggling to find a way to protect you. This is the only solution."

"And you? What would you gain from this *noble gesture?*"

"You would be safe in my keeping, and in return, you would perform certain . . . wifely duties."

"Duties?" she blazed. To hear him reduce what they had shared to a task, vaguely unpleasant but necessary, like bathing bare feet at day's end . . . "You accuse me of taking lovers, then ask me to marry you! You tell me you'll never love me, then in the next breath speak of the *duty* of a wife in her husband's bed! *Damn you,* Sean O'Fallon!"

His eyes narrowed, wariness deepening their blue.

"No! I'll not stand a liar before God and man, making a mockery of what should be—" Her tirade ended abruptly. Should be what? her mind cried. Violent and tender? Madness and magic? Yielding and desiring? Everything that Sean O'Fallon's lovemaking had been only last night.

A spark flared behind Sean's half-lidded eyes. "I was not aware my touch was so distasteful to you." He dropped his hands from her, pacing a few steps away with a shrug of his broad shoulders.

"You mistook my meaning," he said in frigid tones. "A clean shirt and an edible meal were all I required. Never in all my wildest imaginings did I assume that you would share my bed."

God, why did his casual dismissal hurt so much?

He went on. "This would be no true marriage, but a marriage of convenience, Meaghan, for both of us. That is what our union would be. Nothing more. Of course, if you wanted children, we could arrange—"

"Stop it! Arrange children? Arrange marriage? *I can't!*"

"Don't be a fool!" Sean wheeled, knuckles white on his clenched fists. "You and your damnable pride! Would you truly rather be Radcliffe's doxy than live in at least some semblance of respectability with me?"

"Respectability? Selling myself into marriage for safety? For the price of a clean shirt? I think I'd rather be a whore!"

"Damn it, Meaghan!"

"I'm good at playing that, aren't I, Sean? So good you had to boast to Connor—"

"Don't! I was angry! I'd just fought Wilde! For the love of God, I don't know why I tried to hurt you." Sean gripped her shoulders, his eyes so piercing, so fierce, that a needle-thin shaft of fear shot through her. "What happened between us last night was no harlot's bedding. Not for either of us. Don't you dare label yourself—"

Sean's jaw hardened, but Meaghan was too lost in anger to heed the warning there. "A whore?" she goaded. "A woman who lies with a man for pay? That's what I am, isn't it? I'm being paid quite well for the loss of my virginity."

"I'm not trying to *pay* you—"

"Aren't you? Never once have you told me *why* you offered to marry me. Not once! Sean, do you even know?"

He wheeled to face her, raking his fingers through his hair. "I want to help you. I can't stand by and watch Radcliffe destroy your life. I won't let that happen again, damn it. Not after what he did to Alanna . . ."

"That's why. It's for *her.* And because you feel responsible for our . . . for making love."

"Christ, yes, I feel responsible! I saw what was coming the moment I touched you. I should have taken you home. I knew it. But I wanted you, so I . . ."

"So you'll serve your penance and marry me?"

"Yes, damn it! I mean no! Sonofabitch!" Sean slammed his fist into the wall. His head lowered onto his upraised arm, dark curls to sinewy muscles stretched taut against the silk.

A strange sense of loss washed over Meaghan. A tear trickled down her cheek, then another. It seemed they stood there forever, so near, yet worlds apart. She could hear Sean's breath calming, heard him step to her side.

Wordlessly, he smoothed his hand across her wet cheek, catching the tears with his fingers. There was no fight left in her.

"You're right, you know," she whispered. "It's little short of a miracle they haven't already found Ma and the boys. Now that they've seen me . . . it won't take them long to decide that Matthew O'Leary's hoyden daughter must have grown up. But . . . but I can't marry you, Sean. Not this way."

He started to protest, but she stopped him. "I won't *marry* you, but I will *stay* with you until my family has safe passage to America. Not because I want to, but because there is no other way."

Sean lifted her face to his. "If you are to stay here, it will have to be as my wife, Meaghan. Not in the eyes of the church, mayhap, but in the eyes of all others until you leave. It has to be that way."

She nodded.

The deep lines carved about his mouth lightened. "Tomorrow I'll take you to Dublin. It'll be a whirlwind courtship. Then even those who know us will believe that we eloped. There are things I have to do, arrangements to be made, my patients ... Liam can hold things together until we get back," he said almost to himself. "I'll go to MacFadden's. When I come back, I'll hitch up the gig and we'll get your things."

Meaghan's stomach clenched. Ma. Sean paused, and Meaghan could feel his eyes on her. She tried to hide the dread that crept through her. She swallowed. "Fine."

"It will be, Meg." She heard him walk a few steps from her. There was a *shush* of something light being dragged across wood, a tiny click of a fastening unhooking. Meaghan opened her eyes to see Sean slip the catch of a small carved box. His brown fingers closed over something. He replaced the box on an intricately wrought shelf, unassuming and yet so beautiful Meaghan couldn't believe it had escaped her notice the night before. A gold-framed miniature rested there. It was of a girl on the verge of womanhood, dark wings of hair swept back from a heart-shaped face, a shy, loving smile gently curving a mouth yet too tender. Alanna?

"My mother," Sean said quietly, and there was about his face a hint of her, only haunted and disillusioned, as if life had crushed the part of her inside him.

"She is beautiful," Meaghan whispered.

Sean turned away from the shelf, his expression closed. "She was." He opened his palm. A delicate gold circlet rested in its center, banded with tiny blue diamonds. Among the glittering stones shone an oval of green, glowing with emerald fire, a perfect heart cut into its underside.

"I want you to have this." Sean said the words softly, raising her left hand to slide the cool metal loop over her fourth finger. Its clasp on her skin was strange, yet not unwelcome. "It belonged to my mother. She loved it. I think more than anything, except me." An edge of bitterness cut his voice.

"I can't take it."

"I want you to. No one will doubt you are mine as long as it stays on your finger." Sean dropped her hand, as if suddenly aware he had held it cradled in his own all this time. He hurried on. "As soon as you get word on your father's whereabouts, I'll book passage for you on the first ship bound for America. Your family, too. It . . . it's the least I can do."

"Sean, you don't owe me anything." She ran the end of her finger over the emerald's facets, then started to draw it off.

Sean stopped her. "You're wrong," he said. "I do owe you, Meaghan. More than I can give."

He retrieved a set of twin leather pouches linked by a wide strap from its place under the lamp stand and slung it over his shoulder. "I'll be back from MacFadden's as soon as possible."

Meaghan nodded.

She felt his eyes again on the ring adorning her finger. There was a look of loneliness and vulnerability she had never seen in them before. "I want you to be happy here," he said.

She looked down at her hands, unable to answer him, aching to reach up and soothe the lines from his brow. Happy? How could she be happy so close to him, yet still without his touch. She craved it, she suddenly knew; she wanted to smooth the hurt from his face, to see him laugh, to rid him of the demons that drove him.

The sound of the door as he shut it echoed in the hall. Meaghan moved silently to the little shelf, her eyes fastening on the rosy painted face. There was warmth in it. So much warmth, and love and laughter.

Who was she, this woman, now encircled in a gilded frame? Had she kissed Sean, a child with sea-blue eyes and rich brown curls? Had she tossed him in the air, mayhap as Meaghan's father had tossed her when she was small? Kissed his hurts? Bandaged his knees? And had she loved her bastard child more than life, this dark-haired girl with her softly dimpled smile?

Wilde had said Sean's mother was a whore, but it was no harlot's face that stared back at Meaghan now. Had she wanted him, Sean's father, with the same fierce desperation Meaghan felt for Sean, with a driving need that knew no bounds of right or wrong, wise or foolish?

And the price she had paid . . . Meaghan ran her fingers over her own flat stomach. To raise a child an outcast, prey to blade-sharp tongues, despised, with nothing but your love to be his shield. Meaghan felt the walls close in about her. Her fingers tightened. A child . . .

* * *

The crunch of iron-rimmed wheels grinding to a halt on the road behind her forced Meaghan to look up into the last rays of sun. She stood still, fighting that part of her that was glad he had come, though she'd asked him not to in the note she had left pinned to the door. The rigid planes of Sean's face softened as he swung down from the box, running the backs of his fingers down the curve of her cheek. "I've always liked a good fight," he said gently. "Did you think I'd let you go through this one alone?"

"You don't understand . . ."

"Yes I do. It's all in the letter. Enough of it for me to guess the rest."

"If you come—"

"If I come I might be able to help you calm your mother's fears. She has a right to be afraid, you know. You're a beautiful woman, and blindness is not one of my problems."

"It is one of my mother's I'm afraid, at least as far as I'm concerned. Sean, things could get so ugly."

"I'm sure when you explain how Radcliffe—"

"No!" Meaghan snapped, immediately sorry at Sean's questioning look. "Ma can't be told the truth. If she thought I was doing this for her—she's a fighter, Sean . . . I don't know, she's always been the one to take the blows, and sick as she is, I don't know what she'd do if she knew about Radcliffe's threats. And if Tom found out . . . Tom is worse still."

"Tom?"

"My brother. Thirteen, hot tempered, and full of the freedom of Ireland. Da said . . ." she couldn't keep the quaver from her voice. "I promised I'd take care of them, no matter what the cost. And I will."

"Even if it means lying? Angering your mother when with a few short words you could make her understand—"

"Understand and do God knows what? No."

"Meaghan—"

The feel of his fingers soothing her cheek, the gentle timbre of his voice, hurt her. She didn't want to feel anything now. She wanted to wrap herself in a cocoon of numbness that her mother's anger couldn't cut through. She pulled away from his hand. "Sean, if you come with me you have to give me your word you won't say anything. *Anything*. No matter what Ma does."

"If you would just explain . . ."

"No! There will be no explaining. I'll do this my way, or I'll face Radcliffe without you or anybody."

"All right, Meg. All right. If that's the way you want it."

"It is." She lay her hand against the sleek gelding, stroking a rounded haunch. Sean's ring caught the fading sun, glimmering dark upon her finger. "I . . . I'm glad you followed me," she whispered.

She put her foot on the tiny step, and Sean helped her into the gig. She thought he hadn't heard her until she saw him smile. "So am I, Meg," he said, swinging up beside her. "So am I."

He clucked to the horse and the hills rolled under them, the small compartment filled with silence, understanding, dread. And Meaghan *was* glad. Glad of the warm hardness of his arm brushing her shoulder, the feel of his thigh against hers when the rutted road pitched them together, glad that he would be there when . . . Meaghan's fingers tightened on the folds of her skirt. God, she would give anything if the carriage wheels were turning in the opposite direction.

She bit her bottom lip as Sean pulled back on the reins and the wheels ground to a halt beside the rock-bordered path. The dim gold of a rushlight set the window aglow, a stooped shadow passing before it. Meaghan willed her fingers to uncurl where they were clenched in her skirts, but it was as if the threads had woven themselves through the tips of her fingers.

She didn't even know Sean had leapt down from the high seat until his hands spanned her waist. He swung her down, powerful shoulders blocking her from the view of the house, palms lingering just below her breasts. His thumbs moved in gentle circles grazing the softly rounded swells. "Everything will work out, Meg. You'll see," he said. He lowered his head; the blending of his mouth with hers was warm and sweet.

The weathered gray door swung open. Sean straightened up, his hands sliding down her ribs but not breaking contact. Meaghan turned to meet the shimmering fury in her mother's eyes.

"So ye've decided to grace us with yer presence tonight, yer highness." Meaghan flinched at the quiet venom in her mother's voice. She felt Sean stiffen.

"Ma, I'm sorry. I know you're upset—"

"Upset, am I? Connor bounces in here lookin' like he stole the hosts at Mass and tells me ye're with his Mary. So Tom and I, we decide we'll see the new babe, too. But when we get there, there sits Mary all alone. She's not seen ye, not heard from her husband, and when Tom blurts out ye were with Connor her face turns the color of tallow. Ye had him lie to me." Her eyes swept down to Sean's hand, bronze against Meaghan's dress. "Why, Meaghan? To play the fine lady and prance around with this—"

"Sean, Ma. He has a name. Sean O'Fallon."

"O'Fallon," Ma repeated, the name sounding like an insult. "Aye, and I've heard of him before—an Englishman's whelp right quick with his knife and his poisons. And what is the good doctor to ye that ye have to lie to see him?"

"He . . . he's the man I'm going to stay with—"

"Stay with?"

"I . . . I'm going to live with him in . . . in his house, and . . ."

"The day ye see me dead!" Ma gasped. "What do ye think he wants with ye, this fine-dressed man? Pleasant company? Did he ply ye with pretty lies? Trinkets?"

"No, he—"

"Love words then? Meggie, don't tell me ye're fool enough to believe a man like this would give ye anything but a belly full of child!"

"Trust me, Ma. Just this once trust me. I have to—"

"Trust ye? Ye come to me with a lie on yer lips, and tell me that I'm to trust ye?"

"Ma, I—"

Faded eyes fastened on Meaghan's clenched fist. "That's it, isn't it?" The emerald caught the light from the window, glowing warm against Meaghan's twilight pale skin. "A ring. A whore's token!"

"My mother's." Sean's voice was deathly quiet, his fingers compressing Meaghan's waist until she thought the bones would crack. "To protect Meaghan from—"

"You don't have to make excuses, Sean." Meaghan wrenched away from him, eyes burning as she held the ring up to the waning light. "I'm tired of being poor, of having nothing but rags and work and grubbing in the dirt for potatoes that rot. I want more, Ma."

"Meaghan, child—" Her mother's face was gray. "Ye don't know what ye're saying—"

"Don't I?" Meaghan trailed her fingertips down Sean's arm. Her hands shook. Her eyes pleaded. The muscles of Sean's neck

seemed carved from iron. She could feel what it was costing him
to keep silent, and prayed that he would keep his word. "Sean
... my ... my box is in the loft under the window. If you could
carry it ..."

"Meggie!" Her mother's thin hand closed on her wrist, yanking it away from Sean's elbow. Meaghan turned to her mother, a
smile pasted on her face. Bridget O'Leary's eyes were filled with
tears. Her hand lashed out, cracking sharply into Meaghan's
cheek. Meaghan's own hand flew to her stinging face. She
squeezed back the tears that threatened to choke her.

"Go with him and ye're no child of mine, nor Matthew's either! Ye'll never hear from yer father again! I'll tell him ye're
dead! Better Matthew grieve for the child he loved than know
that ye ... Meaghan it would kill him ... listen to me ..."

Meaghan's nails dug into the palms of her hands. She looked
past Ma's haggard face trying to shut out the words, but they beat
down on her like the stripes of a flail until there was nothing but
blinding pain.

She heard Sean's expletive, felt his hands close about her as
he all but flung her onto the gig's black seat. The gig shook as he
slammed his lean body beside her, reaching behind himself to
dump a cloth sack onto the ground beside Bridget O'Leary.

"Food," he snapped. He took up the reins, slapping the dark
leather against the roan.

Meaghan tried not to look back, but she couldn't help herself.
She stared at the figure of her mother, shadowed against the
whitewashed cottage, her frail body shaking with sobs. But it was
not that sight that held her. It was the block of window behind her
mother that filled her with foreboding—the square of light that
cast in sharp relief the freckled, rage-taut face of her brother
Tom.

Nine

Dublin lay dying, her great stone mansions empty of the grace and wealth that had made what had once been the second largest city in the British Isles glisten, a bright cut jewel along the Irish Sea.

Those of wealth and power had deserted her almost fifty years ago when the Act of Union had bound Ireland to England like a bride being dragged to the altar. The forcible disbanding of Ireland's Parliament and the scattering of her leaders had left the city bereft. But to Meaghan there was beauty in Dublin, in the rush of discovery in finding the heavy cornices of Georgian buildings set against the plainness of the street fronts, in the tall windows and the doors, crowned with fanlights.

And in the man who had brought her here.

Sean walked beside her now, his long legs encased in peg-topped trousers, his wide cravat of midnight blue silk wound high above his starched shirtfront, his face kissed with the aura of a boy guarding a secret.

The crisis that had kept him at a patient's bedside, detaining their trip for two weeks, was over, and the purple smudges of weariness smeared beneath his eyes had disappeared as the miles of Wicklow countryside between Cottage Gael and Dublin had rolled beneath them.

She had never seen him thus, the corners of his mouth lifting into smiles in the thin shadow beneath the brim of his gray top hat, his eyes sparkling as the gloom that had enshrouded her since the altercation with her mother faded.

The plain muslin dress he had given her from the chest of

clothes in the room that had been Alanna's was travel stained now, its bodice, pulled tight across her breasts, cutting into the soft skin beneath her arms. Yet she had been glad he had not waited to retrieve her box from beneath the thatched eaves. No, she could not have borne another minute of Ma's condemnation.

"Here." Sean stopped abruptly in front of a shop whose spotless window displayed swaths of silk, printed cambrics, and spools of rich black fringe.

"Here what?"

He opened the door, a small brass bell tinkling from above it. "Here is where you begin to dress like Sean O'Fallon's wife."

"But I . . . I'm not—"

"You have to be, Meaghan, or everything that happened between you and your mother will have been for nothing." Sean stepped inside, doffing his hat and setting it atop a bolt of brown woolen.

"May I help y—" A green curtain sectioning off the back of the shop parted, revealing a sly-faced girl bedecked in a rust-checked dress. "Master Sean!" she squealed, pressing skinny hands to her small bosom. "And just where have you been hiding yourself? We've not seen you in months! Why, if you didn't look so devastatingly handsome I'd—"

The pout in the too-full mouth deepened to a blatant scowl as Sean put an arm around Meaghan's waist, drawing her forward; Meaghan had an urge to shove one of the pins stuck in the cushion tied to the girl's wrist into the plump red lip to see if it would pop. "Delia, I'd like you to meet Meaghan."

The girl's reply was lost as a gold-tressed woman swept from the back room, her eyes alight, her hands held out in front of her. Sean dropped his arm from Meaghan as if she had suddenly sprouted thorns. He grasped the woman's slender hands in both of his, kissing her on her rose-tinted cheek.

"Elisabeth." There was an intimacy in the silken tones, a warmth that made Meaghan want to scratch the woman's eyes out.

"How are you, Sean?"

"Fine. And you? I would have written, but . . ."

"No. It's better you didn't. I . . . I needed time . . ."

Time? Meaghan thought sourly; well *Elisabeth* was certainly making up for it now with those soft eyes of hers gazing up at Sean. Totally amazed that she had done so, Meaghan slipped her hand possessively through Sean's arm and crooned, "Darling, aren't you going to introduce me to your *friend*."

Elisabeth turned very pale, Delia guffawed loudly, and the lines between Sean's brows slashed deep.

Sean released only one of the golden-haired woman's hands, though Elisabeth tried to pull the other from his grasp. "Meaghan, this is Elisabeth Downing. I studied medicine under her father. He died of heart failure in January."

"I . . . I'm sorry . . ." Meaghan stammered, wishing an earthquake would split the floor of the tiny establishment and conveniently deposit her a hundred miles away.

"And this ill-mannered, quick-tempered wench is Meaghan O'Leary O'Fallon," Sean continued. "My wife."

The sudden smile from Elisabeth Downing was completely unexpected, and it galled Meaghan to see perfect white teeth revealed between rose-petal lips as Elisabeth looked from her blazing face to Sean's. "If the poor thing is married to you I can understand her concern," Elisabeth quipped.

"You can, can you?" The fires in Meaghan that had been doused by Sean's cold words simmered to life again at the disarming grin he shot the beautiful woman. They acted as if she wasn't even there! "Maybe I should hustle my wife out of this shop and off to another before you tell her all my darkest secrets," Sean said. "As you can see, Meaghan tends to be a trifle . . . jealous."

"Of all the arrogant, swell-headed . . ." Meaghan stopped herself at the sound of Delia's snickering. She forced her voice to adopt a syrupy sweetness as she laid her hand on Sean's chest. "While *Meaghan* has enjoyed greatly making your acquaintances and providing for everyone's amusement, she would like to see more of the city now," Meaghan oozed, seething at the smug grin that showed no sign of leaving Sean's face.

"I don't think so, *dearest*. I rather swept Meaghan off her feet, Liz." He turned to the woman, one thick black brow arched devilishly. "But in my haste, I forgot a few necessities. Clothes, for example."

"Sean O'Fallon how dare you—" Meaghan fumed.

"You have my heartiest sympathies for allowing him to coerce you into marriage. The man has no manners and even fewer morals," Elisabeth said in tones that could not be mistaken for anything other than kind. "Still, if he's ready to fit you out, I do have some things in the back room that might be suitable... perfect for your coloring. I started them for myself, but when Papa died..." A shadow crossed her face. "Come along." Elisabeth whirled gracefully into the back room, motioning Meaghan to follow.

Meaghan glared at Sean, but he only smiled, prodding her along like a reluctant mule. When she balked at the doorway, he gave her a little push through the curtains. Meaghan stumbled over a narrow board, thudding into Delia who scattered a box of pins to the four corners of the room.

Sean's call from the far side of the curtain cut off Meaghan's apologies and the girl's angry mutterings. "Meg needs everything, Liz, whatever frills and furbelows you ladies are tormenting yourselves with this season, and those lacy things that go on underneath."

"You'll keep a decent tongue in your head, Sean O'Fallon!" Elisabeth warned, "or I'll send you packing." She was perched on a stool, rummaging in one of many large baskets stacked upon wide shelves on the wall.

She pulled a bit of cream-colored cashmere over a woven rim. "Ah, here they are, Delia." The girl abandoned the pins she was retrieving, scuttling over to receive the baskets as Elisabeth handed them down.

Each one held a froth of colorful cloth banded in delicate trims, a half-dozen gowns in various stages of completion.

"Papa promised me a trip to the continent," Elisabeth explained quietly as she ran a length of slate blue linen through her fingers. "We were almost ready when..." she paused, then taking up the cloth again ran her gaze over Meaghan's figure with a critical eye. "You and I are almost of a size, but your waist is so tiny... If we don't lace you into stays, and I take the dress in a little bit here..."

"Don't take in the bust a thread's width or she'll be popping out of these gowns, too," Delia complained loudly, yanking at the fastenings at the back of Meaghan's dress. Meaghan felt her face go crimson as the sound of a choked laugh came from the other side of the curtain.

"Delia!"

"Well, its true! No decent—"

"Curb your tongue before I snip it out with the scissors!" Elisabeth hissed, turning the flame-cheeked Meaghan around to make short work of the jet buttons. In seconds the muslin lay crumpled on the floor, forgotten as layers of peach-colored cambric printed with tiny blue roses were pinned and basted around Meaghan's waist. Taffeta, silk, borders of plaids and laces, satins and velvets fell about Meaghan until the room resembled a field bright with flowers. Meaghan could only gasp, running her fingertips over each new wonder as it was revealed.

"Now for my favorite," Elisabeth said. "I had just finished it, but somehow it didn't look right on me. Now, after seeing you, I know the reason why." Meaghan stared, mesmerized as she shook out layer upon layer of silk taffeta rustling on a bell-shaped skirt. Three bands of pale blue anchored wide ruffles the shade of ripe peach. The fitted blue bodice was topped by a high white lace collar.

Elisabeth slipped it over Meaghan's head. The sleeves dripped ruffles of peach over purest white from the middle of Meaghan's upper arms to the lacy white undersleeves, the collar softening Meaghan's cheeks to the hue of the ruffles themselves.

"They're called 'melting-candle' sleeves," Elisabeth said, fastening the double row of buttons down the front. "This goes with it." She handed Meaghan a round box. Meaghan opened it. The most beautiful bonnet she had ever seen nested in tissue paper.

"N . . . not all of this," Meaghan objected shakily, touching the peach silk rosebuds inside the bonnet's ruched brim. "Sean can't possibly mean for me to . . ."

"Sean most certainly does." The sound of his voice in the doorway made them all start, and Meaghan's heart raced as she tried to guess how long he had been standing there. He leaned against the doorjamb, one booted foot crossed in front of his other ankle, his lazy blue gaze coursing over her body.

He took the bonnet from Meaghan's numb fingers, slipping it over her bright hair. The tips of his fingers felt rough on the soft skin under her chin as he worked the wide ribbons into a perfect bow.

"There, Mrs. O'Fallon." The way he said the words did queer things to Meaghan's stomach. His eyes smoldered as they lingered upon the firm swells of her breasts and her waist, so tiny it needed no casing of whalebone. As his hand fell away from her she felt its brush against the base of her throat like the touch of a brand. There was a promise in it, and a promise in his slightly parted lips.

"As if I haven't enough trouble without someone calling at the shop and seeing you back here!" Elisabeth blustered, grabbing Sean by his coat sleeve. "You can gape all you want when you take her back to your rooms."

"When we get to the hotel, your efforts on Meaghan's behalf will be sadly wasted."

"Sean O'Fa—" Elisabeth began, blushing, then turned to order Delia, "Take this reprobate out front and don't let him out of your sight until I'm finished, I mean it Sean! Behave yourself, or—"

The blue eyes flashed to Elisabeth. With a slow smile, Sean tipped up Meaghan's chin and took her mouth in a deep, deliberate kiss. When his lips came away from hers there was a searching look in his face. His eyes darkened as he stared down at her.

He wanted to shake off Delia's clawlike hands as they closed upon his arm, but he did not. He allowed himself to be pulled into the maze of cloth bolts at the front of the store by the simpering girl and tried vainly to still the trembling in his gut. God! He had meant the kiss to tease Liz, but the feel of Meaghan's mouth opening under his . . . He picked up his hat, hiding the rising clearly visible beneath the fly of his trousers.

Damn it, he'd been fighting to stay away from Meaghan since the day she had taken Alanna's room at Cottage Gael. Even when he'd stumbled home too tired to shuck off his boots he had lain in his cot, aware of her rhythmic breathing on the other side of the wall, trying to convince himself that the mind-shattering release he had found in her arms had been magnified a hundredfold because he had been months without a woman.

He had promised himself he wouldn't touch her again, haunted by her innocence and the torment he had seen in her face, and yet how many times since then had he made love to her in his mind? Damn, he needed a woman, one with no soft reproach in the slenderness of her body, and no innocent trust in her eyes, one he could take pleasure in and give pleasure in return, and then forget. He'd been a fool to bring Meaghan to Cottage Gael; a fool to think he could keep himself from taking her.

Delia's hand on his arm made his skin crawl, her whining voice setting his teeth on edge as he maneuvered away from her on the pretext of examining a swath of garish purple wool, the direction of her affected chatter only then becoming clear.

It was gossip of the most gruesome kind. She seemed almost to thrive on it, but Sean saw enough stark tragedy every day on his rounds. He had no stomach for blood-mongering.

"—when Lettie told us, why, can you imagine, Master Sean?" she squeaked. "Crawling into the hold of one of those ships in the first place? And then to have the thing break apart in the storm. Sinking, with barely a trace and not a week's sail from shore! Why the *Rose*—"

"The what?" Sean dropped the bit of wool, his other hand clenching on his hat brim with the certainty he had heard that name before.

"The *Rose*. Another ship came upon it in the storm, but couldn't get near enough to help."

"The *Irish Rose?*" The sudden intensity of his voice made Delia look away from his muscled bicep and stare, puzzled, into his face.

"Aye, that's the one. Two of the crew were picked up later clinging to some of the wreckage. They say not so much as a rat was left . . ."

Sean grabbed Delia's shoulders to silence her as the curtains parted, and she stumbled hard against his chest, her arms twining around his neck. A look of disbelief replaced the shy beauty of Meaghan's face, shifting then to something akin to pain as Sean's arms went around the girl in an effort to maintain his balance. His hands slid down Delia's waist and the girl wriggled against him. Sean saw Meaghan's fingers touch her lips, still reddened from his kiss, before she turned away.

"There is another bonnet here, and a . . ." Elisabeth stopped midsentence, letting the boxes balanced in her hands tumble to the counter as she looked from Sean's tight face to Meaghan.

The silence in the shop was stifling as Sean tried to put the clinging Delia away from him. The girl's knees wobbled, and she plastered her nonexistent bosom to his shirtfront until he peeled her off, not giving a damn if she fell flat on the floor.

"If . . . if there is a problem . . . or you didn't mean to spend so much . . . I mean, you said whatever . . ." Elisabeth stammered.

"They're fine," Sean said sharply.

"Master Sean and I were just ta—"

"It's damned obvious what we were *talking* about, Delia." Sean's hard voice interrupted, his hand clamping on her wrist until the girl gasped with pain. He could see Meaghan flinch, then her back stiffen. "The gowns are perfect, Elisabeth," Sean said. "Thank you."

"Yes, thank you." The words were as brittle as the smile Meaghan gave as she spoke them. "It wouldn't do for the great and generous Sean O'Fallon's wife to run about dressed like a street urchin."

The pointed giggle Delia gave filled Sean with disgust. Had he ever really found the wench's bold attention amusing? He strode over to Meaghan, his hand cupping her shoulder gently. He could feel the tautness beneath the blue taffeta, and sensed she wanted nothing more than to jam her heel into the center of his instep. He raised her face up to his, astonished at the coldness in her eyes. "Meaghan would be beautiful in sackcloth."

She wrenched herself away from him, hating the subtle shading of pain in his eyes. The feel of his skin through her sleeve made her throat ache, the hurt deeper still when Sean let his hand fall limply to his side.

Sean took up the parcels.

"Delia . . . I mean, I will bring the rest of the things to you as soon as we finish . . ." Elisabeth said uncomfortably.

"Fine."

"Meaghan, I . . . all the best to both of you."

"Goodbye, Elisabeth." Why was it Meaghan felt as if she were leaving a friend? Then Delia was blocking the way.

"You won't leave without saying goodbye this time, Sean?"

"Goodbye, Delia."

The way she arched the flat plane of her chest to brush his arm as she held the door for him made Meaghan ill. A clawlike hand closed on one peach ruffle. "Hang on tight to his coattails if you can," Delia warned with an insidious smile. "I'd hate to count all the hearts Sean O'Fallon has left pining in the dust. Of course, even men like Sean are forced to marry to get an heir, but often as not that does nothing to keep them from . . . other diversions."

Diversions . . . Meaghan thought dully. Diversions like Delia, like she herself had been the night they had made love, distractions all too willing to fall under the magic of his hands. And all of the women he touched were only a bid by him to forget the one he wanted and could never have.

Meaghan could never have him, and she wanted him—she knew this with sudden certainty. She wanted him in a way that tore at her, wanted his slow smiles, his hard, rough hands. Wanted him to . . . *love* her?

No.

Shifting shadows crept through the windows of Kingston House, but Meaghan made no move to light the candles in the grand hotel's room. It was better this way, the darkness shielding tears that slipped from beneath her lashes, spotting the thin lawn of the nightgown she wore, hiding, too, Sean's clothes where they lay tossed across the velvet-backed chair.

"If Radcliffe should get one of his lackeys to check the register there must be no question that you and I are sharing a room," Sean had said. "I swear I won't touch you." How could he have touched her, Meaghan thought bitterly, looking at the brocade-hung bed. He had all but run from the room the minute he had brought her up from the dining room, pulling off his cravat and coat, his dark hair tousled, not offering even so much as a token explanation as to where he was going or to whom.

Had he been running *from* her or running *to* Delia? She picked up the cravat, smoothing the midnight silk against her face. It smelled of bay rum from his shaving and starch, laced with clean male sweat. His hair, curling at his collar, had brushed against it, the textures of fine silk and thick dark waves blending so closely it was near impossible to tell them apart.

Meaghan sat in the window seat, tucking her legs beneath her, as she looked into the streets below. Now that day had fled, the poor and homeless wanderers had taken Dublin's streets, countryfolk, most of them, wrapped in rags, homeless and hungry. She wasn't hungry anymore, but she was hurting, and it would grow worse with each day she watched Sean O'Fallon breeze through her life, kind in the same way he would be in caring for a wounded cat, an abandoned child. Kind only because he didn't know how *not* to be.

A man with a gray shirt whistled a mournful tune as he shuffled under her window, and Meaghan found herself straining toward the sound in irrational hope. The man looked up and she saw faded brown hair and eyes with no joy in them at all. Her heart sank. She hadn't really hoped it could be Da, had she? Da was on the ocean now.

She leaned her forehead against the coolness of the windowpane, closing her eyes as the whistling faded. If the man *had* been Da, what could she have done? Could she have run down the wide staircase and tossed her problems into his hands like so many pieces of a broken toy?

He had depended on her, trusted her, believed in her, and in the space of two weeks, she had failed him. She had destroyed Ma, alienated Tom, been accosted by Lord Radcliffe, and had given herself to a man who didn't want her, a man who had somehow stolen a part of her and made her less than whole.

From the day she had been able to toddle through the cottage door she had been fiercely independent, confident to a fault. Da had made her that way, holding back Ma's hand when Meaghan had walked the fence top, catching her when she had leapt into his arms from the high loft opening.

There was no one to catch her now, but she wouldn't fall. She wouldn't let herself. Meaghan propped her arms on the wide windowsill. She wasn't exactly certain when her head drooped to the crook of her elbow or her eyelids drifted to the blessed darkness of sleep.

Dawn was pinkening the Dublin sky when Sean opened the door. He stared at her a long time, her tear-stained cheek resting on the window ledge, a wisp of dark blue clutched in her hand. His heart twisted as he touched it, the cravat he had torn off in such haste.

Slipping his arms beneath her knees and shoulders, he lifted her slight weight against him, sinking his own lean frame onto the cushioned seat. Tendrils of hair clung damply to her face. The need to shield her seemed to crush his chest. But nothing, no one, could shield her now. Better the cut be quick, clean.

Gold-tipped lashes stirred on her cheeks. He watched her awake. The faint gilding of happiness that lit her features faded to hurt.

"Sean . . . Why did you bother coming back at all? Didn't Delia—"

"I wasn't with Delia, Meg. I was . . ." His fingers brushed the curls from her face, the words barely squeezing past the knot in his throat. "I was at the docks."

"The docks? Why? What . . . what is it? Is . . . what's wrong?"

"I heard a rumor . . . wanted to be sure before I told you . . . to find out all I could. A ship went down a week's sail from the coast."

The sleep-laden eyes widened as she struggled to sit up.

"Two of the crew survived, but—"

"A ship?"

The muscles of his arms flexed, holding her closer. "A storm blew up. The boat . . . it wasn't seaworthy and—it was the *Rose*, Meaghan. The *Irish Rose*."

"No!" She slammed the heels of her hands against his chest, her face ashen.

He gripped her upper arms, and he knew he was hurting her. "I searched all over the waterfront asking every sailor I met to see if there was a chance, but your father . . ."

"He's not dead! He's not! Da wouldn't—"

"Damn it, of course he wouldn't, not if there had been any way . . ."

"I don't believe you! Another boat could have rescued him! He was late starting from home. He might have missed—"

"I saw his name on the passenger list, Meaghan, there's no way—" He caught her face between his palms, holding her so tightly a tinge of color returned to the waxy paleness. "The captain . . . the goddamned captain was afraid of a panic. He ordered a sailor to bolt the door to the hold—"

"The . . . the hold . . ." It was a whisper, a breath.

"None of the passengers even made it to the deck."

Stark agony lanced soft brown eyes twisting deep into Sean. White silence engulfed her delicate features, the sprinkling of freckles standing out against her skin, making her seem fragile and childlike. "Sean, he can't . . . Da can't be . . . Sean . . ."

His name was a plea, and Sean answered it the only way he could. He caught her in his arms, crushing her against him, pressing his lips to her temples, her eyelids. "I wish I could tell you it's not true. I wish I could make it right. God, Meg—"

The sobs that wrenched through her shook him to the core. Sean felt her sorrow like the slice of knife-blades, like tearing claws that ripped away love and security and left desolation—it was his body they tore and he was glad. Glad, to take from her a little of her pain, to feel. But it hurt, God it hurt. And as his hand clenched in the red-gold fall of her hair, pain long buried stirred to life. Pain and something more.

Ten

A single candle burned in the center of the table, chasing the encroaching night across the marble fireplace, casting into pale light the grief-sharpened bones of Meaghan's face. The days since returning to Cottage Gael blended together in a haze of orange-red, shot through with shards of images—Ma crumpling to the floor, keening; Tom shoving Meaghan's hands away from her; Sean catching Tom's wrist with his fingers, a dangerous glint in his narrowed blue eyes.

"If you had married Connor, Da would never have had to leave," Tom had flung at Meaghan, his wide mouth in a snarl too full of malice to belong to one so young as he turned on Sean. "And you, you English bastard, you can go straight to the devil! We don't need your help!"

Then Ma's voice had come, reed thin, hopeless. "Tommy, we have nowhere else to turn."

Meaghan stared into the candle flame, reliving the horrible sensation of being a stranger in the very room where she had been born. She had wanted her mother's arms around her, wanted to cry with Tom, remembering, but they had shut her out as surely as if she, herself, had died.

Now time passed with worried blue eyes searching hers, with meals fixed by Sean left untasted, with watching the shadows huddle in dark corners until even Sean seemed to despair.

She heard the soft shutting of the door below, but it was not the measured tread of Sean's boots that mounted the stairs, but rather a slow swish of bare feet, the creaking of boards under weight. Meaghan closed her eyes. Just one more in the never-ending stream of poor, pathetic souls Sean was trying to save.

The footsteps stopped outside the door, pausing just a moment before the door swung inward.

"He's not here," Meaghan said dully, not even looking up. "The kettle's full and there's bread in the basket—"

"Aye, and I know." The gravelly voice was strangely comforting, and when Meaghan raised her eyes, she saw an expanse of dark green frieze ballooning out over a distended belly. It was the woman Sean had called Grace, the woman who had seen them together . . . The green eyes in the indisputably homely face were quiet, their sparks of amusement gone.

Meaghan couldn't even summon the will to blush.

Grace waved a gnarled hand toward the window. "Sean-o's out making star pictures."

"Star pictures?" Despite herself, Meaghan felt her eyes drawn to the window where patterns of blue dots were beginning to prick the sky.

"For my little one, Annie. He holds her on his shoulders, he does, and points for her shapes in the stars. Then he weaves stories of magic. Tonight he told of a ship that lay broken, and a girl who lost her Da . . ."

The beginnings of anger pierced through Meaghan's numbness. "He had no right to tell you anything."

"He was beside himself with worry, colleen, and looking nigh as bad as ye, yerself. Mayhap he had no call to be spreading the news of yer sorrow to a one ye hardly know, but I swear the lad was that upset he didn't know what else to do."

"He can't bear it, can he? Just leaving someone alone?"

"Not someone he loves."

Meaghan couldn't stop that bubble of bitter laughter that rose in her throat.

"Ye don't believe me, then? He doesn't believe it himself. He's not so much as turned the latch on that bedroom door for three years yet there he was with ye, his face blushing like a lad caught kissing behind the cow byre. He spent an hour growling that it meant nothing till he finally ordered me away. Sean's had his share of women, Meaghan, more than that, maybe, and I well knew it, but he's never needed to deny they touched his heart. They knew it before they began. Sean knew it, too. And he never brought them here, to Cottage Gael. Not since Alanna."

"My dress was torn. He couldn't take me home—"

"Why? Couldn't ye have mended the tear just as easily with yer own needle and thread? With all the sickness about, Sean's been wearing himself raw. Why would he bring ye here when he could have spared himself time and trouble by dropping ye at yer doorstep?"

"Maybe he brought me here to seduce me," Meaghan said recklessly, not caring. "But he made it clear there was nothing else—"

"Clear to ye, or to himself?"

Grace pulled out the other chair, easing herself awkwardly into it.

"The first time I saw Sean was in the ring at the Callewylde Fair. He was angry, then, bitter, but not like he is now. That came later, after..." Grace's moss-colored eyes swept the window before she went on.

"He killed my first husband that day. Not that he wanted to. He tried to walk away, but Eammon wouldn't let him. The wager Eammon had placed on himself was all that we had in the world. I loved him, Meaghan. I begged him not to fight. The last time, he'd had the dizziness for weeks after. He'd be fine one minute, then his sight would blur."

Meaghan felt faint stirrings of empathy. "Your husband, he fought, anyway?"

"Sean sensed something wrong from the first. It was as if... almost as if he were trying to take Eammon out gently, but Eammon wouldn't have it. The fight, it was much more than the money to him. It was his life. But it was over, we all knew it, all but Eammon. Sean was trying to leave the ring. Eammon called him every kind of a coward, diving for Sean, his fist flailing. I think, by then, he couldn't see."

"What happened?"

There was sorrow in Grace's face, sorrow and acceptance. "Sean wheeled and knocked Eammon away. He just wanted it to be over, I could see it in his face. But Eammon fell backward. He was too weak to catch himself. I'll never forget the sound of his head hitting the ground."

"Then did he ... die?"

"I tried to get to Eammon, but Sean stopped me. I felt something inside him breaking, too. First I blamed Sean, hated him when he tried to help me. Then I thought it was my fault, that somehow I should have found a way to stop Eammon from fighting."

A lump of misery too large to hold inside rose in Meaghan's throat. "If I had married Connor, Da would be alive."

"Ye don't know that. Yer father did what he had to when he sailed. There's no way ye could have known the ship would go down. He could have died here in Ireland just as easily, Meaghan, in a thousand different ways. He died. We all die. But ye hold on to the good things."

Meaghan felt the tears burn through her lashes, and suddenly Grace MacFadden was holding her against her breast, stroking her head as though she were a child.

"It hurts so much to remember . . . everything makes me think of Da . . ."

"I know," Grace said. "I know."

"Even . . . even the night . . . and your little girl . . . when I was five I sneaked out of the house late. The stars were so pretty, and I . . . I wanted to sleep in the meadow. When Ma found me she was angry . . . it was damp and she was half-sick with worry. But Da . . . he only picked me up on his shoulder and listened to me tell him how I tried to touch a star . . . That day he . . . he went up in the loft by my bed and he carved out a window . . ."

The floorboards creaked, but Meaghan never heard them, or the stillness that followed. Sean stood, the tiny hand of Annie MacFadden held tight in his as he listened to Meaghan's emotions come painfully back to life. The child looked up at him, tugging until he lifted her in his arms. A little finger brushed beneath his eye and Sean knew she felt a tear.

The massive wooden door banged open, and Annie MacFadden dodged under Grace's arm, bounding out into the waiting embrace of her father. Sean watched the giant of a man sweep her up, tossing her high before he settled her in the two-wheeled cart; her elfin laughter tinkled on the air. "Da, Sean showed me a dragon and a flower princess and told me a story—"

"Ye're good with her, Sean. Ye should have ten of yer own," Grace said softly. "Seeing what I have, well, after listening to Meaghan, it makes me grateful. Seems things slip away, and you never know how much God's blessed you . . . Sounds foolish, doesn't it? Sentimental nonsense, and yet . . . I'm allowed to get soppy now and then, 'specially while I have the excuse that it's the babe talking."

Sean put his arm around Grace's thin shoulders, kissing her sallow cheek. "Thank you, Grace, for helping Meaghan, for getting her to bed, everything. She already seems better."

"Aye, she does. It'll take time, Sean-o, but the wound's beginning to heal." The gentle softness of Grace's face shifted, a tinge of uneasiness creeping through it. "Sean . . . I wanted to tell ye before, but ye've been so worried, and there's probably no damage done. I think I stopped it before . . . It's Trevor Wilde. I saw him a week ago at St. Colmcille's. He was talking to Father Loughlin and the sisters."

"Father Loughlin was going to talk to him about helping with relief measures. I told him it was no use, but, well, if Father can get Trev Wilde to open Lord Radcliffe's purse strings, I'll make him a candidate for sainthood!"

"No, Sean, they . . . they weren't talking about the hunger. It was something else. I . . . I heard him mention Meaghan's name."

Sean's head snapped up. "Meaghan?"

"He was asking Father questions, but you know how close-mouthed Father Loughlin is, at least when he isn't scolding someone. When I heard what was happening, I rushed up to them and started blabbing on and on about the baby's baptism and how Father had promised to talk with me." Grace rested a hand on her stomach. "I'm sure Father thought I'd taken leave of my senses. Wilde left, but he was angry. I could see it. Sean, I know I should have told ye before, but . . ."

"No, Grace. It's all right. I knew Wilde would be sniffing around somewhere. He can't hurt Meaghan here." A protectiveness that astonished Sean in its intensity coiled within him, but he tried to hide it.

"Gracie!" Liam boomed, "ye'd best get yerself over here unless ye plan to stay the night."

"Ye wouldn't dare to leave me. Ye'd starve before morning!" Grace called back, but her smile was strained. Sean kissed her cheek again, raising his hand to Liam who was waiting beside the cart.

"Don't worry," Sean said. "Worrying's not good for the baby. Meaghan will be fine."

"Don't worry, the man tells me." Grace shook her head in

mock disgust. "As if I've done anything else since the day I met him."

The sound of the MacFaddens' banter faded as the cart rattled down the road. Sean listened until it disappeared, then turned grimly into the house.

The door to Meaghan's room was open and he moved silently through it, his gaze running over the sleeping form he had carried to the bed. She was sleeping peacefully for the first time in weeks, her lips parted, her hair tangled about her face. He went to her slowly, trailing the backs of his knuckles down the curve of her chin. She looked so small on the large feather tick, so fragile.

He swallowed hard, tearing his eyes away from the firm rise of breast, the curl of slender legs.

She shifted restlessly. "Don't ... go ..." Her fingers found the tail of his shirt where it had come free of his breeches and closed on it, her hand pressing warmly against his taut belly She quieted.

Sean hesitated but a moment before his hands went to his buttons. The shirt fell away, sliding down his arms to bare his broad chest. His fingers went to the fastenings of his fly, but stopped there as he looked down at Meaghan's face soft with sleep. His hand fell away.

Carefully he eased down beside her, drawing the coverlet over them both. He slipped his arm beneath her, nestling her head upon his shoulder, her body curling around his. She felt so right against him, so strong within herself, yet so vulnerable. He wanted to ... God, what did he want to do? He still loved Alanna, didn't he? He'd always love Alanna ...

He shut his eyes, but no picture of Alanna's face would come to mind. Instead he saw Meaghan, brave, sweet Meaghan with her courage and her innocence. Meaghan who had struck him beside the scalp, not stopping to count the cost; Meaghan who had refused to abandon him to Radcliffe; Meaghan who had given herself to him with a passion that defied reality.

No, he couldn't love again. Dear God he couldn't. Everything he touched, everyone he loved, he destroyed. His eyes flew open, his fingers clenching in the coverlet draping Meaghan's soft shoulder as despair washed over him. Couldn't love again? God, could it be that even now it was too late?

 *Eleven*

Dusk trailed its jewel-toned wings across the hills like a butterfly coming to rest, dripping gold onto the waters of the stream that wound past Cottage Gael. Had it been three hours, or only two, Meaghan wondered, since the terrified scarecrow of a boy had burst into the house begging Sean to save his brother?

She had wanted to go with him, to help him. But though she'd passed the weeks since Grace MacFadden's visit watching Sean's gentle, capable hands bring respite to the ill and injured, this time Sean went alone.

Meaghan leaned back against the crooked stone fence, and shut her eyes, letting the breeze trace her lips with its heather-scented fingers, its touch reminding her of roughened wide palms cradling her cheeks and Sean's mouth searching. She had awakened the morning after Grace's visit, locked in his arms, the sheets a tangle around his bare chest. It had seemed so right, running her hand across the silky mat of hair, upward to the muscled column of his neck. He had groaned, his hands moving down to cup her buttocks and mold her more fully into his body. Then he had come awake with a start, a wary, trapped look in his eyes.

Alanna. Meaghan had known in that instant he was thinking of the dark-haired beauty who still held his heart. The name itself seemed to haunt her, robbing her of her sleep, tormenting her with visions. She saw Sean in the bed they had shared, making love to the woman he had wanted as his wife. *Love*, with a fire and passion that even now haunted him until he cried out for her in his dreams.

116

A wrenching pain knifed through Meaghan as she remembered the hot insistence of his thigh as it looped around her, and the way he had slept, one hand threaded through her hair. He hadn't touched her, no, not since the morning she had wakened in his arms. The wind whispered around her skirts in a melody as listing and sorrowful as a tune from Da's fiddle. It ached inside her.

"Meg." The sound of Sean's voice sent a shaft of longing through her. She looked up to see him standing behind her, ghostly pale, one side of his face swollen and purple.

"Dear God, Sean! What happened?"

"My patient's father was afraid my tainted English blood might defile his son worse than the poison in his body."

"He hit you? But you were trying to cure his child . . . I . . ."

"It's nothing, Meg. It doesn't matter. Nothing matters except the boy."

"Is he . . ."

"He's in the last stages of tetanus. Not a damn thing I can do except try to keep him comfortable until . . ." Sean lowered his head, pressing his thumb and forefinger to his eyes. "They didn't come for me, Meg, even when the leg swelled to double its size. Maybe I could've done something, at least given him something for the pain, damn it!" Sean slammed his fist into the fence with a savagery that ripped skin from his knuckles. "I wouldn't even have expected Casey to pay me. I don't take food out of the mouths of the starving, for Christ's sake! He could've worked it off here, thatching the roof, repairing the fence. He knew that! But no, he'd take no charity from an Englishman's bastard. He had to wait till the filth in the wound poisoned the child. Even then his wife and three older sons had to bind the man with ropes so I could treat the boy. Eight years old and dying, Meaghan. Slowly. God, how he's suffering . . ."

Instinctively, Meaghan reached up to cup the unbruised side of Sean's face, its shadowing of stubble prickling her sensitive palm. He pressed his cheek downward, trapping her hand in the warm cradle of his shoulder. His eyes drooped shut. The corner of his mouth trembled.

He reached for her, burying his face in the fragrant billows of her hair.

"Sean, I'm sorry . . ." she whispered, stroking his tense shoulders, "so sorry . . ."

"Is my English blood so loathsome that a man will watch his son die in agony rather than call on me to ease his pain? Me? In the name of God, no one, *no one* has more cause to despise the English than I do. No one!"

"It's unfair," Meaghan soothed, "I know..."

"Damn it, you don't know!" Sean raged, breaking away from her. "Nobody does!"

"Then tell me."

"You wouldn't understand...couldn't understand hate like this. I've hated so much, so long, there's no room for anything else."

"Who, Sean? Who do you hate? Casey? Your father? Or yourself?" The last words were so hushed Sean bent toward her to catch them. When he did, his head snapped up, eyes simmering with the dangerous pain of a wolf in a trap. A derisive snarl curled his lips.

"You think just because I bedded you you're privy to the darkest secrets of my soul? I've lain with whores who scarcely knew my name!" Even in the heat of anger he stumbled over the word, the slightest curve of his mouth betraying a stark vulnerability that struck Meaghan to the heart. Whore. How many times had he heard it, flung in the face of the mother he idolized, coupled with the word bastard?

The day of Sean's battle with Wilde flooded back to her, the half-crazed fury with which Sean had attacked him, the word Wilde had fired at him with the deadly precision of an expert marksman.

"Whore..." she breathed, not even aware she spoke. "Wilde called your mother a..."

The steely talons of Sean's hands gripped her arms, biting deep into the flesh. His face, inches from her own, a mask of fury. "My mother was no whore, damn you!"

His torment crystallized before Meaghan. He was like a wounded animal, biting where a lance had pierced, but without the power to extract it. And then she read it, the shadow of doubt in the line of his jaw.

"You believe them," she gasped, stunned. "Just a little, somewhere deep inside you, you believe them!"

"I don't! Damn you! Damn you!" The rugged planes of Sean's face contorted, his eyes dragging her with him into the depths of hell. "She was raped! My father raped my mother! Forced his seed inside of her and left her to bear the shame of his half-blooded bastard child alone!"

"No!" she cried. "I don't believe it. Who would tell you such a hideous lie?"

"It's no lie. It's the truth. For thirteen years I wondered why my mother looked at me with such a haunted sadness in her eyes, and why my stepfather, who loved all children, hated me, no matter how I tried to please him." Sean turned away from her. His broad shoulders sagged. "I think the old man took pleasure in it, truly, Meaghan, the shattering of my childhood fancies. You see, my mother told me often of my father when I was small. What pretty tales she wove of a dashing, handsome nobleman who had whisked her away. I even believed he'd come for us someday." His harsh laugh grated.

"Those were lies, Meg. The lies of a loving mother trying desperately to shield her child from the truth. You can be sure my stepfather lost no time in dispelling any delusions of grandeur from my head. He couldn't breathe a word of the truth, not while my mother lived. She loved me. God, how could she love me? She was delicate, gentle, but she'd spring like a mountain cat on anyone who would do me harm. So he bided his time."

"When . . ." Meaghan breathed. "How . . ."

A tremor coursed through his body. He turned, piercing her with his cerulean eyes. "My stepfather was not a man for wasting time," he said bitterly. "He told me everything. Every sordid, agonizing detail on the night my mother died."

Tears rained unheeded down Meaghan's cheeks. Tears for the child, tears for the man. She pressed herself against him, crying quietly against his chest. She could feel his body shaking, and his uneven breathing rasped in her ear.

"I didn't mean to tell you that," he said into her hair. "I've never told anyone before. Not even my grandda. I just sort of turned up on his doorstep, ragged and hungry. I didn't know where else to go."

Meaghan looked up into his eyes. "Sean," she murmured brokenly, "if I'd known I never would have . . ."

Gentle as a whisper, his thumbs traced her cheekbones, and ran over her temples, losing themselves in her hair. His sensual lips were moist as they arced toward her with infinite slowness, his breath warm and sweet. "Meg," he whispered, "Oh, Meg . . ." Seeking, giving comfort, his mouth moved over hers, opening her gently to his loving. She was like a flower unfolding. "Please . . . I need to love you . . ."

She buried her face in his chest, looping her arms around his neck. There was no need for words. Sean scooped her into his arms as though she weighed no more than a breath, carrying her from the waning twilight into the shadows of a sheltering knoll. The air was redolent with the perfume of wildflowers, mingling with the tangy scent of leather, horses, a touch of sweat. Sean lay her there, stretching his long, lean body over hers. Their mouths seemed to melt together as his tongue teased her lips apart. "Sweet . . ." he murmured. "So sweet . . ."

He sculpted the contours of her breast, its thrusting ripeness straining the thin cloth of her bodice. Whimpering, she arched her body into his practiced caress. He played her like a master, strong brown fingers freeing buttons, coasting beneath the cloth to pull the creamy lace of her chemise down over her breasts, opening them to his hungering gaze.

She closed her eyes against the intensity she saw in his. Her breath caught in her throat and her heart stopped as she waited the endless seconds before his mouth trailed kisses to the pink-tipped crest. Then it fastened, hot and wet, upon the swollen peak. She groaned his name over and over in time to his rhythmic suckling.

Shafts of light seemed to pierce her, slashing downward, blossoming in the pit of her belly. Sean caught the taut bud gently between his teeth, tantalizing it with the roughness of his tongue. "Please, Sean . . ." Meaghan gasped, "please . . ."

He rolled off, lips feasting on hers as he lifted her shoulders and slid her dress down. He spread it beneath her, shielding her from the prickly grass. "Take your chemise off," he said, his voice husky with desire. "Do it, Meg."

Her fingers shook as she tried to obey him, but they fumbled with the lacings. The fire in his eyes branded her, seared her. He smiled, and the beauty of it shook her to the center of her being.

The last of the lacings ripped from the chemise's binding. The ribbon drifted to the ground. Meaghan clenched her fist, embarrassed by her clumsiness. Her cheeks flushed.

"You're beautiful," Sean murmured, low in his throat. "So smooth, so soft." His hand closed about her fist, drawing it to his mouth. Slowly, slowly he loosened each finger, stroking the center of her palm in erotic circles. She stared, hypnotized as he wet his lips, pressing them deep into the center. The contact set aflame the passions that had tormented her these endless weeks without him.

With animal grace, Sean swept the blue silk shirt over his head, baring the rippling expanse of muscle beneath. His breeches followed with quick dispatch. She saw him lean over, heard a faint snap. Wildflowers ... the scent grew clearer, headier, deeper as he trailed a scarlet, satiny blossom down her breasts, her belly, and lower.

"I've thought about you," he said. "Every night. How you look, how you feel ... The way you hold your breath, for just an instant before I kiss you ... here ..." He brushed the tip of a breast with his lips.

A wordless cry tore from Meaghan as she clutched his thick, dark hair, forcing his mouth to take her. He drank her in deeply, then wrenched himself free, grinding his mouth into hers. "God ... oh, God, what you do to me ..." he moaned against her throat.

His hand shook as he trailed it down to the gate of her passion. She arched her body toward him, whimpering. "Now, Sean, now."

She didn't need to beg. He braced himself above her to keep from crushing her on the hard ground, the muscles in his arms knotting as she wrapped her legs around his hips, urging him to take her.

A deep throaty roar exploded from Sean as he buried himself inside her. The flames of her love consumed him, nourished him. Soft hands searched his shoulders, his hair. Her tongue probed the secrets of his mouth as she had earlier delved the secrets of his soul. Nails dug into the flesh of his back. He welcomed the pain, a faint reminder of the agony she had shared, the horror of his childhood that until now had been his alone.

With every art of his body he strove to please her, holding himself back, suffering the sweetest of tortures.

Harder, faster, deeper he thrust, unable any longer to curb the raw need of his sex. "Meg ... you're beautiful ... so beautiful ..."

Suddenly Meaghan cried out, grasping the taut muscles of his hips. It was a cry of joy, pain, love. It hurtled him from reality. He was shattering, shattering into a thousand tiny fragments, each shard pulsing, glowing, exploding ... alive.

* * *

The faint stirring of her hair woke Meaghan. She felt immersed in a sea of delicious sensations, and she snuggled closer into the warm roughness that covered her. Lazily, a fingertip traced the satin petals of her lips from corner to corner, then trailed down her chin into the curve of her throat. Her eyes fluttered open.

It was no dream. Sean still lay beside her, braced up on one elbow, his eyes caressing her more intensely than his fingers.

"I was watching you sleep," he said huskily, brushing a lock of his unruly dark mane back from his forehead.

Meaghan pushed herself up, her cheeks burning as she remembered the night's abandon. "You . . . you'll want to be going to Casey's. I'll fix you something to take the edge from your hunger."

"No," Sean said, too quickly, catching the edge of the blanket that covered her. "I'm not hungry."

Meaghan looked down at the blue plaid woolen. Her brow furrowed. "We . . . we didn't have a blanket when we . . ."

"You were shivering in the night. I nearly took you inside, but you looked so perfect here in the meadow." Sean gestured above her. A lavender quilted canopy was draped between a gorse and a seedling hawthorn. A warm glow lit her eyes, but Sean didn't see it. His gaze was fastened intently on the horizon.

"Meaghan . . ." He paused, turning to face her. "I didn't mean for last night to happen."

"Don't." Meaghan felt unrelenting claws close over her earlier joy, dragging her back to the reality of Sean and Alanna, the reality of being unloved while loving. "Not again," she whispered. He hushed her, laying one finger across her lips.

"I have to. The pain I've caused you since we met is inexcusable. I've betrayed your trust, the laws of the church, my own beliefs."

She couldn't look into his eyes. Her own blurred with tears.

"After what happened that first night we were together I swore I wouldn't touch you again. I knew it would only bring you pain." Sean's hand slid down to cup her chin, forcing it upward with a gentle insistence. A drop welled from the corner of her eye, coursing the path of his thumb. "I swore it, Meg. It's been hell to stay away from you. Every night I fought it. You were so close. I had but to take five steps, open the door, come to your bed . . . I wanted you. I knew it was wrong, but . . ." A muscle in his jaw worked. He waited. It seemed an eternity. "But there's something . . . something inside you I need. I don't know . . . an innocence . . . a warmth . . . Meaghan, I've been cold for so long . . ."

His lips were gentle as they moved over hers, not hard and demanding, but searching, seeking. And she wanted to give him anything . . . everything . . . He combed his fingers through her tousled hair, brushing her temples, her eyelids, the curve of her jaw. "Touch me, Meg . . ." he pleaded softly. "Meaghan, make me feel . . ."

Twelve

"You've not paid a whit of attention to me all night, Col," Alanna DuBois complained pettishly, raking a silver-backed brush through her luxurious ebony hair. "Who is she this time? Felicity Tinsbury? The Ratherton girl? Frankly I don't give a fig about who she is or what you do. I just wish you'd take her and get it over with so we could at least conduct an intelligent conversation."

"Jealous, my love?" Radcliffe quirked an eyebrow at her, smiling languidly from where he lounged on the gold-striped settee.

"Hardly!" Alanna snorted. "If I had palpitations every time you dallied with another woman I'd have the heart of a ninety-year-old by now. Besides," she leaned toward the cheval glass, pinching her cheeks to redden them, "I have yet to see the woman I should envy. They're all either ugly or boorishly moral."

"And those are labels that could never be used to describe you, could they?" Radcliffe mused, coming to stand behind her. "Why is it, I wonder, that you and you alone have kept my interest when all others failed?" He lifted her hair, kissing the nape of her neck. "Are you a witch, my delectable Alanna? Or is it that we understand each other so very well?"

"It's that I know you for what you are, a blackguard and a scoundrel," Alanna murmured, leaning back against him. "And that you are never certain of me, as I am never certain of you."

"Even after all these years." Radcliffe's kisses became more demanding. "Since the day I took you from O'Fallon."

"Ah, yes, poor grieving Sean." A smirk played upon Alanna's

ripe lips as she arched her head back, taunting Radcliffe's mouth by offering him access to her slender throat. She leaned back against him. "Although Sean *was* quite an accomplished lover, I must admit. Pity, such talent lying fallow all this time."

"Fallow?" Radcliffe broke away from his exploration, chuckling. "Hardly. I hate to disillusion you, my pet, but Sean's heart, it seems, is no longer buried in your imaginary grave. He's taken a wife and from what I can tell has ensconced the little strumpet as mistress of Cottage Gael. It's enough to make one's stomach sour, the way he flies about in a jealous rage. Why I scarcely touched her and—"

"A wife?" Alanna stiffened. The red pinched into her cheeks vanished. "Sean has taken a wife? I don't believe it!"

"It's true, dear. Regrettably so, from the look on your face. Personally, I found it amazing that O'Fallon stayed loyal to your *memory* this long." He brushed the delicate lace of her peignoir down the slope of her shoulders, pressing a kiss to the flesh he bared. "After all, a man has needs."

"Stop it!" Alanna crossed her arms over her breasts and jerked away from him. Stalking across the room she slammed the brush into the vast array of jewelry on the gilded dressing table.

Radcliffe eyed her reflection in the huge mirror. "My most sincere apologies, my sweet," he drawled. "I wasn't aware I was imposing on you. You seemed quite amenable a moment ago."

"I have no desire to have you pawing me when you're on one of your *maiden hunts.*" Alanna pulled the lacy garment back into place. "The ball at the Rathertons' tired me more than I had realized. I'm going to bed. Alone."

"Quite a sudden bout of exhaustion. Mayhap we should call for the services of a physician. Sean O'Fallon, perhaps?"

Alanna shot him a scathing glare. "The only cure I need is to be rid of you. Go avail yourself of one of the servant girls. I'll not suffer your churlish company tonight."

Amusement glinted in Radcliffe's black eyes, a derisive smile splitting his lips. "Dear God," he laughed. "You love the fool, don't you? You really love O'Fallon in your own twisted way!" He grasped her hair, yanking her head back so his eyes could mock her. "It's the biggest farce of the season! Bedding me but forever languishing over a lost love. Alanna, Alanna, I didn't think you were capable of loving anyone but yourself."

Bright spots of color stained Alanna's flawless cheeks. Pictures flashed unbidden in her mind, the well-honed grace of Sean's body, the gentle worship of his touch. "That's absurd!" she flared, snatching up the lavender sash draped over the delicate chair and whisking the bit of silk around her waist. "You've lost your senses!" She jerked savagely on the slender ribbon. A rending sound made her grit her teeth. "Damn you!" Alanna swore, flinging down the ruined sash. "See what you made me do!"

"Ah, yes. It's ever someone else's fault, isn't it, Alanna? Sean's fault for not leaving Ireland to pamper you in high society, mine for daring to tell you the truth about yourself . . . It would be well for you to remember, beloved, who pays to have you strut about in the guise of a queen. You sold yourself willingly to me. And for quite a high price, I might add. You are as much my property, Alanna, as this . . . bauble."

Alanna snatched the fragile crystal from beneath his fingers, drawing back her arm to fling it at him. An iron hand manacled her wrist.

"Temper, temper, Alanna my love," Radcliffe warned. "This vase is of great value. Unlike you it cannot be replaced. If aught happens to it I will take its worth out of your pretty hide." His eyes left no doubt as to his intentions as he let them roam over her thinly clad body. Releasing her, he ambled to the door.

With a cry of outrage, Alanna hurled the vase against the mahogany panel, littering the room with a million glittering shards. Her hands clutched the edge of the dressing table in helpless fury as his jeering laughter echoed down the hall.

Damn him! Sean married? No! She would never believe that! Sean loved *her!* She had watched him from the tower room when he rode into Radbury Manor the night he had thought her dead, so haggard and pale he had looked like some nightmare come alive.

Springing for Radcliffe's throat, he had seemed a panther enraged with blood lust, his sapphire eyes spitting death.

Colin had crumbled beneath Sean's onslaught, curling in a ball on the ground, trying desperately to fend off the battering fists.

It was then that the others had come, five of them, burly laborers led by Trev Wilde. Sean's scream of fury as they dragged him from Radcliffe had made her flesh crawl. Like a demon he fought them, dodging, parrying, so none could get a grasp on him, all the while dealing vicious, body-shattering blows. The sudden arcing descent of Wilde's hands had made him wheel, but not soon enough to escape their burden. The gray fence stone had glanced off Sean's head, sending him crashing to the turf, dazed.

Two of the men had leapt on him, dragging him up, suspending him between them against the manor's wall for the others to take revenge. Col had beaten him until he could no longer raise his arms, then flung him, face down, into the road.

How had Grace MacFadden known? A shiver went down Alanna's spine even now as she remembered the homely woman appearing out of nowhere, the instant Radcliffe and the others had entered the house. Her skirts bunched high on her skinny legs, her hair tangled, she had ridden astride a scar-faced donkey. In all the time Alanna had known Grace, she had never lifted a hand against a beast, yet now the donkey's rump was scored by the switch she carried. Kneeling in the road, Grace had cleansed the blood and grime from Sean's face with her dress skirt, crooning to him as though he were her child. Her body bent with the weight of him, she had struggled to heave his limp form onto the donkey's back, the usually placid beast shying from the smell of blood.

With her shawl, Grace secured Sean's legs beneath the donkey's barrel. His head sagged down onto the rough coat of its neck, the torn remnants of his shirt lifted by the fingers of the breeze.

Then Grace had stared . . . glowered at the tower window as though to lay a curse on it. Alanna had wanted to scream at her to go away . . . go away! She stood, as if held by some unseen hand, hypnotized by the hatred she saw in Grace MacFadden's face, until at last the lanky woman led the donkey down the hillside.

Had Grace seen her then, with those eyes that peeled away souls? Grace would have told Sean, wouldn't she have, had she known Alanna was alive?

But he hadn't known. He had come back to Radbury Manor again and again until at last Col had taken her to France.

Yes, Sean had loved her. No woman would take what was hers. And Sean O'Fallon was *hers*. If only he had listened to her in the days before they were to marry, when she had begged him to leave Ireland. Then she would have stayed with him. His rakish charm, his reputation as a brilliant surgeon, the glittering recommendations from Charles Downing and the others would have gained him purchase into any parlor in Europe. But he had refused her. He'd not leave those filthy, beggarly wretches who paid their fees in chickens, potatoes, or not at all.

No man was worth a life spent in crude isolation, bearing a brat every year to add to a brood of snot-faced children. Not even Sean O'Fallon.

Alanna's fingers tightened on the white skin of her arms as she recalled his lean brown hands upon her. He had known a woman's body well, pleasuring her until his touch was akin to pain. There was nothing in Colin Radcliffe's bed that tasted as sweet. He knew where to touch, but lacked the tenderness, the desire to please, that had tempered Sean's passion.

Alanna's breasts swelled with remembered desire. She shoved it coldly aside. She had made her choice, a wise trade—the power and riches of the Radcliffe name for the caresses of a man. Besides, there were the others, the pretty-faced boys in Paris and Cannes who brought her pleasure.

Her lips thinned. Beauty fled in the face of the hardness carved in her features. No. She did not want Sean O'Fallon, but no other would have him.

She had sought to drive her knife so deeply into his heart he would never pull it free. Had he forgotten? Memories could be stirred, wounds could be opened.

Suddenly she grew still, the muffled sound of footsteps in the hall creeping nearer. Col . . . was he coming now to extract the payment he had promised to have? She'd not be bullied! She was no frightened milkmaid to cower before him, kissing the hem of his mantle.

The floorboards directly in front of her room creaked. Then there was silence. "Who is it?" Alanna demanded in her most regal tones. Silence. "If you think for a trice, Colin Radcliffe, that I'll allow you to—"

The door swung slowly open on its hinges. Her breath expelled in an angry gasp. "You! How dare you! Have I not told you never to come to my rooms?"

A tiny, thin face looked up at her. Tousled dark hair tumbled about the cheeks of a small boy, his dark hair skimming the collar of his little nightshirt. A ragged plush dog was clutched in his arms.

"Are you mute, boy? When I get my claws in that incompetent nurse I'll—Damn you, quit staring at me!"

The child lowered thick lashes over huge eyes. Alanna wanted to claw him, scratch the sooty fringes from his face. She snatched up the hairbrush, gripping the boy's thin arm, jerking him around. "You'll be taught a lesson this time, my young sneak thief!"

A flurry of nightdress and mobcap whirled into the room, scooping the child out of harm's way. "No, ma'am, don't!" the frazzled being cried, pulling the child behind her broad body. "It's my fault, it is. Take it from my stipend. I deserve it, not watchin' close enough. But don't hurt the little master."

"As if a club could beat sense into this worthless child!"

"He's but half past his second year, ma'am, right smart for his age, he is, but he doesn't understand . . ." The nurse turned to the child. "Oh, Master Rory, whatever possessed ye to come down here in the night?"

"Noise." He pointed a stubby finger at the shattered glass. "Me fix it."

The nurse swallowed hard.

"Master Rory!" Alanna's mouth curled in disgust. "The brat's name is *Roarke!* You'll call him that and quit slavering all over him! He disobeyed me, and you act like he's been granted an audience with the Queen! There will be naught but bread for him tomorrow. Hard bread from the kitchen. You see to it!"

"Aye, ma'am."

"And that . . . *thing* . . . he's dragging around—"

"His pup?"

"Burn it!"

"But . . . he . . . he loves it so . . ."

"Of all the ridiculous—" Alanna hissed as the child clutched the threadbare toy to him. "Oh, very well! Let him keep the filthy thing! But if he so much as sets one foot inside this room again I swear I'll feed it to the fire myself! And you'll be out on the step, Mrs. Duggan. Somewhere there must be a nurse who can tame this incorrigible monster!"

"Aye, ma'am."

"Now out, both of you! My head is throbbing!"

The nurse scurried to the door, trying to hold onto the wriggling child. Just steps from the hall he struggled free, shoving the doll into her hands. Sturdy legs braced apart, chin held high, he faced Alanna with the courage of an innocent mounting the gallows.

"Well?" Alanna stormed. "Speak if you have aught to say!"

"Woarke sorry," the child said, turning the blazing light of his sapphire eyes upon her. "Woarke loves you, Maman."

Nails dug deep into the flesh of Alanna's palms. "Don't love me!" she cried. "I don't want you! I never wanted you!" She shoved the child through the mahogany arch, slamming the door shut behind him. Sinking onto the spindle-legged chair before the cheval glass, she stared into its silvery surface, but it was not her own reflection she saw there. Eyes, crystal blue, looked out at her from a child's face . . . a man's . . . haunting . . . Her shaking fingers closed over a gold-embossed vial, squeezing until the rose-flower pattern was imprinted on her palm. Haunting . . . Her hand grew still; her eyes narrowed. No. She was not the only one who could be haunted by the past.

Thirteen

The biting, clear water of the stream on his naked flesh had done nothing to cool the burning in his loins, Sean mused wryly as he leaned against the doorjamb to watch Meaghan bend over the hearth. Her hair, caught back at the nape of her neck with two ivory combs, glistened like wildfire, and the swell of her breasts strained against the pale rose-sprigged muslin of her dress. It was so good to see the swipe of pink high on her cheekbones and the corners of her mouth tipping up in the hint of a beguiling smile.

She seemed to sense he was there. The spoon with which she was stirring the contents of the kettle fell still and he felt a sudden warmth as the glow of remembered lovemaking shone in her sherry-colored eyes as she turned to face him.

"Sit," she said. "I've all but scorched your breakfast."

"I was bathing in the stream."

"I know." Then she blushed furiously. "When you weren't in bed . . . of course I looked for you!" she snapped at the mocking lift of his brow.

"And saw nothing that hasn't already fallen under your gaze." Sean grinned. "Or have I changed so very much since last night?"

He saw her flush in embarrassment, and he went to her, taking her mouth in a swift, hard kiss. "You should've come with me, Meg. The water was cold. You would have warmed me . . ."

He was alive to her, the scent of wildflowers clinging to her like a veil, the feather-light touch of her fingers on his skin. Now that he had taken her again, his need consumed him. He had had a score of women while he tried to forget his past and a score before Alanna. He had desired them, pleased them, left them. He

131

must have felt this excruciating need for Alanna as well, this craving he felt for more of Meaghan's sweetness. Why then was the memory of his nights with Alanna dulled, their beauty faded like ribbons forgotten in the sun.

"You must be hungry."

"I am. For you."

She didn't seem to hear him as she chipped nervously at a broken nail on her thumb. "You'll be going to Halloran's soon, won't you?" The words were like ice on his desire. Little Timothy Halloran was a fighter, but his battle would soon be over. Sean walked slowly to the table, flattening his palms on the smooth golden wood.

"I'm taking over more laudanum, and then I'll have to see what I can do to ease the sorrow of the rest of the family. Timothy has always been the Halloran's best-loved child, not only of his parents, but of his older brothers as well. There was never any jealousy. I don't know . . . it was just accepted by all that Tim is special."

"Is he?" Meaghan asked softly.

"Yes. Yes he is. Hate's been like a cancer in that family, infecting them all. It's Casey's doing mostly, the father. A British soldier crippled his hand. Casey was trying to steal the man's sword. He was always one for hiding a weapon, starting a rebellion. In truth, the soldier could've thrown him in jail or shipped him off to one of the convict colonies. He probably thought he was doing Casey a favor, leaving him free to support his family. But Casey was a potter by trade. The loss of his hand was the loss of his life."

"How did they survive?"

"The other boys were old enough to keep the family from starving. Times were better then. But they lost everything except their little plot of potatoes and the hovel they live in."

"And Timothy?"

"Tim was too young to remember anything *but* poverty, though he was above that bitterness. He wanted to become a priest. Would've made a good one." Sean fell silent, thinking of the towheaded boy with the earnest, dark eyes.

"I thought . . . I made a stew and a baking of bread. The family will be in no mood to cook."

"That was kind. Thank you." Sean straightened, pulling her

into his arms, her body warm and comforting as she nestled against his.

"And I . . ." She tilted her head back to look at him, uncertainty in her eyes. "I hope it was all right, Sean. There was an old suit of yours lying on top of the things in that old chest at the foot of your cot. I was putting the quilt away when I found it. You told me once that Tim had worn nothing but clothes torn and mended, handed down from four other brothers. I thought, maybe this last time he could be dressed in something better."

Sean buried his face in her neck, unable to speak through the sudden tightness in his throat.

"I know it will have to be altered. It's probably much too large. But I'm quick with my needle and it might do the poor boy's mother some good to have a woman to talk to."

"No. Absolutely not!" Sean pulled away from her, his tone grating even on his own ears. "There is no way on God's earth I am taking you with me on a call where I, myself, may come away with a broken jaw. I'll have enough of a task keeping Casey from *my* neck. I don't need to worry about a woman trailing along."

"Trailing along? I would hardly call fixing food and sewing a shroud trailing behind your coattails! You expect me to sit counting the cracks in the wall while that family needs help?"

"Meaghan, don't be a child! You don't understand the situation in the least. Timothy Halloran won't live through the day. Things could get very ugly."

"Don't you patronize me, Sean O'Fallon!" A chair rasped across the wooden floor as she shoved it under the table, and he could see the golden lights flashing in her eyes. "I know damn well how ugly death can be!"

Sean drew in a deep breath and slowly let it out. Death. She knew about death, about the death of the father who had loved her and whom she had loved, about a maze of aching agony that she was only now emerging from. But what did she know about a man like Casey Halloran? A man whose sanity had been frayed over the years, leaving only a wire-thin band of hate? Hate that might snap at the merest touch of a breeze?

His voice grew gentle. "Meg, I'd take you to Fiona Halloran in an instant, knowing you'd do her good, but I'm truly worried about what might happen when Timothy dies. Casey is half mad with grief, and unpredictable at the best of times. Tim is the joy of his life. I understand how you feel, Meg. And the suit, Timmy's welcome to it, but I *will not* take you with me. Wrap up the kettle in a cloth to keep it hot. I'll take it to Fiona in the buggy. As . . . as soon as it's over and I can gauge Casey's reaction to the boy's death, I'll take you there. My hand to God."

"I want to help them."

"You will." Sean cupped the stubborn thrust of her chin, urging it upward. "Just not now."

"Oh, I can go when *you* decide it's *safe*," she retorted, thumping a spoonful of stirabout into a china bowl. "I've just been through losing Da. I know I could—"

"Meaghan, I realize you feel like I'm ordering you about, but—"

"You *are* ordering me about!" She slammed the bowl down in front of him, splattering his hand with the hot porridge.

"Damn it, woman!" Sean muttered a string of expletives as he plunged his hand into the pitcher of milk on the table, cooling the little burns. Taking his hand out, he dabbed it dry with a towel. "I only want what's best for Timothy! There is no reason that boy has to die in the middle of an angry confrontation. Me, I have to go. But Casey has gotten quieter and quieter each time I've been there. With luck he'll think of the peace of the boy instead of his own anger. Let's not give him fuel for another attack."

"You think I'll goad a man whose son is dying?"

"No. I think Casey Halloran will use you as a weapon to provoke me. Thus far I've controlled my temper. I know Casey is suffering. But if he so much as said a word against you . . ." The very thought of Casey's acid tongue maligning Meaghan set his blood to boil, and the possibility of his hurting her . . . Sean's jaw clenched. "You'll stay here, by God, if I have to bind you to your chair myself!"

There was a stunned silence as fire blazed in Meaghan's eyes. "I'm not your slave, Sean O'Fallon, and you're not my husband. I'll do what I think is right."

"No, I'm not your husband. If I was I'd tie you hand and foot to keep you away from Halloran's. But if you're set on blasting in where you'll only make an impossible situation worse, there's nothing I can do to stop you, is there?" There was a bite in his voice that made Meaghan's hands tremble. She almost backed down before it, but his words still stung too deeply.

"Sean, I only want to—"

"I don't give a damn what you do," Sean snarled. "After all, why the hell should I?" He slammed out the door, crossing the yard with long angry strides, and disappeared into the stable.

The hut was small and crumbling, like mice-gnawed cake. Dirty gray-brown thatch bristled in ragged disarray, clumps torn out by time and weather.

Palms damp with sweat, Meaghan picked at invisible lint on the pile of neatly folded clothes on her lap. Why had she come, she asked herself for the hundredth time. Sean sat beside her, a stony-faced stranger. She could feel the thinly leashed anger within him. He hadn't wanted her help, believing she would only make matters worse. Would she? She shivered, forcing the thought from her mind.

It was as much Sean's fault as it was her own. If he hadn't been so arrogant she wouldn't have forced the issue. But he had challenged her and she had never been able to bear being bullied or condescended to because she was a woman.

This Sean, hard, cold, and angry, would give her no quarter if she made a mistake.

Sean pulled the buggy into the shadows of a dead birch tree, binding the reins to its trunk. He had the taut, swaggering stance of a man spoiling for a fight. Meaghan felt a whisper of foreboding trickle down her spine. She had brought him to this state. A man like Casey Halloran would close in on it like a hound on a blood scent. Damn her stubbornness, damn him for making her so furious!

He stalked to the side of the buggy, fists planted on hips. "Listen to me," he growled. Eyes, like shards of sapphire, glinted at her from beneath heavy dark brows. "I am in charge here. I'm a doctor doing what I was trained for. *You* will do what I say. *Exactly* as I say, the *instant* I say it. Do we understand each other, *Mrs. O'Fallon?*" His implacable face made her bite back the angry refusal that tightened her lips.

"Meaghan, I mean it. Promise me. In tetanus the least little shock can send a patient into convulsions."

"All right! Have it your way! I'll be your obedient servant as long as we're at Halloran's."

Sean held her in his brooding stare, his face strained, pinched with an aura of . . . what was it? Fear? "Damn it, Meg," he began, but he never finished as the boy who had fetched Sean to the house that first day ran up.

"Mammy was just sendin' me for ye," he gasped. "Timmy's bad off. Da wouldn't let us give him that stuff ye left in the bottle. Busted it against the wall. Mammy, she's been cryin'. Cormac and Michael are gone, and Daniel an' me, we can't hold Da."

"Is your father inside, Culley?"

"He's sick drunk, passed out on the floor."

The tension in Sean's face eased a little. "It's just as well," he said, taking the bundle from Meaghan and handing her down from the carriage. His fingers gripped hers, hard, as if to remind her of her promise.

"Don't worry," Meaghan gritted under her breath. "I'll set myself afire if you tell me to." But the fight had somehow gone out of her.

The corners of Sean's lips twitched as he lifted his medical kit from the back of the gig, along with a round basket with a woven rush lid.

Culley preceded them into the hut, dragging the door open on screeching hinges. Putrid air, reeking of vomit and offal and death lay in a thick, heavy blanket over the single room. Meaghan fought the urge to gag. She blinked, trying to accustom her eyes to the semidarkness. A primitive fear gripped her. She saw nothing, yet felt someone else's eyes upon her.

"Ye've come." It was barely a whisper in a voice so tired, so hopeless, Meaghan knew at once it was the dying child's mother. She struggled to bring the room into focus. With the ethereal mistiness of a nightmare Fiona Halloran came toward them. Her skin was drawn like parchment over bones, the pale blue eyes dull with the patient misery of a prisoner serving a life term.

"You knew I would, Fiona," Sean said gently.

"I thought after Casey hit ye . . . I prayed ye would come. I did. It's sorry I am . . ." Meaghan turned away from the despairing woman Sean had drawn into his arms.

Nowhere was there respite for her eyes, nowhere a glimmer of light, of joy. A slat-ribbed sow rooted in the corner of the room, networks of trenches furrowing the dirt floor. Against one wall a boy in his late teens huddled, his low forehead thatched with hair the color of soiled fodder. There was not even a stool for him to sit on. Reeds from the nearby stream lay in a neat stack beside him. Meaghan watched as he peeled back the end of each reed with the broken blade of a knife and fed the next one into it, making a thin pole.

In another corner a pile of straw was heaped. Here Timothy Halloran lay, his face like one of the damned souls in the painting of the Apocalypse behind the church altar. Sweat-beaded flesh seemed cast in iron by a gargoyle maker, his child's lips stretched in a hideous smile, eyebrows arching high on his forehead.

A sharp, welcome pain bit through to her consciousness, and she tore her gaze from the horror around her to Sean's hand which gripped her arm. There was no censure in his face. Anger had fled. His sea-shaded eyes were filled with something deep, calming, and she could sense the need he felt to take her in his arms.

"Mrs. O'Fallon, it was kind of ye to think of Tim. Like yer husband, ye are, always worried about others . . . always . . ." Fiona smoothed the wrinkles in Sam's old suit. Meaghan stared at the clothes she had brought to serve as a shroud, and wondered when she had given them to the other woman. The pressure of Sean's hand spurred her to break the sudden silence.

"I . . . I brought my thread and needle to take them in." Meaghan heard her voice as though it were a stranger's, her eyes never leaving Sean's broad back as he went to the mound of straw.

Heedless of his well-tailored breeches, he knelt in the dirt beside the boy. "Well, now, Timothy-Tim, I've brought you something to help you feel better. And no, I didn't forget that surprise I promised you from my barn." Sean stroked back a lock of the child's hair. "You say you want the surprise first, do you? Well, I suppose—" Meaghan settled herself on a large stone the family used as a stool, biting off a length of thread. She watched in astonishment as Sean unlatched the lid of the basket and drew out a tiny brown rabbit.

"Did you ever see such a beauty? Fox got the mother. This little one is just now old enough to survive on its own."

There was a flicker in the pain-filled eyes as Sean picked up the boy's finger and ran it over the silky curve of the tiny brown ear. With infinite tenderness Sean nestled the rabbit's warm body in the hollow of Timothy's hand. The creature seemed content there, staring out at the world with eyes like jet beads.

"Now, we made a bargain, young man." Sean took a glass

bottle from his case, digging out a shiny silver cup. "You will take your medicine without a fight."

How could he do it? Meaghan wondered as she, along with Timothy, felt the strength coming from this man she thought she knew. How could Sean look at the boy without recoiling? How could he talk to him as though it were a sunny afternoon and they were at the stream, swimming?

Never had Meaghan seen Sean so gentle. He belonged here, the healer, able to shut out the squalor, the hatred, and his own bitterness, able to bring a last taste of happiness to a child.

Arrogant. Insensitive. How little those labels suited him now.

"So ye've brought yer whore to watch the dyin'." Meaghan's needle stabbed deep into her finger, the malice in the slurred voice shaking her as a bundle of rags seemed to rise up and take on human form. Eyes like pits engulfed a stubble-bearded face. Rivulets of drool oozed from slack lips. Fear coiled around Meaghan's throat as she felt herself being sucked into those empty, empty eyes.

"Casey, my *wife* is here to help Fiona." Sean's voice was a wire stretched thin as he got slowly to his feet. "I've brought some more medicine to lessen Timmy's pain."

"Medicine, bah!" Casey spat a stream of yellowish liquid onto Sean's polished boot. "More of yer poison! Ye've poisoned my Tim, ye scurvy English bastard, and come to gloat o're his death throes!"

"It's laudanum. You remember, you were at the rectory when I gave some to Father Loughlin once."

Fiona Halloran twisted her hands in her skirt, shuffling between Sean and her husband. "It helps him to sleep, Casey. When Father was here before dawn . . ."

"That scavenger! Aye, he's another one, cravin' his pound of flesh, and the boy not yet dead!"

"Casey, don't—"

"Quiet, woman! I've my own mouth, I have, and I'll use it as I see fit!"

"You've used your mouth to bad effect since this all began," Sean said, inching closer to Meaghan. "This time use your head. If Timmy could talk, you know he would have asked to see Loughlin."

"But he can't talk, can he? Ye with all yer bottles and powders can't make my Timmy talk. Father Loughlin with all his blatherin' about miracles and God's will can't make him well. Where is Loughlin's all merciful God? I'll tell ye. He's sittin' up there on his fat arse watchin' Timmy die!"

"Blessed Mother . . ." Fiona gasped, crossing erself. "Ye don't mean it, Casey."

"Yes. He does." Meaghan saw Sean's jaw tighten, a sudden flicker of understanding breaking through the wariness in his face. His voice was gentler as he said, "I brought a dram of whiskey for your father, Culley. Get it from the buggy."

"More of yer damned charity," Casey snorted as the boy darted out the door.

"I'm not offering you charity. I expect to be paid—in full. Come planting time you and your boys can put in my garden, and the roof of the stable needs mending."

"Ye think I'll let my babies be fouled by working for the son of an Englishman's whore?"

Sean's muscles knotted, and for the first time Meaghan understood what it was costing him to keep from driving his fist into Casey Halloran's face. Sean looked down at Timmy, eyes slits as he fought to bridle his temper. "Then you'll do it yourself."

"Cormac, Michael and me . . . Culley, too, we'll be at Cottage Gael any day ye say." The boy who had been leaning against the wall climbed to his feet.

"Ye'll do nothing for him! Nothing!" Casey sputtered.

"I'm sorry, Da." The boy regarded him levelly before he turned to Sean. "Whatever ye need, sir, anything. Ask. I'll do my best to find it for ye."

The warmth of his unexpected support thawed the icy anger in Sean's face. He reached out, grasping Daniel by the shoulders.

"No! Ye English whoreson!" Halloran shrilled, dealing Daniel a heavy blow. "Danny, he's yer enemy! He's killin' Timmy!"

Sean caught Casey's fist before it found its mark again, holding it in an iron-fast grip. "Daniel, see what's keeping Culley with that whiskey."

"Aye, sir," the boy said, gingerly touching his bruised mouth.

"Bastard! Ye turn my own family against me!" Casey snarled as Daniel went outside.

"They aren't turning against you, you damned fool! They're trying to help Timmy. Look at him, man! If you love him at all—"

"Sean, something's wrong!"

Sean wheeled. Timothy writhed on the straw, gasping desperately for air that couldn't pass through his strangling throat. His face mottled blue, hands clawing the air.

"Do something!" Meaghan cried, trying to hold the boy down.

"Meg, get the lancet! Now!" Sean arched back the child's neck, his long fingers probing Timmy's throat. "His windpipe. We'll have to try to open it."

"Open it?" Meaghan's eyes were huge in her face.

"Damn it, woman, give me the knife!" With shaking hands Meaghan took the lancet from its slim leather case.

"Hold his head," Sean ordered, one hand firm on Timmy.

Meaghan clamped her hands around the boy's head. Still it moved as though jerked by a diabolical puppeteer. Silver turning to red, the blade bit through the flesh as Sean bore down on it. A swirling dizziness threatened to engulf her, her stomach churning as a ruby drop ran down the rigid throat muscles onto the straw. Skin peeled back to reveal grayish edges as Sean widened the incision. The child's whole face washed blue, his dark eyes bulging from their sockets. "Have to keep the hole open ... A reed ... I'll feed a hollow reed into the opening ... can breathe through the tube ..." Sean said tightly, holding the passage he had cut open with the flat of the lancet blade as he groped for one of Daniel's reeds.

"Murderer!" A high-pitched screech split the air as Casey Halloran lunged for Sean's throat, Daniel's broken knife clutched in his hand. At that instant Sean's hand released the pressure on the lancet in the child's windpipe, the silver edge skating a thin red trail down to Timothy's collarbone.

"You fool!" Sean roared as he dove hard to the right. "If you cost that child any more pain—"

"He'd dead anyway! Ye doin' yer carvin' up on him!" Casey circled Sean, the point of his knife an eerie blue. "Now it's my turn to use the blade, O'Fallon. Now it's my turn."

Halloran flew at Sean, steel slashing. There was a grunt of surprise as Sean evaded the weapon. Grasping Casey's arms Sean planted his boot between them and sent him scudding into the wall, stunning him. Like a cat Sean rolled to his feet, taut, ready.

"Sean!" It was a desperate plea as Meaghan tried to hold apart the flaps of skin opening Timmy's throat. A gurgling sound came from the child as though he were drowning in his own blood.

Sean ran, grabbing up a reed, slicing off a length of it with the lancet. He fell to his knees beside Timmy. His hand, strong and sure, he eased the hollow tube into the opening he had made.

"Damn! We have to stop the bleeding." Sean packed a clover over the wound the attack had caused. "Got to keep pressure on it."

There was the sound of movement on the far side of the room, and Meaghan felt relief spread through her. Thank God. Daniel. He had to hold Halloran. Sean's blow wouldn't stun him for long.

"Daniel, your father—" Meaghan turned to look at the shadowy figure. "No!" she shrieked. She rammed her hands into Sean's chest. Dressings, bottles, and instruments scattered from his bag as it skidded across the floor.

He hurled himself toward Meaghan, but it was too late. Powder blazed orange. Lead bit into flesh. He felt her jerk at the impact, tense with pain as they rolled together over the floor under the force of his momentum.

Warm and sticky, her blood welled in his hand where it clutched her arm. An agony more searing than if the bullet had pierced his own body surged through him.

"Sean . . . hurts . . ." He pressed her tightly against him, as if to take her pain upon himself and force the pain from her. Seconds could be precious. Why was he frozen here, holding her? Because he was afraid, damn it! For the first time in his life he was afraid to look at a wound, terrified of what he might find.

He groped beside him for something, anything, to staunch the flow of blood.

"No! No! Die O'Fallon!" Sean spun around just as Halloran swung the heavy pistol butt in a brutal arc at his head. His leg shot out, throwing Halloran off balance. The metal raked Sean's shoulder, laying open his shirt, leaving bright red tracks scored in the bronze flesh. Lips curled in a feral snarl; Sean drove his shoulder into Halloran's stomach. They crashed to the floor, grappling with an intensity of hatred that paralyzed all within the room. Sean outweighed Halloran by thirty pounds of hard, lean muscle, but the smaller man fought with the most lethal of weapons—insanity.

Sean's fists smashed into Casey's face with a terrible precision, but Casey's stubby fingers gouged and scratched at Sean's eyes. Suddenly an agonizing pain shot through Sean as Casey slammed his knee up into Sean's groin. Sean doubled over in the dirt, that split second giving Casey the advantage he needed. Springing to his feet, Casey swooped up a bottle in his dirty fist. He drew back his arm, bashing the bottle down onto Sean's dark head. Whiskey burned into Sean's eyes. Shards of glass sliced his face as the bottle's end shattered into a crown of jagged blades.

Sean groaned, grinding his fingertips into his burning eyes, staggering as he tried to regain his feet.

A heavy boot cracked into his ribs, making him sprawl backward, the acrid smell of singed hair filling his nostrils as his hair skimmed the peat fire's glowing embers. He twisted his body away from the heat, but Casey tried to shove him back into the fire.

"Did it burn ye, Sean? Did ye feel the flames splittin' yer skin?" Casey chortled, darting out of the way as Sean lunged for him blindly. "By the saints, yer aim is worse than a maid's. I think it's yer wife I should be fightin'. Aye, with that face she'd be a one for sport!"

A new fear shot through Sean. Surely Casey wouldn't . . . not with Fiona here, with his son dying . . .

Shapes, gray and black, blurred before Sean. He threw himself in the direction of Casey's voice, but the cackling went on and on. Halloran danced just out of reach, howling with sadistic glee. Where was he? Damn, to have his eyes clear for one instant!

"Fight me, you coward!" Sean challenged, trying to bait Halloran into revealing his position. "Blind I'm twice the man you are!"

"Still fine and fancy, are ye?" Halloran sneered. "But not for long, I warrant! I'm going to butcher ye now, O'Fallon. Butcher ye and hang yer carcass to dry like a pig out in the yard."

Sean leapt backward, some animal instinct saving him as the glass blades sliced through the air at the level of his face.

"Casey, no!" He heard Fiona scream. A shadowy form seemed to blend with a mass of gray. There was a loud crack, a sob of pain. Fiona. Casey had hit her.

Sean bolted toward the sound, crashing headlong into Casey's bony frame. Glass cut into his thigh as Casey slashed wildly. Grabbing for Casey's wrist, Sean's fingers closed on the knife-sharp points. He clenched his teeth, holding on. If he lost his grip on Casey now . . . Desperately he slid his hand downward until it grasped Casey's wrist, slamming it against the hard earth until the broken bottle rolled from the smaller man's grasp.

Sean staggered to his feet, dragging Casey up with him. He could make out the ragged silhouette of Casey's hair, the stoop of his shoulders. He struck out, and Casey's head snapped back.

Casey kicked and scratched, but still Sean held him there, pinned and helpless. His lip burst with the force of Sean's blow, and his eye swelled and bled.

"No!" Casey blubbered, flailing with his twig-thin arms. "I killed ye . . . I shot ye . . . for Timmy! Die, ye English bastard! I promised Timmy I would kill ye!"

Sean's hands knotted in Casey's shirtfront, forcing him up against the crumbling clay. "Kill me then, you coward! Here. Now. Like a man!"

"Ye're evil, O'Fallon! Ye prey on innocents!"

"Damn you, *I* don't shoot unarmed women!" Sean roared, banging him against the wall. "You made Timmy suffer the tortures of the damned. Now you might have cost Meaghan her life! I *should* kill you!" Casey's head lolled back, his eyes rolling in their sockets.

"No! Ye can't! Blessed Mother, ye can't kill him!" Fiona Halloran sobbed, grasping Sean's arm. "Daniel, help me!"

In a heartbeat the boy was beside Sean, trying to drag him back, but he was no match for the big man's strength. Sean whirled, his fist cocked, his anger like a haze over his face.

White, terrified, Culley stood beside his brother, a broken slane handle clutched in his fingers. "Don't make me hit ye, Doc Sean . . . don't . . ." He whimpered.

"Whatever wrong he's done he'll still my Da," Daniel said quietly. "I can't stand by and watch ye murder him."

"And *you're* going to stop me?"

"If I have to."

Sean looked down to where Casey Halloran had fallen in a crumpled heap, then back to the boy.

He stretched out his fingers, clenched his fists. Culley jumped, wide eyed.

"It's over, Culley," Sean said, pressing his fingers to his eyes. The sensitive membranes still tingled painfully, but his vision had cleared until only the edges of objects blurred. "Keep your father away from me, Daniel." His jaw hardened. "Or I swear I'll finish what he started." The boy nodded.

"Meg?" She was huddled by Timothy, her hair tumbled down from its combs, a fiery cascade around a face translucent as alabaster. Her left hand was on the child, her right arm pressed tight against her rib cage. "Meaghan," he said again.

Reflexively she covered the injury with her good hand, looking up at him. "Not so bad . . ." she managed weakly from between clenched teeth.

"I'll be the judge of that," Sean said softly, touching her cheek. "Here, now. Let me see it." She screwed her eyes shut, turning away in a childlike gesture that wrung his heart. Her slender fingers shook under Sean's gentle ones as he pried them away from her arm.

Crimson spread in a wet stain over the frayed edges of her sleeve. Bits of cloth clung to the path the bullet had gouged out.

"I kept the pressure on Timmy's cut." She blanched as Sean probed her arm, and he could see her fighting to stay conscious. He reached, uncorking the dram of whiskey Culley had dropped in the confusion.

"Here, love, drink," he soothed, putting the amber liquid to her lips. "A big gulp now."

She shoved the bottle away, choking and sputtering as the whiskey burned a path down her throat. "It's like drinking fire," she gasped.

"You think it feels like fire in your throat," Sean muttered grimly under his breath, then said in a louder voice, "I'm going to drench your wound with this whiskey to sear the dirt out of it. Meg, it's going to hurt like hell."

"Sean, wait—Timmy . . . He'll be all right now?"

Sean raked his hand through his hair, his breath coming out in a sigh. "He has lockjaw, Meaghan. It's fatal."

"I know, but it doesn't hurt him so much anymore. He'll be able to breathe easily until . . . until the end comes?"

"I hope so. I've done everything I can." For the first time since the battle with Casey, Sean looked at Timothy. The painkiller had done its work well. The child's breathing was shallow, but regular. Even the cut along his collarbone was free of blood. Meaghan had stopped it.

"Give me your arm," Sean said through a throat so tight he could scarcely get the words to pass.

She held it out to him. Gentle, yet firm, Sean braced it in his strong grip. The hard line of his jaw clenched and unclenched, sweat beading his upper lip as he raised the bottle. For just an instant he hesitated. Then he tipped it, letting the whiskey flow over the raw wound. Sean steeled himself for the scream which must surely come, but it did not. With a strangled groan Meaghan sank her teeth into her lower lip. Her face went gray as the wound was seared clean, but she didn't try to break away from him.

"Feel sick . . ." she choked out.

"I know, love, I know." Sean leaned her back against his chest, resting his lips on her hair as he packed the wound and bound its with strips of cloth.

"You're hand . . . you're bleeding."

"It's nothing, Meg. Just a scratch."

"Thank God it's not more. He would've killed you. I didn't believe it."

"That will teach you to listen to me." Sean gave her the ghost of a lopsided smile and she burrowed her face into the hollow of his shoulder.

"Sean . . . I was so scared. If I hadn't seen him . . ." He felt a shiver go through her, and tightened his arms around her, brushing her temple with his lips.

"Hush, love. It's over."

"Over?" Fiona Halloran swept over to them, her chin quivering. "Ye all but got her killed! It was pure foolishness to bring her here after what happened the time past, and ye knew it! But a little steadier an' Casey—" The shade-thin woman's voice cracked. "How could ye, Mr. O'Fallon?" she cried. "How could ye bring her here an' ye love her at all?"

Meaghan felt Sean stiffen. She struggled to sit up. "No, Fiona, Sean tried to stop me, but I—" She reached her hand up to touch his face.

"Don't," he grated, pushing her hand away. Pain, uncertainty, and guilt clashed like sword points in his eyes. She could almost see the ghosts that rose to haunt him.

"Sean, no. You can't blame yourself. The wound isn't bad and—"

"Blame? Why should I blame myself for your stupidity? I warned you to stay away from here, but would you listen to reason? No, you were so cocksure of yourself. The angel of mercy on a mission from God. Well, your mission is over. You're leaving. Now."

"No. I'm fine. I can still help. I'll bandage your hand and your eyes should be . . ."

"Damn it!" Sean exploded. "This time you'll do as I say!"

Two spots of color stained Meaghan's cheeks beneath the ghostly pallor. "If I had stayed home as you *ordered* this morning, you would be dead! Casey's aim was true. That bullet hit my arm while I was pushing you out of its path!"

Sean's hand closed on her wrist like an iron band, forcing her out of earshot of Fiona and the boys. "You little fool!" he hissed, his voice shaking. "What kind of trap did you hope to lay? Did you think if you were hurt I would come groveling to you on my knees?"

"Trap? I pushed you out of the way because I *love* you—" The words were out before she could stop them. Sean's fingers clenched, a score of emotions flashing like quicksilver across his features.

"Love?" His lips curled in a mocking smile. "You love me? What you and I share in bed has nothing to do with love." Meaghan's breath caught at his derisive laughter. Her hand arced through the air smacking into Sean's cheek with all the force she could muster.

She stood, frozen at the blaze of fury she saw in his eyes, certain he was going to strike her back. "Daniel?" he said at last, his ice-blue gaze never leaving her. "Get *Mrs. O'Fallon* out of here. Take my gig. Stop at MacFadden's on the way and ask Grace to stay with her at Cottage Gael."

"You can't order me out like a child!"

"The hell I can't, *wife*." Sean took a step toward her.

"Please, ma'am," Daniel placed a tentative hand on her waist. "Let me help ye."

"God, no! You're wasting your time. She doesn't need any help. She's perfectly capable of getting killed all by herself."

A strange, raspy sound from the corner cut Sean's raging to silence. In three strides he was beside the straw. He hunkered down, stroking Timothy's hair. "What is it, Tim?" he asked. "What do you want?"

Garbled noises came from Timmy's throat as his eyes darted

about, begging for something. Meaghan looked into the child's pinched face.

"His rabbit," she whispered. "He wants his rabbit." She leaned down, reaching into the shadows, cradling the frightened creature against her. Her lips trembled as she fought back the tears she had held inside her through the horror of the operation and the pain of the bullet wound.

"I'll take it," Sean gritted. "You've done enough damage."

She pushed past him, taking Timmy's stiff fingers in her own and slipping the rabbit beneath them. "Take good care of him, Timothy-Tim," she said, kissing the little boy's forehead.

"Sean," she whispered, suddenly desolate.

His head stayed bent, eyes hooded. Without seeing she knew what they held—the same brooding pain that had been there since the night they made love in the meadow.

Fourteen

Meaghan sagged against the pillows, exhausted, the wound in her arm throbbing as Grace MacFadden again smoothed a pungent salve on the raw flesh. The mixture was soothing, dampening the searing pain that had gripped her arm ever since Sean had doused the wound with whiskey, yet it did nothing for the misery that crushed her heart. She had told Sean she loved him—*loved him*. God, how could she have been so foolish?

She winced inwardly at the memory of his lips curling into a contemptuous snarl, his laughter laced with disgust and bitterness as he shoved her into Daniel's arms.

Two days had passed and Sean hadn't come home. Even Grace's calm presence had begun to crumble. The morning of the second day Liam had gone to Halloran's, returning only to mutter cryptically that "No one's shot Sean-o yet, but by damn, someone should!"

Grace pulled the edge of the lavender coverlet farther down on Meaghan's waist, taking a deeper fold in the white lawn nightdress where it turned down beneath her breast to keep from getting soiled.

Grace's thin hand trailed in a gentle caress over her cheeks. The tenderness Meaghan's own ma had rarely shown her made the lump in Meaghan's throat swell until her tears again overflowed. "There, now, child," Grace soothed. "You don't want yer eyes all red when Sean-o comes home. He'll need yer strength with Timmy dyin'."

"He won't want anything from me. It had been so much better between us, I almost believed . . . but, Grace, when he sent me out of Casey's it was like he hated me."

"Sean doesn't hate ye. He's just tired, an' angry with God an' with death. I've never seen such a man for lovin' those who hurt, an' easin' the sorrow of those left behind. He never lets anyone see, but he carries their grief in him, until it becomes his own. His patients, they feel it, somehow. He makes them believe . . ."

Grace rewrapped the fresh bandage around Meaghan's arm, tying the ends in a knot. "The only one Sean can't comfort is himself. He locks his pain away, an' it stays there, within him, tearin' at his gut. If he rages at ye it's only because ye've touched him where the wound is deepest. He's seen so many die, Meaghan, most all of them beloved and mourned. To Sean-o love means pain."

Meaghan forced the tears down. "I'm beginning to think he's right. I . . . I can't bear living here with him, Grace, loving him and—"

"Lovin' Sean? I know ye love him. Lord, I'd be blind not to. Ever since I've known the lad I've prayed for a child like ye to come into his life, to hold him, to love him. He needs ye, Meaghan. More than ye'll ever know."

"He wants me in his . . . his bed . . . but that's all. I'm nothing but a poor substitute for who he really wants. From the first night he told me—"

"Told you what? About the gentle and saintly Alanna DuBois?"

"Alanna . . . he still loves her and—"

"Loves her, bah!" Grace fairly spat. "She tore his heart out and left him bleeding, bedded with Colin Radcliffe and God knows how many others, threw away every shilling Sean earned, all the while trying to drag him away from the poor folk when no other doctor would touch them. She was a biting, scratching witch with claws all cased in velvet. But Sean didn't tell ye *that*, did he?"

"No." The words were full of quiet menace, as Sean moved into the room. "I didn't tell her that." He let the leather medical bags slide unsteadily to the floor, his features drawn in the brittle stiffness of a flour-paste mask. The faint scent of whiskey clung to his breath. His shirt hung half-open, crisp dark hairs curling in the V. "I didn't tell her anything. Why the hell should I? It's none of her damned business."

The gaze fastened on Meaghan was diamond hard, glinting

bright. "What's the matter, Meaghan? Looking for a new Achilles' heel now that your ploy with Casey's bullet failed?"

"Ploy?!" Gracy exploded.

"Ah, yes. I must say that Meaghan's little scene was much more effective than the one Emily Wallingford staged last spring when she had that gap-toothed gelding 'throw' her at my doorstep. I mean, you should have seen it, Grace, Meaghan declaring her undying love for me in the middle of that hell hole, flinging herself at me in a fit of selfless passion. I've read better trash in cheap French novels. The only flaw in the whole thing was the fact that her judgment was a little off."

He leaned against the edge of the chiffonier, draping his wrist over the curled brass handle. "Rusted as that pistol was I'm sure she didn't expect it to fire."

"Sean O'Fallon, ye'll shut yer yap an' take yerself out of here."

"Oh, I wouldn't think of it. This is my cue to fall on my knees beside the bed and sob out my love and undying loyalty to her for saving my life, only I think the whiskey I had at Kelly's stiffened my knees. Maybe we could skip the sobbing part and get right to slipping her nightgown off—"

Sean let his wrist fall to his side, his gaze lingering over Meaghan's exposed skin where Grace had been changing the dressings.

Meaghan grabbed the edge of her nightgown, yanking it up to cover herself. The sleeve, pulled tight, skated up over her wound. Her lips went gray.

"Don't touch me!" There was a kind of desperation in the cry, as if a hundred nerve ends lay open to the cold.

"Touch you? Isn't that what you've been driving for? After all, I've done worlds more than touch you . . ."

Grace snatched back his hand where it reached to touch Meaghan's bare throat, her green eyes blazing. "Let her be, ye drunken ass!"

"I'm not drunk, only sampling what was offered to me so prettily. When a woman tells a man she loves him, you can damned well bet she wants him—"

"Bastard!" Meaghan choked out. She hurled the word in anger, but the moment it left her mouth she could have bitten out her tongue. Sean's face twisted with torment that she understood too bitingly well. It was as if his soul was bared, and she had taken the many-bladed weapon he had given her in trust and rammed it hot and burning inside him.

But Grace hadn't even heard it, as she blocked his way. "Nay, ye'll not touch her! Go bellow to the winds that the fates have cast ye down, that God and goodness are dead! But ye'll not dare to take the love of this child's heart. Why not, Sean? Fear? Ye're less a man now than I've ever seen ye."

"Less? You can ask Meaghan—"

"Damn ye, ye don't deserve her!"

"No. You're right. I don't." The over-bright glaze of the liquor faded from his sky-shaded eyes. "And she doesn't deserve what I've done to her . . ." His voice trailed to silence. He raked the dark waves from his forehead, the achingly familiar gesture desperately weary. "That's why I drafted a letter to Lance Bowmont in Liverpool today. I'm booking passage for Meaghan and the rest of her family on a steamer bound for England."

"England?" Grace gasped, turning to meet Meaghan's wide-eyed stare.

Sean paced to the other side of the room, bracing his palm on the window frame, his gazed fixed out the window. "Bowmont runs a shipyard there. He'll take Tom on as an apprentice and find positions for Meaghan and her mother in his household staff."

"Ye know what kind of 'position' a fine dressin' man is like to give a beauty like Meaghan?" Grace blustered.

Meaghan could see Sean's knuckles whiten. He went on, ignoring what Grace had said. "I stopped and talked to your mother before I came here, Meg, and she . . . she's anxious to go. The boat leaves next Thursday."

"So . . . soon." Meaghan's fingers clenched on the coverlet, an aching emptiness engulfing her. She had told him that she loved him, and now he only wanted to be rid of her as quickly as possible.

"It took some coin in the right places, but . . . the sooner you arrive the sooner you'll . . . settle into your new life."

"How thoughtful of ye. Ye may near kill her with yer kindness." Grace rolled her eyes in disgust.

"Grace—"

"Ye're damned scared, Sean, an' ye think ye can cast this child aside like a shirt that rubs where the skin is raw! Ye can't! Ye've taken her an' made her love ye an'—"

"Grace!" Meaghan's voice was a strangled plea. It cut through the air, lying between them all.

Grace glared at the broad shoulders silhouetted against the heavy draperies. "Don't worry, child. I'm goin'. I don't think I could stand another spate of Sean's *generosity*."

Sean turned as Grace clanked together the wash basin and the salve tin and stomped from the room. His eyes were lined with hopelessness. "God knows I've hurt you enough, Meg," he said. "And you may well hate me for this. But I told your ma about Radcliffe. I wanted her to understand that there was no . . . no bond between us. You didn't come to me of your own free will."

Meaghan let the coverlet fall from stiff fingers, her gaze riveted on the quilted edging, not daring to look up lest he read the thoughts screaming through her. *No bond!* She wanted to cry. *I would have come to you, labeled a harlot before the whole of Wicklow. I would have stayed with you, taken whatever measure of your love you could give.* She forced her thoughts to silence. Damn him, she wouldn't cry.

The soft shush of his boot soles on the carpet told her he was approaching the bed. He touched her chin, tipping it up, and she could feel the heat of his fingertips. Her eyes slid closed. "Maggie," he said softly, his thumb skimming her jaw, "I never said it was forever."

He stood there a long time, waiting for her to look at him, to say something. She couldn't. Tears burned beneath her closed lids, searing her throat. She pulled away from the touch of his hand, its warm roughness exquisitely painful.

No, she thought, trying desperately to keep from crying, he'd never said it was forever.

Fifteen

The roan skimmed across the heath with the graceful abandon of foam riding upon high-crested waves. Meaghan leaned over its neck, her hair flying free, whipping back, the glossy ends stinging her ears. Sean had promised her the gelding to ride as soon as she was able to leave Cottage Gael, and the hours spent dashing free on its back seemed sometimes the only thing that gave her the strength to keep from begging Sean to let her stay.

The clothes Sean had bought for her in Dublin were packed away in a shiny new bump-lidded trunk, the folds of muslin and silk filled out with tissue paper to save them from being crushed. They would leave tomorrow before the sun rose to pick up Ma and the young ones, beginning their journey to the steamer that would take them to Liverpool and a life unknown. Today, at daybreak, Sean had ridden off with Liam to finish making arrangements for the time he would be gone.

The gelding broke stride, sidestepping a rabbit hole, but Meaghan followed the beast on instinct, hardly noticing. In one way it would be a relief to be gone. The distant politeness Sean had adopted with her since the day he had returned to Cottage Gael grated on Meaghan's nerves until she baited him, goading him to betray an honest reaction—even anger—but he remained kind, aloof, unreachable.

Owing to the strain of heavy pregnancy and the altercations with Sean, Grace had been ordered not to leave home, and the days before Meaghan had been pronounced well enough to go out had ticked by at the pace of wet sand trickling through a sieve.

A wisp of hair flicked into Meaghan's eye. She swiped it

away, along with a tear that stung her cheek. The tie between Meaghan and Grace, forged from the differing loves they bore for the same man, had flourished into something both women cherished. But now she had to say goodbye.

In the distance, Liam MacFadden's rose-draped cottage shone bright beneath its new coat of whitewash. A few chickens scrabbled in the yard and a pink piglet, escaped from its pen, turned baleful eyes on the tightly shut cottage door. As Meaghan reined the horse to a stop beside a post set with an iron ring, the piglet poked his little snout at her as if demanding that she do something about the lateness of his breakfast.

Meaghan reached down and picked up the squirming beast, careful to avoid his mud-caked trotters. "So Grace is a bit slow with you this morning," Meaghan said, plopping him into his pen and relatching the gate. "She's tired, you know, with the babe and all—" The latch was jammed into place before Meaghan's hand froze upon it. Unnatural quiet shrouded even the animals. The shutters blotted out the window glass, and not a sound came from behind the wooden door.

Grace. Meaghan ran the steps to the heavy door, swinging it open. "Grace."

The door to the bedroom was open, and a weak voice called from within, "Meaghan-child. It's about time ye decided to get here."

In three leaps Meaghan was beside the bedstead. The sweat-drenched, pain-pinched face on the pillow confirmed her worst fears. "The . . . the babe . . ."

"Started just after Liam drove off with Sean . . . took Annie with them, praise the saints. I almost got up an' tried to catch them, but they said ye were coming and—" Meaghan watched every muscle in Grace's body tense, the bulging stomach knotting. It was well past noon. How many hours, then, had she lain thus alone?

"I . . . I had some packing to do, and . . . Grace . . ." One bony hand closed on Meaghan's, the nails digging into the back of her hand, the fingers crushing her knuckles together until they ached. The contraction eased and Grace's fingers opened slowly.

"This babe's a mite . . . more anxious . . . than Annie was," Grace managed with a weak smile.

"I'd better get Sean . . ."

"No," Grace said sharply, then more quietly, "No. There isn't time."

Meaghan felt a trickle of fear. "The . . . the midwife . . ."

"I can feel the baby's head. Meaghan, ye'll have to—"

The next spasm tore at Grace's voice. "The blanket . . . take off the . . ."

Meaghan ripped back the dark gray wool. Grace's legs were braced up under the white tent of her nightgown. Her heels and fists dug into the feather tick, and striplike muscles stood out against yellow-tinged skin. Bright vermilion stains soaked the white muslin and the clean rags that were spread under her hips.

Meaghan caught the inside of her bottom lip between her teeth as she smoothed the garment over the tight mound of Grace's belly, her own stomach knotting with panic. God, where was Sean? She knew nothing about delivering a baby. Why oh why hadn't she listened to the other girls' chatterings about birthing brothers and sisters?

Every one of them had bathed her mother's face, watching the miracle of life aborning. But each time Ma's hand had closed on the smoothed knot of wood Da had given her to hold on to in labor, Meaghan had been banished from the room. And seven of the nine times, no life's cry had echoed from behind the door.

Even now, as she tugged Grace's nightgown from under the thin hips, a stab of remembered hurt went through her. Ma had tried not to blame her for each new tiny grave added to the line at St. Colmcille's, yet there had always been a strain to her mouth when Meaghan had slipped into the room and tried to fill her empty arms with a child's embrace. If something happened to Grace or this long-desired baby . . .

Meaghan forced her thoughts away, trying to talk in the bantering, confident voice she had heard Sean use with Timmy, saying anything, saying nothing. Minutes passed. Hours. Grace's hair clung damply to her cheeks as Meaghan smoothed cool cloths over her skin. The weak smiles that had creased her lips faded into dogged determination, then surrender, as forces far greater than her will tormented her. Nails raked furrows in the wooden bedstead, in the skin of Meaghan's arms. Flesh bulged and tore as the tiny wet head battered through.

"Grace, it's almost here . . . I can see . . . That's right . . . that's right . . ." Meaghan sank her teeth into her lip at Grace's scream as the baby's head burst forth in a wash of blood. She held its slippery weight as little rounded shoulders slid free, then tiny arms and legs. The rosebud mouth opened to a squall, infinitesimal fists flailing.

"Grace, it's a boy. A boy!"

"A little lad? Is it?" Grace asked shakily. "He has all his proper parts?"

Meaghan grinned. "It's there all right. Tiny as a thimble."

"Ye know I meant his fingers an' toes, but I'm glad he can pride himself *there* too."

Meaghan laughed, soaring with a mixture of euphoria and relief as she propped the child on Grace's stomach so she could see.

"He's perfect, isn't he?" Grace asked softly, and her raspy voice had never sounded so beautiful to Meaghan. "I'm going to call him Sean."

A lump choked Meaghan's throat at the depth of love in the words, and she thought again of the image of Sean's mother in the gilded frame, picturing the softly vulnerable lips forming the same words, thought of her own secret dreams of bearing Sean's child. She swallowed, and tried to smile. "Considering what I just compared the babe's private parts to, I don't know if Sean will appreciate—"

"Well, if the lad would put his 'thimble' to proper use, he could get his own sons. Red-haired lads, I think, who smile . . ."

At the sudden pucker of loss on Meaghan's brow, Grace took her hand and squeezed it. "Ye're not finished yet, child." She held the bruised knuckles gently, looking long into Meaghan's eyes before waving her other hand toward some string and a clean-scrubbed butcher knife, but though she explained to Meaghan how to tie off the umbilical cord and cut through it, both women knew it was not of this task that Grace had first spoken.

Meaghan wrapped the babe in a knitted white blanket, watching the miracle of the little one's first suckling, the sight stirring needs in her she had not known existed.

"Makes yer arms ache, doesn't it?" Grace asked, tracing the little pink moon of a cheek against her breast. "When ye love a man . . ."

Meaghan shifted nervously, moving to clean away the soiled rags, drawing out a fresh nightgown from a woven basket at the foot of the bed. "What would I do with a baby?"

"Love it. He won't send ye away, ye know. Unless he's a fool."

"Sean's never been known for being particularly wise where I'm concerned." Meaghan dumped the rags into a wooden box. "I don't want to talk about leaving. Not now. I just want to be happy."

"And so ye should be. I want . . . Meaghan, I want ye to stand up for the babe at his christening. I know we've been friends for but a little time, but I feel as close to ye as if ye were my own daughter. That way, if Sean does send ye on that godforsaken boat, ye'll always have a stake here in Ireland. Someone to come back to."

"Grace . . . I . . . I . . ." Meaghan went to the side of the bed, hugging Grace, baby and all. "I don't know how I would have survived these weeks if I hadn't had you," she choked out.

The crunch of wheels at the front of the cottage cut off Grace's reply. Meaghan swiped away the moisture under her lashes, hurrying to the window, peering out.

Sean was jumping with long-legged grace from the floorboards of his black gig. Liam, who had already alighted, put his big hands to work loosening a broken piece of harness from a metal fitting while a garland-bedecked, dirt-streaked Annie looked on.

Meaghan spun to make a face at Grace, and there was a healing inside her. "Wouldn't you know it? They would come now that all the work is done!" The smile she flashed Grace was but a little forced. "We'll teach them! Shh! Quick, let me have the baby!"

She scooped up the drowsy child, blanket and all, nestling him atop the fresh-smelling clothes in the basket, then turned back to Grace, hands on hips, merriment threatening to burst out in giggles at any moment. At the sound of Sean approaching, she took on the tone of an angry lecturer.

"Now you'll stay in bed, Grace MacFadden! If Sean had any idea you'd been washing those heavy blankets in the stream today with the baby so close to coming he'd be in such a fury that—"

"Blankets? Grace was washing *blankets?*" Sean growled ominously, striding into the room. "Of all the idiotic—"

"Sean . . ." Meaghan feigned surprise, the sight of him, tall and taut with very real anger, weakening her resolve.

"Grace, so help me if you—"

"I stopped her before any harm was done," Meaghan cut in quickly, "but all those wet things need to be spread on the bushes before the whole room starts smelling musty. If you could carry them out . . ."

Shooting Grace a murderous glare, Sean stomped to the basket, hoisting it up. At that instant the babe let out a howl loud enough to crack the plaster.

"Good God!" Sean's jaw dropped open as the handles almost slipped from his grasp. Meaghan swept the baby to safety, laughing. Sean's eyes darted from Meaghan to Grace, and back to the baby who was now bellowing his indignation into the apple-green bodice of Meaghan's dress.

"He was in a bit of a hurry. Decided he wanted to be brought into the world by a pretty colleen instead of a stubborn, sour-faced . . ." Grace's stern mien melted. "Ah, well, it's no wonder. The lad has fine taste. Little as he is, the babe takes after his namesake."

"Namesake?"

"Aye," Grace gave him a tender smile. "I call him Sean."

At that instant Liam MacFadden burst into the room as if a banshee was chasing him, a piece of the harness still dangling from his big hand. The look on the giant man's face would have been comical, had he not been so deathly pale.

"Gracie, love, ye didn't go an' have the babe without Sean! He told ye an' told ye not to . . ." Lank blond hair fell over his forehead as he roared, "Sean, don't stand there like a dolt, man! Do something, for the love of God!"

"I'm fine, ye old fool. Fit as can be. Meaghan did a right fine job midwifin' me. Yer precious Sean could have done no better. Now, are ye going to blather away the rest of the noon, or take a look at yer son?"

"My son?"

Meaghan cupped the back of the baby's head with her hand, laying him gently back for Liam to see. Wonder, sheer and beautiful, spread over his leonine features as he lifted a work-scarred finger to the tuft of dark hair on the baby's head. "My son . . ." There was a catch in the big man's voice, and in Grace's soft reply.

"I only hope he'll grow to be as fine a man as his da is."

The babe rooted against Meaghan's breast, hungry again already. Meaghan looked up from the tiny, red face, tears stinging her eyelids.

Sean's gaze raised from the infant's tiny mouth to Meaghan's, delving into her with an intensity that made her heart sing. The carefully schooled indifference was gone, something hot and rich and full touching her in his azure eyes.

A hand tugged on Meaghan's skirt, and she welcomed the interruption of the curl-framed, pixie face of little Annie. "Do you want to see your brother?" Meaghan asked, bending down with the tiny bundle.

"No." Gold ringlets shook emphatically.

Understanding for this child who had been everybody's sunshine tugged at Meaghan. Annie was afraid of being eclipsed. "You're the older sister now. He'll need you to take care of him."

"Don't want to," Annie repeated, her high-pitched voice strained.

"You know I . . . I have to be leaving for England soon, and I'm counting on you to help—"

"I *can't!*" Annie wailed, tugging desperately at her underdrawers. *"Can't!* I *have* to go out *back!*"

Sean's laughter rang through the room. He scooped up the child, hoisting her onto his broad shoulder with a conspiratorial whisper. "Well, then, Annie MacFadden, we'd better get you out there in a hurry, before you—" He whispered something in her ear.

The relief on the child's face was hilarious, and Liam and Meaghan laughed until tears flooded their cheeks. Still trying to catch his breath, Liam took the baby from Meaghan, chattering to little Sean as though he could understand.

Meaghan wiped at the wet spot on her bodice, feeling somehow uncomfortable. Her breasts stung with an unfamiliar fullness that didn't fade. She could feel Grace watching her with those eyes that seemed to know everything.

"Ye'll make a fine mother, Meggie," Grace said.

Meaghan went to the window. Sean was rounding the corner of the cottage, roaring like a monster, pretending to chew on Annie's bare arm. Laughter—how seldom she had heard it from that wonderfully carved mouth.

Annie squealed, kicking her legs against his chest, and Meaghan's stomach churned with the need to lay a child of Sean's own body in those strong arms. Her cheeks burned, and she looked away. Sean was sending her to Liverpool on Thursday. He didn't want her. He didn't want a child. And all the passion burning in those compelling eyes would never change that single fact.

Sean jerked his long legs free of the tangled bed sheets, ramming his fist into his goose-down pillow and muttering an oath! The cursed thing might as well be made of broken glass for all the ease it gave him, and the cot's narrow sides seemed the width of a razor.

He had lain awake for hours, listening to the clock on the mantelpiece mark the time, listening to the soft rhythm of Meaghan's breathing on the other side of the wall until it had grown silent.

Every time he had tried to shut his eyes he had felt the softness of the big bed in the next room, the heat of his hips cradled between Meaghan's thighs, her fingertips coursing over him in a gentle torture that drove him to insanity. Meaghan . . .

God, he still wanted her! Wanted to lose himself inside her, not only his body but his soul. Why? She was no more beautiful than a dozen other women he had taken to his bed, and against the memory of Alanna's ivory-cool beauty, her coppery tresses and fiery courage seemed to blaze too brightly. But there was a mystery there, a fierce trusting that had broken the walls of his defenses and left them in ruin.

And today, seeing her with Grace's baby at her breast had made him want to take her behind closed doors and make love to her, to fill her with his seed, with his sons.

Sons. He had always wanted sons and daughters with mischief in their eyes. A whole brood of them clattering through the silent halls of Cottage Gael, sliding down the polished curved banister, marring the walls with their fingertips, gooey with pie crumbs.

"Sniveling, whining brats with perpetually dirty faces," Alanna had labeled the little bright-cheeked urchins who chased behind them, yanking her skirts. Her nose had wrinkled with distaste as they delved boldly into the broadcloth pockets of Sean's coat for the peppermints he kept there for them.

He had told himself Alanna was young, beautiful, gay, that she wanted to frolic before settling down, that she was little more than a child herself. But the thought of her waist thickening, of her suffering through labor, of her sweating and pushing with legs spread, had seemed even to him somehow coarse, as if pregnancy would defile her.

Why, then, did the thought of Meaghan's body ripening fill him with clawing need, with hunger. Sweet Lord, what was he doing lying here, wanting her, the picture of her with his child in her belly making his body harden and throb?

He was sending her away. A week from now she would be gone, out of his life, unable to hurt him or to be hurt by him in return. That's what he wanted, wasn't it? And after the way he had treated her, didn't Meaghan want it, too?

She had told him she loved him—*loved him*. God, the look on her face as she had said the words—would he ever chase it from his mind? Her delicate cheeks had still been chalky from the bullet wound she had suffered for him, her lips trembling, the sleeve of her dress torn and bloodstained. And he had laughed at her, laughed in despair that she should offer herself so freely to him, because he wanted her, but knew he could never have her. Because he—

Sean flung his wrist up over his eyes. God, no, he wouldn't lay himself bare to that kind of agony . . . not now . . . not again . . . He shoved viciously at the mattress with one foot in an effort to shove from his mind the truth that he dared not think, let alone believe. The solidity of the cot gave way to air, and suddenly he was falling. His right hand stretched out to bear his weight, the wrist hitting the ground at an odd angle. One naked hip banged down onto the hair-sprinkled bend just above his hand. Threads of pain shot through the nerves of his arm as his wrist snapped sideways.

"Damn!" he grated, clutching it with a grimace as he righted himself. "Damn, damn, damn! That's all I need now. A blasted broken arm." He rotated the hand, feeling the bones, then arched it back and down and around again. No shifting, no rasp of bone against bone. Expelling his breath in a long rush of relief, he pressed his good hand and the one that was already beginning to swell to his face.

Falling out of bed. It was absurd! And Meaghan . . . God, how had things gotten so far out of control? He had only wanted to help her, to save her from Alanna's fate at Colin Radcliffe's hands, and now he, himself, was causing her misery far worse than even that twisted mind could have conjured. At least with Radcliffe she would have held her pride, while he had taken it and flung it in her face.

Sean let his arms fall onto his bent knees, an ache growing deep in the pit of his belly as he forced himself to his feet. He was the fool that Grace had labeled him at every opportunity. More of a fool than even she realized. But he couldn't stop himself, even now, from the torture he had borne every night since Meaghan's accident.

Silently, he crossed the floor, striking a match to light a candle that lay on the table. The feeble flame sent its circle of rays toward the shiny wood door in the middle of the wall. Sean went to it, turning the brass handle of the portal leading to the big room. He had come every night to watch her curled in sleep, her eyes red and swollen, with tears still dampening her lashes. He had wanted to wipe them away and with them all thoughts of loving him, to tell her that he wasn't worth a one of her tears, but he had never touched her, and she had never wakened.

Tomorrow she would be gone. He eased the door open, slipping inside it. The cool breeze from the open window tickled his bare flesh as he padded silently across the carpet. The moon illuminated the bed in silver, the mounds beneath the sheets somehow strangely lacking form. He reached down to touch them, a hammering in his heart. Pillows!

A wild fear coursed through him. No, she couldn't have left without saying goodbye, without a word. She had nowhere to go . . . she wouldn't have . . . Damn, he'd been awake all night, hadn't he? Had he dozed off for just a minute without even knowing . . .

He dashed back to his table, nearly upsetting the candle as he grabbed for it, then stumbled back into the room. Her clothes, they were all packed in the trunk, loaded in the wagon he was using to take the O'Learys to the steamer. Only her traveling dress had been left, spread on the spindly chair in readiness for the trip. It still lay there, golden brown folds engulfing the thin gilded legs, her tiny kid slippers peeking from beneath them. No sign could he find of the thin, ruffle-cuffed nightgown she had left out to wear this last night.

He rushed to the window, pushing the velvet draperies as wide open as they would go, searching the moonlit heather as though she might have somehow slipped from the casement into the meadows she loved so well. The meadows . . .

Abandoning the candle, Sean ran back to his own room, finding his breeches and slamming his legs into them.

The grass was wet with dew, soaking his pant legs, chilling his bare feet as he ran, solely on instinct. A wisp of white shone almost eerily in the moonglow, and the stars seemed magically to pick out golden highlights in a halo of flowing hair.

She sat between a hawthorn and a gorse, shoulders wrapped in a lavender comforter, chin resting on her crooked knees.

He stopped, leaning wearily against a scraggly tree.

She didn't turn toward him but continued to stare at the sky. "I wanted to watch the stars. I wonder if they'll be so bright in England."

Sean felt her longing like a physical pain. He stepped to touch her, but his wrist twisted against the tree, and he let out a muffled oath.

Meaghan's head snapped around.

"I didn't mean to scare you," Sean said, his fingertips sliding up his right hand. "It's just my arm . . ." Her sherry-colored eyes seemed to pull at him, and he felt as if he were teetering on the edge of a bottomless crevasse.

"Your arm?" Her tongue darted out to moisten her lower lip, and he knew in that moment he was lost.

"Meaghan, I can't let you leave me tomorrow."

The flash of hope that shone on her face tore at him. He looked away, rushing on. "There are so many sick, and I can't take care of them . . ." The words were a kind of desperate denial.

The coverlet fell from her shoulders, and her skin glowed peachy gold beneath its thin covering. Her lips parted. "You . . . you want me to stay?"

"Yes . . . I mean, you have to help me."

Meaghan saw his jaw harden; there was a twist to his mouth she had never seen before. "A few minutes ago I fell. I checked myself, and . . ." His voice was harsh and somehow hopeless as he continued. "It's my wrist . . ." His shoulders sagged. He ran his fingers through his hair, then let them fall to his side. "Meg, I . . . uh . . . I think it's broken."

The Dublin docks teemed with jaunty sailors and bellowing longshoremen, hair bleached and blown from the harsh salt air, their muscles filling out every thread of their trim uniforms and colorful regalia in sharp contrast to the huddled, ragged forms that were to be their passengers. Scrawny children perched on small trunks, faces wizened like men of a hundred years as they stared out at the bevy of ships anchored in the harbor.

Cluster by cluster each family made its way to board the ship, chests balanced on the thin shoulders of half-starved men, tired women herding flocks of children ahead of them. Tears flowed freely, and here and there a woman keened as though for someone dead.

Meaghan tucked a lock of hair that had tugged free from her chignon back behind her ear and leaned more closely into the support of Sean's hard frame. His breath was warm and comforting against her cheek, chasing away the chill in the air and the much deeper chill inside her. The wind blew in from the waves, whipping at Ma's shawl and buffeting Tom's surly face, the heavy gusts spiced with rain, pitch, tar, and loneliness.

The coat Sean had purchased for Tom lay atop the chest beside them, much the worse for being tramped into the muck by Tom's rag-clad feet, his accusations still swirling in a mire much deeper than the confusion at the dock. A bright red swell on his upthrust chin marked the spot where Sean had cuffed him in desperation to end his ravings, and the blaze in Tom's eyes as he seemed to stare through Sean's face bordered on that of a fanatic. But he said nothing, just glared at Sean with a hatred that made Meaghan shiver to the marrow of her bones.

The queue of families dwindled, and Sean's hand tightened on the curve of Meaghan's waist. She turned her face up to him, and he nodded gently. His warmth stayed with her as he hoisted with his good hand one end of the wooden chest in which the O'Learys possessions lay.

"If you'll take the other side we'll get it aboard," he prodded Tom.

"I'll take it myself, you bloody English whoreson!" Tom O'Leary snarled and Sean let the chest thud to the ground. The weight was too heavy for the scrawny boy, but Tom managed to lift it to the level of his knees. He strained toward the loading area.

"Ma . . ." Meaghan took the few steps toward her mother, laying her hand on the stooped, gray-shawled shoulder. "They . . . I think it's time."

"Time . . . aye . . . it's time . . ." Gray eyes turned from the sea for the first time since they had alighted at the docks. Despite the new dusting of health Sean's gifts of food had brought to the wrinkled cheeks, there was a lost look in her mother's face that made Meaghan's heart ache. Bridget O'Leary reached out, laying the blanket-wrapped Brady into Sean's arms. "Ye'll follow soon, Meaghan Mary?" Rough callused hands framed Meaghan's face.

Meaghan nodded, her throat too tight to speak.

"I did ye great wrong, ye know. Ye asked me to trust ye when ye went with him," she gestured to Sean. "I couldn't. All I could see was yer cousin Maeve as she died, shamed with that devil Radcliffe's child. I didn't want ye to be an outcast, Meggie. I didn't want yer da to—"

"I know, Ma. I . . . I didn't want to hurt you that way, but I was afraid if you or Tom knew the truth you'd do something that would put yourselves in danger."

"And ye were right. Tom there's been itchin' for any cause to blast into somebody. An' I, well, when I'm in a temper my good sense is scarce as meat in a beggar-man's bowl.

"I haven't always been just with ye, have I, child?" She shook her head as Meaghan's mouth opened in protest. "Nay, we both know it. Yer da . . . maybe it was because of the way he loved ye—enough for both of us and then some. Didn't seem there could be any of him left over for Tom an' Brady an' me. But there was, Meggie. I know that now."

"Ma, I . . . I never meant to keep him from the rest of you . . ."

"Ye didn't. It's just he . . . he made ye want so much from life, more than most colleens ever dream of, fillin' ye with reading, ciphering, sendin' ye off on the backs of half-wild horses to run free. That was the one thing I could never forgive him for."

"But—"

"No, child, let me finish. Life's not like that for a woman, Meg. Not now, not here where we are. It's marryin' at fifteen, yer hands gnarlin' from work, yer hair fadin', a passel of babes turnin' yer pink cheeks to ash while they're sobbin' from hunger. Much as I loved yer da, my life was hard, an' I knew watchin' that hopeful light in yer eyes die someday would be the hardest thing I'd ever seen. And the night ye rode off with O'Fallon . . .

"Maybe I was wrong, tryin' to toughen ye, letting ye see that life wasn't the grand adventure yer da had painted. I wanted to tell ye everything—to be brave, to be strong. I guess the only thing I never told ye Meaghan-child, was how very much I loved ye." The words trailed off and tears tracked through the myriad of wrinkles at the corners of Bridget O'Leary's eyes.

Meaghan threw her arms around her mother's thin body, sobs shaking her. "Ma . . . I love you . . ." she choked out, "and I always knew . . ."

A gentle voice at their shoulders made the women pull apart at last. "If you want to get a good berth you'd better board now."

"Aye," Bridget said, whisking away the tears, the no-nonsense strength returning to her bearing as she put Meaghan away from her, and took Brady from Sean's arms. "Where the heaven is that boy of mine?"

"He took the chest with your things. Must've already made it aboard," Sean said, peering through the milling bodies.

"Then I'd best be after him before he sets the ship afire." She shifted the baby to her hip, and Meaghan bent to hold the little body close. "The things Tom said about the both of ye . . . I know they're just a boy's imaginings. Ye're a fine man, Sean O'Fallon. Ye'll take care of her?" She pinned Sean with her gaze.

Sean laid his right hand across Meaghan's back, and she felt the hardness of the splint he had braced it with pressing against her. There was promise in his voice.

"I'll take care of her."

 *Sixteen*

Meaghan took the squalling baby from his basket, and twirled around with him high in the air. "Is this any way to greet your christening day, Sean MacFadden?" she asked, planting a kiss on the black-thatched head. "I'm full aware you may not be so comfortable in your fancy clothes, but you have the look of a little prince."

"Princess, if you ask me." The deep richness of Sean's voice was tinged with laughter as his lips grazed Meaghan's ear. "With all the lace you sewed onto that dress, he looks like a swell dressed for the ballroom!"

"Off with ye an' yer complainin'! It's a fine job Meaghan's done of fixin' his things!" Grace bristled.

"Don't pay him any mind, Grace. He was right there with me the day we stopped at Elisabeth's shop on our way from seeing off Ma and the young ones. He even helped me choose which pattern to make from the books Elisabeth showed me."

"Well, whatever ye chose between ye it was perfect. The babe looks like an' angel from heaven."

"What he looks is damned miserable." Sean gave the starched lace bonnet string beneath the little double chin a tug. "But if you ladies are happy, well, then, I guess he'll just have to suffer."

The fingers of his right hand curved over the end of the splint. He reached out, skimming Meaghan's cheek with the backs of his knuckles. "Will you be coming home soon?" he asked.

"As soon as Grace and I finish mending Annie's new dress. She was skipping around in it yesterday when we let her try it on, and her toe got caught."

167

"Her *toe?*"

"Don't you dare laugh! It was a major tragedy with enough tears shed over it to rival the Flight of the Earls. She ripped out the hem and some of the trim tore—"

"Forget I even asked! When you're done saving the world here at the MacFaddens', try getting dressed yourself. At the last I heard the only thing you'd decided on for certain was your embroidered petticoat and the chemise with the blue silk ribbon . . ."

Meaghan shot him a withering glance, and Grace laughed above the heap of pink cloth on her lap.

"Not that you don't look beautiful in them—"

"Sean O'Fallon, if you don't close that mouth of yours—" Balancing Baby Sean in the crook of one arm Meaghan raised her other in threat.

"All right, all right. I know when I'm not welcome," Sean said with an injured air. "I have to stop by Fitzgerald's before I go to the church, so I'll take your gelding and leave the buggy for you, milady. Unless, of course, you intend to race up to the church with your skirts flying up around your neck."

"And wouldn't ye love that, ye lecherous beast!" Grace goaded from her stool.

"No. No I wouldn't." The words were tender in a way that had crept into Sean's velvet tones often of late. His eyes glowed with a secret sadness, then lightened as though within the sadness was also joy.

The baby snuffled, trying to shove a ruffle away from his cheek.

Sean went to Meaghan, leaning over the baby with a grin. One tiny fist batted at Sean's jaw. "I don't blame you," he commiserated. "I'd want to punch somebody too. As soon as Father Loughlin is done with his muttering and splashing, your godfather, here, promises to rescue you from these two torture masters and their furbelows."

"Ye can rescue him right now, if ye've the nerve to. One more breath in that gown an' he's sure to soil it afore it ever sees the inside of the church."

"I'll leave the dressing and undressing to you," Sean said, arching one brow rakishly. "Except, of course, in very special instances." He retrieved his medical bags from Grace's clean-scrubbed table, looping them over one shoulder. He stooped to kiss Grace on the cheek and surreptitiously pull the thread from the eye of her needle.

"Out with ye, boy! Why I put up with ye I'll never know!" Grace complained. Sean leaned down to her ear, whispering something that made the wide mouth split in a grin. Grace glanced at Meaghan, then back at Sean. "Ye did? Truly? Well, mayhap I *will* keep ye around for a while longer," she said grudgingly, searching out the slip of pink thread on the mound of cloth in her lap.

Sean tilted Meaghan's chin up. "Stop home before you go to the church, now. Little Sean here demands that his godmother be beautiful." The smile he flashed her was heart-stopping, tinged with deep emotion.

Meaghan watched as he swung out the door with lean-hipped grace, then turned to throw her one more look sparkling with suppressed excitement. Home. If only Sean knew how much like home the walls of Cottage Gael seemed.

"I meant what I said about the babe. That dress of his won't look so fine all damp and stained," Grace warned. Meaghan's eyes flicked back to her, then to the door. She slipped the tiny pearl button at the baby's neck free of its loop, then started to slide a little sleeve from his arm.

Hoofbeats faded, muffled by the heather, and Meaghan looked over at Grace's face. She was plying her needle as if the fate of Ireland depended upon it, but the smile on her face had the brilliance of sun, and the edges of her colorless lashes were gilded with tears.

The stairs to the hall held secrets, whispering in the silence as if phantom's feet had tread on the carpeted tiers. Meaghan shook her head ruefully. How many times since she had come to live with Sean had she entered this house alone? So many times that it now seemed as much home to her as her space under the eaves of the empty cottage in the valley. But something was different this time. Something in the stillness as if a smoky veil had fallen over time.

The thought made her shiver. What nonsense! She was no timid flower to be frightened of her own shadow! The secret Sean had held had brought joy to his face. Why then did the air in Cottage Gael seem suddenly sinister?

"Sean?" She called his name, though there had been no sign

of the gelding in the stable, no print of his boots upon the sifting of dust on the veranda. "Sean?"

Her voice echoed and re-echoed through the rooms at the top of the stairs, its only answer silence. "Did you really expect someone to say something?" she asked herself, shaking off her feelings of nervousness. "He told you to meet him at the church. Grace was thrilled at whatever secret he was keeping. If it was something that would upset me she certainly wouldn't have—" Pursing her lips in disgust at her runaway imagination, she hurried through the door to the living quarters. Not a thing was disturbed, from her basket of mending beside the chair to the instruments Sean had been sorting on the table. Even the copy of *Jane Eyre* Sean had surprised her with lay untouched, a brass bookmark partway through it. Why, then, did she have the uneasy feeling that other fingers had trailed across its tooled leather binding, fingers somehow hostile . . .

Her heart was beating in irregular time as her eyes came to rest on the open door to her bedroom. Hadn't she turned back to shut it before she had gone to MacFadden's that morning? She was almost certain . . . Yes, she had forgotten the baby's bonnet, and Sean had reminded her with such a smug look on his face she had flounced into the room, retrieved the missing article, and banged the door in mock anger. Banged it. Sean had accused her of loosening the bolts in the hinges. He had . . .

Slowly she moved to the door, then froze. Again, nothing had been touched. Nothing except the coverlet she had smoothed over the feather tick that morning.

Spread across it like a froth of satiny petals lay a dress so exquisite it defied reality. White lace flowed in abundant softness over ripples of raw silk, little ribbons of palest mint caught tiny bundles of blue silk flowers all around the hem and bodice, and a wreath of the same blossoms lay in a circlet beside it. Meaghan forgot to breathe, all thoughts of creeping evil gone.

She walked the steps to it in a daze, lifting a fold to see if it could possibly be real. White, bride's white. A tiny heart locket nestled in a square of tissue paper on the bodice, its neck ribbon midnight velvet. Could Sean . . . could it possibly mean . . . no, if he wanted her to marry him wouldn't he ask her himself? He wouldn't just . . .

But at Grace's he had seemed so strange, so hopeless yet

hopeful. Was he afraid she had stopped loving him, wanting him? Was that the answer to the pain she saw lurking at the corners of his lips when he thought she wasn't watching? The morose silences, the over-bright teasing, the longing, the self-contempt? So much had happened between them, could this wedding gown be Sean's way of offering her his heart, without risking rejection?

What if he had talked to Father Loughlin already, and was planning for them to be married before the christening . . . Could he have told Grace . . . Meaghan swallowed, letting the cloth fall from stiff fingers. By the time the sun set she could be Meaghan O'Fallon . . . Sean's wife . . . with the right to his body, his children . . . His *love?*

"No," she warned herself sternly, "don't hope. If you do and the dress is nothing more than a gift for the baby's christening, all the hurt of wanting him will come back, only worse . . . so much worse." But when she stripped down to her pantalettes and poured water from the pitcher on the wash stand into the china bowl, she couldn't resist a skip to her step, and as she smoothed the white lace gown over layers of ruffly petticoats, the foot-tapping, joy-springing songs that had rollicked from the strings of Da's fiddle danced on the rose-scented air.

The reins of the gig felt strange in Meaghan's glove-covered hands, and she tried futilely to stretch her fingers against the restraint of the dove-gray kid without dropping the leather lines. Sean's gray shook its head at the sight tugging on its bit. The slender buggy whip danced in its socket and the harness jingled gaily as the horse trotted over the road. She should make it to St. Colmcille's just in time, though she knew she should have left Cottage Gael much earlier.

The flower wreath had proved troublesome, or had it been her hair with its unruly curls escaping in all directions? After heaven knew how long of trying to tame her locks, she had settled for a loosely pinned knot that swirled at the back of her head, glistening with gold fire. Then she had topped it with the delicate circlet of blossoms. Tendrils had slipped through their bonds at the breeze's light teasing, but instead of making her appear untidy, they framed her pink cheeks in a beguiling nimbus of baby-fine curls.

If she was to marry Sean this day, she wanted to be more than beautiful. She wanted to be as perfect for him in this dress he had chosen as she could possibly be with her stubborn freckles and pixie chin.

The sound of a rider approaching behind her broke through her thoughts, and she pulled on the right rein to guide the gig closer to the edge of the dirt road, hoping against hope it would be Sean. The running horse swerved close to the buggy, nearly careening into the swiftly turning rear wheel. Dust swirled, swallowing up muscled legs, huge hooves. Shining black, the horse's coat glowed with blue lights. Meaghan's own horse neighed in fear as a hand shot out and grabbed its reins just under the bit. In barely a minute both animals stood still, sides heaving.

Broad shoulders turned, but Meaghan already knew with a sinking in the pit of her stomach who lay beneath the dark green of the Newmarket coat. There was a new grimness to the thin lips as they drew into a mocking leer.

"Mrs. O'Fallon." Colin Radcliffe's hand slid along the rein and he nudged his horse forward until his knee was inches from her own. "We meet again."

"I have nothing to say to you. Let me pass." Meaghan's hand clenched on the reins she still held, jerking on them in a futile effort to free them from Radcliffe's grip.

"And let you deny me the pleasure of your company? I think not. I've thought of little else the whole time I was closeted away with my grandfather in England, even when he told me my inheritance . . ." A flash of something darkened his soulless eyes, and whatever he had begun to say was lost. He laughed harshly. "The minute I put ashore on this godforsaken land I made it my business to find you, sweeting. I've waited a long while to catch you without your *husband* hovering over you like a buck at rutting time. At our last meeting you seemed quite . . . enamored . . . of my charms and I am in sad need of a diversion."

"Then find it elsewhere! I despised you from the first time I saw you, and if anything my hate for you has grown a hundredfold." Meaghan's anger masked the fear that threaded through her every nerve. Her words were frigid, resolute. "Let go of my horse."

"Ordering about a peer of the realm? Do you truly expect me to cringe and grovel and beg pardon? No, I believe I'd rather see you in that light. And make no mistake, love. I will. I will . . ."

Meaghan's breath seemed to strangle in her throat as his hand neared her. Her fingers crept down the length of the whiphandle Sean kept in a socket near her feet. Her hand closed on it. "Touch me and I'll—"

"You'll what? Do you really think you could be so lucky as to have O'Fallon stumble upon you in your time of distress yet again? Don't even hope it, love. His horse is tied in the church-yard. He'll probably be there all night, plotting ways to strip my purse bare with that meddlesome Loughlin."

There must have been some change in her face. Radcliffe's gaze sharpened.

"Ah, you *were* hoping. Tell me, shall we play at forfeits, Meaghan, my sweet, now that you know your knight will not come charging down upon us? Your wager will be the safety of the people you love against a taste of those delectable breasts of yours and the very, very slim chance that I will be able to release you after savoring their sweetness." A pale tongue snaked over Radcliffe's lips, his hand starting to ease its way into her low-cut bodice.

The whip sliced through the air, slashing down with all Meaghan's strength onto the smooth skin below Radcliffe's cuff. With a brutal oath he clutched the hand to him. "Damn you, I'll see your skin flayed to the bone for this, you little witch!" His fist drew back to strike her, but Meaghan was already bringing the whip down again, this time on her own horse's back. The reins tore free from Radcliffe's hand; his scream was savage and cruel. "Run, run. Just try to escape me . . ."

Meaghan drove the buggy at breakneck speed, wheels jounc-ing out of dips in the dirt, but no sound of rushing hooves pounded after her. When at last the spires of St. Colmcille pierced the sky ahead, her whole body was shaking.

She had struck Colin Radcliffe. *Struck him!* She could still see the shock on his face, the angry red slash where the whip had bitten, and then the malevolence, the bared violence in his eyes. What would he do now? Take revenge on her through her family? No, they were gone, safe.

Sean? Sean had defeated Radcliffe before. But she had to warn him, to think of what to do. God, why was it that she, who had always fought her own battles, now longed for the comfort of a man's arms around her, a sharing of fears, of strengths?

The churchyard was empty as she leapt down from the buggy, not even stopping to loop the horse's reins around a post. She ran up the church steps, wanting only to feel Sean's hands, to see Grace's smile, to hold, to touch those she held dear and know they were safe.

The soles of her slippers slapping on the floor resounded like gunfire in the deathly quiet. The cluster of people at the altar wheeled, and she had the sudden sensation of waking in the midst of a nightmare.

Grace gasped, and Liam's hand reached out to steady her. "My God, Meaghan . . . oh my God . . ."

Sean's face blanched at the sight of her, until the only color in his face seemed to center in his eyes. His lips contorted in shock, almost horror, and the shifting patterns of agony in his face seemed to age him a dozen years.

"Wh . . . what . . ." Meaghan slammed to a stop ten yards from the others, fighting desperately against the confusion.

The lines in Sean's face carved deep, his eyes filled with hatred as he closed the space between them with three savage strides. Fingers closed on her arms, gouging into the soft flesh, the corners of the splint cutting through the delicate lace. Meaghan knew a fleeting confusion that Sean's injured hand could grip her with such force.

"Where?" he hissed. "Where in the hell did you get that dress?"

"I . . . I . . ."

"Here now! Enough of this in the house of the Lord!" Father Loughlin slid his arm between them, pushing Sean back.

Sean shook off the holy man's grasp. "Meaghan, you tell me where the hell—"

"Sean," Grace's voice was desperate as she put herself between them. "Later, after the blessin'. Ye're frightenin' the poor child to death."

"Grace, for God's sake can't you see—"

"She couldn't have known, lad! She couldn't have . . ." There was agony in both of their faces, agony shared, as Sean turned away, and Meaghan wanted to sob. What? Dear God what had she done that was so terrible? What was it that was torturing Sean? Grace?

Father Loughlin's deep baritone boomed out the words of baptism, and the fear Meaghan had felt at Colin Radcliffe's threats faded to nothingness as she watched the fury in Sean O'Fallon pitch and roil.

The final blessing had barely left Father Loughlin's lips, when Sean spun Meaghan around. His fingers clenched handfuls of her hair. The band that held the flower wreath snapped, sending a score of silk blossoms tumbling to the floor as he jerked her face up to meet his. "The christening is over. Now, you tell me, God damn it! Where, Meaghan? Where the hell did you find Alanna's wedding gown?"

Seventeen

Colin Radcliffe paced the confines of his study, the score of papers swiped from his desk in a fit of rage crumpling beneath his boots. He had stared at the meticulously penned records for hours, trying to divine the secrets they held, the people they hid. But the faded ink was as closemouthed as a rogue at confession and a thousand times more dangerous.

Damn his grandfather, the almighty Duke of Radbury! Though it had been almost a month since Colin had left Blythehall, the old man's words still ate at his gut like starving rats.

Ensconced in his huge leather chair, his back still straight as the bore of a rifle, white side-whiskers brushing his perfectly tied cravat, his grandfather had pushed a portfolio across the desk top with his walking stick, then waited as Colin had slipped the buckle and impatiently scanned the leather case's contents. Impatience had shifted to disbelief, then rage.

"What the hell—" Colin had roared. "What is this?"

"I should think it would be quite clear. It is an accounting of my estates, wealth I have accrued over the years separate from the Radbury lands—riches solely under my control."

"Solely? They're mine! My inheritance! Well over three fourths of the estate! This says—damn you! You can't take it from me! I'm your heir!"

"Can't I?" Eyes opaque with cunning evil regarded him over steepled fingers. "The dukedom is not mine to keep, nor the paltry lands your great-grandfather didn't manage to lose at dicing. Those you're bound to have by law at my death, but the wealth . . . ah, that is mine to do with as I see fit."

"And you don't see fit to give it to me?" Radcliffe bit out.

"You're not fit to wipe boots on! Since the day I discovered this 'complication' with your inheritance, I have been trying to find this woman and her child, and destroy them. But by then Jonathan was dead, and my solicitor was clumsy with the information he gleaned. When you came of age, I hoped to stir you to take some action, to be a man for once instead of chasing demireps. But you ignored every letter I sent you, every command. Maybe this other will show more promise."

"Other! You'd make the whelp of some Irish bitch richer than the Duke of Radbury!"

"Yes, if he was the son of your father, though I have my doubts anything that crawled from Jonathan's loins could be worthy of the name 'man'." The Duke of Radbury reached out for the portfolio, but Colin held it fast.

"Why didn't you tell me the reason I was to find the woman? Damn it, I would have ransacked the whole island to dredge her up, had I known—"

"Had you known. Yes, to save your bloody hide I've no doubt you would have played Herod and murdered every boy-child of an age, but you'd not let go of your women's petticoats long enough to take seriously the first responsibility I've ever dared offer you."

"Responsibility! That's what you gave me when you dumped that lot of filthy peasants on my shoulders—"

"A ten-year-old boy could suck monies from that sad lot of scarecrows. The reason I got you the hell out of London was because you shamed the house of Radbury before the whole of England! A damned Irish turf cutter would have more sense than to flaunt his mistress before the Queen!"

"You think this *son* of my *father* will grace a royal ballroom? They sleep in the mud with their pigs in Ireland."

"I would prefer the company of swine to that which you have been keeping." Snake eyes glittered.

"So because of that one night you're going to turn your empire over to some Irish—"

"I'm not certain." The duke had waved his hand in dismissal. "You have to find him first."

"*I* have to find him?"

"Yes. Find him and bring him to me. Then I'll decide between my son's leavings. But make no mistake. You'll be closely watched. If this Irish spawn should . . . say . . . meet with an untimely accident . . . *you*, my beloved grandson, will find your inheritance in the bottom of the Thames."

"With all the other bodies you've managed to put there?"

The gold-topped cane had sung in an arc, his grandfather's blow sending pain shooting outward. Colin had grabbed the polished length, wanting nothing more than to smash it into that smug, wrinkled face, but damn, he hadn't, he hadn't. He'd taken the stick and hurled it into the duke's priceless collection of Ming pottery, then, snatching up the portfolio, left Blythehall without so much as waiting for his valet to pack his clothes.

Colin slammed his fist against his study wall, bringing himself back to the present. The aura of Blythehall fled, leaving in its place the rich elegance of the manor house and the myriad shades of green of the Irish countryside.

No one had ever dared lift a hand against him, except his grandfather and O'Fallon and . . . the girl. The girl. She had lashed him with a whip like some beast. Radcliffe's hand throbbed as if acid had been poured into the raw flesh.

The bitch! A peasant slut who spread her legs for Sean O'Fallon and claimed to be his wife. No, even with gold encircling every finger that hot-blooded wench would still be a whore—a doxy to turn any man's loins to fire.

And he would have her. Now. No more waiting and planning, no more of Wilde's cautions or schemes. He strode to the window, glaring into the stableyard, his pulse pounding with lust unchecked. Today he would have the red-haired beauty, mar the rose tint of her naked skin, hear her cry for mercy.

Would she plead? Beg? The thought singed his flesh with pleasure. But his victory must be complete, total over both her and O'Fallon. He had to find a way to bind her, destroy her, if being forced to submit to him would not be enough to keep her from running back to her bastard lover.

A dappled colt frisked out of the stable door, kicking up slender hooves in a kind of play with the tall, brown-shirted man behind him. Connor MacDonough's broad shoulders stretched against the cloth as he dug into his pocket and held out a lump of something in his palm. The colt crept toward him slowly, his little head cocked, then snatched away whatever the groom had held, skittering off to the far corner of the paddock. MacDonough shoved his cap off his head, and Radcliffe could almost hear him laugh. MacDonough.

When he had asked the big groom about the girl, MacDonough had not been laughing. A predatory gleam sparked Radcliffe's eyes.

The man had been afraid, linked to the wench somehow. There was something the horseman knew, something . . . He had sensed it before, and now . . .

Colin jerked on the bell pull. Wilde, Pinkerton, the others— he would summon them posthaste. MacDonough . . . stiff necked, proud. It would be a pleasure to see him sprawled on the floor, spilling his guts. Yes, he would talk. It was the stiffest necks that made the most resounding cracks when they broke.

Radcliffe's teeth gleamed white. He was weary of the chase and anxious for the kill. Yes, Sean O'Fallon's red-haired witch would receive a lord between her thighs this night if he had to cut his way through Connor MacDonough's heart to find her.

The cool wind lifted the fringe of hair at Sean's collar, buffeting the loosened ends of his cravat against his half-bared chest. The house had seemed to smother him, memories of himself and Alanna seeping from the cracks in the floorboards, sifting through the weft of the carpets until a hundred scenes lined the walls like seconds on a stage. Scenes that he had blocked from his mind ruthlessly, years before, lest they drive him mad.

But now there was no shield, no veil, to keep the pain from spearing through him again and again. He could see Alanna pleading with him, violet eyes spilling tears, lips pouting, begging to be kissed. He could see himself putting her away from him, taking up his medical bag, riding off with a dozen different people to a score of different emergencies.

And he could see her in her wedding gown, the day of her final fitting, bursting into his office against his wishes to spin in slow, seductive circles in front of Grace MacFadden and himself. She had wrinkled her nose, mocking the seamstress's heavy brogue scoldings which predicted bad luck, until he had laughed in indulgence under Grace's disapproving eyes.

But damn it, Alanna, even blushed with memory, had not been half so beautiful in lace and wildflowers as Meaghan had been . . . And never had he seen slanting from Alanna's face the innocent, unselfish love that had touched him in the hall of the church from Meaghan's soft brown eyes.

Nor had he seen shaded in violet the stricken agony his fury had brought. Sean clenched his fist, feeling again Meaghan's soft flesh give under his fingers, knowing the delicate rose was now shadowed with bruises of his making. Damn, he hadn't wanted to hurt her, but the dress ... damn, the dress ...

How could it have been laid out on the bed like Meaghan claimed? The dressmaker had hung it, three years ago, swathed in sheets, in the attic room where she had been staying. No one had touched it since. Only Grace had known what was in the shroud in the tiny room, and Grace would never have ...

Sean arched his head back, feeling the breeze trickle down the corded muscles of his throat. No, Grace had been as stunned as he was.

And Meaghan, she had leapt out of the buggy, her dress catching on the buggy step, tearing its icing of lace as he had accused her of ...

God, what had been in her face that moment that had smashed him awake, as though clawing his way from a world of night terror?

He had vaulted from the buggy seat, running into Cottage Gael to follow her, but the door to her room had been locked, and the walls behind it silent.

Sean kneaded his throbbing temples. Grace had been right. Meaghan couldn't have known.

Instead of fading, the hammering in his head grew worse until it seemed to take on actual sound. His head snapped upright, suddenly alert to the rhythm of hoofbeats. It came all too often, taking him from meals, from sleep, signaling injury or illness on some outlying farm. He shoved his hand through his hair, bolting toward the sound.

The horse was white with lather, and even in the light of the quarter moon Sean could see the scarlet nostrils of the animal quivering and wide as he grabbed for the reins.

"Meaghan ... where's Meaghan ..." The voice of the rider was garbled and desperate as he slid from the horse's back, landing with a thud on the ground beside the dancing hooves.

Sean dropped the reins, sliding his arm around the man to hoist him up. A groan came raggedly from the man's mouth. "She's inside. What's wrong? What do you want with her?" Sean staggered, trying to support the man's large frame.

". . . Radcliffe . . . have to warn . . ."

With his boot Sean kicked the door open, dragging the rider up the stairs to his cot. His fingers felt numb as he fumbled for a flame and touched it to the lamp.

"Meaghan!" he bellowed as the wick glowed orange. "Meaghan, get out here!"

His breath came out in a gust as he turned to face the man on the cot, staring at the bruised and bloodied face which was far worse than anything he'd witnessed, even in the ring. "Dear God," he said through gritted teeth. He grabbed a bottle of whiskey, sloshing some into a glass. "Drink. It'll sting like blazes, but it'll ease the pain." He pressed the rim gently to the swollen lips. MacDonough, Sean realized with a start. Damn, he'd scarcely recognized the red-haired groom. This was the man who had ridden in with Meaghan the day he had fought Wilde. This was the one Wilde had said was her lover. Meaghan . . . where the hell was she?

Connor wiped his lips gingerly with the back of his hand, somewhat revived, each word from his mouth punctuated with pain. "Riding home . . . I heard a noise, stopped. People camp in the ditches, families . . . children . . . I bring them home . . . feed them . . . .But it was Radcliffe. They took me home, beat me. I wouldn't talk . . . God, I wouldn't hurt Maggie, but he . . ." The big man's voice cracked, tears trickled down his cheeks, pink from following the bloody gashes in his face. Sean lay a hand on Connor's shoulder. It gave him the strength to go on.

"My little girl . . . he was going to kill her . . . my baby . . ."

Sean's nails gouged into his palm. His face hardened to granite. Radcliffe. Damn him to hell!

"I told them," Connor sobbed. "I told them everything. Meaghan had told me about you, your plan to keep her safe. When I went to O'Leary's to check on her, Ma Bridget told me she had run off with you to live as your . . ." Connor choked over the words. "Radcliffe and his men headed east, toward the O'Leary holdings. I told them she'd be there . . . wanted to buy time . . . I rode as soon as they were out of sight . . . Mary put me on a horse and I rode . . ."

Sean tucked the wool blanket around MacDonough's trembling limbs. "Quiet, now. You did what you had to. No one could blame you." Cords of fear strangled his heart. If Radcliffe would strike out at MacDonough so boldly, he was done with playing games. Ferret had turned hunter, claws unsheathed. And Meaghan . . . the danger she was in turned his spine to ice.

He swung around to the door, banging it with his fist. "Meaghan! Damn it, woman!" He wrenched the brass knob savagely, and it turned in his hand. The door opened on creaking hinges. Fingers of light from the lamp groped through the darkness like a blind man. Curtains fluttered at an open window.

A mound of lace and silk lay on the carpet, dotted with the remains of silk blossoms. Panic closed Sean in its fist, as his eyes darted around the room, searching. The room was empty.

A square of paper lay white against the pillows. He ran to it, snatching it up. Rushing to the lamp he fought to still his shaking hands. Damn! Damn! If he could just make out . . .

The letters seemed to slide into place like some hideous puzzle. Fear knifed through his body as words leapt at him from the tear-smudged page. *Dear Sean.* He caught the edge of the table, his knees threatening to buckle. God . . . oh, God no, it couldn't be! The curled script crystallized, and Sean felt the color drain from his face. He clutched the paper until the edges tore, forcing his eyes to the swirled line ahead. *Dear Sean*, it read, *I am going home* . . .

 *Eighteen*

The tinker's cart jounced over a stone, sending Meaghan's hip crashing into the hard wooden side again, as the lank-haired driver hit a tuneless note in a song tortured beyond all recognition. Meaghan winced as the rough wood rasped against the thin covering of her skirts, her flesh scarcely padded by the petticoats she wore, and she wished vainly once more that the man would pay attention to his driving instead of trying to deafen her with a voice that would make the angels stop their ears.

But she would have taken a ride with the devil himself to escape the searing pain that had blinded her in the hours since standing on the steps of St. Colmcille's.

Her fingers tightened into fists, tears stinging her eyes, as she thought of the silent ride to Cottage Gael, the look on Sean's face when he had pulled the buggy to a halt beside the steps . . . God, the look on his face! So full of agony, of the same hatred he had shown the night he had told her about the rape of his mother. But to see it directed at her . . .

"A *bride's* dress, Meaghan?" he had spat. "Did you think yourself so bewitching that once I saw you in it I'd sweep you up to Loughlin and demand that he make you my wife?" His eyes had hardened in relentless cruelty as they bored into her, and her face had been scarlet with the truth of the hour before.

"I . . . I thought . . ."

"You thought I would marry you?" Sean had snarled in amazement, his mouth curling in mirthless laughter. "Christ, you really did! It might have worked, *love*, but I've seen this gown on a woman before. It tends to lose its attraction . . ." His hands had closed on her roughly, dragging her into his arms, but the underside of her sleeve had tangled on his splint. Cursing, he had ripped it from the lace, then tore free the lengths of rag that had bound the twin slats of boarding to his arm, hurling them from him with the wrist he had said he could scarcely move.

"You . . . your arm . . ."

"My arm . . . Call it a miraculous recovery." The hard laugh had frightened her as he had crushed her protests onto her mouth with a savagery that had ground her teeth against the inner flesh of her lips, his hand moving up to the tear in her bodice, forcing his way beneath the layers.

"You want to be my wife so badly," he grated. "Then let's get on with the wedding night." His hips had come hard upon hers, and she was terrified to feel him swelling against her.

"Stop it! Sean! Stop!" She had clawed at his face, fearing more to be taken in hatred by this man than in the same way by Colin Radcliffe. She had gained just enough space between them to drive her knee upward. Her strike had been far from the mark, but her ragged sob of despair and the violent trembling of her body seemed to still Sean.

He had stared down at her, still holding her fast, self-loathing in every line in his face, a strange kind of startled awareness about him. Slowly his fingers had loosened. His eyes had slid shut.

She had run up the stairs to her room, wanting only to be rid of the dress that now seemed to jeer at her with evil satisfaction, to be far from the hatred and the hurt in Sean's face. But he had followed, calling after her, trying to open the heavy locked door, until at last he had fallen silent.

Stripped to her shift Meaghan had scrubbed her skin raw, to wash from it the feel of the dress, the feel of Sean's hands, but she couldn't. They stayed, clinging to her, taunting her. And she had hated Sean, as she had stolen out of the house and through the back meadows, hated herself that she had dared hope . . .

"This one, colleen?" Instinctively she braced her feet against the floorboards as the cart bumped to a halt. The tinker jerked his pointy chin at the offshoot of road leading in a downward ribbon.

"What?"

"I say is this the road ye were tellin' me of?" Darkness had come in a swift wing of black, leaving Meaghan no memory of twilight, of moonrise. She peered down the dimly lit lane.

"Yes. This is the road."

"Good thing I saw it. It's a sharp eye this boy-o's got." The man gave her a jaunty smile as he handed her down. "Ye don't have to thank me, for the ride or the intertainmint. 'Tisn't often I have such a 'preciative audience fer me singin'. Wager ye never would've guessed that me grandda was a bard."

Meaghan forced a smile. "No, I never would have guessed."

The man flushed, and she hurriedly tacked on, "I would have thought you were the bard yourself." The tinker's coat buttons seemed to puff out with pride.

"Sure ye don't want me to drive ye down yon? It's dark as sin, an' smellin' like rain."

"No. Thank you. I've been running down this road since I was three years old. And it won't hurt me to get wet."

The tinker jumped back up onto his seat. "Well, Godspeed to ye," he called, setting his donkey to walking. "And God's luck!"

Luck? The wind was moist with the coming rain, and Meaghan lifted her face to it, almost laughing aloud. Her luck could only change for the better. The screechy voice rose again in a tuneless strain as he gave her a wave of his hand. Meaghan turned down the winding road. The walk through the starless night was fraught with memories; the white house, when she reached it, was nested in mist.

It was as if the walls themselves were in mourning, shrouded in dark silence. She paused at the cottage door, wanting to hear the thump of Tom jumping from the loft ladder, smell the fragrant sweetness of the smoke from Da's pipe, see Ma at her loom, her hands keeping rhythm with her sharply scolding tongue. But there was only stillness. And Meaghan knew with an aching certainty that this shell of clay and timbers was no more "home" to her now than a rabbit's warren in the hills.

But tonight . . . tonight it would be enough just to be far from Sean and the bittersweet memory of bodies that loved so deeply it seemed that souls must follow . . .

She raised the latch, sagging against the door frame. Not so much as a rushlight remained, the table, stools, even Ma's loom having been sold to the gombeen-men before the trip to England. But a few of Da's tools still stood in the corner as if waiting for him, and the feather tick in the room off the hearth still lay hidden by the night.

Meaghan swallowed the lump that rose in her throat. Ma had

seemed so numb those last days, obeying almost blindly. The only time a spark of her old spirit had showed was when the gombeen-man had reached down to pinch her marriage bed.

"No," she had snapped, with a suddenness that stunned everyone in the room as she swiped the man's fingers from the worn ticking. "Matthew brought me to this bed that first night when I was but a child. My babes were born on it, all of 'em, an' six of 'em died here. And it was here that he said goodbye to me when he sailed—" her voice had stayed firm. "There's not enough money in Ireland to pay for this bed . . ."

The door shut behind Meaghan with a quiet click, and she fished the candle she had taken from her room at Cottage Gael from her pocket. She fumbled, burning the edge of her finger as she tried to coax the stubborn wick to life, but the candle guttered, sending out a meager, uncertain light that flicked at the blackness, then cowered against the wick like a child clinging to its mother's skirts.

Tallow dripped down the smooth white sides of the taper so slowly that it cooled as it hit Meaghan's hand, crusting there in a hardened layer. More by instinct than sight, she made her way to the room her parents had shared, wanting to feel the softness of the feather tick beneath her as she had a hundred childhood mornings when she and Tom had bounced onto the bedstead to tickle Da awake.

The flame danced in a sudden surge of light, and Meaghan stifled a scream as the tick seemed to come alive. Hooded and black, a figure leaped from its center. Arms closed around her and knocked her to the floor, the candle spinning to the far side of the room. A slurred string of curses seemed to foul her skin from breath stinking with rum.

"Hol' still, damn y'. Hol'—"

Meaghan squirmed free, whacking her fist into her attacker's belly with a crack that sent him tumbling away from her. Her elbow knocked something hard. She groped for it and grasped it, a smooth curve of crockery. "Touch me again and I swear I'll split your skull!" she hissed, scrambling to her feet.

The form on the floor had crouched, ready to spring, but at her words, it slid down to the floor in a heap of drunken giggles. "It won't be the first time you tried."

Meaghan took a step forward, weapon ready, but the candle, now lying against the clay wall, flickered light across the hooded face. A thin hand shoved the tattered blanket back, and sharp-edged features thatched with white-blond hair came into focus.

"Tom!" Meaghan gasped. The thing she'd been holding fell from her hand, shattering, sending waves of wetness splashing onto her skirts and ankles and the heavy smell of rum throughout the room. "Tom . . . you're supposed to be in Liverpool!"

"Sailors helped me jump ship." Tom scooped up the still-burning candle. Retrieving the top of what had been a jug, he pushed the end of the candle into the spout, balancing the whole thing on three pointed ends. "Y' just broke my goin' away gift from 'em."

"But Sean paid for your passage . . . got you an apprentice-ship . . ."

"That fancy fine doctor of yours ain't *my* master! Orderin' me around like he's lord of the manor! Well he's not! I'm my own man, I am, an' I'll stay where I please!"

"Man?" Meaghan echoed, still hardly believing her eyes. "You're nothing but a boy! A stupid, foolish boy! Ma must be crazy with worry! Not to mention the fact that if Radcliffe found you—"

"I blessed wish he would!" Tom faced her defiantly, the drunken haze changing to a reckless anger. "You should have come to me from the first that English swine tried to touch you! I'd have pounded him into pieces so tiny you'd never even see them! I still will! I'll make that English bastard eat Irish steel!"

"Irish steel? What Irish steel? A slane? A pitchfork? Too bad Ma didn't leave her kettle! You could have thunked his lordship over the head with that!"

"At least I would be fighting him on my own, not whining to some stranger, 'help me, Mr. Fancy Doctor, save me from the bad old lord'!" Tom's eyes narrowed with a shrewdness far too old for his years. "Why're you running home, anyway, Meaghan? Did your high and mighty O'Fallon throw you from his bed? Or have you shamed us all with a babe in your belly?"

Meaghan's hand shot out, connecting with Tom's cheek. His head banged hard against the wall. His eyes spit fire.

"Don't you talk to me of shame, Tom O'Leary! Not when your own father told me he couldn't trust you enough to take care of the family because he was afraid your temper would get us all killed!"

Tom's eyes widened, and deep inside them shone a reflection

of her own terrible pain. The words of her mother flashed before her, of how Da had loved her, and of Tom, hanging always on the outer fringes of that special love. So many times she had bounced from the house, shoving away Tom's silent pleas to go with her and Connor, or with her and Da. And now to throw Da's fears into his face . . . She swallowed. "Tom . . . I . . ." She held out her hand. He knocked it away.

"Leave me be! I'm just a stupid boy, remember! Stupid! Worthless! But I don't need you! I don't need Da! I don't need anybody!" He jumped to his feet. The door banged against the wall as he ran out.

Meaghan rushed after him, but he was gone. She leaned her cheek against the clay wall, listening to the wind keen around the eaves with the first cold drops of rain. It seemed fitting, somehow, that the sky should also cry.

As time crawled past, she sank down onto the tick in the corner and waited for Tom to come back. The beat of the rain lulled her, and her eyes drifted shut in sleep.

How long she had lain there, she didn't know, when the harsh cry startled her awake. "Meg! Meg! For God's sake wake up!" The rasp of the bolt slamming home made her jump to her feet just as Tom burst into the room. His face was the color of the wax that had dried upon the jug's spout. "It's him, Meg! Radcliffe and a whole pack of his devils! They're riding up the lane!"

"Radcliffe—" Meaghan tried to clear her sleep-fogged brain. Raucous laughter came through the stout door, mingled with the sound of horses.

"I barely beat them to the door! You have to get out of here!"

Meaghan ran to the window, peeking over the ledge. Torchlight set the yard ablaze, its reflection dripping off the horses in a hellish sheen. "How? They can see us . . ."

"The loft window at the side of the house. There's a rope under my pallet. I use it to sneak out to the Young Irelander meetings at Fitzhugh's. I drove a spike above the window frame. Hook the rope over it and we can lower ourselves out the window."

A deafening shatter of a bottle being hurled against the door made Meaghan's heart leap to her throat, the chain of snarled, lewd threats setting her pulse to pounding. She turned a pale face to Tom.

Tom's cheeks flushed, his eyes over-bright. "The bastard! The bloody bastard. If he—" He checked his words, but his hatred seemed to burn through the palms of his hands as he pushed her toward the ladder.

His hands left her back, and Meaghan turned, her shoe on the third rung, as she heard his bare feet dart across the room.

In the corner where Da's farm tools leaned, Tom paused, tugging the handle of the long-bladed reaping hook. He spun around as it came free in a clatter of falling tools. "For God's sake, I'm two steps behind you, Meg! Get yourself out that window."

Hand over hand, heedless of her long skirts, Meaghan scaled the ladder to the loft, Tom following after. The awkward hook slowed him down, clacking against the rungs, its honed edge cutting tiny furrows in the wood.

The coarse hemp bit into Meaghan's hands as she found it beneath the pile of straw that was all that remained of Tom's bed and ran to hook it over the heavy iron spike. Fear threatened to choke her. God, it would never hold! The spike Tom had driven between the wall and the window frame had pried the rotting support away from the clay edges until a slice of the rainy sky shone gray in an inch-wide gap. Meaghan tugged the rope. The spike moved.

Balling her bare fists, she tried to pound the spike deeper, its head leaving round cuts in her hands. She bound them in the heavy wool of her skirts to muffle the sound, but still the spike would not budge.

The reaping hook thunked to the loft floor and Tom clambered up beside it. "Forget it, Meg. Just go," he said, taking the rope. "I'll brace it."

"But you—"

"You're heavier than me. It'll hold. Go, or neither one of us will have a chance!"

There was thumping on the door, and the shouted curses were near and loud . . . She grabbed the rope, swinging her leg over the ledge, but her skirt was hopelessly tangled on the spike and splintered wood. Desperately, she tried to pull free, Tom's fingers trying to untangle her as well. The sturdy cloth held.

"Get out of it!" Tom hissed. "We can't—" Fingernails raked her throat as she grasped the collar of her bodice, tearing it open. The tiny buttons spattered to the floor, rolling to all corners of the room as Tom grabbed her and ripped the sleeves down her arms.

She struggled out of the skirt and petticoat, kicking them free of her legs. Again she swung out the window ledge, taking hold of the rope that was clutched in Tom's hands, bracing her feet against the wall as the icy dampness struck through her shift like a thousand needles. She looked up at him, getting her balance, trying to stop the wobbling of the rope, but her fingers froze where they held it.

He stood blocked by the window, the cutting edge of the reaping hook a curling slash across his forehead, his eyes glittering with a strange exultation.

He was going . . . dear God, he was going to face Radcliffe!

"Tom—" she cried. "You can't—"

"I have to Meg, don't you see? He'll be proud of me. Da'll be proud . . ." His words were lost as he backed away from the opening, the hideous scraping of metal against wood beating in her stomach as he went down the ladder.

Meaghan clawed upward, desperately, trying to pull herself to the window, to stop him before it was too late, but the slippery, wet rope sliced her palms, skidding her downward. Flesh was scoured from knees and elbows by the rough clay as her bare feet fought for a hold on the rain slickened walls.

There was a rasping of iron, a slamming of oak against clay, then a man's cry of agony shrilled as something slammed into the outside wall. There were bellows and shouts, then Tom . . . oh, God, Tom . . . he screamed and screamed.

Meaghan's feet slid out from under her, toenails pulling back from their anchoring flesh. Her hands clawed at the rope, the wall, the air. Hemp snapped taut. There was the sickening groan of the spike pulling from clay, the splintering of wood, and Tom's shrieks.

Her cheek crashed into the wall, scraping downward as heavy timbers battered her head and arms. A myriad of pointed lights exploded in her brain. She was falling, falling, and then there was silence.

The brace of pistols had been Sean's grandfather's in a time when English law forbid Irish Catholics to bear arms. For seventy years they had lain, hidden in the false bottom of his grandmother's marriage chest. They had guarded many a priest from the priest hunters, and balls from their barrels had blasted the life out of more than one cold-hearted land agent. For never had

Donal O'Fallon forgotten that the blood of Irish kings ran in his veins, nor his responsibility to the people who had been his family's kerns.

But even in his darkest rages, Donal could not have matched the fury in his grandson's eyes as Sean shoved the pistols into his belt and slid a dagger into the high top of his boot.

"God forgive me for the danger I've brought down on Maggie . . ." Connor moaned. "I have to come with you—"

"You can't even sit up, man. How can you stay on a horse?" Sean reached for the laudanum at the back of a shelf, measuring out a dose.

". . . have to . . ." Connor mumbled. "You don't understand . . ."

Sean reached his arm around the quivering man, propping him upright with his arm as he forced the medicine through the swollen lips. "You'd only slow me down."

The green eyes took on a moment of clarity within their blackened sockets. Sean felt them weighing the glint of hardness within him.

"You love her," Connor whispered, and there was sadness in his voice. "I loved her too."

Sean jerked away from him, stung, as he bolted down the stairs. Love? Damn it, did he love her? Had he already fallen into that abyss of pain and uncertainty he had been fighting with such desperation? Her face, proud, defiant, childlike in its innocence, haunted him until he was drowning in her, losing himself inside her until he no longer knew where he ended and she began.

And now . . . was Radcliffe crushing her? Was he shattering her courage, breaking her . . .

The roan gelding pranced in his stall as though he sensed the thinly leashed violence coiled in his master. No saddle touched the horse's back. Sean bridled him, swinging up with one brown hand. The rain pelted him, and twice the big horse nearly went down, but still Sean lashed him onward until a small cottage shone white against the sky.

He sawed on the bit inches from the wooden door, banging it with the toe of his boot. The gelding slammed to a halt and stood, quivering. "Liam! Grace!"

The door swung open, a block of light framing the giant figure of Liam MacFadden. "God's blood, Sean, what is it?" he boomed, grabbing the animal's reins.

"Meaghan . . . she's in danger. There's a man at Cottage Gael, hurt. Go to him."

In a flash of plum-colored frieze Grace flew to Sean's side, clutching his booted leg. "Sean, where . . . what's happened to Meaghan?"

"Radcliffe! God damn me, Grace," Sean groaned, "I sent her straight to Radcliffe! If he touches her I'll kill him!" Even through the leather Sean felt Grace's fingers tighten. "I swear to God, Grace, this time I'll kill him."

Meaghan struggled through giant webs of unconsciousness. She ripped at the strands that held her back, stumbling over screams, faces, and silver-bladed hooks that slashed across the sky. But the webs held her down, sunk her deep in sucking mud, icy wet with terror that seemed to run clammy cold down her breasts.

"Tom . . ." She croaked out the name, her throat swollen, her mouth clogged with hair that strung over her lips in a soaking copper veil. "No . . . Tom . . ."

The web moved of its own volition, a heavy, hard band grinding down onto her hips, another scraping at her throat as it squeezed and kneaded below where the flesh rose upward in a pink-tipped mound.

She shoved at what held her, and the sinews of male fingers took shape as they tightened on her skin. A laugh grated on her ears. "What, love? I've scarcely taken you in my arms and already you're crying for another man?"

Meaghan's eyes flew open, the voice striking her awake with the suddenness of a blow. A torch, its base driven into the ground, lit the night, painting shadows of the leering man who flanked it and the blade of the reaping hook dripping with blood that was clenched in Trevor Wilde's hand. And above her . . . above her . . . Eyes, stygian black, burned as Colin Radcliffe straddled her naked hips with his breech-clad thighs, pinning her to the wet earth. "I'm afraid Tom won't be coming, love, that is unless he crawls."

"Crawls? I—"

"The little bastard took the blade to two of my men. But he paid, my sweet. He paid. Just like you will . . ."

"No! W . . . where is he? What did you do . . ."

"What he did to Pinkerton, Lasley, what he tried to do to me. It didn't take much, the boy was so thin."

"No! Oh God! God, let me go!" Meaghan thrashed beneath Radcliffe, the image of Tom lying in a pool of blood blazing in her mind, but the Englishman rammed her down to the earth, his thighs clamping hard around her.

"Oh, no, my sweet. You're not going anywhere. Let the little bastard bleed. That's one less knife point in the back I'll have to worry about."

"No! I'll do anything you want! Whatever you say! Just let me—"

"You'll do what I want whether your *brother* lives or dies, wench. I have no fear about that. And you and I, we have quite a score to settle." He shoved the back of his hand against her cheek, and she could feel a long welt pressed against her skin. "Your whip left its mark. But the mark I leave on you will be much longer-lasting, and no more gentle. Has O'Fallon taught you ways to please a man, my lovely?" His hand came down to cup her breast, his mouth following and brushing like curled bits of iron. "I can teach you things . . . things O'Fallon would never dream, things from your worst nightmares . . ."

His hands closed on the top of her shift, transparent with the wetness that made it cling to her skin. "Trev, would you like to see the body that's had Sean-o hot and panting these many nights?" Radcliffe's fingers tightened, as the big man jostled closer. "But O'Fallon won't want her anymore. No, Sean doesn't take another man's leavings." Meaghan stared up into the eyes that seemed to swallow her and she had a fleeting image of Sean making love to her, kissing her, coaxing her, and of Tom, with his lopsided grin. The fabric of her shift rent like gauze, as Radcliffe tore it, the rain pelting down on bared flesh. Hands curled like claws, Meaghan slashed at his arms and his face as he stripped away the remnants of the white lawn.

He grabbed her wrists, jamming her hands between the grinding pressure of his knees and the earth as he ground his mouth down upon hers. Meaghan stifled a sob, sinking her teeth into his lower lip. He jerked away, the back of his fist cracking into her jaw. Blood spilled into her mouth in a warm salty rush.

"Bitch! You draw my blood again and I'll—" His teeth were bared, glistening in the flickering light. Then his face went still, with the evil patience of Satan tempting souls. "No more," he said too softly. "I'll take you right here in the slops where you belong." Lips snaking into a smile, he shoved his hand between their bodies to the fastenings of his fly. His knuckles dug into the softness of her stomach, pinching her, his heavy ring cutting her skin as he worked the buttons through their holes

Meaghan saw a fleeting image of Sean as she had watched him the first night they had made love, slipping the fastenings of his own tight breeches with those long fingers that could be so gentle, so full of passion. Sean . . . he didn't want her . . . He would never want her now . . .

A ragged sob tore from her throat as Radcliffe settled himself between her thighs. She felt him probing, probing as she twisted, futilely trying to get away.

Suddenly it was as if the storm had broken in the fury of the gods, crashing, howling, and screaming with a banshee's cry as the night spilled out a rider chased by hell. Fire blazed from a pistol, and Wilde dropped the reaping hook, clutching one plump leg. Hooves sliced the earth, tearing up great hunks of turf, and she could hear Wilde's startled grunt as he was slammed to the ground by an equine chest. There was a hideous snapping sound where the heavy-hard beat of the hoof should be, a gutteral cry, then icy coldness as something seemed to hurl itself from the sky, ripping Radcliffe's body from hers with a force that sent him careening through the muck on his coat-front.

Torchlight glinted over broad white-clothed shoulders, rain-wet hair. "Sean . . ." Meaghan choked. "Oh, God, Sean . . ."

His gaze flashed over her naked form, sobs still shaking her, her huddled body trying to hide her mud-smeared breasts. His eyes seemed to sink into their sockets, cerulean fire spitting death.

"You sonofabitch!" he hissed, wheeling to face Radcliffe, "I'll break your neck!" The Englishman crouched, hands ready on the ground, weight rolled forward on the balls of his feet, the panta-loons that had banded his thighs now yanked up around his hips.

"Kill me for her?" he sneered, shifting backward, a cunning glint in his eye. "Some whore you claim as wife? No, you're the one who's going to die, Sean-o, and this she-bitch of yours will still bear me between her legs."

With a feral snarl Sean launched himself at Radcliffe, wanting to feel his throat crush beneath his hands. Radcliffe sprang to his feet, orange-red firelight glinting on metal as he jerked up the hooked blade Wilde had dropped. Sean tried to twist away to avoid the sharp-honed edge as it slashed toward him, curling his body in a ball and rolling, but the point ripped deep, cutting his side to the ridges of bone beneath. Hot blood gushed down his flesh, and a knifing pain threatened to rob him of his senses.

He forced himself to his feet, groping for the second pistol still shoved in his waistband, his other arm clamped to his wound. The barrel came free just as Radcliffe cracked the reaping hook's heavy oak handle down onto Sean's wrist. The pistol flew from his fingers as shards of pain spiraled through his arm. Radcliffe's boot slammed into the weapon, sending it skidding into the darkness. The hook sliced down again. Sean scrambled backward out of its path, fighting to gain his feet, to tear the dagger from his boot top.

"Running, Sean?" Radcliffe jeered, jabbing with the hook's point. "You've always been so sure of yourself . . . so ready with your fists and your chivalrous drivel. Crawl on your belly, O'Fallon, like everyone else."

"I leave that to you." Sean faked a stumble, judging when Radcliffe would strike. The hook cleaved air, its blade blood-bright. But the split second before it would have slashed into him, Sean lunged under it, the point of his dagger finding flesh. Radcliffe snarled in surprised pain as Sean ripped it upward, tearing into the curve of the Englishman's shoulder. The hook fell from Radcliffe's hands. He clutched the wound with his fingers, stumbling back against the cottage wall.

There was a roaring in Sean's head and a montage of faces— Alanna sobbing while penning the note that would tell him of her suicide, his gentle mother being raped, Meaghan struggling beneath Radcliffe. He raised the dagger, wanting to feel Radcliffe's flesh split beneath it.

"Sean . . ." The broken sob shattered the images, leaving only the image of Meaghan, helpless and hurting. Sean wheeled toward the sound, his head spinning from loss of blood.

The moon, fighting its way from between the clouds, dripped silver over Meaghan's peach-gold skin, her nakedness scarcely hidden by the fall of wet hair clinging to her body and the mud smearing her thighs.

"Maggie . . ." Sean said softly, going to her, touching one cold bare shoulder with his own trembling hand. She jerked away as if he had slapped her, her eyes huge in her face.

"Don't . . . touch me . . . I'm . . . dirty . . . he . . ."

Sean laid his finger on her lips. "No, Meaghan, hush. It's all right now. All right . . ." He slipped his shirt off one shoulder, gritting his teeth against shards of agony as he pulled the fabric from the sticky open wound.

"I'm going to put this around you, Meg," he said, peeling her arms from her breasts and guiding them through the sleeves as though she were a child. Black spots whirled in front of his eyes. He sank down beside her, his knees immersed in the mud.

"They rode in on horses . . . they knew . . . God how did they know I was here?" she sobbed, clutching his wet shirt around her. He held her, and she clung to the heat of his muscled chest, feeling it ripple as he stroked her hair, her shoulders, her face.

"It's all right Maggie, all right now. I have to get you out of here before they regain consciousness . . ."

"No . . . Tom . . . I think they killed him . . . he . . ."

"Tom?"

"When I got here Tom was in Ma's room, drunk . . . Said we couldn't order him around . . . Said he'd get Radcliffe . . . He told me he'd follow me . . ."

"Where, Meg? Where is he?"

"Inside, outside . . . I don't know . . . Radcliffe said . . ."

Sean pulled her to her feet, stumbling around the corner of the cottage, then froze. Tom O'Leary lay in the yard, his left leg hanging at a horrible angle, the femur exposed, white and splintered like a dog-chewed bone, blood mixing with the rain pooling beneath him. Sean bolted to the boy's side, fingers on the scrawny white throat to find a pulse.

"Damn it, he can't be . . ." Blue eyes widened in shock. "He's alive. I don't know how, but damn it, he's alive!" He turned to Meaghan. "Have to stop the bleeding and get him out of here. Get the torch. Move, Meg. He's bleeding to death."

The hours that followed ran together like rain-washed paints —the smell of flesh burning, the sight of Sean's hand holding Tom down as he shoved the flaming brand onto the grotesquely twisted flesh. The sounds of Wilde and Radcliffe stirring behind the cottage, and the feel of the panicked horse as she clung to its back, holding Tom's limp body between herself and Sean, trying to keep the leg from flapping against the gelding's barrel as he stormed out of the valley.

Then Liam MacFadden's giant hands, gentle as he eased her to the ground in front of Cottage Gael. And her fingers clenching in the quilt he had wrapped her in as Sean severed the threads of muscles attaching Tom's shattered leg, rasping the bone to smooth it before he started suturing a flap of skin over the stump.

Sean had stood facing the table where they had laid Tom, his back still bare from giving Meaghan his shirt, his stomach hidden by the height of the table. She heard the clatter of something falling to the wood, saw Liam look up from the other side of Tom askance. Bracing his hands on the oak, Sean's head had dropped in the lee of his shoulders, and a tremor had shot through him.

"Liam..." His voice had been faint. "Better finish..." Sean's whole body had seemed to shake, as he turned to Meaghan. "Couldn't save it...tried to..." The heavy, black-fringed lids drooped down over his eyes in his ghastly gray face. His hand groped for his side. Reality had snapped back to Meaghan with a force that turned her insides to tearing knots as her gaze followed his hand.

The slice of Radcliffe's blade arced beneath the mat of curling dark hairs on Sean's chest, gaping like a leering mouth, filthy with dried muck, still oozing thick, almost black blood that had run down his stomach and caked the waistband of his breeches.

Meaghan threw off the quilt, only then cognizant of a stickiness that made one white side panel of the shirt Sean had covered her with cling to her skin. She pulled it away from her, the pinkish stains tinting her skin. "Sean! You're...you're hurt..."

He wavered, his lean legs buckling. "Sean!" Meaghan lunged for him, nearly colliding with Liam as the big man tried to round the table, but neither of them could catch Sean as he crumpled to the floor with a ragged groan.

Meaghan ran to him, rolling him over so the wound was exposed. Blood flowed; his side was broken open from the fall. She pressed her fingers to it, trying to keep the life-bearing redness from spilling out. It ran through the cracks between her fingers. His skin blazed like fire, hot and dry.

"Liam! Make it stop!" she had cried. But it had been her own hand that had swabbed the filth from the wound, pinching the edges of deathly pale skin together between her fingers, pushing the sharp, clean needle through Sean's twitching flesh under Liam's direction as Liam rushed desperately to close up Tom's leg.

And that night, long after Tom had been moved to the Mac-Faddens' under Liam's watchful eye, she had bound Sean to the bed, unable to hold him down herself, terrified he would rip his side open again as he thrashed in the grips of a raging fever. He had moaned with the sound of the damned, calling her name, mumbling, tears starting at the corners of his eyes as his fists balled and he tore at the strips of sheet that held him. And she had bathed his face with cool cloths, pressing her soft cheek against his tortured one, crying when his moans turned into something akin to sobs.

For two days she didn't sleep, watching the strength drain out of the fever-stripped muscles, changing bandages that pulled away crusted with pus. Grace and Liam came morning and night, Liam pressing hot compresses on the wound, snipping two sutures to allow the cut to drain. "I don't know, Meggie-girl," he said, shaking his great head. "I'm doin' all I know how, but the lad can't go on like this. Ye, yerself, look like death's door. Ye haven't touched a smidgen of the bread or bacon Grace brought. Been layin' on the table, just as she left it. Let Gracie stay an' watch with him awhile. Ye'll do Sean no good sick abed yerself . . ."

"No! I'm not going to leave him! He's not going to die!" She had turned on Liam with a wrath that made the big man flush, and Grace had run to her, cradling her against one raw-boned shoulder, murmuring soothing words in her ear. "Grace, I won't let him die!"

"Child," the homely woman had said softly, "I hope that ye can stop him." She had cried after they left, forcing Sean's long fingers to cup around her cheek, holding them there while her tears made them wet. "Don't die, Sean," she had choked. "God, don't die . . ."

But Liam's warning about taking ill herself made her stop at last and reach for the ivory hand mirror lying on the cluttered dressing table behind her. Purple shadows circled her reddened eyes, the skin stretching over her cheekbones with a thin translucence that made her seem more wisp than woman.

The clock on the mantel chimed three times. Stretching her

stiff legs, she stood and picked up the light that had been constantly burning since Sean had gotten sick, then bent to touch his brow. His face seemed slack, the color of old clay, the waves of dark hair straying around it only accenting his paleness. She had slipped the white loops from his arms and legs hours ago, rubbing a soothing salve into the chafed flesh. He didn't fight her anymore. He scarcely even moved.

Meaghan padded to the big oak table in the other room, the rug seeming to cling to the soles of her bare feet, so heavy had they become. All signs of the surgery Sean had performed had been swept away, the quilt was folded neatly at the foot of the cot, and the instruments, from the tenaculum to the gouging forceps, lay in shining order on the yellow wood beside Grace Mac-Fadden's basket of bread and cooked bacon.

Meaghan tore off a chunk of the crust, sinking her teeth into the yeasty goodness, then gasped, choking on it, Bread! Why hadn't she thought of Ma's jar before? Of the thin, moldy slices she had bound over cuts, swearing that they would keep the wound from festering? Would they . . . could they *stop* the festering after it had already begun?

She ran to where her own last baking still lay beneath a muslin cloth, flipping one of the hidden loaves over, delighting in the spoilage that had crept along the gold baked edges. With a sharp knife she sliced off enough pieces to cover Sean's wound, carrying them with fresh bandages to the side of the big rosewood bed. Only the slightest tightening of his mouth told her that he felt the pain as she peeled the dressing from his side and, cleansing it free of the yellowish matter that clung to the stitches, bound the moldy surfaces to the raw, angry flesh.

She watched his face for any change as dawn filtered through the slit in the draperies, knowing in some dark and secret place within herself that the next few hours would see him better, or dead. His skin stayed brand hot and dry, his breath heavy between cracking lips, his face still. So very still. Yet somehow, somehow it looked peaceful, as if God himself had smoothed his hand across the lines life had carved in Sean's face, wiping away the bitterness, the pain, the guilt. Was that death's gift? Peace?

Meaghan let her face drop down onto the damp cloth she had been using to swab his chest, wishing that she could see him even as he had been in the buggy when he had nearly taken her in fury, the muscles of his finely honed body taut, springing with life. But there was no life in him now. She lay there, her head pillowed gently against his chest, measuring the rise and fall of his breath beneath her cheek, until the candle-glow from the table spun dawn-rays into dreams.

She would never know how long it was she slept there, before she felt it, a stirring, like the brush of a moth in flight, but warmer and heavier in her hair. It trailed down her temple, down the fragile shadowed skin beneath her eye, to where tears she had shed, even in sleep, pooled beneath thick gold-tipped lashes.

"Maggie . . ." The voice was soft, slightly raspy from disuse, but the sound of it sent a shaft of joy stabbing to the deepest parts of her.

Her head jerked up, and she stared unbelievingly into clear ocean blue. "S . . . Sean . . ." she choked out. "Sean . . . you're alive . . ."

His lips curved into the weakest of smiles, and she thought she had never seen anything so heart-stoppingly beautiful. "Must be. My side hurts like hell."

"It should . . . it . . . you got it infected. We thought you . . . God, we thought you might die . . ." Tears poured down her cheeks, cleansing, healing tears that spilled down, splattering his face. "Sean . . . I . . ."

He slipped his hand beneath the weight of her loosened hair, pulling her gently toward him, wincing, as he brought his other hand up slowly to cradle her face in the warmth of his palms. ". . . didn't die, but I found out I had to live . . . Can't keep running, hiding behind things that happened a long time ago . . . things I can't change. I don't know if I love you, Meg. I don't know if I ever will. But I don't want to lose you, what we have together . . . I . . . don't want to lose you . . ."

Meaghan felt the tug of his hushed admission deep inside her heart, his lips crooked with a vulnerability she had never seen there, and an honesty that laid him open to a depth of pain she understood too well. She swallowed hard, her gaze fastening on his chin. "Hush, now, don't try to talk."

"Have to. Been lying here so long, thinking, wanting to say this." His finger eased down to the soft hollow beneath her jaw, tilting it up just a little so he could see her face from his mound of pillows, and Meaghan felt his thumb tremble as it brushed lightly across her lower lip. "Marry me. Stay with me. I can't say what it is . . . what I feel, but Maggie, I want you. Let that be enough . . ."

The feel of his arms as he pulled her against him chased from her mind doubts that nipped at her joy like quarrelsome pups. His wife . . . Sean's wife . . . she would make that be enough. And maybe, maybe someday he would love her . . .

Nineteen

"Oww!" Meaghan yelped, turning to glare at Grace MacFadden as the point of a pin bit into the soft hollow under her arm. "This dress is going to be dyed red by the time you're finished! You've poked me so many times I feel like a pin-paper!"

"Well, if ye'd act like a woman about to be wed an' quit wigglin' around so much mayhap I could see what I'm doin'!" Mouth puckering in exasperation, Grace poked her head around the billowing waves of peachy ruffles that decked the silk taffeta gown. "Somethin's not right here about the bodice, an' the waist —Can't understand it. It fit ye well enough when ye wore it to Mass the last time. Ye must've been doin' nothin' but eatin' since! Eatin' an' Lord knows what else," she finished in a grumble.

"As if you haven't been pushing us toward the 'Lord knows what else' from the first day I met you!" Meaghan teased, pulling away to swirl around on the tips of her toes. The skirt floated graceful as a gillyflower tossed in a stream.

"Don't be layin' yer sins at *my* door, colleen!" Grace scolded. "Ye an' that boy of mine are well nigh indecent! A relief it'll be for me to get ye safely wed!"

"You're just still angry that we didn't wait long enough for you to make as much of a fuss over the wedding as you wanted, aren't you? You've been snapping at everyone for days. If I'd known it meant that much to you . . ."

"Bah, child!" The creases in Grace's forehead smoothed. "The whole of Wicklow will know ye and Sean are to wed tomorrow if my Liam wants his stockin's darned ever again. But fuss or no, a

202

bride should at least have a new dress for her marriage day, not some rag her man has seen her in a dozen times."

"I'd hardly call the prettiest dress Sean bought me in Dublin a rag, and besides, we've had enough of wedding gowns, Grace. Both Sean and I." The bantering tone left Meaghan's voice, and the heels of her slippers dropped back to the floor.

Grace touched her cheek. "Ye know ye'd be prettier than Alanna ever was even if ye was wearin' sackin', Meaghan," she said softly. "An' better for Sean. I know he still holds back from ye, I see it in yer face, when ye watch him, like ye're waiting fer a door to open. It will. Ye've given him the heart to smile. 'S been so long since I've seen my Sean smile."

Meaghan fingered a pale peach ruffle at the sleeve. "Sometimes . . . sometimes I wonder if I'm being foolish, if I should turn and run back to my ma and the boys. Sean loved Alanna so much."

"Has he told ye, Meaghan? Anything about her?"

"Only that she died because of Colin Radcliffe. That he found them together in . . . in bed. That he was going to marry her. And . . . that he loved her."

"Love? It was more like a sickness with Sean. Alanna DuBois knew less of real carin' than the tip of the pin ye were yowlin' about, an' she had the gift of playin' a man's heart like a fiddler plays his strings. She wanted Sean. Bad enough to coax out cryin' tunes from the rain. Though God alone knows why. Alanna wasn't a one to be tied to a man. Especially one like Sean, who was so caught up in his work an' his dreams. Sean made it no secret that he wanted a home, and cradles full of little ones. Alanna . . . she couldn't stand Ireland, and children . . ." Grace paused, looking over to where her own two played on a quilt on the floor. "Saints help any child Alanna DuBois mothered."

"Why, then? Why would Sean choose her?"

"I guess maybe he just needed someone to love so bad he forgot to be wise. She was comely enough to tempt any man when she set her mind to it, poison in a rosy wine. But the bitter taste was comin' through. A day, a week . . . who can say? Things would have been different. She was the curse of his life. We all knew it. If she had lived but another month Sean would have known it, too. Mayhap what Sean never got over was the fact that he was falling *out* of love with her."

"But if that was true it would have been easier for him. He would have grieved, but let go. Not held on to her all these years."

"No. Not Sean. He thought her dyin' was his fault for not loving her enough. Thought she sensed it, that he drove her to Radcliffe's arms with his doctorin' an' carin' for others. When she died there . . . he forced all of his doubts out of his mind, wouldn't hear a word spoken ill of her. It was like . . . like she became too holy to touch. A dream. That's what she was, always. A dream. He never really knew her."

"But you did?"

"Aye. I knew Alanna DuBois better than her own mother. When other babes were nursin' at their mammy's paps, I swear Alanna was already plottin' how to dry up the milk. She was a pinching, biting, scratching woman with claws all cased in velvet. But ye, Meaghan-child, ye're warmth, heart, flesh to be touched, to be held."

Meaghan flushed, pulling her lower lip through her teeth as she smoothed her hand down the fabric tightly stretched over her waist. "A little too much flesh, if this dress is to be the judge. Grace, I'm getting married tomorrow. What if we can't get it to fit?"

"I'll sew in a strip of somethin' at each side an' cover it with a touch of lace. No one'll be the wiser. We'll have ye lookin' like an' angel yet." Grace helped her unfasten the straining buttons down the bodice front, easing the pin-laden cloth down till it puddled on the floor. Her troll face crinkled. "Meaghan, ye haven't been feelin' sick like, have ye? Tender?"

"Sick?" Meaghan echoed, her voice muffled by the slate-blue day dress Grace had flipped over her curls. "You've all but said I'm fat!"

"Sometimes . . ." Grace hesitated. "Sometimes a woman feels changes."

Meaghan's head popped out of the dress. She flushed, a touch of shyness tingling through her veins as she slipped her arms into the tight-fitted sleeves. "I feel changes, but not from being sick. It's like I'm so full of loving him sometimes I'm afraid."

"I know." Grace's gnarled hand smoothed the hair from Meaghan's forehead. She smiled, changing the subject. "I'll stop by Cottage Gael on my way to the market an' get the dress cuttin's to set in. Ye have things to do fer Sean-o, I'm sure, keepin' that old Fitzgerald eatin' an' such."

"I *do* need to stay there for a while. He won't take 'charity food', but if you come to visit and bring along some stew and bread he'll pull out what little he has and play lord of the manor."

"Well, he'll love to be entertainin' someone pretty as ye," Grace said, patting a strand of Meaghan's flyaway hair into place. "But before ye go, I have somethin' for ye. I was meanin' to save it till just before ye wed, but I feel the need to give it to ye now."

Walking to a shelf, Grace drew down a paper-wrapped package, bringing it to Meaghan with a soft smile. Meaghan took it, pulling at the string that bound it, folding back the crinkly covering.

A froth of delicate white lace lay within it, webbed of finest silk. Meaghan took it from its nest of tissue, testing its softness against her face, and she felt that she would burst from a joy too great to hold. "Grace, it's beautiful . . ." she said, "but there are so many things you and Liam need, and you've given me so much already. . ."

"Ye know how much ye mean to Liam an' me, Meaghan. Both ye an' Sean. Saw some fancy lady on the church steps when we went to Dublin, one of these things drapin' her hair. When we were takin' Tom to the docks to ship him off to England there was a girl sellin' laces from a wooden box. When we saw it, well, seemed fittin' ye should have it. A million little knots, there are, woven in, an' ye an' Sean have had more tangles between ye than any two people I've known. Tom, he helped me pick it out. It made him smile."

A tiny bit of sadness pulled down the corners of Meaghan's mouth as she remembered the pinched, subdued face of her brother three weeks ago, his twig-thin form perched in the back of MacFadden's cart, a new wisdom turning his fanaticism to a maturity that made Meaghan's throat ache. "I'm coming back, you know, to Ireland, as soon as times are better," he had said. "I'll have a trade, then. A way to earn my praties without only the harvest to depend on."

Tom had raised his eyes from where they were fixed on the tip of his crutch, giving Sean the ghost of a smile. "I'm not going to stop fighting the English, either. Any more than you have."

"There's time, Tom." In those simple words had been a wealth of understanding, of forgiveness.

Tom had swallowed, his Adam's apple bobbing in his gangly neck as Liam touched the scar-faced donkey lightly on the rump with his whip. "Bye, Meg..." Meaghan shut her eyes. Why, why did it seem she was always saying goodbye?

Lace, feathery soft against her temples, brought Meaghan back to the present as Grace let the delicate veiling drift down over copper-bright hair. "Though I'll have yer dress, at least ye'll have this to hold tonight. Ye'll look beautiful tomorrow, child," Grace said, a tinge of unease in her voice. She stared at her hands and started, as if to say something. Then she stopped and whispered, "Be happy, Meaghan. I can't ask more for ye than what I have already. The love of a man an' babes to fill yer arms. Don't let anyone take that away from ye. For in the end, it's all that matters." Meaghan turned her eyes to Grace's moss-green gaze, surprised to see colors clashing like troubled seas, the wide lips trembling under a sparkle of unshed tears.

Grace hitched the baby higher up on her hip, her fingers tightening unconsciously on the blanket that wrapped him as a sense of impending evil trickled down her spine. It had crept through the cracks in her joy since that morning on the church steps when Meaghan had run through the doors dressed in Alanna's gown, jabbed at her while Sean lay close to death, until now it seemed to jeer from every shadow in the heath, and taunt her from the squat hut that cowered on the windswept hill.

Itha O'Byrne was somewhere within, her ceiling strung with herbs flavored of magic, the dirt floor littered with overturned baskets where little creatures scratched, her face falling into a million tiny wrinkles that puffed diamond-shaped pillows of skin out like the tufts on a horsehair sofa.

Grace could feel it, the pull of spirits evil and good swirling around the thatch-straw in their never-ending war, the tug on her skirts as if an invisible hand were trying to keep her away. She shuddered.

She had been to Itha's but once before, when years had passed with no child born of her union with Liam. The old witch-woman had smiled her toothsome smile, and ground up herbs and potents in a crockery pot, bidding her to sprinkle them on the wind. Months had passed, the packet of herbs lying secreted in the loft beneath an aged rag rug because Grace had been afraid of what the witch-magic would spawn. But at last, one night she could bear her empty arms no longer.

The charm had been chanted to an azure sky, but an hour had scarce passed before the clouds had roiled—gray, black, blue, and orange—a storm ripping at the cottage she shared with Liam, pitching debris against its walls. Liam had taken her and loved away her fears.

Annie came of that night. Grace knew it with a certainty that had made the months before birth an agony of waiting to see if the babe she carried was somehow tainted by the spirits that had quickened life within her womb.

When the babe had blossomed like a perfect flower, Grace had rejoiced, but never had she forgotten the terror of the night the storm had come, the feeling of helplessness against the things that Itha had unleashed, things far beyond the control of a mere mortal. It had been hard to come back to this hut. But the evil whose mist was prickling over her flesh was closing in around Sean and Meaghan, fangs bared like a wolf at the kill. She knew it, knew that only one person could have laid the blossom-decked wedding gown on Meaghan's bed those weeks before. Only one. And she was dead.

The baby gurgled, his tiny fist tugging at a loosened strand of her hair, and Grace gently untangled his fingers, straining her eyes to where Annie frolicked ahead in the sheep-bitten grasses. She had had no choice but to come here on foot, children in tow, Liam having taken Sean to tip some poteen in honor of the morrow.

Now, suddenly, she felt stranded, isolated, exposed, and as much out of place as the fine-boned mare of Arabian stock tied outside the tumbledown hut. The cottiers sought Itha often, in hopes that her conjuring could cure what mistrusted doctors and harried priests could not. Hope to the hopeless . . . and yet . . . this was no poor farmer's horse, with its soft leather sidesaddle and rose-blushed dapple-gray coat.

Those of high blood slunk to the hut on the hill for only a few reasons . . . to rid themselves of babes conceived in shame . . . and other things, things too shameful or frightening for Grace to put a name to.

Grace felt a hand on her elbow, and looked down to find Annie staring at the cottage with a sudden stillness in her pixie features. Silently, Grace took the little fingers in her own as they neared the door with its interlocking circle design worked in polished nailheads. The door stood partway open, revealing a slice of the small room within. Slowly Grace pushed it open, suddenly unable to so much as call Itha's name.

Though it was still day, the walls inside seemed aflame from the rushlights as their golden light flickered over the black folds of veiling that fell around the form of a woman, and glistened orange along a white crockery vial still clutched in Itha's hand.

Itha looked up, meeting Grace's gaze, her strange gray eyes lost in deep pockets of flesh, and for a moment, Grace could have sworn she saw regret.

"Ye shouldn't have come, Grace." The almost whispered words sent chills squiggling through Grace's body. "I told ye not to."

The black-clad woman's shoulders jumped. She wheeled, the top of her veil catching on a gnarled, berry-ladened branch that hung from a peg above her head.

Grace gasped as the plumed hat pulled free, dangling from the branch like a felon from a gibbet. "Alanna . . ."

Hate too virulent to come from a specter swept perfectly molded features, as Alanna DuBois's violet gaze flayed her. Grace felt herself falling into a pit, spiked with the sudden frightening realization that she had known in the secret recesses of her mind all along that Alanna DuBois could not truly be dead.

Alanna whirled, her ring-bedecked fingers grabbing the vial from Itha's hand, as she bolted out the doorway, knocking little Annie to the ground.

Grace swept the child up in her other arm, starting toward the retreating figure, aware of the death-pale terror in Annie's face, but Alanna had already flung herself onto the mare's back, and was tearing down the hillside. Alanna, the evil. A milk-colored vial.

"Grace!" Grace heard old Itha's voice shrilling after her as she ran down the stone-blemished slope in the opposite direction, her thin legs pumping at a speed that threatened to throw both herself and the children to the road that wound below. "Stop, Grace! Ye mustn't go—"

The old woman's warning was lost to her as the fear that had stalked Grace for weeks tightened its coils around her heart. She ran for what seemed like hours, carrying Annie when she could, dragging her alongside when she could no longer bear her weight, tumbling at last onto the steps of a silent Cottage Gael.

There her eyes flew to the school slate, searching for the scrawled backhand message Sean left whenever he was gone, but for the first time since the board had been nailed by the heavy door Sean hadn't marked where he could be found. Meaghan would be at Fitzgerald's still. But she couldn't tell Meaghan. Not yet.

Grace took up the slate pencil, writing in the clumsy letters Sean had schooled her in years ago: Alanna alive. Come. Grace.

"Mammy, I want to stay here." Annie's round eyes filled with tears. She swiped them away with one pudgy hand, sinking down beneath the slate. "That lady's gonna hurt me . . ."

"I won't let her, love. We have to get home. If yer da's in his cups Sean'll bring him home." Grace took Annie's other hand, but the little girl clung to the wooden slate frame.

"No! Can't run anymore."

"We'll take the horse Sean keeps in his stable, Ann," Grace said. "Put yer arms around my neck." Crooking one aching arm about the child, she dragged her up to straddle one hip, her other arm clutching the babe as she stumbled toward the darkened outline of the nearby stable.

Night dripped ebony down the canvas of the sky before Grace tucked the two exhausted children into their beds. She listened to the night sounds weaving their spells around the cottage walls, each minute that slipped past feeding her dread.

Alanna . . . dear God, Alanna . . . *She* had somehow slipped into Cottage Gael, setting into motion the chain of events that had nearly cost both Meaghan and Sean their lives. And now . . .

Grace hugged her sides, trying to ward off the gooseflesh that crept up her arms. What lengths would Alanna DuBois go to, now that her ruse had been discovered? What stygian secret swirled in the vial the witch-woman had given her?

The tiniest sound outside the door made Grace jump. She rushed to the window, taking in the darkened yard at a glance. Empty. Quiet, as if someone had taken a pillow and smothered all sound. The door was bolted, she tried to calm herself, and the night was often quiet before a storm.

Quiet . . . The sudden sharp crackling at the corner of the

house iced her veins with terror as a shadow darted past the window. Straw . . . the thatch . . . God, no! She ran panic-stricken to the corner, as though there were some way she could stop the flames, but the thick, choking smoke rolled into the room with a speed and heat that knocked the breath from her body. She dashed to the cradle, scooping up the baby, yanking at Annie's hand as she dove for the door. The bolt was fiery on her hand as she threw it back, pushing her weight against the heavy panel, knowing in a sickening instant no power could make it budge.

She ran to the window, letting go of Annie to shatter the panes with her hand. Jagged edges slashed Grace's arm, razorlike bits of glass crashing from the window onto her bare feet.

Smoke clogged her lungs, her eyes, as she reached down to lift Annie to safety. Her fingers closed on air. Gone!

She clawed through the roiling smoke, coughing, choking, screaming Annie's name. In the corner she found her, huddled behind the loft ladder, her little arms wrapped tight around the post, eyes huge with mindless horror.

"Annie!" Grace heard timbers supporting the roof groan, the burning thatch buckling the turf layer beneath it, spraying flames across the floor. She clawed at Annie's fingers, trying desperately to get them free, but it was as though terror had fused them to the wood. "Annie! Let go!"

The baby shrieked as sparks showered his tender cheeks. Grace clutched him to her breast, eyes blinded with tears, lungs screaming for air that singed her nostrils and lips. Her eyes flashed heavenward as the first flaming timber crashed down. She hurled herself over Annie and baby Sean, feeling Annie kicking and clawing in terror against the suffocating weight of her body. She felt the babe's weaker struggles.

There was a horrifying crack as the roof caved in.

Twenty

Azalea blossoms rioted in joyous color over the pristine starched cuff of Sean's shirt as he trailed their silky petals over Meaghan's lowered lashes. She stirred, lips parting in a sleep-blurred sigh, nuzzling closer to the pillow she held in her slender arms. His pillow, Sean thought, his fingers tightening on the ribbon-decked stems in time with the strange squeezing in his heart, the pillow he had slept on the first night he had made Meaghan his, the pillow where he would take her this night as his wife, where their children would be conceived and born, where he and Meaghan would wake together the rest of their lives.

He swallowed, running the backs of his knuckles over the innocent blush of her cheek. She deserved so much more than he could give her—this child-woman who loved with a fierceness that risked all, forgave all—more than a man whose past was tainted by a hundred mistakes, whose heart was more wary and scarred than a battle-worn soldier. And yet, he could no more release her sweetness to another man than sever his own hand.

"Meaghan, I know I've hurt you, so many times," he whispered, not even aware he spoke the words aloud, "but I'm trying. I'm trying to forget."

He started as eyes, rich, deep, and warm as golden-brown velvet drifted open beneath a heavy fringe of lashes. She reached up, her delicate fingertips brushing his lips, the very lightness of her touch stabbing him with a sharp surge of desire. He took her fingers in his hand, pressing them hard against his mouth.

She smiled sleepily, burrowing her face against his taut belly, her breath moist, warm, dampening his skin beneath its covering of white cloth. "G' morning."

He felt the vibrations of her mumbled words strike in a downward path to fire his loins. "Good day to you, Mrs. O'Fallon. Do you intend to spend your entire wedding day abed?"

"... promised you'd sleep till noon . . ." Meaghan murmured. ". . . headache . . ."

Sean gently pushed her away, his brow furrowing with concern as he smoothed the tangle of hair back from her face, feeling for the heat of a fever. "Meaghan? You have a headache?"

"No. You do." A smile tipped one corner of her mouth, the fairy-dusting of freckles across her nose making her seem more child than ever as she came awake. "'Least you're s'posed to. Grace said you 'n Liam'd be moaning an' groaning for hours. We'd be lucky if Father Loughlin didn't take a stick to your backsides."

"To our backsides, eh? Well, Grace would be horrified to know that the good Father tips a few himself now and then, and not just the holy wine. In fact, it was Loughlin who gave us our first bottle . . ."

"Don't you be maligning the church, Sean O'Fallon, or blaming your excesses on a poor priest! Why—ooff!" Her breath came out in a gasp as Sean fell half onto the bed, pinning her beneath his chest.

He grinned. "You'd better hope he did no thrashing, or tonight you might be *sorely* disappointed . . ." He arched one brow, letting a devilish glint show in his eyes as the accented word made her giggle. The tinkling, unaffected sound made him cup his body more fully over hers, bracketing her face in his hands. "Besides which," he continued, "Liam and I got almost no drinking in because some prankster sent us riding hell bent for glory to a nonexistent medical emergency. By the time we got back, we were both so tired we couldn't even lift a mug." He took playful nips along her jawline, delighting in her unabashed laughter. "So you think that's funny, do you?" he teased. "Maybe I'll just spend my wedding night on the cot and teach you a lesson."

"Don't you even think it! You've been sleeping on that blasted cot from the day you asked me to marry you! You and your blessed notions of honor! If I'd known sleeping alone this long was a part of the bargain, I'm not sure I would have agreed . . ."

He caught the sensitive cord at the base of her neck between his teeth. She arched her head back, giving his lips better access to the vulnerable white curve, and he felt a shiver of answering need sluice through her. "Sean . . . It's been so long . . ."

The scent of crushed flowers taunted his nostrils, blending with the warmth of Meaghan's body beneath the coverlet, and suddenly there were no more games between them. He fastened his mouth upon her parted lips, his tongue thrusting hard between them, wanting to sip at her openness, her innocence, to take it within himself . . . to heal whatever hurt he had caused her.

"Meaghan . . . sweet, sweet Meaghan . . ." he murmured, skimming his hand down her neck, her shoulder, tunneling under the coverlet to close over the tip-tilted softness of her breast. The feel of her nipple hardening, veiled by the slight roughness of finely woven lawn, tantalized the center of his palm as he eased it in ever narrowing circles. He tugged the coverlet from between them, laying his lips on the heated, cloth-covered crest. "God, Meg, I want you!" he said against it. "Right here. Right now."

"Too bad . . . we're waiting . . . till the wedding . . ." The husky taunting in her whisper, coupled with her fingers skating a ticklish path up his ribs made him burst out in laughter. "You're trying to get even with me for having such an iron will." He braced himself on his elbows above her, looking down at the mischievous spark in her eyes, feeling the slight swell of her womanhood beneath his hardness, seeing within her a lambent desire matching his own. He flicked the tip of her upturned nose with his tongue. "Just remember, my pretty, tonight I'm sleeping on the cot . . ."

She gave him a playful shove away, but as he rolled to his feet, her hand on his sleeve stopped him. "Sean . . . what's this?"

He looked down at the bedraggled bunch of azaleas, half crushed in their tussle. "Flowers for the bride from the meadow . . . our meadow." She lifted them to her lips. "They're a little bit worse for the wear."

"You're not supposed to lie on them," she said, a tremor in her voice belying her words.

"And a bride's not supposed to drag her intended down onto her bed, looking for all the world as if she were making love to his pillow . . . I mean my pillow . . ."

She flushed prettily, color tinting her cheeks a perfect rose. "I wasn't—"

"Oh, yes you were, but I don't have time to argue the point. If

I don't get over to MacFadden's, Father Loughlin won't need to take a stick to my backside. There'll be nothing left of it when Grace gets finished."

"Grace is coming here with my dress . . ."

"Not until she's fed me breakfast, she's not. She made me swear I'd come first thing in the morning so she could make me all my favorites one last time. I think she believes you'll starve me."

A fluffy pillow hit him in the face. "More likely she's giving *me* a little time to rest, knowing how demanding you *men* can be!"

Sean let his amusement dance on his face, and Meaghan went scarlet. "That's not what I meant, and you know it!" she squeaked, her nightgown slipping off one shoulder to bare a glimpse of creamy smoothness. "You can sleep on that cot till they cut ice blocks in hell!"

Sean's eyes wandered over the shadowy hollow beneath her breasts, wanting to touch, yet now savoring the anticipation of the night to come. "You'd best send Satan some sawdust for the packing." He ran his tongue slowly over his upper lip. The second pillow puffed toward him, but he caught it, firing it back at Meaghan with an accuracy that muffled her cries of protest in a flurry of kicking arms and legs until he had bounded down the stairs and out onto the veranda.

Every pore of his skin tingled with life. He hadn't felt this way since . . . God, how long had it been? Had he ever felt this rushing, surging pleasure as he did at this woman's slightest smile? At the crinkle of cinnamon-colored freckles as she wrinkled her nose, the burning sensuality of her fingers on his lips? Had he even felt this body-shattering need with Alanna, whom he had loved?

The very thought was like probing the bright pink scar on his side. He leapt down the veranda's steps, and was nearly to the fence when he remembered. He had never forgotten before, but here he was, wandering off like some lovestruck boy, with no thought to those who might be seeking him. He turned, retracing his steps, taking up the slate pencil to mark the church on his map at the rail. His gaze flicked up to the slate at the door. Taking the stairs two at a time, he rushed to the slate, cursing himself for not reading its message last night. But when he reached it, the child-like letters formed there turned his scowl into a grin. He leaned one brown hand upon the wall, squinting his eyes, as he tried to decipher the words Grace had written. A scolding, no doubt. She had left them countless times before, tinged by her own wry humor. But the least Grace could do when upbraiding him for all the world to see would be to keep Annie's hands off the message so he could find out what he had done. Somehow the most irate of messages lost their sting when little handprints wiped out part of the words.

A—alive . . . Com . . . race

Sean shook his head. Perhaps it was healthier if he *didn't* know what she'd written. As angry as Grace had been when Liam had insisted on *takin' him fer an outin' his last night as a free man,* there would probably be poison in his stirabout this morn. It would be a wonder if either he or Liam showed up at the church alive. He bounded down the steps, stooping to pluck another bunch of azaleas before he swung up on his roan gelding. Setting the horse into a rhythmic canter he breathed in the flower's delicate fragrance. Today he could almost believe there was nothing in the world their glowing colors could not mend.

The muscles in Sean's arms strained in corded ropes against his shirt as the gelding spun yet again, bolting off the dirt road. Sean set his heels deep in the animal's sides and jerked on the reins whose thick leather lengths seemed to stretch in his hands. Flecks of foam from the horse's mouth spattered Sean's chest and arms, the sweat drenching its sleek body sending the smell of animal terror to blend with the stench that clung in a cloying shroud over the dew-bright morning.

Smoke.

Sweet Christ, it was smoke!

The knowledge lay in his stomach like a stone. With a savage oath, Sean slammed his heels into the frightened gelding again, driving him up the rise with a desperation that conjured a dozen other times when this cloud of sickly sweetness had hung in the fresh Irish air, times he had been called to soothe flesh seared by flames that swept through thatch like brush fire. Times he had helped to bury . . .

Half-formed prayers clashed with mindless threats to Grace MacFadden's God, and through it all one face seemed to glow through the mist of his clawing fear. Grace, years younger, her moss-green eyes striking up at him across her husband's body.

Grace, heavy with child, standing in the bedroom at Cottage Gael, mouth agape as she took in the scene of Meaghan half naked and himself wrapped in a sheet. Grace, when he'd told her he'd asked Meaghan to marry him. She had kissed him full on the mouth, and for the first time in all the years he'd known her, she'd stood unable to speak . . .

The gelding stumbled as it crested the hill, shying at the view that seemed almost to leap in front of them. Sean felt his heart plummet.

Blackened, charred, empty as the shell of his heart, the cottage stood, tails of smoke still rising from its belly like damned spirits. Partially burned timbers stuck out at odd angles, and the roses . . . Grace's roses . . .

"No!" he cried aloud, slashing at the horse with the reins, but the smell that had terrified the horse now filled Sean's nostrils as well.

Death.

Flinging himself from the gelding's back, Sean crashed to his knees, then pushed himself up, running to where the door space stared, an empty, blinded eye. The beast's pounding hoofbeats faded into the distance; a thick piece of iron three feet from the doorway caught the toe of Sean's boot. He skidded into the ruins, the remains still warm to his hands. He struggled up, seeing the room Grace MacFadden had loved, a tangle of broken dreams, shaded in black and gray.

A choked sob came from the corner, and Sean dragged his tortured gaze to the soot-smeared figure huddled on the floor.

"Liam . . . for God's sake, Liam . . ." Sean cried. "Where's Grace? The babes?" The giant of a man seemed to shrink into himself, his lank blond hair dulled with ash, eyes rimmed as though someone had taken crimson and outlined the lids. He rolled aside, and Sean shut his eyes against the three twisted shapes Liam's bulk had hidden, but not soon enough to block their image from his brain. One long, and two tiny, so small . . . Sean felt a scream rise in his throat, but it died there . . . died . . .

"She told me not to go . . . begged me, she did . . . But I laughed at her . . ." Liam sobbed. "She'd never asked anythin' the like of that before. Said she had feelin's . . . bad feelin's . . . I wouldn't listen, Sean . . . didn't listen . . ."

Sean forced his eyes open, and it was as if the destruction

around him had fallen in a brittle layer over his soul. He staggered to Liam.

"Why, Sean?" Liam pleaded with the pathetic confusion of a child. "Why would anyone want to hurt Gracie?"

"What?"

"The door was blocked. They jammed it . . ."

"Blocked? Who jammed it? Damn it, who?"

"Them . . . both of them . . . I saw them on the hill." Liam stared at his own big fists, tears trickling through the soot on his face. "I tried to find them . . . Grace . . . Annie . . . It was hot . . . so hot . . . I couldn't find the baby . . ."

Sean grabbed Liam's arms, shaking him. "Who did you see on the hill?"

The big man opened his hands, slowly turning them beneath Sean's grip. Sean's breath hissed between his teeth as Liam's palms caught the light streaming through the hole that had once been the roof.

What little skin was left curled like the burst casing of a sausage, edges blackened, flesh seared off until the entire surface was a weeping scarlet wound, broad fingernails broken and torn away. Liam's glazed eyes were fastened on the injured palms with shocked detachment, as if they had been severed from his wrists.

"Why, Sean-o? Why would he want my babes dead . . ." Liam begged, his voice an aching void. "He never even knew them . . ."

Tentacles of hatred strangled Sean. "Who?" he croaked.

Liam's vacant gaze found his. "His lordship . . ." the big man whispered. "His lordship, Colin Radcliffe."

Horror started at the marrow of Sean's bones, creeping outward until even his skin was stiff with it. *Why would he want my babes dead?* Sean dropped Liam's hands, Radcliffe rearing to life in his mind's eye, the knife wound in his shoulder gushing blood, black eyes spitting promises of vengeance. Twice Radcliffe had struck at him through someone he cared about—Alanna, then Meaghan. This time . . .

Sean's throat constricted. Dear God, had Grace and the little ones died because he, Sean, had loved them?

Sean stumbled to his feet, feeling the blackened walls closing upon him, crushing him as he ran out the door. He fell into the grass, face down, clutching handfuls of earth in fingers gone numb. No . . . God, no . . .

His eyes burned with a fire no tears could stem, a fire that destroyed the joy budding inside him. They blazed until there was nothing left. At last he raised his head. One of Grace's rose-bushes was but an arm's length away, the leaves shriveled from the heat of the fire, the petals withered. Had it been but yesterday they had shimmered with satiny beauty beneath Grace's loving hand, while he had watched her pluck the most perfect bloom to dangle over her babe's tiny nose?

"Ye'll be havin' a one of yer own soon, ye gettin' wed an' all," she had said, tossing the blossom to Sean with a wide, loving smile, "an' I'll be enjoyin' it greatly if yer babes give ye but half the trouble ye've caused me these many years. Yer wed-din' day . . . Lord, an' I thought I'd never be rid of ye . . ."

His wedding day. God, the morning with Meaghan seemed a million years ago. Sean reached toward Grace's rosebush, his touch crumbling the scorched petals. They drifted to the ground, and he watched them, hand still frozen by the naked stem as he caught a glimmer of gold in the grass beneath it.

His fingers closed on the object, and he turned it over so it lay in his palm. It was a leaf, so carefully wrought that each infini-tesimal vein was etched in its airy surface. The border was notched, every cut of the goldsmith's tool the stroke of a master, the only jagged edge was the place where it had been torn from whatever piece of jewelry it had adorned.

Sean's hand tightened until the point bit into his palm. The metal was cold and hard, no pain could touch it. He felt the coldness flow up his arm to wrap around his heart and harden there in a shell of icy rage.

Grace, Annie, the baby—they were dead because of him, because he had dared to love them. But this time Radcliffe would die as well, though not in fury whose tempest could betray a man. No.

Sean righted himself, climbing to his feet, to stare at the fire-gutted house. Today he would kill Colin Radcliffe, yes, as coldly and methodically as the dark lord had murdered the children Sean O'Fallon had loved.

A frightened neighing made Sean look to the hill where his gelding fought the lead of a pair of whip-thin boys. Daniel and Culley Halloran both clung to the leather reins, the gelding's tossing head all but lifting their feet off the ground. Pointed bones stuck out on their shoulders, tenting their torn bawneens over hollow stomachs, their arms so robbed of flesh the bones stood out against their skin in sharp relief.

More of Radcliffe's victims, the tenants whose only sound harvest stuffed Radcliffe's bursting granaries while they, themselves, starved and died. These people would be coming here hours from now for the wedding feast Grace had insisted on taking charge of. Sean's eyes narrowed. Yes. They, too, deserved their pound of Radcliffe's fatted flesh.

He took the reins of the skittish roan, and the animal calmed a little, as it recognized its master.

"What happened? We saw the smoke," Culley rattled. "Did anybody—"

"Culley!" Daniel cut the boy off, regarding Sean with world-worn eyes. "Is there buryin' to be done?"

"No." Sean's mouth set in a grim, white line, his fingers clenching on the gold-wrought leaf in his hand. "No burying, Danny," he said with hollow menace. "Killing."

Layer upon layer of petticoat flounced around Meaghan's ankles as she sucked in her breath and struggled to fasten the last straining catch around her waist. Even though she had snipped off all the buttons on the undergarments and resewn them at the very edge of the bindings, she could scarcely draw a breath through the bands cinching her middle. If Grace hadn't been able to alter her dress, she might well faint in the middle of the wedding from lack of air!

Wouldn't that be perfect? Sean standing so dashing and solemn beside her while she tumbled to the church floor in an undignified heap! A flush crept up her cheeks as she remembered the way he had looked just that morning, his dark hair gleaming in silken waves upon his forehead, the stray wisps of curls he could never seem to tame at his collar. And his kisses . . .

She fingered the ribbons of her chemisette where the rounded swells of her breasts pushed upward, heat pulsing inside her at the very thought of what Sean's mouth had done to her, what she would do to him this night. Her eyes drifted shut as she let her hand trail down the delicate curve of her breast, her fingertips skating below the cutting waistband to her stomach.

She caught her bottom lip between her teeth. The hope, so

terrifying before, was now achingly sweet, thrilling through her body like the most dulcet of chimes. She had not had her woman's time since before Da ha sailed, but often in the past her flow had come erratically, lasting for nearly two weeks, then disappearing until Ma had glowered suspiciously, growling around the house. Yet never had it been absent this long.

Could it be that Sean's child already nestled within her womb? A babe with eyes sea-blue, with wavy hair, thick and dark? Joy spread through her like sun-warmed honey. She started as the tiniest of flutterings whispered in the center of her womb, the brush of moon sprite's wings beneath her hand. Tingles of wonder swept over her. A babe. *Sean's* babe.

Tonight, after the wedding, she would tell Sean as she curled beside him, their passion spent. She would kiss him, take his strong bronzed fingers, and lay them . . .

The sound of footsteps on the stairs made her jump guiltily, pressing her palms to her burning cheeks as the heavy door swung open. She wheeled and froze, all thoughts of the new life within her shattered.

"Sean?"

He stood in the block of the doorway, shirt torn and matted with ash, the hands she had been dreaming of but a moment before battered and filthy. Slashes of soot blacked his face into a hideous mask. But it was his eyes that sent terror spiking downward through her limbs.

Meaghan swallowed and stepped toward him, then stopped. "Sean . . ." she whispered. "Wh-what happened? Where's Grace?"

He stared back at her, eyes cold, barren as a winter sea. She felt her lower lip tremble, her voice shaking. "Where's Grace?"

"There was a fire. Grace and the babies were trapped—"

"Trapped? No! The . . . the wedding's today! She can't be . . . they can't be— Grace!" Nausea ripped at Meaghan's stomach, the breath leaving her body as though a giant fist had plunged into her belly. She gulped down the bile that choked her, and fought to push past Sean into the hall, but he caught her, slamming her against his chest, crushing her into his body.

"She's dead, Meg."

"No! She promised me—" Sobs strangled her, Sean's fingers bruising her flesh. His hand knotted in her hair, forcing her head into the crook of his shoulder. "Sean, she promised me— I need her!" Meaghan heard the broken babbling of her own voice, knew she should stop, couldn't. "I need her!"

The violent tremor that racked Sean's body at her words pierced through her consciousness when nothing else could have, the force of it setting her teeth to chattering. Like the irons of a vise, his grip on her tightened, crushing her ribs until she felt they would pierce her lungs. Grace . . . Sean's conscience, his friend, the one who made him laugh at himself . . . the one person he had allowed himself to trust fully . . . *We die, child*. Meaghan could hear Grace's voice in her mind, repeating the words that cut gently through her pain. *We all die, Meaghan child, but you hold on to the good things* . . .

Good things . . . A warmth, a strength deeper than herself, flowed through Meaghan as she shoved her fingers through Sean's hair, kissing him, tasting her tears upon his cheeks, wanting to take from him the pain that had robbed him of hope. "Sean . . ." she murmured. "Oh, Sean . . ."

She felt his body melt into hers, his hard lips pressed to her temple, his broad back rippling beneath her hands. Tears burned her eyes again, trailing down her face. "Sean . . . Grace loved you so much . . ."

In that frozen instant he stiffened; his muscles seemed molded in stone. Fingers manacled her wrists, clenching cruelly around the fragile flesh as he peeled her away from him, forcing her to step back.

A new kind of chill swept through her as she met his gaze, a fear more devastating than even the word of Grace's death. Each plane of his face was shifting subtly, tightening, closing the once crumbling walls of his defenses, fusing them into place as though by a sorcerer's wand.

She twisted her hand free, trying to touch him, to force some warmth into him, but he pushed it away.

"No." He cut her off, arm raised as if to warn her away. "There are things to be done . . . take care of . . . I have to go."

"Let me help you. I'll get Father Loughlin . . . tell him about . . . about postponing the wedding . . . the . . . wake . . ."

"We won't need the damned priest! Grace is already in the ground. The little ones, too. If Loughlin's all powerful God had given a damn about them in the first place—"

"Sean—"

"And there'll be no wedding, Meaghan. No marriage. Ever."

"Ever? W-what? I . . ."

"I killed Alanna. I killed Grace, the babes. I killed my own mother. I'm not going to kill you."

"You didn't kill anybody! It's not your fault they died!"

"Isn't it? The fire was no accident."

"Wh . . . what do you mean it wasn't—"

"Colin Radcliffe *set* it. Made sure Grace couldn't get out."

"I don't believe it! Why would he—" Meaghan felt a shiver breathe up her back. Gooseflesh raised on her arms, the nape of her neck prickling as she trailed into silence.

"You tell me why Colin Radcliffe would fire a cottage that didn't even belong to one of his tenants. Why he would murder a woman and two children he didn't even know. Why would he do that, Meaghan?" Sean challenged.

Understanding trickled over her, seeping inside her. "No! It's not your fault!"

"It is and you damned well know it! But that sonofabitch will never harm another person I care about. Never. I'm leading a raid on Radcliffe's granaries as soon as it's dark."

"Sean! You can't—"

"There's a load of grain being readied right now to be taken to port and shipped to England. It's not going to happen, Meg. Half the county is hungry. The celebration we arranged to have here after the wedding will go on as planned this afternoon. We'll laugh, dance. None of Radcliffe's hounds will be able to ferret out our plans. Come nightfall the men who go with me can take whatever spoils they can carry. And me, there's only one thing I want now. One thing."

"To die?" Meaghan flung back at him. "That's it, isn't it! You told me once how easy it is to die in a blaze of courage, and how foolish. Well, this will be just perfect for you, won't it? Blasting into Radcliffe's house in a fit of self-righteous rage to avenge Grace! Grace who hated killing! Bloodshed! Damn it, don't you dare even *try* to convince me you're going to kill Colin Radcliffe for Grace!" Her voice cracked. "Grace loved you, Sean. Don't do this to her, to us. I can't lose both of you! Sean, I love you."

"Don't love me. I don't want you to love me. There's not enough of me left to give you, to give anybody."

Not the slightest change of emotion stirred in his face. No warmth, no anger, no life. Meaghan wanted to scream. Don't shut me out, Sean, don't die! But he was dying in a way Colin

Radcliffe could never have managed to inflict, dying inside.

She wanted to kick him, shriek at him, hit him, anything to bring a spark of life back into his eyes.

"Damn you! Go ahead then! Get yourself killed! Why don't I just herald your arrival to Radcliffe myself so he can put you out of your misery with one clean bullet? Bury yourself in the ashes with Grace and the babes! It's where you want to be! Just the excuse you needed! *Dead* Grace MacFadden is more alive than you'll ever dare to be!"

Blue eyes narrowed just a fraction as he started out the door. She grabbed his arm, trying to stop him. "No! Sean don't! I didn't mean it! Sean . . ."

"We'll be here in three hours. Be ready." He freed himself without gentleness, without anger, grasping her wrists and putting them from him.

She stared at him, his gray-tinged cheeks and pinched mouth deadened, cold. A stranger's face, a stranger's eyes. Not Sean's. No, not Sean's.

"Sean, I love you . . ." she pleaded brokenly.

His eyes held hers for a heartbeat, then he wheeled, stalking out the door. The tiny flutter of life brushed again in her womb. Meaghan sank to the floor, holding her hands tight against it, sobbing for all she had lost.

Twenty-One

The women in the room stood silent and still, as though listening for battle sounds they could not hear, the cries of husbands, lovers, and sons who had set out for the gray stone walls of Radbury Manor hours before. Even the children huddled in small groups like kits cowering in a vixen's den, watching for the rising of the moon. For it was then that the men would sweep up the hill, weapons drawn. It was then that they would die.

Meaghan moved to the window, pressing her cheek against the pane, feeling her skin would shatter if she tried one more time to smile.

They had all been so brave, these half-starved women, when their men had ridden off, shouting encouragements to the pathetic army, as though it was mounted on coursers instead of clinging to sway-backed horses and donkeys, or else scuffing the miles in rag-wrapped feet.

But as soon as the last of the men had vanished over the rise, saber had changed back to pitchfork, silver mace to tree branch. The eyes that had stared out from the shade-thin faces had become frightened, seeking strength. Meaghan's lips tightened at the irony. The women had turned to *her*.

And she had calmed them, though God knew how, because in her there was no comfort, no peace. It had ridden out to die astride a sleek roan gelding.

Meaghan shut her eyes trying to dispel visions of Sean, his face smeared black to hide it in the darkness, the pistols Liam MacFadden had retrieved at the O'Learys that long-ago day after

Tom had been hurt, shoved in the waistband of his breeches.

With the still-dazed Liam but a pace away on his left, Sean had leaned to talk to Connor MacDonough, who sat the horse beside him, the big groom's arm looped around his baby daughter who was perched on the saddle before him, the back of his other hand, bearing the reins, resting gently on his Mary's mouse-brown hair.

Meaghan slid her hand down to her stomach, remembering Connor's teasing grin as he handed the little one to his wife, and kissed the downy head. She had almost cried then and run to Sean to tell him about the babe she carried. But he hadn't so much as let his eyes skim her face, and the tenuous thread of her pride had held her.

Yet now pride was no shield against the pain that crashed over her in waves, against the loneliness, the fear for the baby inside her. All she wanted was to cry, to lick her wounds, to be alone. Quietly she slipped toward the stairs, seeking the sanctuary of the rooms she had shared with Sean.

The door stood partly open, and she entered, fingers already opening the fastenings of her binding dress. The bands of skirts and petticoats snapped free, and the gasp of air that burst into her lungs was mingled with despair.

A tiny noise in the corner made Meaghan spin around to face a small figure huddled in the leather chair. Huge, tear-reddened eyes caught hers for just an instant above a blanket-wrapped baby as Mary MacDonough skittered from the seat like a startled fawn, swiping the back of one hand across her wet, mottled cheeks. "I'm sorry," she said, pressing the baby against her shoulder. "I didn't want to . . . to be a bother and I didn't think anyone would come here."

Meaghan tried again to force her lips into a smile. "You're welcome to stay as long as you need to. Can I get you any-thing—"

"No. I . . . I just wanted to be alone for a while."

"So did I. If I had had to listen to one more minute of silence I swear I would've—"

"Don't." Mary turned away, but not before Meaghan saw a wistfulness in the pinched little face. "You . . . You don't have to pretend. I saw you looking at Mr. O'Fallon in the yard, and . . . and crying when they rode out . . ." Her voice quivered as

Meaghan stared at the straight white part dividing her mop of soft hair. "Connor talks . . . about you all the time. I know . . ." Mary's voice trailed off.

"Connor has told me about you, too. I've never seen him so happy."

Mary's lips tugged into a weak smile. "I'll always be his second choice, but it's enough. I love him." Her narrow shoulders squared. Meaghan thought of Sean and Alanna and understood Mary's feelings too well to murmur platitudes. Connor *did* care about Mary. Mary knew it. But to feel that someone had come before and maybe still did . . .

"I was standing downstairs, watching all the others try to keep up their courage," Mary was saying softly, "and I couldn't bear it. They have to know, don't they? I mean, no matter what happens at Radbury Manor, win or lose, they'll be turned out of their homes. Tonight, if they get the grain, they'll be eating like princes, but tomorrow the children . . ."

Meaghan turned away, running her hands up and down her arms as though to ward off a chill. She had used just that plea with Sean as the sun sank inexorably toward the horizon. "They're dying by inches right now. Burying whole families," he had said with a calm that terrified her. "Better to die like men than to hide in corners and rot."

"And while you *men* go to your glorious graves we *women* will have to live," she had cried, "live to watch the children *starve.*" Starve like the woman she and Sean had found the day they had met, burrowed in the hillside? Meaghan shuddered, covering her own stomach with her hand while the crude holy medal the woman's babe had worn glowed silver in her mind. It seemed as though all Ireland lay clinging to each day by the tips of skeletal fingers, watching the winter months bear down like millstones, crushing . . .

"I'm sorry." Meaghan felt Mary's thin hand at her waist. "You've had enough to worry about already. It's just that if you have a child of your own, you—" Mary stopped midsentence, and Meaghan saw her eyes glance from the unfastened garments that gapped open to her face, and back again.

Meaghan's chin tilted defiantly. "I *am* going to have a child." She said the words as though daring the girl beside her to be horrified. "Sean's child."

Soft understanding lit the wide eyes. She could see Mary MacDonough fumble for the right thing to say.

"I'm sorry. . ."

"Sorry? I'm not! I—"

"No! I didn't mean it like that." Mary flinched. "I . . . I meant I'm sorry your wedding was ruined, that you . . ." she stammered to a halt.

The stillness that fell between them was splintered as the sharp staccato of an approaching rider broke through the night. They stared at each other for a moment, then Meaghan shoved the lace curtain out of the way, peering down onto the ink-shadowed yard. There was something familiar in the skinny form clinging desperately to hanks of mane with both hands, sliding about on a sorrel's broad back with all the grace of a child jouncing on his father's knee. As the horse slammed to a stop, the boy lost his hold on its mane, tumbling to the ground in a tangle of bone-thin arms and legs.

The face turned up, catching the candlelight streaming from the glass pane, and Daniel Halloran stumbled toward the house. Meaghan spun, bolting down the stairs with Mary bare inches behind her.

By the time they reached the landing, Daniel was leaning on the bottom newel post, white-faced, gasping for breath. He grabbed Meaghan's sleeve. "Mrs. O'Fallon, where are they?" he begged. "How long ago did they leave? Da—" Meaghan took him by the shoulders, a horrible sinking in her stomach at the mere thought of Casey Halloran.

"They left hours ago. Why? What . . ."

"Culley an' me got home from helping raise the alarm . . . Da was there, drunk, mean drunk. Made Culley tell him where we'd been. Culley was scared . . . told him we'd been with . . . O'Fallon . . . everything. Da said he was coming to Cottage Gael, to help. But he stumbled back in before dark . . . a big sack of food over his shoulder . . . He left again, but he was heading in the wrong direction. Toward Radbury Manor, talkin' like Timmy was right there beside him, promising O'Fallon would die. Doesn't care how many others are killed as long as O'Fallon—"

"Mother of God!" The gasp was from some faceless woman behind them. Meaghan felt Mary MacDonough's fingers tighten on her wrist, but the rest of her body had gone numb. The only advantage on the tenants' side had been surprise, to hit swift and hard and melt into the night. With Radcliffe warned . . . waiting for them . . .

"I tried to stop him," Daniel cried, tears swelling at his eyelids. "He was too strong. I ran two miles to find the horse, but I couldn't get a bridle and I kept falling off—"

Meaghan turned to Mary. "The moon . . . Sean said they had to wait until the moon had risen so they could see." Running through the door, they both took in the horizon. Pale gold, the moon was creeping upward in the sky, the bottom of its crescent defining the tops of a distant stand of scraggly trees in a maze of twisted shadows. Had the ragged army waited? Were they breaking from the cover of night even now for their meeting with disaster?

She shook off Mary MacDonough's hand, the wide, child-eyes holding hers. "They had to move slowly for the men who were on foot—" Meaghan said. "I have to try to catch them."

"You can't . . ." Mary pleaded. "Let the boy . . ."

"He can't even stay on the horse's back! I'm the only one here who rides well enough to reach them in time." The sorrel shifted nervously as the women and children poured outside. Meaghan grabbed the loop of its halter rope, catching up her skirts, swinging onto the high bare back. Petticoats whipped around her thighs as she clamped her legs around the horse's barrel, slamming the low heels of her satin slippers into its ribs.

"Meaghan!" She heard Mary MacDonough scream her name as the beast surged forward, and then there was nothing except the heavy rhythm of the hooves flying beneath her, the moon inching a path toward its crest, and the desperate need to see Sean O'Fallon alive.

The sorrel's coarse, sweat-soaked hide scraped the insides of Meaghan's thighs, rasping against the fine lawn of her pantalettes until the skin beneath was raw. The sting of the horse's sweat bit into her flesh with the same sharp tang as the fear gnawing at her mind as she drove the sorrel on toward the manor house that crouched, a sinister giant, upon the hill. It was quiet, too quiet.

Her eyes searched the grounds, illuminated in a faint, silvery light. She had watched Sean and Connor map out the estate on the burn-scarred oak table, deciding at length that their best chance would be to steal up the hill behind the stables, that the little used wooden segment of the manor would give them cover until they were close. If they hadn't changed their plan . . .

Jerking on the halter rope, she guided the horse toward the canopy of trees that flanked the outbuildings in precise columns, their leaves making patterns, like lines in a primer's copybook.

A mass of shadows shifted in a hollow thirty yards away, one tall, strong form silhouetted clearly against the night sky, the lines of his body as familiar to her as her own—Sean . . . alive . . .

A rush of relief coursed through her, and she swallowed, her eyes flashing skyward in mute thankfulness, but her throat froze in horror. Moonlight skated a glimmering path down a long metal barrel hidden in the leaves, the myriad of black shadows in the treetops taking on shapes more menacing than the imagined figures of specters long dead. Legs were slung over branches, arms weighted with weapons, eyes she couldn't see watching, their evil boring into her. Each thud of her mount's hooves on the turf seemed to explode with the force of a cannon.

At that moment, Sean's head snapped around. His hand raised in signal, slashing downward.

"No, Sean! Run! It's a trap!" she screamed the warning as his horse plunged out into the open. A pistol blazed inches from the sorrel's rump, a shriek of agony ripping through the night as the ball buried itself in a shadowy figure hidden somewhere among the raiders.

"Meaghan!" She heard Sean's bellow of disbelief, saw in his face a flare of stunned recognition. That instant the night-shrouded stable doors to her left crashed open, spewing out horsemen, sabers drawn and gleaming with a sinister whiteness that seemed to reflect even from a distance the blood-drunk euphoria of the men who wielded them. "Sweet Christ! Connor! Get the men the hell out of here!" Sean shouted.

"No! Maggie!" The report from Sean's pistol drowned out the rest of Connor's reply. Bright orange flashes rained death in a ring that clamped its jaws tight around Meaghan, closing to the rear of the men charging into the fray behind Sean. They fought, and many fell. Bullets whistled through the air, tearing through the billowing material of her skirt, grazing the brownish hide of the horse beneath her. The animal leapt sideways, bolting in terror among battle cries and death cries as the riders swooped down from the stable.

She clung to the sorrel's back desperately, the single loop of rope over its nose no help in controlling the frightened creature as the other horses bore down on them with terrifying speed. A hand grabbed at her arm. Yanking it away, she bit back a scream as Trevor Wilde jerked and fell, red blossoming in his porcine face as a bullet slammed home. She had a glimpse of Sean's roan gelding hurtling toward her through the mass of men, saw a flash of blue-black glossed in the night, the leering countenance of Colin Radcliffe three yards from her shoulder.

Ramming her heels into the sorrel's sides, she struggled to force it toward Sean. The gleaming edge of Radcliffe's saber arced downward as his stallion pulled abreast. A scream lodged in Meaghan's throat as the horse beneath her gave a hideous shriek of pain, then faltered and fell. Earth rushed up to meet her as she was hurled into the crush of hooves, the air driven from her lungs as she slammed into the unyielding turf.

A howl of triumph sounded above her, a rough arm catching her beneath her breasts, hauling her back up against Radcliffe's body. The scene before her swirled and pitched as she fought for life-giving air, the sound of Radcliffe's sick laughter smothering her, then the scene snapped into focus with stomach-wrenching immediacy as the click of a hammer being pulled back echoed in her ear. Cold and hard, the nose of a gun barrel nudged her temple.

Only then did she see Sean again, afoot now, five strides away, his own hand locked around the grip of his pistol, his eyes spitting hatred.

In a horrible backdrop behind him, the men who only hours ago had filled Cottage Gael with their boasts and their jests were crumpling to the blood-slicked ground, as Connor battled at their head to lead the bulk of the raiders through a break in the circle of gunfire.

Those few tenants on horseback had formed a scraggly barrier to the rear, pitting their makeshift weapons against hopeless odds to gain the others escape time.

"You sonofabitch! Let her go!" Sean's hissed words blotted out all else as Radcliffe tightened his grip, using her body as a shield against Sean.

Radcliffe barked a laugh. "Let her go? I think not. You want the little slut so badly? Come and get her, Sean. Of course, it would be a pity if you forced me to blow away half of such a lovely face . . ."

"You touch her and—"

"Drop the gun, O'Fallon. Save the threats for your hangman."

"No, Sean, don't! He'll kill you!" Meaghan cried.

"I won't have to kill him. The courts will do it for me. Nice and slow. The great hero, Sean O'Fallon, dangling from a gibbet. A common murderer for all the world to see."

"You're the murderer! You burned Grace MacFadden and her children alive!" Meaghan cried.

"What magistrate would believe that a peer of the realm would stoop to killing peasants? What proof do you have? Some fool's word? Some idiot notion that you're all-seeing, all-knowing? There's only one issue Sean has to settle here, and that is what I do to you before he dies. Well, O'Fallon, tell me. Are you taking her with you into hell?"

Sean's hand flexed on his gun, his eyes fastening on Meaghan's for a long minute. "She's been there already." The words were soft against the fading sound of the retreat as Radcliffe's men closed in around them. Sean's fingers loosened, the gun falling from their grip. He raised his eyes to Radcliffe. "You have me now. Kill me. Hang me. But let her go."

"And spoil the fun? I could have had all of them. All those louse-breeding fools who followed you. Emptied my land of the scum that infests it. But she had to warn you, so they eluded me. Now I intend to get my pleasure in the only way left . . ." The slightest movement from Sean sent a chuckle rumbling from Radcliffe's chest. He shoved the gun harder against Meaghan's skin. "Ah, you're so predictable. You'll kill me with your eyes a hundred times, threaten me with tortures that would make Satan cringe, but I could flay the skin from you an inch at a time, and you wouldn't flinch if by doing so you would cause *her* harm. Shall we see how much *she* is willing to suffer for *you?*"

"You sonofa—" Sean lunged forward, but a rifle butt slammed into his stomach, the mob of evil-faced men falling on him like beasts rending their prey. The struggle was over in seconds. They jerked him to his feet, mouth bleeding, eye blackening, his arms wrenched upward at a sickening angle as he still struggled against them. Their mouths stretched in wolfish grins as another man yanked a leather thong from his pocket, ready to bind him.

"No, no. His hands in front, Murdsty." The grizzled man looped the thong around Sean's wrists, twisting it until Meaghan saw Sean's lips tighten in pain. She flinched as Radcliffe moved the pistol. He lowered it, setting the hammer gently back into place. "We're going to let Sean here dangle another way, before we turn him over to the executioner."

"I don't give a damn what you do to me. Whatever your sick mind can think up. But let her go. She's nothing to you."

"There you're wrong," Radcliffe snarled. "Your doxy and I have had several trysts, Sean, but never one that ended to our *mutual satisfaction*. All that will change now, you can be sure. Did you know she has a penchant for whipping?" He shoved the back of his fist at Sean's face. A thin red scar sliced across the hair-stippled skin. Radcliffe's eyes raked Meaghan. "You remember this, don't you, lovely? You took great pleasure in it. Cutting me with your lash. I wonder how it would feel on your own soft skin . . ."

With a scream of fury, Sean threw himself at Radcliffe, a move desperate, futile. A meaty fist cracked down on the back of his neck, sending him sprawling as a second man drove his boot into Sean's kidneys.

"Stop it! Sean!" Meaghan broke away from Radcliffe, running to where Sean was struggling to his feet. Her arms went tight around him, and for a second she buried her face in his neck. Every muscle beneath her hands was wire-taut with rage. She raised her head, drawing strength from the feel of Sean's body, from his steely pride. Her chin jutted defiantly as she met Radcliffe's eyes.

Their black depths seemed to swirl with unearthly light as his lips drew into an eager sneer. "So stiff-necked, both of you. So much better than everyone else. Tell me, do you bleed red, O'Fallon? Just like the rest of us?" Radcliffe jerked his head at his hirelings. "Get them up to the stables. My grandfather left some very interesting legacies for us to entertain them with."

Rough hands bruised Meaghan's arms as they pulled her away from Sean. She could feel him straining toward her until other hands, even more savage, closed on him.

The ground was littered with dead, as they were dragged toward the building that had been Connor MacDonough's domain. Glassy eyes stared unseeing; faces were slack, bodies limp. Meaghan couldn't tear her eyes from that blood-christened earth, or the men who lay there. She pulled back from her captor's restraining grip, pausing just a moment at the base of a gnarled tree to look down into two faces she knew well.

Casey Halloran lay, his body as shriveled in death as his soul had been in life, an arm's length away from another, dearer figure. Blond hair was tousled in a cap about a face free of grief, of torment. He was at peace. "Liam . . ." The name squeezed past Meaghan's lips, but she could not mourn for the gentle giant who had lost all that he had loved.

The stable door creaked on its hinges, the merest breeze clacking it in an eerie staccato against the wall as she and Sean were shoved into the musty interior. A lantern suspended from an iron hook in the rafters flickered over a half-stripped haunch of beef and a dripping keg of wine. Paying no heed to the half-empty bottles dotting the floor, Colin Radcliffe strode to a wooden chest in a hidden corner and lifted its web-veiled lid. He rose and turned. Dangling from a heavy handle closed in his fist, nine knotted cords twisted like a madwoman's hair. Lead-weighted ends thunked against each other in a dull, skin-crawling chant.

"We were having a bit of a celebration before you . . . *arrived,"* he said silkily, fingers trailing over the cat-o'-nine-tails in a satanic caress. "How thoughtful of you to provide the entertainment. Show us how brave you are, O'Fallon. How much your whore loves you."

The weapon's lashes cracked into the stable wall, the sound of it cutting into Meaghan as surely as if it had struck her in the face. Radcliffe jerked his head at Murdsty and the man who had struck Sean with the rifle butt.

"String the rutting bastard between the posts," he ordered, lips snaking into a savage smile. "You're about to hear the high and mighty Sean O'Fallon beg."

Twenty-Two

"No!" The strangled plea stuck in Meaghan's throat, trapped there by the warning that fired Sean's eyes. The message flashing from the dark-fringed blue was cold and clear. *Don't crawl before these animals. Don't let them break you . . .*

But as the men yanked him around, Murdsty's thick fingers closing on the neck of Sean's shirt, ripping it from his broadly muscled shoulders, it was all she could do to keep from screaming. And as the coarse rope bit deep into Sean's wrists, his arms spread wide between twin posts sunk in the stable floor, the lengths of hemp seemed to cinch *her* chest, crushing whatever vestiges of strength remained within her.

Sean's face, half turned toward her, was visible over his shoulder, the rippling muscles across his back the color of burnt honey, his silky hair skimming the nape of his neck.

Murdsty took hold of the rope, jerking on it, shifting Sean's weight to the balls of his feet. "Tight enough for you, Radcliffe?" Sean goaded, wincing as the bindings grated along his flesh. "You wouldn't want me to break loose and show all your fine friends what a coward you are. I'm sure they'll be astounded at your bravery by the time you're done—whipping a lone man with twenty to one odds."

"Oh, I'll not be doing the whipping," Radcliffe said. "I have something much more . . . interesting . . . in mind for you." He trailed the cords across Sean's back. "A whip is like a woman, isn't it, O'Fallon? Pliant beneath your touch, but turning on you, tearing at you with the slightest threat." He let the weighted ends of leather drip over Sean's shoulder. They fell, thudding gently

234

against his naked stomach just above the black line of his breeches. The muscles they struck were stone, unyielding as the stubborn pride that cast Sean's face in the taut lines of a captive king's.

"How long will it take your woman to shred your hide, O'Fallon?" Radcliffe asked, letting the whip fall away from Sean's flesh. "What will it take to persuade her that your pain is much more tolerable than her own?"

"Damn you! Leave her out of this!"

"I think not. She is going to suffer for what she did, learn lessons far beyond your wildest imaginings. But since I want her hot beneath me, I don't want her *body* scarred."

Meaghan's breath came out in a gasp as Radcliffe caught her around the waist, dragging her in front of Sean. The lord's fingers clenched on her wrist, crushing the bones until her hand fell open against her will. He pressed her back tight against the front of his own body as he forced her fingertips to glide over Sean's chest. Sean's heart hammered beneath the silky heat of his skin, and she wanted to sob at the achingly familiar feel of it. Her stomach churned as Radcliffe defiled what had once been a caress of love. She tried to pull away, but Radcliffe held her.

"Feel good, O'Fallon?" he asked. "Now we'll unsheath her claws." Something hard was forced into Meaghan's hand, strands tangling from its end around her fingers.

"No!" She tried to fling the hideous whip away, but Radcliffe stayed her.

"I wouldn't do that, love. I'm quite prepared to use more subtle torture on your own precious hide."

"Go ahead! I don't care! I'm not going to—" Her words were cut off as Radcliffe wrenched her arm behind her back, forcing it brutally toward her shoulder.

"Meaghan!" Sean cried. "For God's sake—do it!"

"Yes, do it, my pet. Listen to your lover. Such fragile, delicate bones..." Radcliffe's breath crawled across her neck in a chuckle of delight. "How much farther do you think I'd have to twist to break them, O'Fallon?"

"I'll kill you if you hurt her! I swear to God somehow— Meaghan!" The ropes sliced into Sean's wrists as he struggled, helplessness and a searing tenderness tearing inside him at her white-lipped refusal to cause him harm. The tawny velvet of her eyes caught his, and he saw love in them, and pain.

"Maggie, do it!" he pleaded, his voice breaking. "Do what he says!"

"I can't." She cried, throwing the whip to her feet with her free hand.

Radcliffe flung a sneering laugh to his cohorts. "How disgustingly touching! Well, if threats against your own body won't make you turn on your lover, perhaps there is another way." Casting her to the ground, he paced over to Sean, drawing his pistol, pulling back the hammer. "Well, whore? Tell me. What will it be? O'Fallon battered? Or O'Fallon dead?"

"No! Don't! I . . ." Sean's heart wrenched at the sight of her, scrambling to her feet, her eyes wounded, lips trembling.

"Don't what? Don't pull the trigger?"

"Don't . . . do this . . ."

"I'm not going to do anything, my pet. It's you who will be doing the devil's weaving tonight. You'll beat him until I give you leave to stop, or I'll blast a hole in his skull the size of your fist. My finger is getting tired, wench."

The cat-o'-nine-tails lay at her feet. She touched it as though it were some live and slithering thing, the handle ludicrous in her slender fingers. The devil's weaving . . . could Satan himself have devised a more diabolical form of torture than the Lord of Radbury Manor?

"Sean . . ." Meaghan breathed, the single word a plea.

She looked into the eyes that had been so dead hours before and felt their warmth and strength seep through her. "I know, Maggie."

The murmur of voices from the men surrounding them rose like rabble at a gladiator fight, hideous and sadistic as she drew the whip back.

"Hit him," Radcliffe snarled.

The cords seemed to dance in her shaking hand, writhing and twisting as she cracked the cat-o'-nine-tails down onto the smooth, sleek muscles of Sean's back. The lashes bit deep with a sickening sound, the sensation as they struck his flesh vibrating from the whiphandle up her arm. Welts streaked across his skin as though a lioness had clawed him. A shiver went through the taut muscles. There was silence.

"You hit me harder with the buggy whip," Radcliffe purred. "I know firsthand that you can break the skin, my pet. Show your lover here the *cat's* sweet caress." His voice changed, sharpening to an evil hiss as he jammed the gun against Sean's temple. "Blood, girl! Now! Or I swear I will draw it myself!"

Meaghan's fingers slipped on the whiphandle, its round surface slick with the sweat from her palm, the weighted ends dragging at her arm as she brought them down in a whistling, gut-wrenching arc. The strength of years climbing trees and throwing rocks was in the blow as it tore into Sean's flesh, the leather slicing across the rippling muscles. Trails of bright crimson welled in their path. He arched his head sideways, and she could see the tendons in his jaw knot with pain.

What little she had eaten that morning forced its way up in her throat, burning her, choking her as she cracked the "cat" into Sean's back a third time. *The devil's weaving*—it crisscrossed the taut muscles in gashes, their pattern writhing before her eyes.

She tried to lift the whip again, her whole body quaking with horror and nausea, but couldn't. The stable walls spun, and Sean's blood revolved at their center. Then she was retching, crumpling to the ground, barely able to keep her face from the hay-strewn floor.

"Meg!" Sean's worried cry penetrated her haze.

She could hear Radcliffe's satanic laugh, hear in his voice a trill of amusement. "I warned you, witch. I warned you not to stop!"

Meaghan tried to struggle up, to lunge for Radcliffe as his eyes narrowed with deadly intent, but it was too late. The toe of his boot caught her full in the chest, knocking her backward as his finger tightened on the gun leveled at Sean's head. The pistol's hammer was a silver blur as it cracked down toward the pin. Meaghan's own screams rang in her ears, desperate and hopeless, but no explosion of gunpowder split the sound. There was laughter . . . only laughter . . .

The gun was empty.

A raging fury broke over her, piercing hatred of a depth she had never dreamed possible. She wanted to kill Colin Radcliffe . . . to feel his flesh split beneath her hand. She wanted to . . . Her fingers brushed something hard and round, still warm from her grasp. She groped for it, feeling cords wet with Sean's blood.

"Did ye see her?" Murdsty was roaring, clutching his belly as he leaned against the stable wall for support. "Did ye see the wench? She really believed ye were going to blast the bastard!"

"Did you ever see anything so amusing?" Radcliffe asked.

"God, the things O'Fallon must have done between her legs—"

"Christ! Look out!" a man in the crowd squealed.

Radcliffe wheeled, his words severed in a shriek of pain as Meaghan slashed the whip into him with all her strength. The cat-o'-nine-tails smacked his face with a force that knocked him back against one of the posts, its knotted cords gashing his cheeks, forehead, and nose, splitting his lips. He tried to rake them away, but she was hitting him again and again, flailing wildly, sobbing.

She could hear Sean shouting and struggling, could feel strange hands grabbing her, yanking the whip from her hands. Radcliffe's battered face contorted in a mask of rage, his fist cracking into her mouth as he regained his balance. Blood spurted from cuts torn by her teeth, filling her with its sweet-salt taste. She spit into Radcliffe's face, hating him . . . hating . . .

"Bitch!" Radcliffe slammed the back of his fist into her other cheek. "You goddamned bitch!" He swept up the whip that lay at his feet, hurling the whipcords back ready to strike her.

"Radcliffe! You sonofa—God damn you—" Sean roared, tearing at the ropes.

Meaghan gritted her teeth, awaiting the blow, terrified of Radcliffe's bloody, contorted face, yet exulting in its ruin. But the strike of the leather did not come. Instead the blaze of rage in Radcliffe's eyes shifted, a strange diabolical gleam glinting in their blackness. "No . . . no . . ." he hissed to himself. "There's another way . . . a better way . . ." He turned to Murdsty. "Hold her. I want her to see this. Every stroke."

Brutal fingers knotted in Meaghan's hair, bulges of stinking male bodies pressed against her as she fought.

"You want to see a man lashed to a bloody pulp?" Radcliffe snarled. "Well then, *by damn I'll show you one!*"

The "cat" flashed out, powered by a rage that snapped the bounds of sanity, of brutality.

Sean felt the first rush of air as the lash arced down, steeling himself for the agony that exploded in its wake.

Like liquid fire, the whipcords snaked across Sean's flesh again and again, flaying the skin from his back and shoulders, tearing the muscle, sending blade-sharp shards of agony spinning to every nerve cell in his body.

The bite of the lashes when Meaghan had struck him had been tempered by the knowledge that he *must not* cry out, must not make it harder for her. And Colin Radcliffe—he vowed he would never let that sonofabitch break him.

But as the "cat" slashed again, Sean's hands knotted around the lengths of rope that held him, the coarse hemp digging its needlelike slivers into his palms, sweat drenching his body and mingling with his blood, the hissing bite of the whip shoving him to an ever-higher plane of torment.

They held Meaghan where he could see her, the fawn-soft brown of her eyes—terrified, horrified—but he couldn't even glance at her. The sight of her shattered and sobbing clawed at his gut with a pain that far surpassed even the physical torture, and Radcliffe knew it—knew it . . .

Instead, Sean turned his head away from her, trying desperately to picture her face breaking the surface of the stream, her coppery hair shining, clinging to her breasts. He thought of her diving beneath the crystal blue, tugging his feet out from under him . . . of both of them sputtering, splashing . . . of seeking lips made hotter by the cold, clear water.

But then the pain came again . . . the pain that turned the water to flame, that ate away courage and left a man cringing, cowering, begging for mercy . . .

No . . . no . . . he wouldn't . . .

The "cat" bit down again.

Dear God, don't let him beg!

"Had enough, O'Fallon?" Radcliffe's voice penetrated the orange-red haze of misery. "Your woman is crying, O'Fallon, sobbing . . . Can you hear her? Do you care? Beg me to stop it, O'Fallon . . . Scream . . ."

"No . . ." Pain-glazed eyes caught Meaghan's for an instant, and then jumped away. She tried to shut out the sight of them, block out the horror of his back, now a mass of bloody pulp, torn as though a hundred sharp-clawed ferrets had tried to dig their way into his body. But whenever she closed her eyes, a fat, callused hand slapped her face until she opened them. Gray beady eyes and slack drooling mouths feasted greedily on her torment.

At last, sobbing, she stared at Sean. She saw the blood-sodden leather flashing, the glistening crimson flesh, skin-stripped muscle. Incongruous images of the previous day played in her mind, images of smoothing Sean's shirt across his broad shoulders, of him laughingly teaching her to tie his cravat, of standing behind him in the half-light of dawn, pressing her cheek into the spicy-warm brownness of his back as he rasped the straight-edged razor over his jaw...

But she couldn't lean against him now...the blood...it soaked the back of his breeches, spattered her dress, her face, dripping down her skin with each slash of the "cat."

"No...no please..." Meaghan heard her voice as though it were a stranger's, choked, pleading, through the maze of blood. Begging. "Don't...don't hurt him anymore. I'll do anything you say..."

"Meaghan! No!" Sean's voice was slurred, distant.

"No! I'll do anything—"

"Damn!" He struggled at the ropes, pain-ravaged muscles quivering, jumping, his feet barely holding him.

Radcliffe's laugh twisted through the rafters. "Do you hear your woman beg, O'Fallon? She'll do *anything—anything*—to save your hide. And we both know what that means, don't we, Sean-o?" His eyes flicked to Meaghan. "How much is the bastard worth to you, whore? How much?" He jerked his head at the men who held her. "Let her go."

The hands loosened and released her, and Meaghan felt a painful surge of feeling burst into her arms. "Come here, bitch." The command was low, gloating. "Right here in front of your lover."

She stumbled forward, Radcliffe's black eyes pulling her deeper into hell. "Show me how much you love O'Fallon. Show *him*. I'd like to see what I'm being offered in place of this... amusement." He let the cat-o'-nine-tails slither to the ground, wiping the blood that smeared his hands on the leg of his pantaloons. "Your bodice, wench," he said. "Open it."

"Meg! Please!" Sean's words were almost a sob. "They're going to hang me anyway!"

The crowd around her jostled forward, hurling lewd comments, smacking lips still reeking of sour wine, as Meaghan's numb fingers fumbled with the tiny buttons at her throat. One by one they came open, baring the delicate wedding lace Grace had sewn on the white of her chemise weeks before.

Radcliffe reached one finger into the tiny slit between the first ribbon-tie. Hooking the finger around the satin bow, he yanked it, tearing it free with a studied savagery. Meaghan flinched as the chill night air touched the bared top curve of her breast.

Slowly, Radcliffe ran his finger over it, leaving a cloying stickiness on her flesh. "Prime, O'Fallon. Prime." Radcliffe purred. "Like Cathay silk. What does she like you to do with them?"

She could hear Sean's curses as he fought to break loose, his pleas for her to stop. She shut her eyes, wanting to die . . . only to die. Other sweaty hands groped, tearing the last of the covering from her breasts. She could feel them bruising, kneading.

The sound of a fist hitting flesh and a howl of pain made her eyes snap open to see Murdsty clutching his face, one beady eye purpling. "What the hell'd ye do that for?" he whined to Radcliffe. "Christ! Ye were offerin' her up here like some piece o' meat on the block! The least ye could do is share a little squeeze of 'er!"

"The day I share with the likes of you—" Radcliffe snorted. "I just wanted Sean, here, to get a sample of what I'll be doing tonight, and every night for as long as the bitch wants him alive." Radcliffe tugged the edges of the chemise back over Meaghan's breasts, then slid an arm around her waist.

"Bid goodnight to O'Fallon, love," he sneered. "We have a long and *eventful* evening ahead of us." There was a chink of glass as Radcliffe's boot bumped a corked bottle lying in the straw. He picked it up, yanking out the stopper, raising the flask high.

"To a night your whore will long remember, O'Fallon," he laughed, tipping the bottle up over Sean's back. The gold-tinted liquid gushed down over the maze of torn flesh. Sean screamed, animal sounds of agony ripping from his throat.

"No!" Meaghan broke away from Radcliffe, running to Sean, trying to hold him, comfort him as he writhed, his wrists bleeding, his muscles twitching, jerking. "Sean . . . oh, God, Sean."

Barely intelligible words squeezed between his clenched teeth, his eyes fighting to focus. "Don't . . . go with him . . . Maggie . . . Don't let him . . . touch you . . ."

"Cut him down," Radcliffe ordered. A long-bladed knife appeared from somewhere in the gang of men, hacking through the thick ropes.

Meaghan tried to brace Sean's weight, as he toppled face down to the stable floor, but he fell, clutching handfuls of hay, of her skirt.

She felt Radcliffe's hand close on her arm to drag her to her feet. Sean caught at her fingers, trying to push himself up, but failing.

"Don't go, Maggie . . . don't . . ."

"I love you, Sean," Meaghan whispered brokenly. His hand dropped to the stable floor, and sooty lashes fell in thick crescents to his death-pale cheeks, as he slipped at last, she was certain, into the blessed release of unconsciousness.

Radcliffe's fingers tightened on her arm, and she stumbled against him, her eyes still clinging to Sean's lifeless form twisted on the stable floor.

"I love you, Sean," Radcliffe mocked, his hand trailing down the swell of her breast. "We'll see, my pet. We'll soon see just how much you love him."

Twenty-Three

The copper tub glistened with firelight reflected from the rich marble hearth, its now-tepid water filling the room with the cloying odor of boiled violets. Meaghan pushed back the hair that strung over her shoulders in a mass of snarls, letting it slap in a heavy, wet curtain against the mist-thin cloth that draped her body. The strange, foreign gown Lord Radcliffe had ordered her to wear—to make herself ready in—

She huddled closer to the fire, shivering, though the strands now sticking to her back were warm from the flames, seeing in the orange-red flickerings above the grate Sean's face, Sean's eyes. Eyes shimmering with the cerulean tint of a clear Irish sky, darkening with fury, glazing in agony, closing.

He had lain so still on the dirt, his breath scarcely stirring the weight of his chest, his face gray-tinged, taut. How long could he live like that? His back shredded, matted with stable filth . . . But he didn't want to live. He wanted to—

Meaghan wheeled away from the fire, her heart clenching at the thought. No! She wouldn't even think the word. He wouldn't —couldn't—

But even as she tried to block it out, the image her thoughts had conjured forced its way into her mind with other beloved faces. Grace, little Annie, Da . . . Dead. All dead.

And her own child, Sean's babe, still inside her womb, could it cling to its fragile thread of life through what was to come? For she had no illusions about what Lord Radcliffe planned for her.

The curl of his lips as he had locked her in this silk-lined prison had warned her only too well. She had promised the payment of her body for Sean's life.

Radcliffe would make certain that price was high.

The click of the lock made her heart leap to her throat, her eyes darting to the door. The portal swung open, but no tall evil presence was revealed behind it, only a stout, graying woman, her plump hands balancing a silver tray laden with food and wine, her white cap askew, stained on one side with three smears of purple.

"Are . . . are ye done with yer bathin'?" Her head bobbed toward the tray. "I was told to bring this up for ye an' the master, an' then be emptyin' the wash water . . ."

"Fine," Meaghan said dully. "Whatever . . . whatever he said." The woman's gaze was fastened on her in a way that would have made her squirm, had she cared enough to bother. But though the poppy-shaded gauze clung like a harlot's robe to her curves, Meaghan couldn't summon will enough even to shield her breasts from the older woman's eyes.

"I . . . I be Mrs. Duggan . . ." the woman faltered. "And if ye . . ." Her eyes flicked to Meaghan's, then away, a blush reddening her faintly wrinkled cheeks as she let the sentence dangle unfinished in the air. She turned, bustling toward a cherry-wood table to deposit her load, then whisked over to the huge bed, turning the coverlets down.

Even through the fog of numbness that had settled over her, Meaghan could feel Mrs. Duggan's eagerness to quit the room. The eyes in the round face were kept scrupulously away from her, as though to look at her would be to taint them. Another one of Radcliffe's whores, the woman's straight back seemed to accuse.

Legs trembling, Meaghan sank into the heavily scrolled chair by the fire, letting her face fall into her open hands. Radcliffe's whore. That she would surely be before the sun rose. For how long? How long before he tired of tormenting both her and Sean? How long before he set his teeth for bigger game—hanging. God, how would she even know if Sean was still alive?

She sensed a quiet in the room, a watchfulness, and raised her head, trying to hide the tear-bright glistening on her lashes. When she faced Mrs. Duggan it was with a touch of her old defiance. "Well? What is it?"

"Mistress . . . I . . ."

"Don't call me that!" Meaghan winced at the word's double meaning. "I'm Meaghan . . . Just Meaghan."

"Mistress . . . a . . . Meaghan . . . Is . . . is something wrong?"

"Wrong?" Meaghan leapt to her feet with a wild little laugh. "Here I am trapped in this . . . this place and the man I love is—"

"Here at last." The low-pitched voice made Meaghan's stomach cave in upon itself, and she looked up into Radcliffe's whip-battered face. "Did you miss me, my sweet?" he asked silkily. "I'm sorry I'm late, but I had to *dispose* of another guest. See to his discomfort before I . . . sought . . . more pleasant *diversion*."

"Is he—"

"You really mustn't trouble yourself. He gave not a word of complaint, though I must admit the accommodations were a bit cruder than these. Not every visitor to Radbury Manor is treated to a welcome this extravagant." He gestured to the ornately carved wall panels around them with one hand, then let his eyes travel down her slender form. The corner of his mouth tipped up in a knowing smile. "Of course, I've been eager to entertain *you* for some time."

"Damn you, I want to see—"

"Always so demanding!" Radcliffe chided, pressing cold, damp fingers upon her lips to stop her words with mock indulgence. "'I want this,' 'I want that.' You should really learn to control those grasping little hands of yours—at least in front of the servants." Meaghan followed his gaze to the stout woman scrubbing up a bit of spilled water beside the tub as though the fate of Ireland depended on it, the rolled copper rim not quite hiding the odd look on her face. "After all, my pet," Radcliffe continued, "Mrs. Duggan might think something amiss—and I know you're as eager for this night to come to a *satisfactory conclusion* as I am."

Meaghan started to wrench away at the thinly veiled warning, but his fingers tightened around her jaw. His lips ground down on hers, raping her mouth, and she knew the full horror of what was about to happen and the shame that their kiss was being witnessed by the maid. Then as suddenly as he had swept to kiss her, he broke away. "What the—" he sputtered, eyes widening. "Did they boil you in that bath? You're on fire!" He pressed his hand to her cheek, and it burned her, ice to heated flesh.

Fire . . . she'd been sitting in front of the fire . . . in the stable she had thrown up . . . A desperate seed of hope took root in

Meaghan. She had played pirate queen on the moor, fought as Finn MacCool with apple branches, but this . . . Never before had she acted when so much was at stake . . . She swallowed hard, trying to remember the scores of symptoms Sean had told her about. She glanced at Mrs. Duggan. The woman had seen her in front of the fireplace, had been watching her . . .

"I . . . I've been . . . cold all day," Meaghan managed, pressing her fingertips to her temples. "And my head . . ."

"Cold? You're hot, for God's sake!"

"I thought it was just . . . just a headache . . . that when Sean got home he could give me a powder. But it keeps getting worse. The boy we buried a week ago had the same—"

"Buried?!"

There was a catching of breath to the side of them, a rustling of skirts. "The boy?" They both wheeled at Mrs. Duggan's gasp. "B-begging yer pardon, yer lordship, m-mistress . . . but . . . but not the one who died last Tuesday?"

"Uh . . . last Tuesday . . ." Meaghan stammered, knowing there had been no death the week before, knowing somehow that the older woman was well aware of that fact. "I . . . uh . . ."

"Mother of God! That child died of road fever! Heard it myself from those 'at was carryin' him!" Mrs. Duggan said, hastily crossing herself.

"Fever! Christ!" Radcliffe snatched his hand away, swiping his other palm across his kiss-wet lips as he took a step back.

"I . . . there was no one to nurse him . . . Sean brought him to Cottage Gael . . ."

"Fever! You brought fever into this house!"

"I didn't bring it! You forced me to—"

"Damn you, witch! I should snap your neck!" Radcliffe screamed, eyes wild, face purple with rage. He took a step toward her, then stopped, backing toward the door.

"I . . . I can't be sure it's fever yet."

"Can't be sure? What do you expect me to do? Wait around until you're certain? You think a night in your bed is worth dying for? You can rot in here! Rot!" The curved door handle rattled beneath his shaking fingers as he grasped and turned it. "But if it's not fever . . ." he said. "If there is anything left of you after . . ." The threat hung unfinished in the air as he slammed the door shut behind himself. Crystal pendants on the wall sconces tinkled together, the oil flames reflected in their facets dancing, then stilling at last to silence.

Only then did Meaghan realize that hanks of the poppy-red shift were clenched in her fists, her nails punching tiny slits in the fragile material, digging into her palms. She let her hands fall slack, pressing them to her already cooling face as she turned to Mrs. Duggan.

The other woman's eyes were frightened, wary as though she was suddenly conscious of what she'd been a party to.

"Thank you," Meaghan breathed, sagging against the bedpost. "I don't know why you did it, but thank you."

"Don't be thankin' me!" The woman cut her off. "I did nothin' fer ye. Nothin'! I want no part of what ye're about . . . why ye're here." Her glance darted to a small door cut in the wall beside the bed, then to the door through which Radcliffe had disappeared seconds before.

"Please, just tell me one thing. There was a man Lord Radcliffe had flogged tonight in the stable. Have you seen—heard anything—"

"No!" Mrs. Duggan clutched the soaked towels against her breast, stumbling back against the brass woodbox at the hearth. "They'd take him from me if they knew I'd told ye—ye don't know what she's like, the lady. She'll give him to somebody cruel. She'll—"

"Give who? Oh, God, please! I have to know—"

"I can't help ye!" Mrs. Duggan cried, fleeing across the room. The door slammed shut behind her, the outside key scraping in the lock as Meaghan caught at the handle.

"No! Don't!" she sobbed, pounding on the panel. "I have to know!" The sound of running footsteps faded down the hall. Meaghan leaned against the door, sliding down, crumpling to the floor. "Please," she cried to the silence, burying her face in her hands. "I have to know if Sean's alive."

Darkness faded to tints of the new day's dawn before Meaghan surrendered to sleep, but no nightmare born in the pit of hell could surpass the dream that snared her in its talons the instant her eyes fell closed . . .

Running . . . she was running, legs aching, lungs burning as she stumbled down a twisted labyrinth of pitch-black corridors. Moans echoed through the darkness, seeping through the damp stone walls, through the iron-barred windows of a hundred cell-like alcoves, clutching at her throat like the bony hands that tore at her skirts. Meaghan clung to the candle stub in her fingers as she stumbled down yet another midnight passage. For there were screams, screams that pierced all other sounds of human pain, screams that surrounded her, smothered her. Sean's screams.

She crashed into a shadowy wall, trapped yet again in a hall that led nowhere. Slime stuck to her cheek, her arm, and some small wet-bellied creature slithered down her neck. She shrieked, swiping it away, running, still running. But this time the end of the passage opened, and an odd, red glow shimmered inside.

Meaghan bolted toward the light, flinging away the guttering candle, hurling herself through the stone archway, Sean's sounds of agony becoming clearer, louder. Then suddenly she was falling, hurtling into a mist that spotted her skin with blood, hurtling down toward a huge gilt-framed mirror, alive with the blue of Sean's eyes, alive with his torment.

She reached out her hands, trying to touch him as she fell, trying to help him, but he was trapped in the mirror's silvery depths. His arms strained toward her, corded muscles drenched with sweat and blood, but someone yanked them back. Not Colin Radcliffe—hands, they were a woman's hands, white, cruel, dripping with gems.

Meaghan screamed Sean's name, saw the anguish in his eyes, felt the hopelessness tearing at her as her body slammed into the glass, crashing it into a million cerulean shards. Desperately she tried to claw through the pieces, to find him, but there was nothing but the stark agony of his eyes staring up at her from a hundred blade-edged fragments of shattered mirror... and fingers trying to pull her away. She struck at them, trying to fight her way out of the dream's horror, but they shook her, feather-light, so small...

She started awake, then wheeled and screamed. Eyes, rare crystal blue, stared at her from another face, a child's face, her terror reflected in their dark-lashed depths. At her cry the little boy snatched his hand back, clutching at something in his arms as he dashed for the open door by the side of the bed. Instinctively Meaghan leapt from the bed, grabbing for him just as one bare foot snagged in the tail of his nightshirt, but even as he was pitching forward he squirmed to avoid her, smashing himself into the door.

The crack of his side into the heavy panel resounded through the room, the ragged cloth animal flying from his arms, as he careened to the floor. He scrambled toward it with a pathetic little wail as it skidded across the slick marble hearth toward the flames that still lapped the charred underside of the log, his plump little hands but inches from the fire as Meaghan swept him away.

Popping and hissing, the log rained glowing sparks onto the aged cloth, stinging Meaghan's hand as she snatched the toy from beneath the grate. A forgotten towel lay in a heap upon the floor. She grabbed it, smothering the tiny smoldering holes that speckled the stuffed animal, trying to fend off the child's groping hands until all chance of harm was past.

She sank to the floor, pulse hammering in her chest as she hugged the child against her, finally letting him claw through the towel to the toy beneath. "It's all right, all right, now," she soothed, smoothing a hand over the boy's dark curls, pressing her cheek against his. "See, it's scarcely burned at all, we moved so quick. You scared me half to death, little one—diving for that fire! If my ma were here she'd paddle the life out of you!"

She felt the boy stiffen and tremble, his expression fearful and wary as the lame foal she and Connor had found a dozen winters ago, cowering in the nettles while a covey of boys threw stones at it.

Da had had to kill the foal, the delicate bone in its foreleg having been broken by one of the blows. She could remember trying to stop him, Connor holding her back, the foal's soft bruised innocence as Da had carried it away.

It was a look she had seen too often in the days since her own childhood had fled, since the praties had failed. But in this child's eyes it tugged at her heart in a way nothing had since that long-ago winter, in a way she hadn't experienced since she had realized that Da was not God, that all hurts could not be healed, that people could be cruel and murderous instead of kind.

"Easy, now. I didn't mean to frighten you. It just scared me when—"

A tiny whimper of pain made her jerk her hand away from where it had been smoothing over his side. "What's wrong? Did you hurt yourself?" Meaghan asked gently, picking him up, stuffed puppy and all, and laying him on the bed. "That was quite a tumble you took. Let me see—" She froze, stunned, the tangled white muslin he wore clutched in her numb fingers.

Light streaming in through the leaded glass window spilled down over his pale skin, accenting several deep-purple splotches edged by angry cuts as though something sharp had struck him. Meaghan ran her fingers gently over the new welt on the little boy's hip, horrified at the injuries that marked his body.

"Wh . . . what's been done to you? How did you get these—"

The child tugged the nightshirt down over the bruises, cheeks paling in his pinched little face, guilt touching the soft pink of his mouth. "Falled. Stairs hit Woarke."

"The stairs? But, did a doctor—"

"Me bad. C'umsy."

"Bad?"

"Maman say—" He stopped, biting his bottom lip.

"Maman?" Meaghan prodded gently, picking him up, cradling him closer. The child curled against her side, warm, soft, his dark brown curls brushing the crook of her shoulder. She shut her eyes. She had thought the brutality she had witnessed in the stable had numbed her, deadened her spirit, but at the sight of this bruised and terrified child, a fierce protectiveness blazed inside her. This crisscrossing of bruises had been caused by no fall. His mother—someone had—

"Rory! Master Rory!" The distressed call was followed by the sounds of someone scuttling toward the small doorway. Meaghan glared at the opening, still cradling the child against her as though to shield him as Mrs. Duggan burst into the room.

"Master Roarke! I have half a mind to tie ye to yer bed!" the woman blustered, her face more white and frightened than the boy's. "I've been nigh out of my mind searchin' for ye, thinkin' ye'd wandered off again, an' ye not even healed from the last—"

"The last time he *fell* down the *stairs?*" Meaghan challenged, icily.

"The stairs? Master Rory, ye didn't hurt—"

"Didn't hurt?" Meaghan echoed as the little boy's arms twined around her neck. "You can scarcely pick him up without hurting him somewhere!"

"*Ye* think *I*—" Mrs. Duggan halted, the eyes beneath her stubby, colorless lashes widening as she stared.

Meaghan felt Rory's tiny smooth palm pat gently against her cheek, his little fingers splayed, warm upon her skin.

Tears stung Meaghan's eyes. She leaned her cheek against his soft one, wanting to soak up the innocent caring of this child who, by all appearances, had known little love himself.

"To your room, Master Rory." Mrs. Duggan's voice was quiet, almost gentle. The boy looked up, obediently stretching out his arms, but the older woman did not return the childish hug, only set him on his feet, pushing him toward the door.

At the opening Mrs. Duggan stopped. "'Is lordship's been called away by his grandfather, the old duke," she said, without turning. "Rode out at cock's crow."

"He's gone?"

"Aye." Mrs. Duggan hesitated. "And that man . . . the one ye asked after—"

"Sean?" Meaghan's heart seemed to choke her.

"Lord Radcliffe hasn't had time to finish the killin'. Yer man, 'e's here on the manor, though God knows he'll die soon enough where they've locked him away."

"Please— Is . . . is he all right? Can . . . can you tell me where he is?"

"A half-breath from hell, child." Mrs. Duggan's hand stilled on the door's iron bolt. "He's a half-breath from hell."

White-hot spikes of pain pierced Sean's arms, driving into his shoulder sockets and shooting down his spine. He was held upright by heavy iron shackles, which cut into his wrists, yanking his raised arms. He struggled to open his swollen eyes, but something thick and sticky seemed to have fused the lids together. A coarse rough plane of stone ground against his back, grating the torn flesh. He twisted, trying to arch away from it, but the shackles forced him back into the pitted wall as another wave of unconsciousness threatened to break over him.

Meaghan—he had to find Meaghan. Even through the blood-red cloud of agony that engulfed him, he clung to that thought, trying to anchor himself in the dim half-light that filtered through his mind before he slipped back into blackness.

He held on to the image of her face, her hair, the feel of her hands on his body, soft and trembling, the only coolness in a hell of whip cracks, savagery, and hate. And the sound of her voice —that broken angel's voice whispering her love to him as Radcliffe and his jackals closed in around her. Her love—the thing that had delivered her into Colin Radcliffe's hands, the single thing that kept Sean fighting for every tortured breath.

The sound of something rasping against stone made Sean try to raise his head, to rip through the dark gray veils that webbed his mind, but even that slight movement made his stomach churn sickeningly. Boot heels? Someone—the scraping noise stopped.

"Wake up ye whoreson bastard!" a slurred voice hissed, the sound of it stirring in Sean's memory, pictures of thick groping fingers defiling Meaghan's breasts, of slack drooling lips. Murdsty. "Wake up, O'Fallon!" An elbow jabbed sharply into Sean's stomach sending spasms rippling outward.

He twisted in his chains, a blurred sliver of pale light and muddy-brown cloth visible as he struggled to focus his eyes. Something arced toward him, smacking into his cheek. Sean's head snapped against the wall, his back sliding in an excruciating path across the stone. He bit back a scream, fingers clenching around the lengths of chain that held him, bright, piercing rays of light knifing into his eyes as a lantern was thrust up to his face. He blinked and moaned, taking in the crumbling block walls and sagging wood beams, the rusted tangles of iron from another age with its own more blatant brutality, their hideous purposes gripping Sean's gut in a fist of fear.

"So ye're not dead yet, bastard."

Sean tried to swallow, to force words past his parched tongue and battered jaw. "Where . . . Where's Meg . . . you sonofa—"

"Wonderin' about yer woman when Lord Radcliffe's entertainin' ye so lavish?" Murdsty taunted, taking a swig from a nearly empty bottle. "Ye surprise me, Sean, boy, bein' so ungrateful—Now yer woman, there's a one knows how to show her 'preciation. All but screamin' it out as Radcliffe—"

"God damn you, Murdsty, you tell me—"

"Tell ye what yer precious whore is about? Wipin' Radcliffe's seed from between her thighs, I'd wager, 'er openin' them to take someone else's thrustin'. 'Is lordship likes to watch sometimes when 'e's in a sharin' mood, see how another man rides 'em. Is yer bitch broke to take two men, O'Fallon?" Murdsty goaded, cupping a wine-stained hand over his crotch. "Or will this be her first—"

Bile rose in Sean's throat, gagging him with impotent fury as he lunged against the chains like a crazed animal. "God damn you, I'll kill you! You touch her and I swear—" He heard his own voice as though from a distance, anguished and distorted. A hundred pain-edged razors slashed his back and arms as the shackles tore at his ravaged flesh.

"Save yer threats for the rats, O'Fallon," Murdsty chortled. "They'll be feastin' on yer back soon enough. An' me..." He smacked his pink lips. "We both know what *I'll* be feastin' on..."

With a feral snarl Sean hurled himself against the chains, the taut lengths slamming him brutally back into the stone midst Murdsty's laughter.

Sean struggled to breathe through the crushing agony, drowning in a sea of unconsciousness as odd fragments of the room around him registered in his mind. The incongruous flash of a woman's face in the doorway, the slightest shift of chain bolts within stone, Murdsty's voice as it faded into nothingness.

"Ye can come in now," Murdsty called over his shoulder, turning to spit the whiskey he was swilling onto the floor. "Sean-boy here'll be seein' nothin' but the devil fer hours."

The figure in the shadowed entry glided forward, lantern light dripping over chine silk and Honiton lace as Alanna DuBois slapped an ancient spider's web from her gown. She stopped two feet from where Sean hung, her eyes skating over him as she fished a scented handkerchief from her dress pocket, pressing it to the tip of her delicately wrinkled nose to ward off the stench of blood. His once proud head sagged to his dirt streaked chest, the muscles in his arms standing out in tortured ropes beneath his skin.

Sean... the virile, bronze-bodied lover who had bedded her with such consummate skill, brought her to such heights of pleasure, beaten now into a filthy broken wretch.

Irritation prickled through her, setting her teeth on edge. How typical of him, wasting his life on some idiotic noble gesture, seeking justice for his infernal Irish peasants. To die on a gallows like some vengeful holy martyr. But it was all of a piece with the way he had cast *her* to the winds three years ago, caring for nothing but wiping runny noses and poisoning people with his bitter concoctions.

"Tore up good, ain't 'e, the murderin' bastard," Murdsty said, scratching his belly. "Like to sliced the skin right off 'im, Lord Radcliffe did, he was so riled after that red-haired witch went flyin' at 'im."

"Red-haired witch?"

"O'Fallon's slut. Got 'is lordship right in the face with the whip, she did, screamin' an' carryin' on. An' O'Fallon— Jesus, I never saw such killin' fury. If he'd got loose, I swear he'd 'a ripped through Satan himself to save 'er. *Love!* Bah!" Murdsty snorted. "As if the rest of us gettin' a piece 'o her'd hurt a wench like that! Made to take a man, she was. If O'Fallon there—"

"Quiet!" Alanna snapped. "I didn't come down here to listen to your lecherous drivel, you sotted fool. Lord Radcliffe bade me check on the prisoner. To make sure that you weren't wallowing about in a drunken stupor."

"A drunken stupor? If 'is lordship was so all-fired worried about my whiskey why didn't he stick someone else in this slimy hole? O'Fallon ain't goin' nowhere."

"He'd better not be. Lord Radcliffe would be most displeased if he were cheated out of this hanging . . ."

"Makin' an example of him, is he? For the ones 'at got away? Good thing if 'e did, the scurvy lot! We'd 'a had every last one of the sniveling scum if O'Fallon's woman hadn't—"

"Quit your babbling! You just keep him alive, Murdsty. Even if you have to drip food down his throat with a spoon."

"I ain't bein' no damned nursemaid to the likes of him!"

"Fine. Let him die. Just remember, if he does it may be you that dangles from Lord Radcliffe's gibbet in his stead."

A soft moan broke the icy standoff between them, as even in his unconscious state Sean made a feeble attempt to ease some of the weight on his arms. Alanna spun so her back was to Sean, pulse hammering, a flush of color reddening her cheeks.

She felt Murdsty's beady eyes upon her. "What's the matter, mistress? No stomach for blood?" His slobbery lips creased into a sly smile. "This is a garden party, compared to what yer holy lordship has planned for this buck. And his woman . . ."

"I couldn't care less what his lordship does with that carrot-headed slut!"

"May not have t' do anything with 'er. Got the fever, I heard. Did 'is lordship get a sample o' her before she—"

"I don't care if she has the plague!" Alanna said, hands knotting at her sides, as she beat down the urge to scream in the slavering lout's face. "You just take care that *you* do *your* duty, Murdsty, or you may well find yourself as dead as O'Fallon will be."

"Don't ye be worryin', mistress. I'll do my *duty*." Murdsty chuckled, his eyes flicking back to Sean's half-naked form. "Aye. I'll do my duty and then some."

Twenty-Four

"The devil take your excuses, Strathmore!" Colin Radcliffe blazed, the mourning ring bedecking his finger snapping sharply against the paper-strewn desk as he slammed his fist down. "You've been dragging your feet about settling this mess since the day that Grandfather died. Six weeks! By damn, I could've parceled off the Queen's lands by now!"

"Your Grandfather has been dead but a month's time, your Grace," Barrett Strathmore arched one woolly eyebrow as he looked up from the pen he was scratching across a page crowded with figures. "Certainly a man of your intelligence can understand that disposing of such a large estate is a lengthy and difficult procedure . . ."

"Lengthy and difficult! Have your years under Grandfather's thumb put too much strain on you? If you find this task beyond your capabilities we can take the issue to someone more able. There are most pressing matters I've yet to attend to in Ireland."

"Ah, yes. Radbury Manor. All England knows how conscientious a landlord you've been there. It's little wonder you're so eager to return."

Radcliffe glared at Strathmore, detecting a barb underlying his statement, but whatever the thoughts going through the balding man's pate, they were well hidden in his scrupulously bland expression.

"Please, your Grace, sit down. I have but a few more notes to make here and then I will be done. Even as the newly made duke you must accede to your grandfather's last wishes."

256

Radcliffe paced to the giant bookshelf that constituted one wall, leafing through a volume but an instant before he flung it onto a squat leather chair. Damn his *beloved* grandfather! From the moment Radcliffe had set foot on English soil it was as though the old man had set out to infuriate him one final time—though from the first the duke had been too weak to say a word.

For a fortnight the old man had lingered, bony fingers folded on the coverlet, ice-cold eyes staring at the crimson brocade of the bedcurtains as if woven in their patterns were the haunting images of the wretches he had wronged over a lifetime.

Day by day what little color had remained in the haughty lines of his face had seeped away, the transparent skin revealing traceries of swollen, blue-gray veins that bulged and twisted across his shrunken skull. And Radcliffe had waited—chafing with impatience at each labored breath the old duke drew, measuring each rise and fall of his chest beneath the bedclothes, each throb of the pulse in the old man's temple. And still the Duke of Radbury had lived.

But at the end, with death's kiss upon the thin, blue lips . . . Radcliffe shuddered, tugging the knot in his cravat, loosening it with unsteady fingers. The bastard . . . the old bastard had pierced him with those glacial eyes and for the first time in his life Radcliffe had heard his grandfather laugh—laugh until the death-grimace twisted his face, rattled in his throat. Laugh . . .

Beads of sweat dampened Radcliffe's brow, and he could almost feel the slick edges of the portfolio his grandfather had thrust into his hand the last time he had made the trip to Blythehall. Had the duke made good his threats? Found this Irish spawn of Jonathan Radcliffe? Were the infernal figures Strathmore was even now scribbling stealing away the riches the dead duke had hoarded, leaving Radcliffe only the lands linked to the title of Radbury, barely one quarter of the old man's estate?

Radcliffe seethed at the very thought. What pleasure that pompous ass Strathmore would take in robbing him of his birthright! And his grandfather . . . no doubt the old bastard was laughing even now, peering through the gates of hell.

But if either of them expected for a penny's weight that Colin Radcliffe would come to heel like a cowering dog, they were sadly mistaken.

At the clink of the lion's head inkwell being closed, Radcliffe turned, glowering at Strathmore as the solicitor sanded the page he'd been working on.

"Don't tell me you've made an end to it at last! Surely, you can find something else to waste my time," Radcliffe goaded.

"Everything is in order now, your Grace."

"And just what do you mean *in order?*"

Strathmore stared at him blankly. "Lands, titles, the duke's treasury. If you want a full accounting . . ."

"I never want to hear another word about your blasted acreage, leaky roofs, and mended fences. My grandfather certainly must have hired competent men to oversee his estates. Although in one instance I question his wisdom."

"As did I." Barrett Strathmore returned Radcliffe's pointed glare levelly. "The men his Grace left in charge of his *English* estates are more than able, I can assure you."

Dull spots of anger darkened Radcliffe's cheekbones at the subtly accented word.

"And then of course, you, yourself, have been in charge of the Irish holdings, haven't you, your Grace? With that—what was his name? Childe?"

"Wilde."

"Ah, yes, the unfortunate who was killed in that tenant uprising just before you left. Ungrateful, aren't they? Those wretched Irish. Stealing and murdering when you have been so just with them." Strathmore rose from the chair, not quite concealing the glint of irony in his eyes. "So now you have it all. The money. The lands. The power. All but one last thing . . ."

Strathmore drew out a velvet bag, its once bright blue dulled with age, the outline of something rectangular having worn away the nap along its edges. Almost reluctantly, he put it into Radcliffe's hand.

"Here. The duke's final command was that I give this to you upon his death."

"A moth-eaten sack? I'm overwhelmed." He saw a muscle in Strathmore's jaw tighten as the solicitor gathered up his things.

"Tell me, Strath, what's inside it?" he baited. "Some holy Radbury bauble *Grandpapa* couldn't trust out of his sight?"

For the first time there was the smallest shading of defeat about Strathmore's bearing. Without a word he turned and walked to the door.

As he watched the solicitor's thin shoulders disappear, Radcliffe fingered the ribbon ties of the bag's drawstrings, then slipped them open, dumping out what the bag contained.

A richly enameled case the size of a bandbox clunked onto the desk, rays of light dancing over the prancing unicorns, frolicking maidens adorning the box's glistening top. He opened it, running a finger over the small, filigreed key that rested on a bed of yellowed papers.

My Dearest Love—a cynical smile twisted Radcliffe's mouth as he caught the faded line on the topmost page. Some lover's slop? Was that the great treasure his grandfather had entrusted to Strathmore? He took out the note, one brittle edge tearing as he unfolded it, impatiently scanning the spidery lines.

His jeer froze, face chalk-white. Sweet Christ, no! It couldn't be— The letter fell from his hands, the sound of his grandfather's hellish laughter echoing in his ears.

Childish peals of merriment bubbled through the room as Meaghan brushed a quick kiss across Rory's rosy cheek, dodging his outstretched arms as he whirled around. She reached out a hand to steady him as he almost toppled over, giggling as the three-year-old stuck one finger beneath the edge of the dress sash covering his eyes, and peeked beneath it.

"No, no, Rory! You have to leave the blindfold *on!*" she warned, but the little boy was already flinging himself into her arms, collapsing them both into a squealing laughing heap.

"Wory got you! Wory got you, Meggie!" he crowed in delight, his eyes dancing as though a million stars had been scattered in their depths. He pulled the sash the rest of the way off, pushing it at her. "Your turn. You find Wory!"

"Oh, not again!" Meaghan cried in mock dismay. "You always get away! You're too quick for me!"

"Me won't run too fast." The worried pucker in the brow, dusted with fine, dark curls tugged at Meaghan's heart. She cupped the boy's cheeks in her hands, smoothing back the wild tangle that reminded her so hauntingly of other deep brown waves that could not be tamed.

"Oh, Rory!" she whispered, a catch in her voice. "Run as fast as you can! I love to chase you!" She slid her arms around his thin little body, hugging him tight, as love for this child who had crept terrified into her life seven weeks ago swelled inside her, mingling strangely with the aching pain of wanting Sean, of wondering . . .

How would she ever have borne these endless days without the little boy? His first wary sorties into the room, the slow blossoming of smiles, the fading of fears, his warm little hands reaching out to her—these were the only things that had kept her sane during weeks of desperately plotting how to save Sean, how to escape. And when all hopes had proved futile, the precious days of Radcliffe's absence slipping between her fingers, it had been Rory who had given her the will to go on with his love, with his innocence. And she had come to love him fiercely, as deeply as she loved her own unborn child.

Every day she had waited, pacing the confines of her silk-lined cell until she heard Mrs. Duggan unbolt the door by the bed, letting Rory slip inside before she locked it behind him. And every day, as the marks on his little body healed, something inside him had seemed to heal as well, changing the wide-eyed child who had slunk about the corners to an enchanting, teasing imp.

Only one thing had dulled the new light in his face, one subject Meaghan had never broached again after her first gentle probing—"Maman."

"Meggie, *your* turn!" The exasperation in the three year old's voice brought Meaghan back to the present as he stuck the sash in her hand and tried to fold her fingers around it. "You got to find Wory."

"And what would I want to find *you* for?" Meaghan asked tweaking his button nose until he grinned.

"'Cause you *love* Wory. Now *you haf to put the bind-old on!*"

Meaghan slipped the sash over her eyes to hide the glisten of tears that rimmed her lashes. "I do love you, Rory," she said.

But the child didn't even hear her. He was already bouncing about, clambering over the furniture. "You can't get me, Meggie! You can't find me 'hind the bed!"

He howled as she pretended to search for him inside the pillowcases, tugging at her skirts, dodging in and out on short legs to plant wet kisses on her nose and chin, and the ache in her heart became an almost physical pain.

She felt a little hand snatch at one of the combs that bound up her hair, and the chignon at the nape of her neck loosened and fell free.

"Roarke, when I catch you—" The sound of a door being opened cut short Meaghan's teasing threat. "Mrs. Duggan, just look what this scamp has done! Catch him quick so I can— Rory?" She called the child's name, tentatively sensing, even blindfolded, the tension in the boy, the unsettling silence as her fingertips brushed something just in front of her. Silk.

An almost physical evil emanating from the cloth seemed to coil around her hand. Meaghan jerked her fingers back, yanking the sash from her tumbled curls, a rise of panic choking her. But as the length of satin fell away, it was not the dreaded face of Radcliffe she saw.

Instead, framed in the open doorway stood the most icily beautiful woman she had ever seen. Exquisitely molded lips were curled in disdain beneath eyes the color of frost-struck violets, and raven-black hair fell in luxuriant ringlets about a proud, slender neck. Yet in that too-perfect face lurked the poison of a jewel-colored serpent, scented with the essence of roses.

Meaghan whisked the web of curls back from her cheeks, an eerie sensation of familiarity prickling the back of her neck.

"M . . . Maman . . ." Meaghan barely caught Rory's whisper from the corner where he now stood, rigid with fear. Without sparing him so much as a glance, the woman flicked the skirt ruffle Meaghan had disturbed back into place, the rich purple gown accenting slender, gem-laden hands. Hands so deceptively flawless and delicate they might have adorned a madonna . . . Hands so cruel they could batter a child . . .

Meaghan reached out to Rory, his terrified pallor confirming her suspicions as he crept warily up behind her. She rested her hand on his head. "I . . . You . . . you must be Rory's mother."

"And you are Sean's new whore."

The venom in the woman's tone struck Meaghan like a fist.

"Sean—" she echoed, stunned at the hatred with which the violet eyes weighed her, scorned her. "You . . . you know of Sean O'Fallon?"

The woman gave a low, sensual chuckle, deep in her throat. "Oh, to be sure—the way that he kisses, the feel of his hands, that delicious scar that arches down his left side—" She stopped, the words trailing off as though swept from her tongue by the memory, her fingers tracing down the line of her neck. "Oh, yes. I know Sean O'Fallon in ways that a dull-witted urchin like you never could. Never will. Because I swear to you," she hissed, eyes narrowing to malevolent slits, "I'll see him dead before I let you take what's mine."

"Yours!" Meaghan's stomach knotted as she felt her own lips pressed to the thin white line running down Sean's ribs, heard the hungering growl that had rumbled in his chest as he had rolled her beneath him. Never had he hidden from her the fact that there had been women in his past, many women, none of whom had touched his heart, and now this woman was threatening to kill him . . .

"I . . . I don't know who you are, or what you are to Sean, but he asked *me* to marry him! Told me there has never been anyone . . . anyone except Ala—"

It was as if the floor beneath her had suddenly vanished, hurling her through a maze of images—the bedroom at Cottage Gael the day of baby Sean's christening, still as though death itself had crept over it; the wedding dress she had found tearing beneath Sean's rage-driven hands; the torment that had changed him from lover to stranger; Grace's warnings . . . evil—roses . . . essence of roses . . .

"No! You can't be . . ." she gasped, her fingers clenching on Rory's shoulder. "She . . . Alanna is dead!"

A full-throated laugh, cruel and cold, rippled from the scarlet lips. "Dead? No, alive— Alive to watch Sean writhe in his guilt."

"But why? How could you—"

"Easily! As easily as I'll watch him hang. He could have had everything—wealth, power, me—the finest drawing rooms in London, even though his mother was some Irish slut. But no! He chose to throw his life away on peasant filth like you— So when Colin offered me more—"

"God damn you!" Meaghan flared, fighting the tears that rose to choke her at the thought of Sean's agony the night he first told her of Alanna. "He's wasted three years grieving, blaming himself— For God's sake, he *loved* you!"

"Yes, *loved* me!" Alanna hissed. "Like he'll never love you! Because I won't let him— I've always stood between you—"

"He asked me to be his wife!"

"Wife!" Alanna snorted, her gaze flickering from Meaghan's expanding waistline to Rory. "More like his broodmare. Nothing but a body for his rutting—to grow fat-bellied and haggard bearing the screaming, whining brats he wants year after year. As if one time wasn't enough!"

"One?" The warmth of Rory's little body beneath her hand seemed to shoot up Meaghan's arm, the sudden certainty twisting like a dagger in her breast as she looked down into the child's haunted, terrified eyes—cerulean eyes, so clear, so deep—eyes she had drowned in in the face of a man. "Rory..." she breathed. "Rory is—"

"Sean O'Fallon's son."

"That bastard's son!" The shriek of rage from outside the open door made Meaghan jump, Rory burying his face in her skirts, as a blur of travel-stained frock coat and rumpled trousers burst into the room. The savagery in the mottled, beard-roughened features struck terror to the core of her as Colin Radcliffe spun Alanna around, the self-satisfied look swiped from her beautiful countenance, changed now to raw, primal fear.

"You bitch!" he screamed into her death-pale face, crushing her pathetic struggles. "You lying whoring bitch! You made me believe that brat was mine, *my son,* when all the while you knew I was harboring O'Fallon's whelp!" In a vicious arc, Radcliffe slammed his fist into her cheek, sending the beautiful woman crashing into the mantel. Meaghan heard a sickening crack as Alanna struck the marble mantelpiece, blood welling from the corner of her mouth as she scrambled to her feet, dodging for the open door.

Radcliffe grabbed for her as she fled the room, the purple flounce of her dress barely brushing past his fingers, her escape fueling his insane fury as he wheeled on Meaghan.

Her blood froze as she saw the murder in Radcliffe's eyes, felt Rory's arms lock around her. "Lying whore made a fool of me, but no more...no more..." he snarled, hands curling with deadly intent.

Meaghan tried to sweep Rory into her arms, to get him to safety, but he clung so tightly to her legs she couldn't get free.

"No...Please..." But it was like pleading with Satan. Radcliffe's eyes dropped to Meaghan's waist, the bulge of her pregnancy outlined in stark relief as Rory pinned her skirts around her legs.

"Another of O'Fallon's bastards! That one will die before it takes a breath!"

With Radcliffe's first move toward her, Meaghan yanked desperately on Rory's little wrists, breaking his hold, swooping him awkwardly into her arms as she evaded Radcliffe's lunge. She bolted for the door, knowing that encumbered by the child she would never reach it, knowing, too, that regardless of the consequences to herself or her own baby she could not leave Rory.

A tearing pain shot through her head, as Radcliffe caught a handful of her flowing hair, yanking savagely. Meaghan careened to the floor, still clinging to the boy, seeing a flash of the door adjoining the nursery opening and Mrs. Duggan's terrified face.

At that instant Radcliffe dove for Meaghan. Desperately she kicked upward, driving the heel of her slipper into his groin with all the force she could muster.

Radcliffe's face crumpled with pain as he doubled over, clutching himself, screaming threats and curses. Meaghan grabbed Rory, hurling him toward Mrs. Duggan.

"Get him out of here! Get him out—"

"Meggie! Meggie!" She heard Rory screech, kicking and flailing in Mrs. Duggan's arms, then the slam of the door, the scrape of the bolt as Radcliffe raised his head. Death. Meaghan saw it in the brutal twist of his mouth, the blaze of his eyes. She struggled to her feet, pulling herself up with the carved bedpost, one arm cradled protectively around her stomach as she fought to breathe.

She tried to leap aside as Radcliffe grabbed for her, but his hand knotted in the daffodil-colored satin of her gown, yanking her against him.

"Stupid wench!" Radcliffe jeered. "Do you think that fat old woman can lock me out? Keep that brat safe?"

His fingers closed on the material at the base of Meaghan's throat. "You can be sure I'll kill both of O'Fallon's whelps even if I have to rip the one out of your belly. But first . . . first . . . I wouldn't want the chill of death on your body when I sample what I've waited for for so long."

He threw her back onto the feather mattress, still rumpled from her frolic with Rory, then bore his weight down on top of her, grinding his mouth onto hers. Meaghan felt his frame seeming to crush her stomach, his hips, though still sheathed by his trousers, thrusting against her. The babe in her womb kicked and turned. Meaghan struck at Radcliffe's face, clawing and biting as his hand shoved up her skirts, his teeth closing painfully on her now-bared shoulders.

"So you have fangs, little hell-cat. Use them. Use them while you can..." His fingers clenched in the firm flesh of her inner thigh, digging until she cried out. With a malevolent laugh he fumbled for the buttons on his trousers.

"Yer lordship! Yer lordship!"

Cursing savagely, Radcliffe broke away, wrathfully turning to face the source of the blubbering wail. Meaghan rolled from beneath him, catching the edges of her gown together with shaking fingers as the battered form of Murdsty staggered into the room. Horrible purple welts slashed his face, one beady eye was swollen shut in its pocket of flesh, and his lips were torn, bleeding.

"Murdsty, what the hell—"

The fetid stench of stale whiskey and sweat assailed her; she could see smears of filth on the man's slack skin as he cowered near the door. "It wa'nt my fault!" Murdsty whined, clutching the rim of a table for support. "I swear it wa'nt. The chains must'a broke loose! 'E could scarcely walk, but 'e came at me like the devil hisself, bashin' me— Made me tell 'im... made me tell him where *she* was—"

"Who? What?"

"O'Fallon!"

Meaghan felt a surge of joy shoot through her at Murdsty's cry as the slobbering man buried his face in his dirt-streaked sleeve, blubbering. "Christ, I thought 'e'd kill me!"

Sean—alive! Meaghan's heart screamed. *Free! Wherever they had kept him, however they had tortured—*

"You let O'Fallon get away!" Radcliffe bellowed, his hands closing on Murdsty's throat. "You drunken ass, I'll—"

"No! Ye don't understand," Murdsty choked, his face mottling blue as he clawed at Radcliffe's fingers. "He's comin' fer *her*. O'Fallon's comin' here!"

Meaghan felt a lump of dread knot in her throat. No, Sean couldn't—

"Here—" Radcliffe repeated, his grip loosening enough to allow Murdsty's rasping breaths to reach his lungs. "No... no, he wouldn't leave her... Not the great and noble Sean O'Fallon."

With a brutal shove Radcliffe smashed Murdsty into the doorjamb, the stygian black of his eyes soulless as the angels of hell.

"Raise the alarm then, you incompetent fool! I want every man on this estate armed and waiting when O'Fallon comes to claim his slut." Meaghan shuddered at the blood-lust contorting Radcliffe's face. His smile was hideous. Triumphant. "I want to see that bastard dead, Murdsty. Here. Tonight." Meaghan's stomach churned as he yanked a huge diamond ring from his hand, thrusting it into the man's bruised face. "This will go to the man who brings me O'Fallon's corpse," he snarled. "This ring and a night with Sean O'Fallon's whore."

Twenty-Five

Meaghan . . . he had to get to Meaghan . . . the single thought pounded in Sean's pain-fogged brain like a hellish litany as he staggered down the deserted hall, blood dripping from his iron-savaged wrists. He wiped them again on the tattered remains of his filthy breeches, leaning against a mahogany wall panel as he tried to stave off the waves of blackness that threatened to sweep over him.

God, how long had it been? A month? Two? Of trying to lap like an animal what little rancid food Murdsty shoved in his face, of no light, no hope, Murdsty's vile allusions of what was being done to Meaghan the only mark of passing time. Time he had spent, hour after torturous hour, clutching the links of chain above his shackles, working the loosening bolts back and forth in the stone. Each slight, grinding rasp as he had pushed the chains to their limit had sliced the torn skin that ringed his wrists beneath the heavy iron circlets, each shift of his muscles grating his half-healed back against the gritty wall.

But in every shard of agony that spiraled up his nerves had been the image of Meaghan's face as he'd last seen her, an angel's face, loving him, offering herself up to Radcliffe like a sacrifice at the devil's altar. And in all the dreams that had tormented him, when the pain had won and his mind lay shrouded in hazy orange-tinted half-worlds, he had heard the wounded echo of her words— I love you.

Sean's jaw clenched at the memory that had clawed for weeks in his chest. Damn it, she'd be all right . . . she had to be. But how could any woman survive the hideously perverted torments

Murdsty had taken such pleasure in recounting...and cling to her sanity.

Sean levered himself away from the wall with arms so weak they quivered, doggedly forcing himself down the corridor. A single oil lamp burned on a stand beneath the portrait of a young, handsome man, his too-tender mouth and wide-set eyes staring out at the world with dreamy idealism, oblivious to the wretched peasants crawling through the dirt beneath his nose.

His detached expression made Sean want to slap the lean, clean-shaven cheek above the immaculately tied cravat, to rip the canvas from its frame and shove it in some rotting mud hovel where half the family lay dead.

He shook his head, trying to clear it. God, it was *he* who was going mad—mad with fear of what he would find when he reached Meaghan, with the fear that he would never find her at all in this maze of darkened corridors and alcoves.

He stumbled, thumping against a tightly closed door, cursing as the fang of a vixen carved upon the panel bit into his wrist, his blood trickling warm, wet rivulets down his arm. He clutched at it with his other hand, the sweat and dirt coating his palm making the raw flesh burn.

Sean's eyes stung, his vision blurring. Damn, where could it be, the hunting scene Murdsty had said was worked in the wall beside the room where Meaghan was being held? Was it possible the drunken pig had had the wits or courage to lie as the links of chain had bit deep into his neck? No. Murdsty had cowered, whined, begging for mercy; the lout would have killed his own mother had Sean asked it of him. Meaghan was here, somewhere close, if he could only find her...

A sudden sound penetrated his mind. Heels. They clacked on the glistening marble of the floor, closer, closer, seeming almost to be fleeing...

Sean tried the knob of the door he was leaning against, a rush of relief washing over him as it turned in his hand, but just as he was slipping into the sanctuary of the room he saw it. Blood. A smear of dark, sticky red staining the shiny wood of the door. God, they'd see it...but it was too late. He dodged behind the door, easing it closed as he heard the approaching steps round the corner.

His rasping breath seemed to crackle through the silence like gunfire, waves of dizziness threatening to drive him to his knees.

The room he had entered blazed with light, its piercing silver glow dripping from gilt-striped wallpaper, a dozen discarded gowns, a dressing table groaning under enough jewelry and trinkets to feed the starving of Glendalough for a year. But whichever of Colin Radcliffe's pampered wenches lived in this squalid luxury, she was nowhere to be seen.

Scanning the armoires and tabletops, Sean spied a heavy candelabra, scooping it up in tightly clenched fingers as the rise and fall of voices drifted through the crack in the door.

"God's wounds, Denny, ye'd think that poor bastard had the Queen's army behind him, the way his lordship's driving us," a gruff voice complained. "A dozen men standing guard outside the wench's room, twenty more combing the grounds. Near's I've heard this O'Fallon ain't nothing but a skeligan with a little skin throwed over."

"A skeligan wi' enough strength to break chains as had held fer two hundred years and leave a man the size of Murdsty layin' in the dirt trussed up like a Christmas goose. If that kitchen boy hadn't a run down wi' the extra bottle o' whiskey Murdsty'd ordered, I vow the drunken sot'd'a still been tryin' to worm his way up the stairs on his belly."

"Mayhap he'd a wore off a little of the fat there," the deep voice chuckled.

"Well, whoever finds O'Fallon'll be wearin' out more 'an just 'is belly. Owen says the master's got a ring the size of a lumper 'e's givin' to whoever brings 'im the bastard, and 'e's throwin' in a night wi' the wench fer good measure."

"Ye mean the one as was out in the stable that night?" Sean's fingers clenched, his knuckles whitening at the raucous laughter as the other man went on. "Glory, and wouldn't I like a tumble wi' her. That wench had enough fight in her to make a man pure ache fer a piece of it."

"Bah! Can't get myself excited no way o'er a woman wi' her belly sticken' out wi' another man's babe. An' Radcliffe's already got that red-haired witch o' O'Fallon's bulgin' out right ripe. Now that other wench o' his lordship's—"

Sean heard no more of their words, only a roaring in his head that made his stomach heave. Sharp edges molded into the candelabra's silver base bit deep into his palm, his mind screaming denial at the image that branded itself in his brain. Meaghan, *his* Meaghan, raped, screaming, her stomach swelling grotesquely as if some hideous gargoyle had been shoved inside. Shoved inside as a permanent reminder of hatred and ugliness, like he had been forced inside his own mother's womb over thirty years before. "No . . ." Sean's face contorted with inner agony more savage than any he had ever known, a huge invisible fist seeming to crush his throat. "Not Meg . . . God, not . . ."

But the wild-wind beauty of her face pierced through his very soul, twisting in a hundred montages of hideous violence, roiling there, along with the gentle, dark-haired innocence of his mother.

Despair gnawed at the edges of Meaghan's sanity, shredding even the slightest ray of hope she had buried in her breast as she paced her dusk-shrouded room—knowing nothing, hearing nothing but the tic-tic-tic of Radcliffe's nails upon the tabletop, where he had at last tired of his tauntings, the scornful jests of the men stationed outside her door waiting there for Sean. Burly, pistol-bearing men with blood-hunger in their eyes . . . and lust.

She shuddered, averting her eyes from Radcliffe's cruel, handsome face, remembering how he had yanked her out into the hall hours before, displaying her in front of the slavering pack like a choice haunch of beef. "I can guarantee a night with her is well worth hunting down a half-starved wretch like O'Fallon," he had told them. "Bring him to me—*dead*—and this will be yours." He had dangled the key to Meaghan's room on his finger.

The key . . . Meaghan stared at it, where it lay, now, at the edge of the table, inches from Radcliffe's drumming fingers. So close, so tempting . . . so hopeless. God, even if she could reach it, if she *could* get past Radcliffe, she would never get through the animals that milled outside the door. But if she didn't try . . .

Her body tensing, she glanced from the iron of the key to the door, gauging the time it would take her to reach the handle.

"Try it. I'm sure the wolves are . . . hungry." Her head snapped up at Radcliffe's mocking jeer, a hot flush of guilt and anger firing her cheeks.

"Ah, yes, your wolves. How would you dare to face Sean without them?" Meaghan started at the blue-black spark flaring in Radcliffe's hooded eyes, the muscle in his jaw tightening as though she had struck raw nerve.

God, what was she doing? Baiting him when he was already bare seconds away from a raging fury? Endangering both herself and the babe to fling words in his face? She spun around, her skirt catching on a sharp corner of the brass woodbox beside the hearth, half expecting Radcliffe to leap from his chair as she pulled the sun-yellow taffeta free, and took the few steps to the window at the end of the room. But she had scarcely reached the leaded glass pane when her attention was arrested by a figure stalking in the shadows below. The face turned up, moonlight skating a path across rugged cheekbones and wide shoulders.

Sean.

It was Sean . . . Her heart leapt into her throat, choking her with joy and terror. Dear God, he was all right—she had to warn him—

The sound of Radcliffe's chair rasping against the floor made her jump then wheel. "Why so pale, my pet?" he jeered. "Afraid you might see your high and mighty O'Fallon slinking away on his belly? Perhaps Sean-o decided a *soiled* woman wasn't worth risking his pure untainted hide for."

The words plunged into Meaghan's stomach like a sharp-toed boot, driving the joy from her body in a nauseating rush. Soiled . . . could it be that Sean was leaving her, sickened by the thought that she had gone with Radcliffe? She could almost hear the agony straining from his throat the night he had first told her of Alanna—told her he would rather have died than see his woman dirtied by Colin Radcliffe's touch.

Evil as Meaghan knew Alanna to be, Sean had loved her, and still he had driven the icy beauty from Cottage Gael the night he had found her in Radcliffe's bed. Meaghan fought back the tears that burned in her eyes. Sean didn't love *her* . . . but would he leave her . . .

"Ah, so the possibility of O'Fallon deserting you has crossed your mind." Radcliffe's voice snapped her back into the present as he paced slowly toward the third-story window, his black, ravening eyes fastening on the glass pane. "Perhaps you and I should keep watch for him cowering . . ."

"Sean cowering!" Meaghan flung the derisive laugh desperately, trying to draw his attention away from the yard below. "You're the one who is hiding from a single unarmed man behind a score of guards with more weapons among them than the Queen's first brigade!"

Her nails dug into her palms as Radcliffe slammed to a halt a split second before he reached the window. But she spun around, moving with a light mocking gait toward the cherry-wood table.

"Do be careful," she taunted. "Even now Sean might be scaling the walls with a cannon in his teeth."

Radcliffe lunged toward her, his face mottling with anger. Pain exploded in her skull as his fist connected with the side of her head, sending her reeling. Her hip caught the edge of the table, the oil lamp upon its polished surface teetering dangerously on its delicate base as she stumbled.

"Bitch! You peasant whore! I swear you'll not be laughing—"

Meaghan clutched at the bedpost, trying to gain her balance, but the roaring in her head suddenly seemed to burst, its waves reverberating through the entire room. She tried to clear her head, but the roaring shook the very walls, in a shattering, earsplitting explosion.

"What the hell!" Radcliffe's eyes bulged in his face as he ran to the window, and his curses mingled with the shouts of the men outside the door.

There was a loud banging on the wood panel. "Yer Grace! Yer Grace!" Radcliffe swooped up the key, jamming it into the lock and throwing the door open. The whites of Murdsty's eyes ringed opaque irises in their nests of loose flesh, and his mouth went slack with fear.

"Yer Grace, 'e musta got to the gunpowder. That bloody bastard's blowed off half the west wing!"

"Imbeciles!" Radcliffe screamed, livid. "If you had been doing your duty instead of lounging here like a bunch of fools O'Fallon would have a bullet in his brain by now! Get down there and find— Damn! The west wing! It's wood, and dry as tinder!"

"Fire!" Meaghan heard the cries echo through the hall, accompanied by the sound of coughing, choking, and running footsteps. A spindly youth sagged against the stag carving outside the room. "Yer Grace, the whole place is ablaze! We're tryin' to keep it from spreadin' but it's already nigh to the new part of the manor an'—"

"Shut up! Get down there, you fools!" Radcliffe shrilled. "O'Fallon can't have gotten far! Damn! If that fire singes so much as a slop pot in the Red Room I'll flay every one of you to the bone!"

The footsteps retreated, thundering now, as the lad was joined by the guards, seeming almost eager to face the inferno rather than stay and fall prey to their master's wrath.

Meaghan hugged the roundness of her stomach, thrills of hope and fear running down her spine. Sean . . . Where was he? God, what was he doing? She glanced up, suddenly aware that the last hint of slapping boot heels had faded, veiling the room in an eerie, heavy stillness.

A chill prickled Meaghan's arms as she met Radcliffe's gaze. His eyes darted away, flickering about the room as though searching for something he couldn't see, couldn't hear, an almost mystical fear lurking in the darkness beneath his brows.

"They . . . they'll soon have the sniveling bastard." Radcliffe leaned down, fingering the hilt of a jeweled dagger in his boot top. He pulled it out, turning the silvery blade on his palm. "He's half-dead now."

"Half-dead, Sean is more than a match for you. And you know it." Meaghan said the words quietly, no goading now in her tone as she gave Radcliffe a level stare.

"Bah! I all but starved him! Beat him . . . No man could survive treatment like that and—"

"Live to murder you?" Low, silky with hate, the voice crept across the back of Meaghan's neck in timbres that at once thrilled and terrified her. "Ah, Radcliffe, didn't anyone ever warn you that an animal is most dangerous when it's wounded."

Both she and Radcliffe spun to face the open door. There, outlined in the shifting flickers of light from the oil lamp stood a man, so changed, so savaged, that Meaghan cringed at the sight of him. Once crisp dark hair was plastered to his skull, dirt coating the bones of a visage stone hard, sharp-featured, as though the flesh beneath the prison-pale skin had been shaved away. Corded sinews stood out in ropes on his naked chest and arms, his teething gleaming in a slash of a mouth beneath eyes that glittered with tight-coiled violence.

"Sean!" she breathed as those storm-blue eyes raked her, locking an instant on the mound of her belly, cradled now in her hands.

"No!" The denial was torn from his throat, jagged edged and filled with an agony that pierced her to the core as he wheeled on Radcliffe. "You sonofabitch! I'll kill you! Kill you!"

He hurled himself at Radcliffe with a feral scream of rage, knocking the Englishman to the floor as he drove a fist into Radcliffe's white, pinched face. The jeweled dagger glittered in Radcliffe's hand, slashing wild arcs inches from Sean's throat, but Sean seemed not to notice at all, bearing down on him with a crazed fury that twisted Radcliffe's features in fear.

Fear . . . it wrapped thick fingers around Meaghan's lungs, crushing her as she stumbled out of their way. Radcliffe's blade sliced through the air again and again, desperation and raw terror making the Englishman more deadly than ever. The dagger point bit flesh, a thin scarlet line of blood shining in its wake across Sean's sweat-glistened collarbone. Sean faltered just an instant, and Meaghan could see his body shudder, his eyes close.

"Sean!" The scream clogged her throat. He shook his head, as if to clear it, cerulean eyes slitting open at her cry. His hand flashed out, catching Radcliffe's wrist just before the dagger plunged home. She could see Sean's fingers shaking where they clenched on Radcliffe, sweat beading in a clammy layer on his skin as the Englishman struggled to force the blade down.

Tired . . . dear God, Sean was tiring . . . she could see it in the taut lines of his face, the twist of his mouth. A dozen times she had watched Sean's lightening reflexes and powerful grace. His movements now were slower, almost clumsy. They ripped at something inside her.

She grabbed for Radcliffe's arm, trying with all her strength to pull it away. With a savage oath, Radcliffe slammed his elbow back. Sharp pain jabbed through her stomach, driving the breath from her body, but in that flashing instant, Sean rolled to the side, releasing his hold on Radcliffe's wrist as he dodged from beneath the blade.

Meaghan clutched at her stomach, seeing, in pain-frozen horror, the dagger point graze Sean's arm, driving through the thick Aubusson carpet to the flooring below. Sean struggled to his feet, the rage now on his face that of the hunted and cornered beast. His hand groped for the smooth marble of the fireplace, clutching onto an edge, and Meaghan could see him fighting for balance and consciousness, as Radcliffe yanked the dagger free.

With a demonic laugh, Radcliffe turned on Sean, all traces of his earlier fright gone. Black eyes looked down, the cruel mouth curving in a malevolent leer, before his gaze jumped back to Sean's face.

Sean leapt back, avoiding the blow as the dagger cut the air a whisper away from his belly, but his leg slammed into the heavy brass woodbox with a force that crashed against the marble hearth. Meaghan's heart stopped as she saw Sean falter, then smash down backward onto the sharp-carved box.

An animal cry tore from his throat as his back grated down the brass corner, his face waxing gray. His eyes rolled back in his head as he gulped for breath, hands grasping at nothing, struggling to catch hold as Radcliffe stalked toward him. Rubies glowed like congealed blood between Radcliffe's fingers, and blue lights shone along the silver-kissed blade.

"You're going to die, now, O'Fallon. Die . . ."

"No!" Meaghan screamed. Her eyes darted around, searching for something, some way to help Sean. Her fingers closed on the delicate base of the oil lamp, the flame leaping and writhing as she bolted toward Radcliffe. In an arc of living fire, she smashed the shimmering crystal base down on the Englishman's head. Glass shattered as Radcliffe wheeled.

Screams exploded through the room as one side of his face was washed in a blaze of orange, the once handsome features contorting in a hideous burning mask. Meaghan stared in horror as skin split and curled, oil and flame spilling down his neck, filling the room with the acrid stench of seared flesh. His hands clawed at his face, ripping it, as he threw himself toward the bed and writhed, smothering the flames in the coverlet.

She jumped back, biting her knuckle to keep from screaming as he rolled from the mattress, his head cracking into the floor a sword's breadth from where she stood. It lolled to the side, features still twisted in a frozen grimace of agony, his eye staring at her, unseeing from a socket nearly stripped of its lids.

Meaghan wavered, grasping the footboard, as the sight branded itself in her mind—his burnt fingers twitching, the slight stirring of his chest.

There were cries in the corridor outside, the sound of men approaching. "Meg!" She felt Sean's fingers grab her upper arm, shoving her toward the door, his body still quaking. "Out . . . have to get out . . ."

"No!" Meaghan jerked free, running to the small door by the bed, pounding on it.

"Meaghan! What the hell—have to—"

"I can't! Rory! Mrs. Duggan! Open the door! Open—" The door banged against the wall, the plump face revealed behind it almost swallowed by wide, frightened eyes. Meaghan grabbed Sean's arm, pulling him after her, slamming the door closed, shooting the bolt.

"Have to get Rory—" she gasped, catching up her skirts to

dash to the top of the staircase. "They'll kill him—"

"Was goin' to take the lad myself. Got him ready—fought me like a wolf cub—didn't want to leave ye."

They clambered up the stairs, bursting into a stark, white room.

"Meggie!" In a bundle of dark curls and tear-streaked cheeks, Rory hurtled himself into Meaghan's arms, sobbing.

She crushed him to her, kissing his forehead, tears stinging her own eyes. "Hush, little one, shh. It's all right."

"Meg! For God's sake we can't—"

"There's no time," Mrs. Duggan cut Sean off. "The place'll be crawlin' with men any minute. We'll have to—"

"Christ! 'Is Grace! They got to 'is Grace!" The cries from below made Sean stiffen and Mrs. Duggan pale. The sudden banging on the door at the foot of the staircase rooted Meaghan's feet to the floor. "Open the door up there! Open—"

"We'll have to get ye out the back way.", Mrs. Duggan whispered, prodding them toward the other exit. Sean hooked his arm around Meaghan's waist, but even the warm comfort of his body could not drive from her the hideous scene of death below.

"Quick now." The crash of splintering boards drowned out Mrs. Duggan's words as they slipped into the empty corridor, running down the seemingly endless hall. "There's a way nobody knows about . . ." she told them. "A door Master Rory found . . ."

"No! Rory no want to! Dark!" the child whimpered, burying his face in Meaghan's neck as Mrs. Duggan led them into a tiny room.

"Shh. It's all right," Meaghan choked out, hugging him tighter.

The latch clicking behind them seemed to echo through the room as Sean shut the door, his breath hissing between clenched teeth. He sagged against the panel. "If . . . if you can get us to a horse . . ."

"Aye. This'll lead us nigh down t' where 'is Grace's men tied their mounts." Mrs. Duggan slid aside a damask curtain, fumbling with something behind it. "Follow me," she ordered. "Careful now."

They stepped through the small opening in the wall onto stairs so narrow and uneven they threatened to pitch them all into the sea of blackness below. Dark and twisted as the devil's wiles, the passage wound downward. A mass of unseen cobwebs clung to faces and stone crumbled beneath feet. Tiny, unseen creatures scuttled out of the way, their claws scratching against the dark walls.

Meaghan's arms ached from holding Rory, the skin of her shoulder breaking beneath his gouging nails, his arms clutching her neck as she made her way after Mrs. Duggan's shadowy form. She fought the sense of rising hysteria that engulfed her from the image of Radcliffe's grimace of death, and the feeling of being buried alive in this dank, black tomb.

She could hear Sean stumble and curse, his warm hand at her back the only thing that kept panic at bay.

And then, just as the air seemed too heavy to draw one more breath, there was a scraping sound of wood being shoved aside. Skeletons of trees suddenly appeared before them. The bulky outlines of horses set against the shadows of outbuildings were just visible in the haze of smoke that had settled over the hillside.

Meaghan's body quivered with exhaustion and relief as they stepped into the night. Sean moved stealthily up to the line of horses, untying a chestnut's reins.

Meaghan turned to Mrs. Duggan. "How . . . how can I thank you? For . . . for helping us. For Rory?"

"Bah! It's little enough I've done, scared as I was o' his Grace. I'm sorry, colleen." Mrs. Duggan dug into her apron pocket, fishing out a heavy pouch and shoving it into Meaghan's hand. "Take this. Go t' Dublin an' ask at the docks for Paddy Duggan. *Paddy Duggan*. 'E'll be comin' in on a timber brig, th' *Sara Day*. Tell 'im Pegeen sent ye. Give 'im this." She pressed a small wooden cross into Meaghan's palm. "He'll get ye out o' Ireland, t' America, the provinces, somewhere yer man'll be safe."

Meaghan looked up to see Sean upon the chestnut's back, his hands held out to take the child. Distant shouts of discovery resounded down the passageway, closer, closer.

"I'll keep 'em here as long as I can," Mrs. Duggan said.

"Mrs. Duggan—"

"Nay, I'll be all right." The older woman's eyes misted and her hand trembled as she laid it on the little boy's head. "God-speed, Master Rory."

Meaghan handed the child to Sean. Then, because of her pregnancy, she clambered awkwardly up behind him, her arms linking tight around his waist. He wheeled the chestnut around, driving his heels into the animal's sides, setting it at a run toward the pastures beyond. Meaghan pressed her face against his shoulder, unable to contain the sobs of horror now racking her body.

"It's over," Sean said above the sound of the chestnut's hoof-beats. "Over."

But even as he said the words she could feel something inside him pull away from her; even in the darkness she could see Radcliffe's hands clawing at burnt skin. And she could see a black staring eye that would forever haunt her dreams.

A chill swept through her, as if those blackened fingers had crawled across her spine. God, would it ever *really* be over? She had attacked a peer of the realm, maybe killed him. Nowhere would she be safe from the Queen's justice. But it was not the Queen she feared most, not soldiers or prison. There was something far more dangerous and menacing. She dared a look back at the burning manor.

Scores of windows blazed alight beneath curling smoke, like demon eyes glowering into darkness. The older part of the mansion was all but destroyed, tongues of flame now licking at the newer stone. But Meaghan scarcely noticed the fire. She bit her lip, the eerie sensation of being watched and followed trickling through her. Yet nowhere could she hear the sound of horsemen thundering or see the eyes . . . Eyes . . .

Her gaze locked on a balcony far from the blaze. There, on the stone abutment stood a woman silhouetted in orange and gold, her depraved beauty untouched, an image from hell.

Though she could not make out the woman's features, Meaghan felt the evil promise there. She shivered, her arms tightening protectively around Rory and Sean, knowing that in that wicked, beautiful face lurked the power to destroy them all, fearing, even as the chestnut carried them away, that she had not seen the last of Alanna DuBois.

Twenty-Six

Soft rose ribbons of dawn unfurled across the tips of the hills, kissing them awake as gently as a mother caressing her baby's cheek. Meaghan leaned against the crude wall of the ancient cow byre Connor MacDonough had brought them to the night before, tugging the frayed but clean blanket more tightly around her shoulders, watching the day being born anew. It was as though there had never been blight, or fire, or death. As though Alanna DuBois had never stolen into Sean's life, taking his joy and his son, twisting her knife in his heart until there was nothing left . . .

Meaghan reached out, the breeze from the Wicklow Mountains trickling through her fingers, whispering promises of dancing and music, autumn swims in lakes, crystalline blue. But the wind would see a hundred dead today, carry with it tales of fever and hatred, while Radcliffe's men hunted for her and Sean with the savage purpose of a pack of hounds.

Yes, even the wind lied, in its untouched beauty—

She turned, looking back into the shelter where Rory lay curled in a warm little ball beneath one of Mary MacDonough's quilts. It had felt so right to hold him and comfort him, to croon her own da's lullabies as she soothed away the little boy's fears. And after he had fallen asleep she, too, had wanted comfort, the strength of Sean's arms around her, his lips on hers. Instead he had watched her with an odd wariness, his gaze flinching away whenever she caught the troubled blue depths upon her abdomen. And even when he had finally held her, his body had been stiff, as if somehow he was warring within himself . . .

She smoothed a hand over the mound in her tightly stretched

skin. How she had wanted to tell Sean she cherished the tiny son or daughter safe within her, to share with him the lusty kicks of the babe who already seemed impatient with its gentle, protected world. But though she tried to warm his aloofness, he had fended off any mention of the babe, as though it were almost too painful for him to speak. When he had slept she had felt tears of disappointment swell her throat.

No, he didn't want her, didn't want their babe. Only his sense of honor had forced him to come after her in Radbury Manor. The child she carried meant nothing to him but chains that bound him to her as certainly and unwillingly as the shackles that had eaten at his wrists. The last thing he had said to her the morning of the disastrous raid on Radcliffe's manor was that there would never be a wedding, that he would never love her.

The stain of Sean's bastardy had always festered inside him, a wound that would not heal. No matter how he felt about marriage and love, would he feel duty bound now to make her his wife? A sickly little laugh bubbled up in her throat. Sean's wife . . . God, had she truly thought she could live with him, knowing he didn't love her? Believing that it was enough?

And what if he knew that the woman he *did* love . . .

The mere thought of Alanna DuBois made her stomach churn. For three years Sean had suffered guilt, shut out love, and hated himself for Alanna's supposed death when all the while Alanna had been yanking at the strings of his emotions with the twisted amusement of a sadistic puppeteer.

Already it was almost impossible for Sean to reach out to anyone, to risk the pain of loving. If he ever found out the truth about Alanna and Rory it would destroy him.

Meaghan's fingers clenched on the blanket, digging into the wool. Or would it destroy *her* . . .

A splashing, gurgling noise from the stream that wound below drew her gaze to where Sean's lean, naked figure was just visible through the clumps of gorse and heather. He stood waist-deep in the water, his wide-spread fingers skimming over the glistening muscles of his chest as he scrubbed the filth from his body with slivers of lye soap. His dark hair shone, wet and clean in the nippy autumn breeze, but the sharp lines of his face showed despair.

Tears welled up in Meaghan's eyes. She could see the pain in him, the hurt. He didn't want her. She wouldn't saddle him with a wife and child he did not want. And the sooner they got things settled between them, the easier it would be for him to leave . . .

The blanket trailed on the ground behind her as she made her way to the edge of the stream. Sean was stretching, trying to reach the tender flesh of his back, but every time the scar tissue pulled, Meaghan could see him wince.

"Can . . . can I help you?" she asked softly.

Sean's head jerked up, a flush of red darkening his cheekbones. "No," he snapped, his eyes flickering away from her. "I can get it. I— Damn!" His breath hissed between clenched teeth as he stretched too quickly, a flash of pain crossing his face.

"You have to get that clean, Sean, and there's no way you can reach it." Though she tried to keep the hurt from showing in her words, she saw Sean's jaw tighten as she dropped the blanket to the ground. Tearing a ruffle from one of her petticoats for a rag, she tucked the rest of the muslin layers, along with her skirts, into the waistband of her dress.

"Don't be an idiot. It's blasted cold! If you get your clothes wet, you'll damn well get pneumonia. You—"

"Fine." Meaghan glared at him, ripping at the buttons down the front of her dress. "I won't get my clothes wet."

"Damn it, Meg, I didn't mean—"

She stripped off the layers until she was clad in only her chemise and pantalettes, barely aware of the thickening in Sean's voice as she picked up the piece of muslin she had torn off and waded into the water. "Believe me, you don't have to worry, Sean," she said, unable to keep the tiniest of quivers from her lips. "I promise I'll touch you as little as possible."

His eyes snapped up to hers. "Meg . . . I . . . "

She shook her head, dipping the rag into the water, drizzling the chilly wetness over the mass of scars on the back that had once been smooth and sleek. An angry red cut from his fall against the woodbox slashed across the weals. The tears she had been fighting welled to the surface as she touched the ruin of Sean's back with the tips of her fingers. She had not seen it this close before, felt it . . . A choked little sob rose in her throat.

He turned and cupped her chin in one warm palm, his eyes gentle. "It's not so bad. Doesn't hurt unless I bend too far."

"It's horrible! What they did to you—and I couldn't . . .

couldn't help . . . I tried to get out and find you, but they kept me locked in. It was so long . . . I was afraid you'd die . . . and they . . ."

"Shh." Sean's voice was a strangled whisper as he crushed her against him, his hand knotting in her hair, pressing her against his naked shoulder. "Don't . . . don't talk about it. They can't hurt you anymore."

"But they'll . . ."

"No, I'll take you to America, a new life. It doesn't matter what happened. What they did to you. I'll take care of you . . . the boy . . . the . . . the baby." He lifted her face to his, his lips skimming her cheeks, her eyelids, her mouth. "When I think of you with Radcliffe—" his voice broke. "God, Meg, what I wouldn't give if that baby was mine . . ."

"Y . . . yours . . ."

"I've been acting like a fool. It's just knowing that they raped you and I was so helpless . . . Meg, if I hadn't—"

She pressed her fingers to his lips, stopping his words. "Sean, he never touched me. I tricked him into thinking I was sick . . . had the fever. Then he went to England. He'd just gotten back when you escaped."

"But Murdsty said that they—"

"No. He was lying. I was going to tell you about the babe two months ago on our wedding night." A loving, joyous laugh bubbled from her throat as she watched his face suffuse with wonder. She took his hand and placed it gently on the rounded swell. "Sean, this is *your* babe. *Ours*. And no child was ever loved more."

"Mine?" His long fingers trembled. "Maggie, I . . . if it's Radcliffe's I'll still . . ."

"If it was Radcliffe's child I'd scarce be showing!" she said. "Grace knew that I was . . . with child when she fitted my dress. And the first time I felt life was just before you came in and told me she was—" her voice faltered. "Dead."

"You . . . you knew you were pregnant when I went riding out after Radcliffe? When you followed me?"

"I wanted to tell you, but you never gave me the chance . . ."

Sean's hand moved as the babe kicked, and his eyes jumped up to her face.

"All the things I said . . . did, and you were . . . God, Meg, oh, God!" He crushed her to him, his mouth fastening on hers, hot and wet, incredibly sweet, taking from her all doubt and fear. The heat of his body seared her through the thin wet layer clinging to her skin. His hands slid down her thickening waist, down the curve of her hips and her buttocks, nestling her full against his burgeoning hardness. His tongue stroked inside her mouth, taking it, loving it. "I thought . . . I was so afraid that . . . Meg . . ."

He cupped her breast, its milky ripeness filling his hand, spilling over as his mouth traced a path to the tie of her chemise. His teeth locked on it, tugged it free, and then he was kissing her, suckling her. Broken sentences came from his lips—profanity and prayer. He lifted her into his arms, not with the easy grace of months past, but gently, so gently.

Water ran off them in sparkling rivulets, dripping onto grasses, bedecking the emerald strands with watery diamonds as the two of them broke out of the stream. Sean laid her on the discarded blanket, sipping at the drops that glittered on her skin as he peeled away the damp muslin that veiled her from his eyes.

"Maggie, it's been so long . . . I don't want to hurt you . . ."

"It's all right. I want you so much. I thought we'd never . . ." And then her words were swallowed in his mouth, his kiss changing from tenderness to driving need. She tasted of his tongue, his passion. She buried her hands in his hair, releasing her hold on him only when he pulled away to take the deep-rose tip of her breast into his mouth with an almost savage sweetness.

One hand trailed to the soft nest of down between her thighs, and the feel of his touch there sent quivers of white-hot pleasure whirling through her body.

She felt his muscles shaking under her hands, his heart hammering. "Meg . . . you feel so good, so right . . . an angel after all this hell. Touch me. Oh, God, I need you to touch me!"

Her fingers slid down the hard ridges of his chest, down the flat plane of his belly to where the dark mat of curls narrowed, then widened. The backs of her knuckles skimmed velvet-smooth hardness. Her hand closed over him, stroking him, loving him.

With a low groan Sean shuddered, rolling her beneath him. "Can't wait . . ." And then he was inside her, the rhythm of his body as it thrust into hers mystical, spinning her through a thousand rose silk clouds that blossomed into dawn.

The gentle feathering of his breath against her hair brought Meaghan softly back to earth. He held her cradled tightly against him, and the edge of the blanket draped over them in a warm cocoon.

"Meaghan, you're so beautiful." His fingers whispered over her abdomen. He smoothed the blanket back, pressing his lips softly to the warm swell. "My babe . . . here . . ."

He sighed, a sated, peaceful sound, as he drew her again into his arms. "I wish we could stay hidden away like this forever. Like we're the only two people on earth."

A rustling in the brush made Sean sit bolt upright, his face battle-ready as he spun toward the sound. Meaghan caught his arm, throwing one of her petticoats over his naked hips.

"The only *three* people on earth," she giggled, sweeping the blanket in a band covering her breasts just as Rory burst upon them.

"Me woked up," he informed them, his cherub's face wreathed in a triumphant grin. He thrust one grubby fist out, opening his palm to display a shiny rock. "Pretty. Me found pretty for Meggie."

"It's beautiful," Meaghan said, taking the translucent stone and holding it up to let the sun filter through.

"You must've looked very hard to find it." The boy's brow puckered a little at the sound of Sean's voice. He eyed the big man warily.

"Meggie's."

"And I see you're hiding another rock from Meggie." The child flinched as Sean touched him, fingers flashing past his ear. But before Rory could even jump away, Sean opened his hand. There, upon Sean's broad palm lay a shiny pebble even prettier than the first.

Rory's blue eyes widened, his mouth a perfect O.

"Well," Sean prodded gently. "Aren't you going to give it to her?" Rory reached out half-afraid, taking the rock.

"He maked it come out of me!" Rory said in awe. Meaghan's laughter tinkled on the air.

"Sean's a man of many *hidden* talents." She let her gaze flicker brazenly from Sean's dancing eyes to the strip of bronze flesh covered by her petticoats.

"Go find some more pretties," Sean said, ruffling Rory's curls. "I'll show you another trick."

The boy bounded away, squealing with delight as he bobbed along the stream bank like a frolicsome pup. Meaghan arched her head back, letting her loosened hair sweep in a silky tangle across her bare back.

She felt Sean's hand slide under the heavy mass, tracing the delicate curves of her shoulder blades, the tiny bumps of her spine. He gave her a lazy smile.

"I guess we'd best be getting used to this, Mrs. O'Fallon. I have a feeling we'll be having quite a few little interruptions— what with my 'hidden talents' and all."

"Mmmm." Meaghan closed her eyes, reveling in the feel of his callused fingertips. He tilted her head toward him.

She opened her eyes to see him staring intently down at her. "This babe will be no bastard. We'll have Connor find a priest to marry us when he and Mary bring the hay cart to take us on to Dublin."

She nodded.

"And about the boy. . ."

Meaghan bit the inside of her lip, fingering frayed gray wool. "Rory?"

"You haven't told me anything about him, where he came from, how you befriended him when you were locked in that room. I've seen the marks on his legs and arms. I know he was mistreated. But he must belong to someone."

"B . . . belong?" The word stuck in Meaghan's throat. She looked to the little boy who was at the bend of the stream, chasing ripples in the water with his toes. Alanna didn't deserve him . . . had no right. And Sean . . . "He . . . I don't know who he belonged to. Just that he was untended, abused. He was so little . . . and they hurt him." She could hear the rising note of defensiveness in her own voice and hoped that the tremor of fear didn't draw his attention.

Sean's jaw hardened. "Probably some serving maid's poor bastard. He was lucky he found you." Sean turned back to her, smoothing back a wisp of hair from her forehead, kissing it into place. "Like I was." Meaghan felt a wrenching guilt and a melting need as Sean caught her gaze with the tender blue light of his. "I'll never let anything hurt either one of you again. And I'll love him, Meg. I promise you," he said, his eyes warming as they skimmed away to follow the scampering child. "As if he were my own son."

Twenty-Seven

"Rory, no! Look out!" Meaghan cried, trying to regain her hold on the dark-haired moppet's hand as he pulled from her grasp to dash across the crowded deck of the *Sara Day*. Vainly she tried to catch him as he bolted toward the ship's rail. He dodged in a flurry of little elbows and heels through a bevy of stern dowagers and between the legs of fierce-looking sailors bearing litters for the sick. But at the child's squeal of joy and the deep answering laugh, Meaghan gave a heartfelt sigh of relief, the crowd parting just long enough for her to see Rory throw his arms around a man's black pant leg and scale the tall figure as though he were a tree.

Sean. The child had scarcely seen Sean the last weeks they had pitched and rolled in the timber brig's belly. Fever, the final legacy from Ireland, had swept through the hunger-weak immigrants, leaving few families untouched. Sean had done what he could to alleviate the suffering, both of passengers and crew, until he had fallen into a berth at the other end of the hold, too exhausted to mumble so much as a word.

He had wanted to keep fever from them, hardly daring to come near her and Rory, but the sickness had been everywhere, breeding at the cookfires where they had warmed what little food they had, at the stagnant water barrels soured from old wine, in the berths where the healthy cowered, waiting for the chills to begin.

Meaghan saw Sean give a weary nod to the men taking the sick ashore. Then he lifted Rory into his arms and settled his little bottom on one broad shoulder as he pointed to the island floating like a fairy ring in the St. Lawrence River.

Grosse Isle. Haven. Hell. The launching point to new life in Canada, the first leg of the journey to steal across the American border, the end of a futile flight from death's sharp scythe. She had overheard the whispers of the seamen about the quarantine station, the fever sheds stuffed to overflowing, the tents thrown up to shield the sick from the rain. She had heard of those who helped the doctors abandoning their tasks to steal whatever the ill had of any worth, and of the few doctors and priests courageous enough to stay, often dying of fever themselves beside the poor wretches they were fighting to save.

Meaghan drew her shawl tightly around her against the chill October wind that stung her cheeks and looked at the pathetic souls around her. They had little money, only the thin rags upon their backs—no warm clothes to ward off the savage Canadian winter. Where would they go if they escaped death here? How would they live?

How would she and Sean have managed if Mary and Connor had not been able to slip a few things from Cottage Gael for them before Radcliffe's men closed in—a little coin and the few special treasures Meaghan had asked Mary to bring?

A tiny smile tipped the corners of her mouth as she remembered her gift to Sean after Father Loughlin had presided over their wedding vows. Sean had looked so solemn as he had made her his wife, slipping his mother's ring over her finger with a hand so warm, so strong, she felt safe and cherished. They had made magical love that night, and after the tumult came, she had gone to the bundle Mary had left and put into Sean's hand the small oval-framed portrait of his mother.

Only later did the guilt creep in again, lying like a stone in the pit of her stomach when Rory had run to snuggle in her arms after a nightmare, asking in a pitiful little voice if "Maman" was going to get him.

Meaghan cringed inwardly at the memory of how Sean had come groggily awake, cuddling the boy between them, mumbling soothing, nonsensical words of comfort.

She had lived in fear since then, waiting for Rory to inadvertently betray her lie, waiting for Sean to discover...

Meaghan shivered, her eyes flashing back to the figures beside the rail. No. Mrs. Duggan had said Rory had rarely seen Alanna. He was so little he'd forget her cruelty, and even her name. Yet the possibility of losing both Rory and Sean twisted inside Meaghan as she watched the man's dark head bend over the child's. She loved them. God how she loved them.

Through the danger-filled, nightmare-racked days while Radcliffe's men had hunted them in the wilds of the mountains, she had been terrified the Englishmen would somehow trace their flight to the *Sara Day* and discover their destination. But surely no one would trail them all the way to Canada, risking the perils of a winter voyage, not even to capture the woman who had attacked as important a man as Colin Radcliffe.

They would be safe in Montreal until spring, when they could lose themselves in the vast westlands of America. Then the Queen's justice could not reach them, nor the wicked poison of Alanna DuBois.

Unless Rory...

A shaft of dread shot through her as Sean's deep laughter ended abruptly, a strange look creasing his haggard face as he seemed to study the eyes so incredibly like his own.

Scooping up her skirts, she rushed across the deck, heedless of the coiled ropes, barrel stays, and trunks.

The toe of her shoe snagged the round wooden handle of an abandoned litter. She caught a flashing glimpse of Rory leaning to look down at the water, wobbling precariously on Sean's shoulder. She felt herself pitching forward, tumbling toward Sean's legs.

She tried to scream a warning, but it was too late. Her shoulder crashed into the breech-encased lengths with a force that drove them out from under Sean. There was a guttural cry, as Sean tried to keep hold of Rory, a splintering of wood.

Pain tore at her arm as her elbow cracked into the deck, but she stumbled up, trying to get to her feet. "Rory!" She cried the child's name desperately, hopelessly, her eyes catching the broken rail, certain he had fallen.

There was the sound of other passengers running toward them while Sean shouted, scrambling toward the rail. And then those sounds were broken by the lilt of childish giggles from a pile of sailcloth a few feet away. Meaghan whirled, as tousle-haired Rory poked his head up from the white mound.

She caught the child up, clutching him to her, sobbing in relief as his warm little body squirmed in her grasp. "Wory flied. Oww! Too tight!"

Sean's hand closed roughly on her as he pulled both her and Rory into his arms, his face deathly pale. "Meg, what in God's name were you thinking of, running across the deck like that? You almost knocked him into the river, not to mention hurting yourself! God, are you all right? The baby?" His fingers tangled in her hair, stroking, soothing her as sobs racked her body. "I'm sorry, love. Didn't mean to snap at you. I was just so scared . . ."

He murmured soft words into her ear, love words, but Meaghan barely heard them as she stared into the foaming gray water swirling against the hull far below. *What had she been thinking of?*

Running footsteps pounded up to them. "Doctor O'Fallon, yer lady safe? Yer boy?" Meaghan felt Sean's nod against her shoulder. "I told an' told the cap'n t' fix that rail. Child like that'd sink t' the bottom afore ye could cut butter an' the current —oh, sorry, ma'am, it's just . . . well, I hate doin' this t' the doc, now, ye upset an' all, but they be needin' him t' head ashore with the sick. Got so many t' carry it'll be nightfall afore we can tend t' 'em all."

"Tell Paddy I'll be there in a minute." Sean eased Meaghan over, setting her on the sailcloth, kneeling before her as he took her trembling fingers in his. "Maggie, I don't want to leave you now, but I have to go with them. I'll be back as soon as I can." She swallowed, then nodded, the tenderness in him cutting into her as he gently twisted her wedding ring around her knuckle. "You and Rory go with the others who are still healthy to the part of the island where we'll be staying until our quarantine time is over. I'll come the second everything at the fever sheds is settled . . ."

"The fever sheds! You can't—"

"Shh, don't worry. I've been dealing with typhus for weeks. A few more hours won't matter." He brushed her lips softly, his own warm with promise. But day passed and night fell, and though Meaghan lay awake long after the other immigrants slept, Sean did not come.

It was nearly a week later that the skinny, long-shanked boy put the note in her hand. She sank onto a stool, hastily scanning the bold scrawl.

Can't leave. Not enough doctors. Get off of this island the minute they clear you. Sean

Her fingers clenched on the scrap of paper as she looked up at the boy who was shifting uncomfortably from one foot to the other. "Is . . . is he sick?"

"Doc Sean?" The boy gave a snort of laughter. "Not hardly. But the lagabouts are a might sick o' him, I can tell ye! An' the other docs are nigh 'bout to kiss 'is feet. He's blastin' through the sheds like the devil's on 'is heels. Like to took my head off when 'e asked me t' bring this t' ye. Said I'm t' see ye on the next steamer out if I have t' nail ye t' the boiler."

"Oh he did?" Meaghan bolted to her feet, the thin leash of control she had held through days of frantic worry snapping at the unabashed male arrogance revealed in the scrawny boy's banter. "Well you can tell *Doc* Sean that he can go *straight to hell!*"

The boy's eyes widened as though a baby rabbit had suddenly sprouted talons and flown in his face. He took a step back. "I . . . a . . ."

Meaghan's hands balled into fists. "You tell your wonderful doctor that for three days I've had him dead and buried, or at the very least delirious with fever. I've agonized every minute whether to leave our little boy and risk infecting myself and the baby to find him, and now he dares send you to—"

"Meggie?" At the soft, pleading fear in Rory's voice, Meaghan bit her lower lip, trying desperately to keep her temper in check.

"It's all right, Rory." She took the child's hand and turned back to the gaping lad. "As long as you'll have his attention, you can tell my husband something else for me," she said between gritted teeth. "I'm not stirring a step from this island until he talks to me himself, and furthermore there aren't enough nails in this whole blasted country to hold me on his bloody steamer!"

Flinging the last words like a gauntlet, she strode away with her chin held high.

But brave words did little to shelter Rory as the nights waxed colder. And as those who had been healthy grew weaker—banished to the fever sheds—Meaghan's resolve began to crumble.

When the gray hulk of the steamer rounded the island fifteen days after the passengers of the *Sara Day* had first set foot on Grosse Isle, she regarded it with the belligerence of a child facing a spoonful of castor oil. Bundling together blankets and clothes, she had slammed them into the trunk with the rest of their belongings, banging the lid shut with a resounding crack before two kindly immigrant men had carried it up to the deck. Then she had lowered herself onto a battered wood bench on the shore, wanting both to rage and cry as the queue of ragged scarecrows started to wend its way aboard.

"Meggie . . ." She felt Rory tug on her shawl, and looked into his woeful eyes. "Me can't leave Da. Wory wants him."

"I know you want him, moppet." Meaghan drew the boy close, her words seeming to ball in a lump in her throat. "I . . . I want him too, but he can't come with us now. He has to take care of the people who are sick."

"Like Lucy?"

The lump grew as Meaghan thought of the little red-haired imp who had been Rory's playmate on the voyage. She could almost see the child huddled on a lumpy pallet in the belly of the ship, her slight body tossing in the throes of fever. "Yes, like Lucy."

"Will Da come get Wory when Lucy's better?"

"When all the sick people are better. By then you and I will have picked out a new home for us to stay in in Montreal until we can go the rest of the way to America. Just think how much fun it will be to surprise Da."

"You said me could 'prise him with my letters." Rory's lower lip quivered. "Me knows A B T's. An' 'CAT' but he never comed."

"I know, darlin'. But maybe on the steamer you can learn some more words to show him. Tell me, what would you like to . . ." Meaghan's voice trailed off, all thoughts fleeing as she stared at the achingly familiar form of Sean striding from the direction of the fever sheds at a measured, angry pace. The autumn sun picked out gold strands in the mahogany waves of his overly long hair and limned the taut planes of his face in its light.

"Da! Da!"

She clambered awkwardly to her feet. Happiness at the sight of Sean surged through her as Rory ran to meet him, but one look at the ominous set of his features after he sent the boy scampering toward the shore dashed her joy.

"So you *are* going." The bite in his voice jabbed at her pride as he shot her a disgusted glare. "You told Rob you wouldn't leave until you saw me personally. Well, here I am, at your command, while God knows how many suffer for want of a doctor."

"Ah, yes, and *God knows* how many of them will survive without *you!*" Meaghan felt as if a tub of ice water had been dumped over her. Even seeing he was tired and frazzled, she struggled through the pain to blaze back at him. "Of course, Rory and I, we have to learn to live without you, don't we? To board this steamer and sail to a strange city in a new country where we don't know anyone? That's just expected."

"Expected!" Sean barked. "Hah! I don't know what the hell to expect from you! What do you want, Meg? Do you want me to leave children riddled with fever lying in their own filth? Dying? Damn, we can't even keep enough people healthy to dig their graves." He slammed his fist into the trunk of a small tree, not even glancing at the blood on his torn knuckles.

"I know . . . I mean you can't—"

"You don't know! You haven't seen them, heard them crying for water when there are a hundred others to get the dipper before them. Watched husbands searching for wives that have been dead for days, mothers dumping children in the dirt outside the door, running away as the little ones scream for them."

For the first time the meaning of his words pierced through her anger, her own insults sounding shallow, childish as he raked his hand through his hair.

"Damn it, Meg, I can't just leave them! I couldn't live with myself!"

"No. But what are Rory and I supposed to do if you don't live at all?" She heard the quiver in her voice, saw Sean's eyes leap to meet hers.

"I—"

"Ma'am?" One of the men who had loaded her trunk onto the steamer shuffled forward sheepishly. "They're about to cast off. If you're coming . . ." She looked over her shoulder to where only a smattering of departing immigrants still stood ashore, jostling up toward the broad open deck, Rory's small head bobbing near them.

The boy ran over to Sean, stretching out his arms to be tossed in the air, but Sean only clutched the child to his chest in an almost desperate hug before heading him off toward the others.

Then Sean turned, his warm hand brushing Meaghan's chin, tipping it up. "Maggie, I'm not going to die."

She nodded, her throat too tight to speak.

"Send word where you're staying. I'll come as soon as I'm able. Before the babe is born, I promise. And the money Connor brought us, and Mrs. Duggan . . . use whatever you need."

"We'll be fine." She knew that tears shone in her eyes, couldn't stop them. "Be careful, Sean. I . . ." She looked down. "I love you."

She felt his fingers tighten on her chin, heard him start to say something, then stop.

"I know." There was gentleness, a reverence, in his voice, and sorrow as he bent to kiss her. "Good-bye, Meg."

She boarded the steamer, then watched him stride toward the distant sheds as the ship's boilers fired up, and she felt the first sluggish lurch of the steamer that was to carry Rory and herself away.

It was only much later that she was haunted by the memory of his touch, his kiss, the almost final sadness in his soft 'goodbye.'

Twenty-Eight

Meaghan sank shakily onto the lid of her trunk, feeling as though she, too, had been dumped and abandoned in the midst of Montreal's teeming waterfront. Six days of braving the driving wind on the open deck of the steamer had left her deadened with cold and listless, her stiff muscles aching whenever she tried to shift the now uncomfortable bulk of her pregnancy.

And as if he also felt Sean's desertion, Rory had spent the trip clinging to her skirts, the miserable voyage over the choppy waters giving him his first case of seasickness. She looked down at the shivering little body huddled so forlornly against her side, and fought the urge to cry.

Much good it would do anyway, she berated herself. No one would so much as glance at one more bedraggled wretch. The docks were full of crying women, hurling themselves into the arms of husbands, lovers, and sons who had sent for them, sobbing over those lost on the voyage. Gaily dressed sailors' wives flitted about like summer's last butterflies welcoming home their men.

In the hour since the immigrants had been put ashore, awaiting transport to Point St. Charles, the stopping-off place from which they were to be dispersed through inner Canada, Meaghan had tried to ask someone for guidance. She wondered where to go, what steps she should take to be allowed to remain in the city. But the coquettish maidens and surly seafarers who had spoken in English ignored her, and the others, with their lilting tones of French, had stood waving their arms in accompaniment to instructions she could not understand. If she and Rory were forced to leave Montreal with the others, how would Sean ever find them?

She choked back the tears of frustration and exhaustion, staring out at the sullen, fog-hazed slope of Mount Royal that fell in a gray-green backdrop behind the quaint city. Sean and his damned notions of honor! She didn't care about the people on Grosse Isle or about anything but getting Rory warm and dry, eating food more than half-cooked, and having this baby that pressed up against her lungs until she could hardly draw a breath.

Sean should be there, carrying the trunk and taking care of Rory and of *her*, damn it!

"Damn *him!*" She said the words aloud, taking absurd pleasure in the odd looks the people passing by gave her. But the satisfaction was short-lived as the first drop of slushlike rain struck her cheek.

Rory whimpered, muffling his face in her breast. "Cold."

She cuddled him closer, torn between seeking some kind of shelter and staying with the trunk that now constituted everything they owned in the world. Perhaps if she offered someone money to help them, made them understand that she could pay, they would be allowed to find a room on the island . . .

Slipping Mrs. Duggan's pouch of money from her pocket, Meaghan pulled some of the crumpled pound notes out into her hand. The sudden almost feral gleam in the eyes of those around her made her quail inwardly and wrap her fingers over the currency.

"Rachel?" The feel of a hand on her shoulder made Meaghan start, turning to face a woman who stood behind her. At her movement, the woman jerked her hand back into the folds of her somber cape, her other fingers fluttering to a hank of brassy-gold hair straying from beneath a prim bonnet. "I . . . I'm sorry. I thought you were my cousin," she murmured apologetically, wetting cherry-red lips. "We've been waiting so long. She should've been here long since."

"It's all right. I . . . I don't know how anyone can find anything here." Meaghan forced a little smile as she looked into the keen hazel eyes so at odds with the woman's face, pretty but mildly garish like an overblown rose. A slight bluish shadow darkened one side of her rice-powdered cheek.

"Is someone supposed to be meeting you? Your husband?"

"My . . . my husband is a doctor. He stayed behind at Grosse

Isle and sent me to find us a place to live, but they say they're going to send us on to the mainland and if they do I don't know how he'll find us before the babe . . ."

Meaghan curved one hand protectively over the mound of her stomach as she felt the woman's gaze fix on its swell. The eyes now raised to Meaghan's were almost stricken as the woman spun away in a swirl of plum-shaded cloak and started off into the crowd.

"Ria! Ria, love!" A dapper little man rushed up to stay her, clasping the woman's hand in a grip that even to Meaghan seemed strangely tight. "You mustn't run off like that! I've been beside myself with worry! Heaven only knows what could happen to you here!"

"I was looking for Rachel. She's not here. I want to go home, now." Meaghan sensed the subtle emphasis on the last word as the woman tried to pull away again.

"Of course you do. And I'll take you there. But you haven't introduced me to—"

"She's *not* Rachel."

"But, cherie, then we'd best enquire who she is. After all, we can hardly leave a woman who is *enceinte* here on the waterfront alone. Perhaps we could be of service." He gave a little bow to Meaghan, raising his top hat from his balding pate. "Allow me to introduce myself. Osgood Parsons, Esquire, and my lovely wife, Ria."

"Meaghan and Roarke O'Fallon."

"Roarke. A fine boy." Rory flinched away as the man poked out a hand to pat his head. Parson's smile turned brittle.

"He's not used to strangers, and we're both so tired," Meaghan said. "If we could just find someone . . ."

"Say no more. I overheard your predicament as I was approaching." Mr. Parsons eased a solicitous hand under her elbow and helped her to stand. "Fortunately for you, I do wield a certain amount of influence here on the waterfront. If you've no objections, Ria and I would be happy to aid you."

"Osgood, I don't think—"

"Now, now, dear." Parsons shot the woman a quelling glance, rubbing his knuckles across his jaw. "Obviously this poor woman has no one else to help her. We can hardly allow her to be shipped off God knows where, before her husband returns. We'll take her to the establishment we are residing in, and if Mrs.

O'Fallon, here, can't afford the room, I can certainly supplement..."

"No," Meaghan objected, uncomfortable at Ria Parsons's reluctance. "Rory and I can pay our own way. We...we don't want to impose..."

"Impose? Don't be ridiculous!"

"If I could just draft a note to my husband and send it back on the steamer to let him know we're all right..."

"Let it wait until tomorrow. By then we'll have you settled in somewhere, and I'll bring the note down for you. I'm certain your husband will be most relieved to know that you are safe."

"Mr. Parsons, I..." Meaghan started to protest, but Parsons waved it away, motioning two roustabouts to carry her trunk. A tiny thread of unease curled through her as the men hefted the burden, the smiles in their bestial faces reminding her strangely of wolves who have closed for the kill.

But the odd image vanished when she saw the plump feather tick in the room Parsons secured for her at the *L'Auberge D'Etoile Cassée*. And as soon as she was able to dig a night rail out of the trunk deposited at the foot of the bed, she snuggled beneath the quilts with Rory and fell into an exhausted sleep.

It was well past midnight when she heard a tiny scraping sound. Rory whimpered and stirred. She cuddled him closer against her, unable even to raise her eyelids before she drifted again into dreams.

The afternoon sun slanted across the bed when she came awake to the sharp rapping of a servingmaid at the door. Pushing herself upright in bed, Meaghan started to call out, but the words froze in her throat. The battered, travel-worn trunk was gone.

Meaghan twisted the band of her wedding ring around her finger, the prongs holding its emerald cutting into her skin as she looked from the dirty, bewhiskered landlady who had thrown open the door moments before to what was little more than a warren dug in the wall. It was a room like all the others she and Rory had seen since that morning when they had left *L'Auberge D'Etoile Cassée*, dismal and filthy. A room to foster sickness and smother souls. A place to house the hopeless.

Fallen plaster from the low ceiling lay in clumps, half-buried in refuse that littered the floor, while pages from an old newspaper rattled about, borne by the wind that whistled its chill breath through the shattered glass of a window. With her toe, Meaghan nudged the stinking straw mattress that lay beneath the broken panes, unable to keep her mouth from puckering against a wave of nausea as the black leather of her shoe came away from the ticking dulled with a scum of mildew from the rain-sodden cloth.

"If it's the royal palace you're after you should'a married the prince," Elbertine Fenwick taunted, biting off the end of one filthy fingernail with rotted teeth and spitting it onto the floor.

She barked a laugh, her eyes traveling an insulting path down to Meaghan's stomach. "'Course if I was a bettin' woman I'd lay my coin on the chance that you ain't got *any* kind of husband a-tall, fancy or otherwise. Not that I'd mind you startin' up business here after you drop your brat, but there's others that would, right certain. They got a boomin' trade right round the corner, an' the mister, he wouldn't take kindly to you cuttin' into his profits. Now, if you'd like me t' be settin' you up with him—"

"No." Meaghan choked down the bile rising in her throat long enough to get out the word. "If . . . if you would let us stay it would only be for a little while . . . until my husband comes. People I met at the docks stole—"

"Stole?" Elbertine blustered, indignant. "Don't be wasting my time with any weepin' tale! I got a dozen people'd fight fer such fine fixin's as these an' be glad to get 'em 'stead of turnin' up their pointy little noses like they was a duchess. Either you pay your way or you walk the streets!"

"My husband will come as soon as I can get a message to him. I promise we'll find some way to—"

"I ain't fallin' for no story about some imaginary husband, and I don't take me no charity cases. By the looks of those scrawny little hips you'll die bearin' that babe anyway, and then where will I be? No money and a dead carcass on my hands, not to mention your other snot-nosed brat."

Meaghan cupped a hand over her abdomen, a shiver of fear creeping up her spine, as her worst fears were put into words. Rory alone, Sean never finding him . . . "Please, I—"

"Save your pretty tears for the sotted fools that pay you for your favors. They'll gain no ground with me. You give me your silver now, or out with the both of you."

A gust of wind brought another wash of rain through the window that was now laced with night. "Meggie, me tired," Rory whined, huddling against her skirts.

Meaghan laid her hand on his drooping shoulder, trying to find the long-spent strength within herself, knowing that Rory depended on her.

Tired? God, she was tired, too, but where would they go? The wind whispered of winter, and the child was half-sick already. Her own ankles were so swollen from walking she had had to leave the shoe buttons unfastened, and the weight of the baby kicked and jabbed inside her stomach until she wanted to scream for peace.

Even if she could send word to Sean with someone on the steamer, it would take the boat twelve days to make the trip to Grosse Isle and back, and that only providing it left Montreal immediately. Twelve days of no shelter, no food . . .

"Humphf! Just as I thought!" Elbertine snorted, banging the rickety door against the wall with such force another powdering of plaster fell from the ceiling. "Blasted idiots come with no money and expect those of us 'as had had to work to pour the world at their feet. I don't want to so much as see your face around—"

Meaghan's fist clenched, a sharp, cutting pain slicing into the flesh between her fingers as the woman began to flounce out. Her wedding ring . . . "Wait!"

In the instant it took for Elbertine to jerk around, Meaghan's other hand closed over the glowing emerald Sean had given her. The ring with which he had made her his wife, the ring that had belonged to the mother he'd loved. Meaghan swallowed hard. "Wait," she repeated softly. "I can get you the money."

"Sure, and I'm the Queen of—" Elbertine broke off midsentence as her filmy yellow eyes fastened on the glittering gem. "Glory God!" she croaked.

"It's my wedding ring. Tell me where I can pawn it."

"Pawn it? There ain't a shop round here could give you half of what that thing's worth!"

"Then I'll have to take whatever they *will* give me." She touched the tiny carved heart in the emerald's center with fingertips that trembled. "I have no other choice."

Raucous sounds of sailors returning from shore leave and ruffians out for sport split the cold sea air hours later as Meaghan dragged herself and the exhausted Rory toward the place the steamer had landed the day before. But even in the darkness,

Meaghan was too sick at heart to fear the drunken men. She rubbed the empty place on her finger, feeling a smoother band of skin where her ring had been.

She had felt more defiled than when Radcliffe had touched her when the greedy pawnbroker had snatched up the piece of jewelry, trying to bend the gold band, holding the emerald up to the lamp to let the fireshine shoot through it. He had not set it down even as he had counted out a miserly amount of money from the box he kept hidden under a floorboard. He had given her enough to get herself and Rory through the time it would take Sean to come once he got the note she now crushed in her hand, if she was careful . . .

But as the waning moon broke through the clouds, something in the pit of Meaghan's stomach wrenched horribly. For no silvery light reflected down the lines of the ship, no sounds of the river lapped against its hull, only the rush of waves upon shore shushed at the empty space where the steamer had lain anchored the day before.

Meaghan's grasp tightened on Rory's hand as she felt panic shoot to her fingertips. She stumbled to where a young seaman was weaving drunkenly toward a brig nearby.

"Stop! Please wait!" She grabbed the man's sleeve and he toppled over, plopping the seat of his britches into a puddle of water. He looked up with a disarming, lopsided grin, wiping his muddy hands on the scarlet linen of his shirt.

"Prettish damn fashe I ever dreamed outa a bottle," he slurred, giving her an owlish stare. "But I can't shay I ever dreamed 'em quite so big 'round the belly a'fore."

"Please . . . I'm trying to find the steamer that came in from Grosse Isle yesterday. Do you know—"

"Groshe Isle? You don' wanna go to that hell hol' angel. Sick out there . . . got the fever."

"I have to find the captain—"

"Avery? Then you'll haf t' go for a shwim. Stupid bastard left hours 'go. Said 'e was makin' one lash trip a-for the ice set in."

"Last trip?" Meaghan felt her knees quiver, heart stop.

"Aye. Won't be nothin' sailin' for that island 'til shpring thaw. Hey, angel! Careful! Don't—"

Meaghan heard Rory's wailing and the man's frantic protests, felt his hand make a grab to steady her. Her head spinning crazily in time with the roiling of her stomach, she fought to keep her legs from buckling. Spring . . . God, they could never survive until spring . . . Her hands clutched at the rain-soaked ends of her shawl as she stared, vacant eyed, into the harbor.

The rags stuffed in the broken window whipped and tugged in the winter gale as Meaghan tore her eyes from the large woven basket beside the slat-backed chair. For the first time in two months it stood empty of the mending that had kept Rory and her alive since that horrible day at the waterfront. Empty, with no chance of being filled again.

Not after Miss Doolittle's performance that afternoon. Meaghan's hand shook as she stirred the meager kettle of soup bubbling at the grate, her cheeks flushing hot as she remembered the accusations the butcher's waspish daughter had flung out for the benefit of her staid, plodding mother. Nose pinched and white, Lirabeth Doolittle had dumped Meaghan's work onto the fresh-scrubbed floor, pawing through the neatly folded garments, ranting that Meaghan had stolen a pair of embroidered pantalettes.

Pantalettes, for the love of God . . . Meaghan gave a sick little laugh, the end of the wooden spoon she was stirring with snagging her protruding stomach. As though she could even squeeze the bony Lirabeth's undergarments up to her hips! But the girl's straggle-haired mother had believed every lie, puffing up with indignation when Meaghan had dared to defend herself. Double chins quivering, Mrs. Doolittle had vowed to make certain Meaghan would never have the chance to steal any decent person's clothes again.

Steal? Meaghan thought bitterly, remembering Lirabeth's sly, lascivious smile. No doubt the sneaking chit had *given* them away.

But not an hour had passed before Mrs. Doolittle made good her threat, the other dour, self-righteous women Meaghan had sewn for coming to snatch up their things, none of them bothering to pay for the hours she had spent laboring over seams and tears.

Hours she had spent pricking her fingers until they bled, marking the time until she could take her earnings to the market place, to buy food to fill the barren shelf. Meaghan stretched awkwardly to pick up one of two wooden bowls, ladling into its crudely carved hollow the last scraping of withered carrots, potatoes, and turnips.

Trying to stem the pangs of hunger that gnawed her own stomach, she looked to the window ledge where Rory sat glaring sullenly out at the blinding snow.

A pang of guilt jabbed her as she remembered how she had snapped at him after Mrs. Doolittle had made her grand exit, his endless stream of questions having worn on Meaghan's nerves until she wanted to scream. When she had caught him snipping the buttons from his coat with her sewing scissors, she *had* screamed at him, and the look of pain in the little boy's eyes had made her want to cry.

But she couldn't . . . she had to think of something, some way to earn money to pay the infernal rent, to buy food to tide them over during the time she was bedfast from the babe's birth. Enough to survive until Sean came.

The thought of him made Meaghan ache—fear, love, and resentment all warring inside her as she pictured his rugged, handsome face. Was it even now covered with dirt, nameless in the grave mound where Grosse Isle's dead lay buried? Or was he still fighting to save those he could, risking his own life in a deadly gambit? Meaghan's hands clenched on the rough edges of the bowl until her knuckles turned white. He had promised he'd come. Promised. But even if, by some miracle, he got off the island, how would he ever find them in a city teeming with destitute Irish widows and orphans?

She shook herself, picking up a spoon to plop into the steaming bowl. No, she dared not even think that Sean might be searching somewhere nearby. The steamer would not leave again until spring. She had met it on the day it had returned to set its winter anchor in Montreal, watching as the last of the season's wretched immigrants had straggled off, but Sean had not been among them. Only the ragged passengers' stories of his untiring care, compassion, skill—and temper—had traveled the storm-gray St. Lawrence.

But even the thought of his temper's notoriety couldn't conjure a smile from her now. Compassion didn't put food on the table. Anger shielded no man from death.

Or woman . . .

She swallowed hard, running a shaking hand over the huge bulge of her pregnancy. Every time she had seen Elbertine Fenwick, the woman had regaled her with yet another birthing story, seeming to take the greatest of pleasure in painting each tale more horrible than the last.

At first, she had been able to discount them as a sick old woman's lies, forcing herself to remember the day Grace had given birth long ago. But as the babe swelled within her, stretching her body until she felt her skin would burst, her fear of the ordeal to come had grown, and with it her terror over what would happen to Rory if she died.

The bowl in her hand tipped, a little of the hot soup splashing onto her thumb as she grabbed the wooden rim with her other hand. Her nerves strained, snapping at the stinging pain. Her temples throbbed as she cooled the burn in her mouth, tasting on her skin the tang of vegetable broth. She had not had a chance to eat that morning, the Doolittles having burst in just as she had given Rory his breakfast. Her mouth watered, and she swallowed.

"Rory, time to eat," she managed, hearing the crackle of tension in her own voice. She moved to the window where he sat, setting the bowl on the wide ledge that served as a table. "Finish this up and we'll—"

"Me *hates* soup!" Meaghan leapt aside, but not fast enough to escape the splash of hot liquid as the child shoved the bowl away, toppling it off the ledge.

A shattering sob tore through her, her hand whipping in an arc toward Rory's cheek. She saw him cringe and freeze, stunned terror contorting his face. "No!" She slammed her fist into the window frame, horror at what she had almost done clawing through her hysteria.

A rending spasm ripped through her abdomen as she crumpled to the floor, warm liquid gushing between her thighs.

"Mama?" she heard Rory cry, felt his warm little arms go around her. "Mama, me sorry. Me didn't mean to—"

"Shh, I know, I know. Mama..." she choked over the word he had used to describe her for the first time, burying her face in his little neck. "Mama's sorry too. Rory, listen to me. You have to go upstairs and get Mrs. Fenwick. Tell her the babe is coming."

Wide, frightened eyes met hers.

"It's all right, moppet. Now hurry. Run fast. The babe will be here before you know it."

But hours passed, and night melted into dawn. The world outside hushed with new snow as the life within Meaghan's womb fought to burst free. She bit her lips until they bled, sweat dampening her body as she tried not to scream with the ever-increasing pain. Rory was there, terrified, tiny, huddled in the corner whimpering, as he watched her with Sean's cerulean eyes. Eyes that she needed desperately—not frightened, in the face of a child, but strong and reassuring in the lean bronzed visage that was the core of her very soul.

"Sean . . ." she whispered brokenly. "Sean . . ."

"Soon?" Mrs. Fenwick's brow furrowed as she bent close to Meaghan's face. "No, girlie, I don't think so. You got a ways to go yet, an' that's for sure." She clucked her tongue against blackened teeth, prodding the torturous ball of Meaghan's abdomen with rough, pudgy fingers.

"It ain't goin' right," she mumbled. "Just ain't—"

Stark terror exploded in Meaghan as the old woman's words penetrated through the pain. "What . . . what's wrong? My babe?"

"Can't say. It's like . . . like somethin' is caught somehow . . ."

"Oh, God . . . God, no!"

Meaghan screamed as the next wave of agony clamped its jaws around her, tearing like some savage beast. She clawed at her stone-hard stomach, feeling the child's life-struggle and wanting to rip open the flesh that held it prisoner, that bound both her and the babe in a world where white-hot pain battled death.

The glare of sunlight piercing her lids faded again, replaced by the smoky tongue of a single flame. She clung to its faint glow, fearing that when the flickering orange went out, she too would die . . .

A waft of icy air bathed her sweat-soaked skin and she was vaguely aware of a black-robed figure gliding into the room. Fragments of voices drifted through the haze of pain that gripped her.

". . . can't last much longer . . . mumblin' some Latin gibberish. Know you papists set great store by . . ."

"Per istam sanctam Unctio—"

The sound of the priest's deep voice above Meaghan snapped

the room into painfully sharp focus for an instant. Extreme unction . . . litany of the dying . . .

"No! Rory . . . babe . . ." Meaghan tried to push the cold fingers away from her, crushed in talons of agony that seemed only to dig deeper into her flesh.

She shrieked and fought as Mrs. Fenwick's meaty hands forced her down into the mattress. Oil dabbed Meaghan's forehead, slick and warm from the priest's fingertip. "Easy, child. Soon it'll all be over."

"Over . . . No! Help me! Sean! Sean!" She screamed his name into the hell that consumed her but no one . . . no one answered.

Twenty-Nine

He felt sick. Gut-wrenching, hideously sick. Sean swallowed the gorge that rose in his throat as he stared at the room around him, but the churning in his flat belly came not from the throes of the fever he had battled, nor from weeks of torturous travel over snow-drifted roads. He gripped the edges of the dirty, gilt-edged note in his hands, panic rushing through him like wildfire as he stared again at the scribbled message, then raised gritty, blood-shot eyes to the sign scrolling above him. *OSGOOD'S O. Parsons, proprietor.*

No, it couldn't be! he thought wildly. Meaghan and Rory at a brothel? Meaghan wouldn't . . . couldn't . . . For God's sake she was over eight months pregnant!

His gaze snapped down from the sign to see one of the many women, gaudy with face paint, spilling her full breasts from beneath an icing of lace into the pawing hands of a drunken customer. The man buried his face in her brassy-gold hair, then, staggering, he let her steer him toward the elegant curving stair.

The woman fixed keen hazel eyes on Sean, a smile parting her lips with practiced sensuality as she perused him. "I'm good for more than once a night, Irish," she said huskily, trailing long fingernails down Sean's unshaven cheek. "That is if you take a bath."

Sean jerked away, a muscle in his jaw knotting. "All I want is to know where the hell my wife is!"

"Your wife?" The woman laughed, her wobbly-legged customer tumbling onto the stair. "Shouldn't you be looking under your *own* sheets?"

"Damn you—"

"Ria, love, is there some difficulty?"

Sean wheeled on the balding worm of a man who had appeared beside them, an ingratiating grin splitting his pale face.

"It seems this gentleman has misplaced his wife, Osgood." The woman's eyes danced over Sean's travel-stained breeches and torn greatcoat.

"Like hell!" Sean shook off the hand she had laid on his arm and shoved the crumpled note into Parsons's face. "Two weeks ago a priest at Grosse Isle found this among the possessions of a dead man. It says my wife is in trouble, to come to Osgood's. Now, you can damn well—"

"Come now, let's be reasonable, Mr. . . . ."

"O'Fallon."

"Mr. O'Fallon," Parsons repeated, reaching a hand under a flap of broadcloth to scratch at his embroidered silk waistcoat. "I'll be happy to try to help you find your bride, if I can, but as you see for yourself, I deal with a great volume of women. Most of whom have run away from something or some*one*. Perhaps your wife—"

"Meaghan didn't run away! She's going to have a babe!"

"Babe?" Something flickered in Parsons's cunning eyes, then vanished. "Come now, Mr. O'Fallon, even you must admit that in my line of work, I would hardly have any use for a pregnant woman with a boy in tow."

"Who said anything about a boy?"

Sean heard a soft intake of breath to his side. His eyes flashed to Ria's face, dark red above where her fingers fluttered upon the lace draping her decolletage—lace worked through with wild-flowers, like Grace had given Meaghan . . .

"You sonofabitch, you tell me—" Sean lunged toward Parsons, only to be halted by the six-clustered barrels of a pepperbox pistol yanked from a pocket in the man's waistcoat.

"Now, now, Mr. O'Fallon," Parsons chided silkily, his finger curved around the trigger. "I must insist upon civil manners in my establishment. My clientele has a tendency to become quite . . . restive . . . at times, so at *Osgood's* we have one hard and fast rule. Anyone causing a disruption is no longer welcome. I think that you should leave."

"That lace belongs to my wife. Now you damn well tell me where—"

Sean started to grab for him, then froze as the pistol barrels jabbed closer. Ria dodged between him and the gun, laying her hands on his arms.

"The . . . the waterfront," she said, her gaze darting fearfully to Parsons. "Check the old buildings near the waterfront."

Parsons's eyes were rock hard as they pierced into the woman. "Sound advice, Ria love. Mr. O'Fallon had best search among the garbage if he is looking for something he's cast away."

Sean's muscles tensed, the guilt that had festered inside him since the day he had watched Meaghan and Rory board the steamer flaring to rage. Ria's fingers cut deep.

"Don't," she pleaded. "You won't do her any good dead!"

"And just how much good did *you* do her?" He shook off Ria's hold, then turned, glaring at Parsons. "If anything has happened to Meaghan I'll be back. And I swear I'll break the neck of whomever is responsible."

"Then you won't have far to look, will you, Mr. O'Fallon?"

The quiet comdemnation in Ria's voice struck him with more force than Parsons's bullets could have, the sick feeling tightening in his chest as he stared into her keen, accusing eyes. Color drained from his face. He tried to speak, swallowed, then spinning on his heel, he stalked into the darkening street.

Snow lay over the rise of Mount Royal in a thick, white pall, as though shrouding something beautiful that had died. Sean shivered at the macabre image, his eyes blurring from exhaustion as he watched the dappling of stars fade in the night sky.

He ran gloved fingers gingerly across a bruise swelling his cheek, a legacy gained in the hours he had combed the waterfront's streets, pounding on uncounted strange doors, rousing the people behind them from bed or drink to ask for any word that might lead him to Meaghan and Rory. But through both rages and vain attempts to help, there had been no shred of hope, no bit of information to lift the horrible sinking despair inside him—only sadly shaken heads, or barks of laughter from those more cruel than kind.

Finally, he had even gone to the nearest Catholic church in hopes that the priest there might have seen them, but the nightcapped housekeeper at the rectory had crossed herself, telling him that the good Father was off with some poor soul who was like to die. He had asked her to tell him where the priest could be found, more in hopes of helping whomever was suffering than in hearing news of Meaghan, but even as he had tried to follow the sour old crone's directions, he had become lost in the unfamiliar streets. Lost, as Meaghan was . . . Alone . . .

Clenching his teeth against the frigid air, he kneed his mare forward, the crunch of her hooves upon snow a hollow, aching sound in the stillness. With each movement of the horse's back beneath him, he could see Meaghan astride his gelding, dashing like a hoyden across Irish meadows, her skirts flying, her face thrown back to the wind's sweet kiss. He could feel her loving him, rolling naked in grasses as wild and delicate as her own beauty, making him forget everything but the wonder they made together. And he could see her boarding the steamer, her chin held high, her body so heavy with his babe it seemed impossible her fragile form could bear its weight.

He had wanted to hold her, to tell her . . . but he had turned and walked away, unable to stand the reproach in her velvet-dark eyes. Hadn't he always turned away from her, afraid of what she did to him, afraid because her honesty and her open loving had lodged in the very center of his being?

God, where was she now? Not so much as a single oil lamp cast light from inside the buildings that loomed, shadowed on either side of him.

Awkwardly gripping both reins with one hand, he ground the coarse tips of his gloves into his burning eyelids, despair and fear clotting in his throat.

"*Meaghan!*" He arched back his head, hoarsely crying her name to the indifferent sky. Night bore the sound back to him. The nape of his neck prickled as a high, keening noise seemed to cling to the air. Or was it his cry he heard?

No. Pulling his horse to a stop, he listened, then tensed, instinct gleaned from years of gauging human suffering snapping in tiny, stinging sparks down his nerves. He had heard it often enough, the screams of someone injured, some tortured soul in the jaws of excruciating pain.

Grabbing the reins again with two hands, Sean jammed his heels into the mare's sides, forcing the winded horse in the direction of the sound. The tiny side street branching off to the right was worse, even, than the other streets he had followed. The stench of human waste bit the insides of his nostrils through the numbing cold, through shadows of old crates and garbage discernible in the faint light of the coming dawn. A flicker of light cut a lopsided pattern from a window, and a small huddled form was silhouetted against its glow.

The shriek came again, and Sean could almost sense the figure in the window flinching from the sound of it. He lashed his horse with the ends of the reins, the beast surging forward just as the agonized cry crystallized in his mind.

His whole body snapped taut. Sweet Christ, the person was screaming his name!

Flinging himself from the mare's back, he ran to the door, hurling it wide, then stumbled up the rickety staircase that was barely visible in the dimly reflected snowlight that filtered through the opening.

A crack at the foot of the first door in the hallway gave off an eerie glimmer. Sean threw it open, taking in the scene with one horrified glance.

Rory, frozen and terrified, Meaghan writhing and screaming beneath the hands of a slovenly woman, a black-robed priest intoning in Latin. Rites of the dying . . .

Raw, primal fear raced through Sean's veins with the force of a curragh storm-hurled to the cliffs. "Shut up, damn you!" he bellowed, bolting across the room. Half-crazed with the terror gripping him, he knocked the priest away from Meaghan's side, oblivious to both the man's startled blusterings and the burly woman's indignation, unaware of what he shouted at them as, ignoring Rory's wails, he stuck the boy into the woman's arms and shoved all three through the door.

White-ringed and glazed eyes locked on his face as he ran back to the bed. Pain contorted features still piercingly beautiful, childlike within the sweat-soaked mass of hair.

"Babe . . . Not right . . . help me, Sean," The plea ripped at his soul, his name on her lips changing to a screech of sheer agony as her stomach contracted. She twisted, digging her head back into the ticking, clawing at the mound of their child beneath her nightgown.

"I'm here, Maggie, I'm here." He grabbed her hand, feeling her nails tear at his flesh, her grip crushing his fingers.

"Can't . . . get it out . . ." she sobbed as the spasm passed. "Can't . . ."

Sliding his hand beneath the cloth, he gently probed the tight-stretched skin, his gut churning as he felt the distorted shape of her stomach. *No! God, no!* his mind roared, as he identified skull, shoulder, and buttocks lodged crosswise in her womb. She wouldn't . . . he wouldn't let her die.

Yanking free of her grasp, he pushed up her gown, a dirt smudge from his fingers on the pale curve of her thigh stopping him for an instant. He spied a bowl of water and bits of soap on a shelf, and rushed to scrub away the dirt that clung to his fingers from weeks of travel, not knowing why he did so, knowing only that he could not touch her until he did.

When he hurried back to her side, another contraction was waning, and the shape of the baby was outlined in the thin wall of muscle. She gulped for air, tears squeezing from beneath her eyelids.

"Dying . . . have to . . . tell you . . ." He barely made out her words. "Rory . . ."

"Damn it, Meg, you're not going to die! Listen to me. I have to go inside you, try to turn the babe. Meg, can you hear me? Understand?"

Clammy sweat broke out in a layer over his body as he positioned himself between her upraised knees. He eased his fingers inside her. Hot, tortured flesh ripped as she thrashed in mindless agony, shrieking as his hands forced their way through the mouth of her womb.

The tiny warm column of an arm and the curve of a chest slid across his palm. He cupped the baby's body in one hand, its skull in the other.

Please, God . . . please . . . The unaccustomed prayer came rough against his tongue. Shutting his eyes he shoved with all his strength, fighting the binding sheath of muscle, and the horror of Meaghan's inhuman screams.

Then suddenly the baby turned, the soft features of its face pressing against the inside of Sean's other arm. Another contraction built around his hands. He waited, straining as the head was forced downward toward him.

"Meg, that's it. Push, Meg. Push with it!"

He felt the babe start to break free, his own wet arms cold as the air struck them.

Meaghan arched back, and he could feel her bear down with each new contraction as the baby's head and then its tiny round body slid from within her. Sean cradled the child in his big hands, staring in wonder at the wrinkled, red-faced mite as its high-pitched wail split the room.

"Meg, it's a girl. We have a daughter," he choked. The babe wriggled, nearly slipping from Sean's grasp as she flailed tiny limbs, her face crinkling in high dudgeon as she thumped tiny heels against his chest. Quickly, he tied and severed the umbilical cord with the string and knife laid out beside the bed. Wrapping the baby in a tiny clean blanket warmed near the hearth, he settled her gently in the crook of Meaghan's arm.

A stab of heart-stopping terror shot through him as his eyes locked on Meaghan's death-pale face. Her gold-tipped lashes drifted shut upon the bruised half circles at the crest of her cheeks. "Meg!"

At his cry her eyelids fluttered, lips parted. "Tired."

He knelt beside her, his eyes closed. He was unable to speak through the myriad of emotions sweeping over him as soft, trembling fingers traced his mouth, nose, and brow.

"Came . . ." He opened his eyes at the breath of a word, her voice scarcely a whisper as her mouth tipped in the tiniest of smiles. "You . . . came, Sean. Knew you would . . ."

He leaned down, pressing his lips to her cheek. "I came, Maggie."

"My babe . . ." Her hand flopped to the mattress, and she nuzzled her face against the tiny bundle. "Tired . . . so tired . . ."

She sighed, the childlike sound wrenching his heart. His jaw knotted against the stinging in his eyes, the straining in his throat, as he smoothed the tangle of damp curls back from her forehead. "I'm sorry," he rasped. "Sorry I sent you to face this alone. Maggie, I—" He faltered, the truth he had been fighting for so long striking deep into his soul. He loved her . . . *loved her*.

A helpless despair washed over him as the words died in his throat. Now, even now, he could not say them.

Thirty

"Ceara Rose O'Fallon, if you don't quit eating so often you'll be plump as a piglet!" Meaghan giggled, snuggling the squirming baby to her breast as the tiny, pink mouth fastened greedily on her nipple. "Ouch!" She winced as the little gums bit down hard on her slightly tender skin, and then she grinned, love and contentment swelling in her heart until they seemed too great to hold.

Two days after Ceara's birth, Meaghan had finally awakened from her exhausted sleep to a world so changed, it was as though the sparkling snow had buried all evil, leaving enchantment in its place. The room had shone bright with a cheery fire and smelled deliciously of the thick, rich stew that bubbled over the grate. She had been warmed, so warmed by Sean's tender smile as he had brought her the baby, and they had marveled together over the perfect little being who was their daughter.

"She's beautiful," he had said softly, caressing the tuft of carrot-red curls upon the little head. "Beautiful like her mother." His eyes had shifted from the baby to Meaghan's face, cerulean depths glowing with a new, deep light that made something inside Meaghan quiver and hope. Then his lips had closed over hers, and the haunting sweetness of his kiss had stolen Meaghan's soul.

For well over a month Sean had coddled her, forcing bowl after bowl of the inevitable stew into her hands, not allowing her to lift so much as a sewing needle, until idleness grated on her nerves. Finally, one day after he and Rory had gone to the market, she had fairly leapt from her chair and thrown together a big meat pie. Two hours later Sean had opened the door to find her gobbling it down with great relish, a heaping spoon in one hand, a wooden paddle in the other as she had alternately stuffed the crusty goodness into her mouth and stirred the kettleful of clothes she was washing.

At his protests she had pulled the paddle from the boiling water, brandishing it like a saber. "One more word and so help me, I'll tie *you* to that Godawful chair and make you eat your own cooking until you beg for mercy!"

"Was it really that bad?" He had thrown back his head and laughed, pointing to where Rory had dodged behind her to pilfer her spoon, his pie-smeared three-year-old face a study in ecstasy.

"No, it was wonderful." Her voice had been hushed and love-filled as she had put her arms around him, paddle and all, standing on tiptoe to share the spicy heat of his lips with hers. "I love you, Sean O'Fallon."

But it was that very night when she first noticed the moodiness in him, the odd tension. Cuddled with her in bed, he had prodded her into telling how she and Rory had come to be at Mrs. Fenwick's. And she had told him all—the day at the docks, the horrible morning after when she had awakened to find Parsons, Ria, and the trunk gone, the pawning of the ring she had treasured above all else.

He had been so quiet, then, it had frightened her.

When Ceara had stirred for her midnight feeding, he had still been awake, staring into the darkness. But he had held them both in the circle of his arms as Meaghan had nursed her, and in the morning all traces of his black mood were gone.

She glanced up to where he now stood, stripped to the waist, his own jaw foamy white with shaving soap as he lathered Rory's cheeks with the brush. The hair Meaghan had cut just that morning waved back in glistening mahogany from Sean's forehead, and rich gold light toyed with the silky strands.

"Look, Mama! Look!" Rory squealed, grabbing up the tin spoon and scraping at the foam. "Me an' Da's *shabing*."

"So you are." Meaghan's eyes danced to Sean as he picked up his own bone-handled razor and began carefully divesting himself of two months worth of beard. "Well, you'd both best shave those whiskers off in a hurry so Da can find some doctoring to do," she teased, gently disengaging Ceara from her breast and switching her to the other side. "He's going to need a great many patients to feed you and your sister. I swear, Sean, if your daughter ate real food, the kettle would be bare!"

The razor in Sean's hand wavered for a second. He swore, a tiny line of blood welling on his cheek.

"Sean, are you—"

"I'm fine, damn it!" The sharp blade whisked across his jaws so savagely, it was a wonder any skin was left in its wake. He slammed the razor into the bowl of water as soon as the last black stubble was gone and then wheeled. "No. I'm not fine. We're not fine." Rory went still beside Sean.

"What..." Meaghan swallowed, dread knotting in her stomach at the stubborn jut of his chin.

"There's no more money, Meg. It's gone. Everything they gave me when I left Grosse Isle. Tonight I'm going after what is rightfully ours."

"Ours?" Ceara fussed as she lost her hold on the nipple, but Meaghan was too stunned by Sean's hard words to glance at the babe.

The storm she had sensed in him that night so long ago raged in his eyes and body. She could see it now and feared it. Knowing... somehow knowing...

"I... I don't understand..."

"I think you do. I'm going to Parsons's."

"You're *what?*"

"I've only waited this long to be sure you were well enough to take care of yourself and the babes. This morning I talked with Father Tyson so if anything should happen to me you'll all be taken care of—"

"Nothing is going to *happen!"* Meaghan plopped Ceara onto the bed, and turned to Sean, furious. "If you think you're going to leave us again to dash off to one of your noble causes, you can just think again! Last time it nearly got me killed, not to mention the fact that it almost left your son an orphan in a strange city! Now with Ceara, too... Oh, no, damn you! For once your blasted pride can just go to the devil!"

"This has nothing to do with pride!"

"It has everything to do with pride! I know that wall you've built around yourself! That bloody stubbornness of yours that won't let you bend no matter what the cost because you're afraid the seed of your father has tainted you, made you weak!"

She could see the color drain from Sean's face, felt a sick horror at the wounds she was inflicting, but she couldn't stop.

"Damn it, Meg, you leave my *father* out of this!"

"I can't! You're not accountable for the sins of your parents, Sean, any more than Rory is! And blasting into Parsons's like an idiot won't prove—"

"What do you want me to do? We don't have any money! The swine stole everything we had! How the hell do you expect us to live until spring? How do we get to America?"

"You could *doctor,*" she flung out bitterly. "Unless, of course, you forgot to bring your bag of instruments in your *great haste* to reach us."

Sean's jaw set in a hard line. He snatched up a freshly ironed shirt, shoving his arms into the sleeves. "I'm going."

"Oh, yes, you're going! Just like you always do what you please! Right the wrongs of the world, Sean, but for God's sake, don't bother to take care of your own family!"

The beauty of the past weeks vanished, leaving a hollowness inside her. It had all been a lie. All the time she had been so happy he had been plotting to go after Parsons. The thought terrified her, infuriated her. She wanted to scratch his face, to shred the silk cravat he had pulled from among the things he'd kept with him at Grosse Isle, wanted to hold him so he couldn't go.

"You bastard!"

His lips twisted in a mocking smile. "Is that the worst thing you can think of to call me, to call anyone?" Jerking on his coat he wheeled toward the door, but stopped as something fell from the pocket of his coat, clinking to the floor.

Rory grabbed the bit of shiny gold, staring wide-eyed at the tiny wrought leaf. Sean snatched it from him, the dark rage on his face seeming to blaze even brighter as he stamped out the door. The portal slammed with a resounding crack, rattling on its hinges, but Meaghan's eyes were locked on the boy. A chill of foreboding prickled down her spine as she stared at his impish face, frozen now in a mask of terror. With stiff white lips he whispered one word.

Maman.

Whiskey seared Sean's throat as he bolted down another glass of the amber liquid, but it burned inside him not a wisp as much as Meaghan's words of the hour before. Hands shaking with suppressed fury, he shoved the glass toward a bartender decked out in Osgood's green and gold, who filled it and shot it back to him. Damn Meaghan! She had flown at him like some kind of she-cat, slashing him with truths that lay open wounds deeper than the whip scars on his back. Truths he had wanted to deny, but couldn't.

He had planned to blast into the brothel, to collar Parsons and vent his fury with his fists. Getting back their things had been secondary—important, yes, but not as important as saving his own pride. He glanced around at the five men strategically placed about the huge room. They took no part in the debauchery around them, but watched, always watched, flexing huge muscles, spoiling for a fight. They were Parsons's men, trained no doubt like savage dogs to rip open the throats of any troublemakers. Had he followed his first instincts, Sean knew he would have been beaten by now, or dead.

The mirror across the room caught his eye, and he smiled grimly at his reflection there. At least no one would suspect that the well-dressed rake leaning against the curve of the bar was the same man as the bearded wild-eyed "Irish" of the month before. Parsons himself had brushed right past him, not even sparing him a glance as he carried away a money sack in his bony clutching hands.

Sean's fingers clenched around the fresh glass of whiskey before him until the crystal threatened to shatter. Damn it, there had to be a way . . .

He started as something cold and sharp bit the nape of his neck.

"Easy, handsome, easy!" His heart slowed again as he saw a brown-haired prostitute of no more than fifteen yank back her hand, pressing long fingernails to her lips. She giggled, insinuating one wetted finger between the buttons of his shirtfront to swirl in the mat of chest hair beneath. "You don't have to worry, love, I won't bite you. That is, at least not anywhere you don't want me to."

Fighting to conceal the revulsion he felt, Sean forced a lazy smile. "Sorry. I like my women a bit . . . riper. At least past the stage when they should be playing with dolls."

The girl's lips plumped into a childish pout. "I'll see if there is anyone ancient and wrinkled enough to satisfy you snoring about in a rocking chair somewhere."

"That won't be necessary, Josie. I'll deal with this gentleman." The genuine amusement that had been twitching at the corners of Sean's mouth stilled. His eyes snapped up to the piercing hazel ones of Ria Parsons. "How is your wife, Mr. O'Fallon?"

Every nerve in Sean's body tensed as he waited for Ria to summon Parsons's lackeys, to expose him. With studied nonchalance he reached past Josie for the neck of a whiskey bottle to use as a weapon. "Fine."

"The baby? She *has* had it?"

Sean nodded, eyes skimming for a second over the crowd to find the nearest way out before they flashed back to Ria.

"Wife? Baby? Oh, Lord!" Josie pulled a face. "I guess I'll leave you two old folks to talk about rheumatism and sugar teats."

Ria Parsons's mouth set cold and hard as the ice in the St. Lawrence as the girl flounced off. "You get upstairs with me now," she hissed under her breath, draping one lavender-scented arm around his neck.

Sean started to yank away, but her fingers cut into his shoulder.

"Do it, you ass, or I swear I'll kill you myself and save your wife a lifetime of misery!"

Gritting his teeth, knowing he had no choice but to follow her, Sean let himself be guided through the crowd, then up the curved staircase, Ria throwing out lewd, witty comments about his sexual prowess to those they passed. When she had shut and locked behind them the door to one of the rooms on the first landing, the pretense of their journey up the stairs vanished.

"What kind of an idiot are you, anyway?" she blazed. "Waltzing in here, easy as you please, guzzling enough rotgut to poison a sailor when any minute Osgood could've recognized you? You think he'd wait for an explanation before he had his watchdogs beat the life out of you?"

"What concern is it of yours, anyway?" Sean bristled, the censorious tone of the prostitute playing moral judge grating at his nerves. "Parsons walked right past me. Didn't even—"

"Well, then you're damn lucky! I knew who you were the minute I saw you!"

"Then why didn't you call Parsons yourself?"

"I should have, damn you! I can't believe I haven't! If Os ever found out . . ." She rolled her eyes skyward with a sick little laugh. "Why the hell aren't you home taking care of your wife, Mr. O'Fallon, since you were lucky enough to find her alive?"

"I almost didn't. She and the boy were in a filthy hole with no money, no food, the babe coming. If I had gotten there an hour later—"

"Spare me. If you'd been with her where you belonged, none of that would've happened in the first place. I sent that note the very day Os found her, thinking that you'd come. But then, you men never can be bothered with such unimportant matters as wives or childbirth."

"I came as soon as I got it!"

"You shouldn't have needed it! She was sticking out to *here* when she stepped off of that cursed boat! She was in no condition to be thrown up onto shore to fend for herself! You're a bastard, Mr. O'Fallon. You make me sick."

The word twisted Sean's gut. Guilt and rage convulsed him. "You're the one who stole everything she owned and left her to face God knows what!"

Ria's cheeks went scarlet. She turned away, her fingers fumbling with the edge of her bodice. "I tried to stop him, but it was too late. I did what I could for her."

"Did you?"

"I thought she was safe. When you didn't come here, I figured she must've reached you somehow herself, or . . . I don't know. Osgood, he beats me and I . . ." The hard features softened. The hazel eyes glittered strangely bright. "I just tried to block her out of my mind. I couldn't. No matter how hard I tried. See, I was like her once. Pregnant. Alone. Only my baby died."

Sean's roiling anger cooled and died, to be replaced with an uncomfortable sensation of sympathy as he saw the play of emotion on Ria's normally stone-cold face. "I'm sorry."

"I'm not. What kind of life would it have had? Men like Osgood pawing at it, just waiting till it was old enough to take up whoring or thieving. Don't know nothing about being a mother, anyway. But your wife . . . She looked at that little boy of yours like he was the heart right out of her. I don't give a damn what happens to you. But her . . ."

Ria walked over to the window, peering down into the street. "I'll help you however I can, for her."

"Then tell me where I can find the things you stole."

"Osgood's room. There's a tin box under his bed where he keeps the money. It's locked, but I know where the key is. The rest of the things . . . I don't know. It's been so long they could be anywhere. We'll have to hurry. He'll be coming to count the receipts for the night any minute."

The hall outside was empty as they slipped down it, the echoes of the revelry below discordant and sour, making an almost eerie sound. At Parsons's door, Ria turned the knob quietly, easing the door open so they could both enter.

"Stay here, listen, in case he—"

She never finished the sentence. Her eyes in the moonlight streaming through the window grew wide and frightened as the steady tread of footsteps moved toward them down the hall.

Laying his finger against his lips, Sean motioned her back into the shadows as he moved stealthily against the wall. Parsons? One of his men? He gauged his chances, body whip taut. It would have to be a swift, clean blow. One cry would bring the whole house down upon them.

Candle-glow edged beneath the door, shone in a crescent as it swung open, illuminating Parsons's greedy face. Sean could see his beady eyes search the shadows where Ria's light dress was just visible. The slack mouth fell open. "Who . . . who's there?" He dropped the moneybox clutched in his hands and groped for his pistol.

Locking both fists together, Sean bashed them down on the balding pate, feeling in himself a surge of savage joy as Parsons tumbled to the floor.

The candle rolled across the rug, igniting tiny sparks in the weave. Ria snatched the taper up, stamping out the glowing embers as Sean grabbed the worm of a man by the collar, his fist cocked back.

"Forget him! He's unconscious. Get the box. There should be enough there to make up for all you've lost. You have to get out of here now, before someone sees you."

"But Parsons—"

"Believe me, nothing you could do to Osgood would hurt him more than the loss of his money. He's not worth dying for!"

Sean let the little man fall in a pathetic heap to the floor; the sight of Parsons's cringing, bony frame lying there only disgusted him.

"And you?" He looked up to Ria. "What if they find out that you . . ."

"They can't . . . They won't if you do what I say! Now get the damn box . . ."

The trip down the back stairs seemed to take a hundred years, each creak of wood, each sigh or sound of pleasure from behind the doors they passed pulling tighter on the cords of tension that bound Sean's chest.

Wintry air stung at their faces and lungs as Ria opened the door and slipped into the night. He turned, seeing in the flickering candlelight a shadow of the girl she had been.

"If anything should happen . . . If they should find out . . . come to Mrs. Fenwick's. Elbertine Fenwick's."

"I'll be all right."

"Ask for Sean or Meaghan O'Fallon if you ever need—"

"I won't. Go!"

Ria watched him mount his horse and melt into the darkness as he cantered across the powdery snow.

It was two weeks later that the woman came, her violet eyes dripping tears and concealing lies as she pleaded for news of her beloved lost brother, Sean.

Thirty-One

Meaghan swiped at her eyes with the back of her hand, biting her lip against the fear that threatened to tear her apart as she stared at the pitiful little figure of Rory huddled in a ball beneath the bedclothes. He had clung to her for hours after Sean had left, his eyes round, his whole body quivering against her as she had tried to soothe him. But no lullaby, no hushed, gentle stories of fairy queens and princes had had the power to banish the terrors that stalked the child this night.

The terror had a name, a face that clutched at them both with ring-bedecked fingers. Alanna. Maman.

Is Maman going to take me away?

Meaghan cringed at the words that still haunted her, seeing, yet, on Rory's pale, sleeping face traces of the tears that had welled from beneath his lashes, the pallor that had stolen the rose from his cheeks as he had stared up at her with his huge blue eyes.

No, angel, no. She's never going to hurt you again. I promise.

Is she going to hurt Da?

She had hugged Rory tight, a fierce protectiveness screaming inside her. *No. Your maman is far, far away, across the big ocean in Ireland. She can't hurt Da now.*

Then why did he look so sad?

Sad? She had wanted to cry remembering Sean's face as he had spun out of the room. He had been furious, sarcastic, biting. But had there been a hint of something else in the shadings about his eyes? An emotion he had been fighting hard to secret away from her?

322

Meaghan paced to the hoarfrosted window, blowing on it, scrubbing off the ice with the side of her fist to peer into the dreary, empty street below.

The image of Sean's face shifted in her memory, the stubborn jut of his jaw no longer quite concealing his stunned pain. She had slashed open wounds with a sword so sharp it had cut through the core of him, in the same brutal arc imbedding its blade in her as well. It had torn at her so badly—the chance of losing him again, the agony of waiting and not knowing—that she had wanted—had tried—to hurt him.

Meaghan pressed her hands to her face, her unshed tears balling in a lump in her chest.

He had slammed out the door in the wake of her vicious words, hurting and blazing with anger. By the time he reached Parsons's brothel his fury would rage out of control. He had been gone so long. Even now he might lay dead . . .

"No!" She said it aloud, the sound of it snagging in her throat. They had come too far, she thought desperately, too far from the solitary, bitter man at the roadside and the naive child she had been to lose all they had gained.

Sean was hers. Rory was hers. Hers! Alanna DuBois had tried to destroy them, had tormented them with her evil lies, had cast them away. She could never find them . . . never . . .

But where had Sean gotten the golden-wrought leaf?

Rory whimpered, and Meaghan rushed to him, smoothing back his sweat-dampened curls, tucking one little leg back beneath the blankets. Haunting fear coursed through her whole body as she felt the warmth of his tear-streaked cheek and saw the fire-glow cast shadows upon the features so like his father's.

Lies . . . lies . . . What of her own lies that had at once given Sean a son and robbed him of one, only to protect herself? Could she truly go through the rest of her life, loving both Sean and Rory as deeply as she did and keeping from them the blood tie that bound them? Yet if she told Sean . . .

Meaghan let her hand fall away from Rory, drawing the cheery calico curtain she had hung around where the children slept to shut out the firelight that shone in the little boy's face. She turned to the wooden cradle where Ceara lay, her angel's face plump against the soft, knit blankets, her little bottom sticking up in the air. "If I tell your da he'll hate me," Meaghan whispered to the sleeping child. "I'll lose him, Ceara. And I love him. I love him so, so much."

A tiny sob escaped, and Meaghan bit her knuckle, trying to battle off the storm of misery that threatened to engulf her.

Her teeth sank in so sharply she tasted blood as she heard the door handle rattle and turn. The door opened.

"Sean!" He let something heavy fall to the floor as she cried his name. She took no notice of what it was because she was running, flinging herself into his snow-dusted, outstretched arms, which clutched her to the winter-chilled length of his body. Horrible, racking sobs choked her as she drove her fingers through his thick, unruly hair, and she felt him, tasted of him, as she buried her face in his neck, warm, wonderful, alive.

"It's all right, love. Hush now," he murmured softly, soothing and petting her. "I'm home."

"Sean, I'm so sorry . . . the things I said . . . I didn't mean . . ."

"Shh. Yes you did. You were right about so much, Meg. I didn't want to listen, but all the way to Parsons's I thought about what you said. With my usual self-control, I was going to go in there and break that sonofabitch's scrawny neck, the devil take the cost." She could feel his smile against her ear. "But if I had I'd be dead. I didn't want to die, Meg. I wanted to come back to you, to our babies. Because . . ."

He nudged her head from his shoulder with a lightly whiskered chin, his big hands cradling her cheeks as he tipped her face up. He swallowed, his husky warm voice faltering. "Because I love you, Meaghan O'Fallon."

The cerulean of his eyes washed over her in waves of intensity so great, so sweet, Meaghan felt herself sinking in them.

"I love your gentleness, your innocence, the way you take my pain inside you, and make it yours." He traced the pad of his thumb over her lips, his eyes strangely bright. "All my . . . all my life I've seen the cruel side of people—hatred, murder, lies. But you . . . you made me believe again . . . and I . . ."

His hands threaded back into her hair, his lips taking her tear-dampened cheeks, her chin, her eyelids. "Meaghan, I . . ."

The words were lost as his mouth fastened on hers. The play of his tongue was rough and wet, and he delved into the recesses of her, as though he would take her all within himself. And she wanted him to take her into the haven of his love, to make her his, shutting out all else. Because if he knew...when he knew...

She met his kiss with driving passion born of desperation, her lips grinding against his seeking ones, her tongue meeting his in a union so wild, so fierce it left them both shaken.

Her fingers tore at the buttons of his coat and shirt, the tiny discs ripping free to roll on the wooden floor, her teeth taking tiny nips of his neck, his collarbone, the muscled hot flesh of his shoulder. His hand slid down to capture her breast, its nipple taut, straining into his palm.

Dragging his mouth to her ear, he rasped, "Maggie, it's too soon, we shouldn't..."

But the tip of her tongue flicked out, skimming through the mat of hair furring his chest, to find his nipple and teethe it. The velvety wetness of her mouth upon his skin sent rivers of fire rushing to his loins. He groaned as her fingers slid down his taut belly and beneath the waistband of his trousers to cup that part of him already stone-hard with wanting her.

Swooping her up, he strode to the bed, his whole body burning at the boldness of her hands, her mouth. Clothes were shed by fingers suddenly awkward, and he felt her helping him, shoving his trousers down his legs. He kicked free of them, starting to pull her up to the bed, but she stayed him, her fiery tresses spilling about her naked back and breasts, pooling over his feet. Her eager mouth seared his hair-roughened thigh, kissing and nipping, her tongue running up the hard length, taking him, taunting him, loving him. His hands clenched in her hair, his head arching back.

"Meg..." The guttural cry dragged deep from his chest, as every fiber of his being exploded with agonizing pleasure. Unable to bear her sweet assault another second, he gripped her arms, pushing her back into the bed's softness.

"Love me, Sean..." she whimpered, her dark eyes oddly pleading and desperate, tearing at his heart.

"I do, Meg, I..." His mouth and hands were everywhere, touching her, arousing her as he drove himself into her silken sheath. He felt her stiffen as though from pain, tried desperately to slow himself, but she clutched him to her, her legs twining around his hips, urging him, giving no quarter, wanting none.

The sharpness of her nails clawed the flesh of his shoulders and buttocks, and Sean felt the tremors shake her, rock her, her cry of release firing in him an ecstasy beyond the wildest reaches of imagination. He thrust once, twice, and then, he too was swept away, by a torrent that blended their very souls in a flood of molten gold.

They lay still a long time, awed at what their bodies had wrought together, the sheen of sweat from their lovemaking mingling as they both gasped for breath.

"Maggie . . ." Sean eased off her, his throat clenching as he saw her lips quivering, her eyes full of tears. "Oh, God, Meg, I hurt you!"

"No! No!" Her fingers traced his mouth, his nose, his brow, her voice a broken whisper. "It was beautiful . . . just so . . ."

He kissed her as the tears poured down her cheeks, gently skimming his mouth across the bridge of her nose and under her eyes, tasting her tears. "I never . . . never knew it could . . . could be like that . . . making love. Never knew what it meant . . . God, Meg," his own voice cracked with emotion. "I fought it so hard, for so long . . . admitting I loved you. After Alanna . . ."

He could see her flinch, the wounded, haunted look deepening in her dark eyes, and he cursed himself for a fool, wanting only to banish it, to make her understand.

"No more lying to myself . . . no more lies. I love you, Meg. Love you . . ."

The words she had longed to hear poured over her like sea spray breaking across raw flesh, scaring her conscience with guilt. The trust in his once-wary face lanced into her soul.

With a sob, Meaghan caught Sean's face between her hands. "I love you, Sean." She choked out the words, kissing him, pleading again for the comfort of his body. Even as his hard-muscled warmth moved to cover her, she shivered with cold.

Tonight he loved her, but one day he would despise her.

Sean stared down into the dismal street, feeling as bleak as the filthy, trampled snow below him. She had been crying again. He could see it in her red-rimmed eyes, her mouth that never tipped in its pixie smile anymore, the droop of her head, once tilting up at him so beguilingly as she teased him with her loving banter.

For two weeks she had gone about her tasks dispiritedly, moping by the fire, gazing into its flames with a hopeless despair that made him ache inside. Yet when he'd asked her, probing gently for whatever was making her unhappy, she had grown quieter still, or else urged him to their bed with a consuming passion that left him oddly hurt and confused.

He had told her he loved her, but it was as if the very act of his loving was causing her pain. She had been honest and open for so long, gifting him with her love freely as a child casts petals to the wind. He had thought she would embrace his confession with the same unabashed joy. But he could see her now, curling in upon herself, cocooning herself in some grief she would not let him share. It was as if in reaching out to her, she had slipped through his hands. And the thought of it left him emptier, lonelier than ever before.

He walked to where she sat in the chair, Ceara on a blanket at her feet, Rory playing listlessly with wooden animals Sean had carved for him. Even the child looked lost.

"Meaghan . . ."

She flinched as he laid a hand on her shoulder, the anguish in her face visible for a fleeting second as though the light touch had been a blow.

His hand feathered through her curls to her cheek, her flesh stiff and taut beneath his fingertips. He hunkered down. Her eyes were like those of a savaged fawn, hunted and hurt, and the desolation within them was his own.

"Meaghan, tell me what's wrong," he pleaded, cupping her chin in his hand. "There is nothing so terrible we can't heal it together."

He felt her delicate jaw tighten. Her pale lips pressed together. Pulling away, she stood and paced to the hearth, leaning her forehead against the mantel. "It's just so cold here all the time, and gray, and I miss Ma and Tom, and Ceara keeps me up half the night. And God, I wish it was spring!" Tear-dewed lashes swept her cheeks. Her fingers chafed unconsciously at the place where her wedding ring had been, the habit, so ingrained, tugging at him. Then her hand fell still, and she slammed the ringless hand against the wood.

"Can't you find something to do besides hounding me? I don't . . . I can't . . ."

Sean levered himself to his feet. "Maybe it would be best if I went out for a while. Father Tyson said he found a house we could rent until spring. I'll go look at—"

"Fine. Go."

The sharp words cut him. Taking his greatcoat from the peg beside the door, he ruffled Rory's curls.

"Can Woarke go too, Da?" the child begged. Sean leaned down to plant a kiss on the top of his head.

"No, son. I won't be back till past your bedtime. You be good for your mama, now."

Even as Sean let himself quietly out the door, Meaghan's mind was locked on the picture he and Rory had made, Sean's big, bronzed hand on Rory's tousled hair, the little boy's childish pout a caricature of Sean, impatient.

She pressed her fingertips to her burning eyes. God, what was she doing to them? To herself? Each day guilt ate at her until she couldn't bear to look at either of them, wanted to scream *Don't love me! I'm not worth it!* Wanted it only to end. End? To see the love so lately won harden to hate and contempt. No. Meaghan stumbled to the bed and sank onto the coverlet.

"Mama?" She felt Rory's soft palm on her hair, patting her with an innocent concern that tore out her heart. "Wory loves you, Mama."

"Oh, Rory," Meaghan crushed the boy in her arms, drowning in the hopelessness that washed over her.

No more lies, Meg . . . Sean had said.

No more lies.

The ruffled edge of the night rail seemed to cut into Meaghan's flesh as she looked from the small, white-wrapped package to the boyish eagerness that lit Sean's face. He had burst in, breezy-fresh, the chilly scent of winter clinging to him. The package he thrust toward her glittered in the light of the single candle she had left burning after tucking the children in bed. The words she had been rehearsing for hours lodged in her throat.

"Oh, Sean . . . I . . ."

"It's a gift to mark our new beginning. The house is perf—" Sean's voice faltered. "Oh, I wouldn't give a damn if we were moving to a castle! I just wanted you to have something to remind you that . . ." His face stilled, his expression almost shy. "That I love you."

He reached out, yanking at the package string, his lips curving in a devilish grin. "Besides, with the way you're always twisting at that knuckle of yours, I was afraid if I didn't do something fast, you'd have no fingers left. And I *do* love the way you use your fingers, Mrs. O'Fallon."

Meaghan tried to smile but failed as she slowly smoothed off the crackly paper wrapping and lifted the box's lid. The icy knot in her chest tightened past bearing, blurring the deep green stone set in the gold circlet upon the bed of cotton.

Sean's hand, warm and strong, covered her shaking ones as he slipped the ring on her finger, his voice hesitant and hopeful. "I thought if anything could make you smile again . . ."

She looked up at him with pain too great for tears, a horrible, cold pain that froze all hope inside her, leaving her bereft, barren as an ice-swept wasteland. The joy in Sean's face shriveled into hurt, confusion, anger.

"Damn it . . . I thought . . ." He spun around, his back to her, an odd quaver in his voice. "What the hell do you want?"

Meaghan stared at the ring on her hand, unable to speak, to tell him. *I want you,* she screamed inside. *You! But you're not mine. You never were.*

Until dawn they lay silent in the bed they had shared through their weeks of loving, not touching, not speaking.

The first rattles of carts were echoing in the street when a frantic pounding sounded.

Cursing, Sean rolled from the bed, shoving into his pant legs, fumbling with the buttons of his fly as he stumbled to the door.

Meaghan's bare feet struck the floor the instant he turned the handle, slamming it open. Bewilderment and dread uncoiled in her breast as the blood drained from Sean's face, his hand suspended midair. Meaghan stepped toward him, then froze, sick panic stabbing deep.

The powerful curve of his shoulder was silhouetted against lilac silk and ebony hair, smothered by them as, with a practiced cry, Alanna DuBois hurled herself into Sean's arms.

Thirty-Two

"Sean, Sean, thank God I found you!" Sean staggered back, waves of shock and disbelief exploding through him like cannon fire as the wailing, silk-clad woman crashed against him. Small breasts grated into his naked chest, and arms twined about his neck. She was so cold it was as though he were holding death. But she was alive. Alive.

"'Lanna." The name croaked from his throat, as wet lips plastered onto his, smothering what little breath he had been able to suck into his lungs. And he felt himself whirling, dazed, into a reality with sensations so excruciatingly sharp and piercing they seemed to flay his very soul.

"Sean, where is he? What has she done with him?" The shrill cry stabbed into his ear as she spun away, branding a dozen images into his brain—Alanna swooping toward the little bed where Rory huddled, death-still and chalk-white, the boy's screams, Meaghan flying like a she-wolf, a blur of loose copper hair and rumpled nightgown as she snatched Rory from the tangle of covers and wheeled, slamming her fist into Alanna's face with a force that sent her reeling to the floor in a heap of silk, ruffles, and blood.

Sweeping up the clinging Rory, Meaghan pressed his little head into the crook of her shoulder. "Don't you touch him!" she hissed between clenched teeth. "Don't you ever touch him again!" An icy spike of confusion and dread pierced through the trance that had frozen Sean as he heard the raw hatred burning in Meaghan's voice, saw it blazing from her eyes while she glared

330

at Alanna sprawled below her. Hatred, as though she knew . . .
Meg knew . . .

"What the hell—" Sean shoved between them, reaching down
to pull Alanna to her feet, but as soon as he touched her, she
again wrapped herself around him so he could scarcely breathe,
her huge tears soaking his skin.

Cold dread settled in the pit of his stomach like a stone. He
needed to know . . . fearing to . . .

God, if Alanna would only quit wailing and let him think.

"Make her give him back to me, Sean. My little—"

"Give him back? What the devil—" He forced Alanna's arms
away from him and wheeled, his gut churning with a new, more
horrible fear he dared not name. *"Meaghan!"*

She looked up at him, silent and still, holding Rory like a
condemned madonna, and he wanted to scream at her, to beg her
to speak as claws ripped inside him.

"She won't say anything!" Alanna accused, pressing a handkerchief to her bleeding nose. "She can't! She knew Colin was
holding me at the manor house, but she didn't tell you! She stole
Roarke from me because she knew that you loved me, *me*, not
her! And she couldn't bear for me to have anything of yours, not
even your son!"

"Son—" Sean's gaze locked on the dark curls, the cerulean
eyes peering fearfully from the lee of Meaghan's shoulder, the
lips, so pale and innocent, but already bearing the shape of his
own. Son . . .

"—been searching for months, even risked going to Grosse
Isle . . . told me you'd gone to Osgood's . . ."

Sean thrust Alanna out of the way, bearing down on Meaghan
with a devastating pain that spiraled through him, tearing in a
way his grief over Alanna never had, in a way nothing in his life
ever had.

"You *knew?*" he grated, inches from Meaghan's face. "You
knew Alanna was alive? *Rory* is my *son*. Mine, and you . . ." He
tried to steady his voice but failed.

"She—"

"'Lanna, shut up!" Sean hissed, his gaze never leaving
Meaghan's flushed, drawn face.

"Damn it, Meaghan, answer me!" His hand clamped on her
jaw, forcing her eyes to his. The brown depths stared back at
him, dark with guilt, not even attempting to conceal or defend,

their very openness shattering something inside him. *"Answer me!"*

Meaghan flinched at the pleading note in the deadly soft words, knowing in all their time together she had never seen Sean so angry. He was begging her to explain, to make it right, not wanting to believe... But she couldn't speak, couldn't tell him...

The muscle in his jaw jerked so tight she could almost hear it snapping, breaking like the fragile thread of trust and love he had put into her hands.

"My son..." The tiny choke in the words slashed Meaghan. "You knew how much I loved Rory... knew... but you never told me. Your sweet, noble gesture, taking in some poor abandoned child! Christ! I thought you were so gentle, so innocent ...But it was all a lie. Some warped trap." A bitter laugh scraped in his throat. "I told you I loved you, *loved you* and you—"

Meaghan felt the tears searing her cheeks as he yanked his hand away from her, his lips twisting in revulsion. She reached out, her fingers shaking, but he struck them away.

"Don't touch me!" He spun around, grabbing his boots and shirt, slamming into them. Alanna's triumphant smirk filled the room like venom. The wash basin teetered on its stand as he snatched his coat from beside it.

"Sean..."

"Damn you!" The curse ripped across Meaghan, savage and hate-filled, his eyes glazed with the pain of her betrayal.

She bit back the tears as he slammed out of the room, the agony within her wrenching, bursting, as Alanna DuBois swept after him. For even in Sean's fury Meaghan had seen it, heard it... his stark, soul-shattering despair.

Sean moaned, grinding his fingers into gritty eyelids as he kicked at the welter of sheets that smothered his whiskey-numbed body. Damn! The Queen's whole army was warring in his skull, blasting him with rose petals that curled up his nose, filling his stomach with a bubbling queasiness at their cloying stench.

What in the name of God had Meaghan stuck into the washtub to make the bed smell like this? He burrowed his nose into his bicep, seeking with his other hand the fall of her coppery hair where it usually lay on the pillow beside him, its silken mass always smelling faintly of cinnamon and wildflowers.

But she wasn't there . . . wasn't . . .

He shifted his weight, the lush mattress sucking him down into its softness, far different from the firm straw of the bed he had shared with Meaghan. Where the hell was he—

The sick feeling in his gut knotted as a sudden sharp awareness bore through his befuddled senses, bitterness swirling inside him like the whiskey in the countless glasses he had emptied during the hours since leaving home.

No. It didn't matter where he was, didn't matter as long as it was away from Meaghan. Because she had lied . . . Behind his closed eyelids he could see her, more beautiful in her rumpled muslin than Alanna had been swathed in silks and furs, the soft brown of Meaghan's eyes touching him in a silent plea.

A plea for what, damn it? He had given her love and trust and she had torn out his soul with her deceptive innocence. Yet still he wanted her, needed her to hold him, heal him as she had so many times before. Her betrayal ripped inside him, leaving wounds deeper than any he had received in a lifetime, because from her . . . from her he had never expected . . .

A pickaxe slammed inside his temples as someone jounced down onto the strange bed beside him. A cold hand crawled across his ribs. He opened one eye, squinting up at the person bending over him. In the light of the oil lamp, the cheeks inches from his face looked lopsided where the edges of rouge had worn off. A woman. Alanna. He'd forgotten she was alive.

"It's about time you woke up." Her petulant voice grated inside his skull like a blacksmith's rasp, as one sharp-nailed finger wriggled beneath the waistband of his breeches. "I've been sitting around this room for hours while you lay here snoring."

"Where . . . how long . . ." Sean winced, failing to finish the sentence as she nuzzled up against him, the potent stench of her perfume causing his stomach to heave as he tried to push himself up on an elbow.

"Not nigh long enough." She gave a low, throaty chuckle. "I spilled something all down your shirt and didn't want you to catch your death out in the cold, so I brought you here to my room about three hours ago. We started to . . ." She stopped, feigning a pout, then slipped the ribbon tie to her lacy peignoir, trailing the satin strand over the hair matting his chest. "You never used to fall asleep when we shared a bed."

"Shared a ... we ..." Sean jerked his head up, the sudden movement shooting shards of pain through him.

"Not yet. But I don't intend to wait any longer."

He turned his face away as her lips came at him, their wetness dampening his nose.

"'Lanna, quit," he grunted, reaching up a hand to try to force her away.

"Never." She caught his fingers in hers, arching her back like a cat as she rubbed his palm on her breast. "Remember how it was with us? You couldn't be in the same room with me without wanting to—"

Sean shoved himself upright, his groggy drunkenness fading as the reality he had tried to escape prized its way into his senses. He pushed her hand away. "Three years is a long time. Must've slipped my mind."

"Then I'll make you remember. Forget her. After what she did to us—"

"Us?" Sean slung his legs over the edge of the bed, kneading his throbbing forehead. "There is no *us*. You threw all that away."

"No. I told you why I went with Radcliffe. I had to. I thought you didn't want me! That you wouldn't believe the baby was yours."

"You never asked me, never tried. I would have taken that boy and loved him even if he had looked exactly like Colin Radcliffe."

"And would you have loved me?" Her scarlet lips quivered, the rich white lace about her neck skimming the curve of her chin as she clung to his arm. "My only sin was loving you too much to burden you with—"

Sean gave a vicious bark of laughter, batting her hand away. "You *burdened* me with enough guilt to turn my life into hell for three goddamned years. You'll forgive me if I wait until later to weep over your great sacrifice."

"Oh, yes, later. Isn't that how it always was with you? Too busy to listen, too stubborn to trouble yourself with *my* needs. If you knew what I've suffered ..."

Sean raised his head, his eyes raking the richly appointed room, the riot of gowns cast about in bright disarray, the mound of jewelry winking from the dressing table. "I can see exactly how much your needs have suffered."

"Do you think *things* mattered when I didn't have you? You know how much I loved you!"

"So much you slept with Colin Radcliffe days before we were to be married. And you let me believe you were dead while you were living with him, keeping my son from me. Tell me, did you enjoy elite society as much as you always thought you would?"

"I did it all for you!"

Sean snorted in disgust, levering himself to his feet, avoiding her fingers as they plucked at the unfamiliar linen shirt that hung open from his shoulders.

"Go ahead. Laugh. But if I hadn't gone to Col, I would never have discovered—" She stopped, hurrying to the dressing table to tug a square object from the lowest drawer. "Look." She thrust it at him. "I can give it all to you! This holds the key to everything we ever wanted. More wealth than you can imagine . . . a title . . ."

"What?" Sean stared down at the whimsical motif of unicorns and maidens that frolicked across the enameled box Alanna shoved into his hands.

"After the fire, I knocked this off the table in Col's study. Papers fell out. Papers that prove that you're his older brother. He—"

"What in the devil are you talking about? I—"

"No! Listen! As soon as I found it I started searching for you to tell you. We can have it . . . you and I . . . like it should have been from the beginning. *You* are Colin Radcliffe's brother, heir to the Radbury wealth."

"Brother?" Sean felt the blood surge to his head in an excruciating rush. "No . . . My mother was ra—" His mouth clamped shut over the word too painful to think or say. He shoved the box back at Alanna, but she folded her arms across her unfettered breasts, her mouth slack with an eagerness that repulsed him.

"It doesn't matter that she was just some light-skirt peasant wench. She was cunning enough to get a son off a nobleman—"

"Shut up!" Sean roared, the last webs of alcohol swept from his mind. Radcliffe . . . Radcliffe's father had been the one who raped . . . Sean wheeled, the feel of his own flesh revolting him as though some hideous disease had suddenly eaten it away. No. It couldn't be . . . couldn't . . .

"Sean, it's true!" Alanna clutched at his chest, licking the drops of saliva pooling at the corners of her lips. "That's why Col was trying to kill you! Just open—"

"No!" He cried the denial aloud, shoving past her to slam the box down onto the dressing table's littered top. Jeweled baubles scattered in all directions, but the horror Sean had felt at Alanna's claim paled to a scarlet haze as his gaze locked on a huge opal brooch, glowing like a devil's eye. His numb fingers reached into the tangle of silver and gold, grasping the circlet surrounding the stone. Leaves . . . delicately notched golden leaves.

Sean's hand clenched around it, the sharp, empty end of a broken leaf stem piercing his skin. "Where . . . where did you get this?"

"Why? I—"

"Tell me, damn it!"

Her eyes widened. "It was designed especially for me by Raoul LeVignon. I . . . I keep meaning to return it to him for repair. I lost one of the leaves . . ."

"Like this?" Sean snarled. He grabbed his coat where it hung on the bedpost, jamming his hand into the pocket to yank out the tiny bit of gold he had carried with him for months. He shoved the perfectly wrought leaf inches from Alanna's startled face.

"Yes . . ." Alanna stammered. "Exactly . . . Where on earth—"

"I found it ground into the ash and rubble outside of the Mac-Faddens' cottage the night Grace and her children burned to death."

"M . . . MacFaddens' . . ." She paled. "No! No! I just lost it somewhere. I didn't . . . wasn't . . ."

"You didn't what?"

"I didn't do anything! Col ordered the fire . . . he blocked the door and—" The pristine beauty in the face before him withered into a sly malevolence so palpable it cracked into his gut like a cudgel.

"You . . ." Sean rasped, grabbing Alanna's arms in a bone-crushing grip. "It was you—"

"Sean, it doesn't matter." Her fingers curled into his bare chest, stroking, pawing, the nails cutting deep. "We'll get the boy, go back—"

"You murdered Grace, Annie, the baby . . . *burned them alive.*"

"She was nothing, a filthy turf cutter. I had to get rid of her so we could be together."

"Why? Why the hell would you kill—"

"She would have ruined everything! She was going to tell you—"

"Tell me that you were alive?"

"She always hated me! She would have said horrible things, turned you against me. I—"

"The note. The night she died she left a note on the slate . . . but I couldn't read it. She was trying to warn me . . . and you *set her goddamned house on fire*."

Sean slammed Alanna back against the wall, rage searing through him as his fingers closed on her slender, pale neck, crushing . . . crushing. She arched back her head, her face washing blue, but no terror distorted her eyes. She laughed, a hellish, crazed laugh that gurgled from her throat, clawing through Sean's consciousness, forcing his fingers to freeze and loosen.

"Go ahead!" she croaked, her hair snaking around her like a harpy. "Kill me! Save me the pain! I'm dying anyway!"

"Dying . . ." Sean shoved her away from him, the marks from his fingers purpling on her flesh, the feel of her like filth on his palms.

She sagged against the wall moulding, the sight of her making gooseflesh prickle down Sean's neck. "Dying! Slowly, slowly. In a way far more terrible than even you could have managed. The pox. French pox!"

"Syphilis . . ." Even through the hate that consumed him, cold horror iced through Sean as he pictured her ravaged by disease, insanity in the years ahead as the pox ran its course . . .

"I even went to the witch-woman's for a cure . . . saw your blessed Grace. The witch said my face . . . my beautiful face will be ruined . . . I'll go mad . . . and there's no one . . . no way I can stop it . . ." She clawed at her own cheeks, raking gashes into the skin. "I'll be ugly . . ."

"You always were." Sean backed away from where she leaned like a nightmare vision, as twisted and hideous as the soul inside her. Why hadn't he seen the truth lurking behind the sugared words and siren's body. Hers was an evil more twisted, more dangerous than even Colin Radcliffe's, because it was layered under a facade of beauty—deadly nightshade in bloom. The vision of Meg that had haunted him earlier rose again in his mind —the violence he'd never seen in her before . . . Meg had known

338

what Alanna was, tried to shield him and Rory...

Rory—scars, screams, and terror when Alanna had tried to grab him... Sean wheeled.

"Wait!" He paused, then turned at Alanna's scream. Once exquisite eyes glassed wild purple, bulging in sockets black-ringed and sunken, as she spit the last of her venom. "I would have killed your brat, too, if I could have. I tried. Even when he was in my body I tried..." Her hands curled into talons and she tore at her nightgown. "But your cursed bastard clung inside me. Bloating my beautiful body. I wanted the midwife to cut him out of me. She couldn't... but you... you were a doctor... you could have..."

Sean grabbed his coat, then the unicorn box, not knowing why, not feeling...

"Go! Try to run back to your wife and brats. If you can find them! If you can ever find them—"

The shrieks of laughter and the shattering of glass that echoed after Sean sent chills down his spine. The fine linen shirt suddenly scraped against his skin. A man's shirt...

A terrifying sense of foreboding shot through him. Meaghan ... He bolted down the hall.

Night had stolen in like secrets whispered behind a druid's hand, dark secrets that maimed, destroyed, and taunted in the firelight as it played across the silence of the room, casting its glow upon the emptiness.

For hours after Alanna had left, Meaghan had knelt beside the big bed, trying to coax the terrified Rory from where he had hidden beneath the bedropes, trying, also, to banish her own fears. But at last, exhaustion borne of the sleepless night before had numbed her past bearing, and she had crawled up on Rory's rumpled little pallet, the poison threads Alanna had woven about the room entangling her even in the numbness of sleep.

Webs of faces and feelings snagged on the edges of nightmares that spun just within Meaghan's grasp, and she could see them—Rory cowering in the tiny space beneath the bed; Sean jerking away from her as though ʰer touch defiled him; Alanna coiling like some jewel-hued serpeแ around Sean's throat, laughing and laughing, a succubus spawned of hell. And shadows, shadows of devil wings gliding in patterns of firelight. Shadows...

Meaghan bolted awake, a scream frozen on her lips as the flowing blackness took on substance, blotting out the knotted wood of the cradle three feet away from her. Ceara. Someone was bending over...

"No! Who—" She leapt from the bed, her foot catching on a swath of coverlet trailing on the floor, pitching her forward toward the broad, midnight-cloaked figure. She crashed against it as the form wheeled, one gloved hand shooting out to clamp over her mouth in a smothering grip.

Raw terror raced through Meaghan's veins as another hand clenched brutally in her hair, yanking her head back against a hard shoulder, a low, satanic laugh rumbling beside her ear. The laugh she had heard in a hundred nightmares, yet different, shaded with madness.

She recoiled as a mass of gnarled flesh pressed against her cheek, tightening in a leer, and she could feel sharp edges of teeth cutting her flesh. "I wouldn't scream, my lovely, unless you want me to crush your brat's skull."

Dizzy, roiling horror sucked at Meaghan, threatening to drag her below churning waters of unconsciousness as her gaze strained back to be clutched by a hideous, deformed eye. The hand on her mouth fell away, knotting at her other temple to force her inches from the mangled ruin of Colin Radcliffe's face.

"Did you think you and that bastard's whelps could escape me, after you did *this?*"

Meaghan struggled against the binding hands, terrifyingly aware of the soft rasp of Rory's breathing from beneath the bed; Ceara, so tiny, so helpless in the cradle; and the barely leashed glitter of insanity in the features looming over her. "What... what do you want..."

"Want?" Radcliffe snarled. "I want you to pay, bitch, for what you did to me, you and your bastard lover. I want you and O'Fallon to suffer. And you will. Mark me. You will. Every nuance, every type of pain you can imagine. But not here, not now. No. I have a much more intriguing plan in mind. Get dressed. You and your brats are going on a little journey." Radcliffe shoved her toward the line of pegs where the clothes hung, then leaned over the cradle.

"Don't..." Meaghan pleaded, grabbing a pale blue dress, dodging to squeeze herself between him and Ceara as she jerked it over her head. Her body brushed against his, nearly pinned as she was in the small space between him and the edge of the cradle. "Don't hurt her..."

"Hurt her? Oh, I'll do worlds more than hurt her. Now where's the boy?"

"Rory?" Meaghan managed, praying desperately that the child would stay quiet and hidden. She could feel his terrified gaze on her as she met Radcliffe's stare with her own. "He's dead."

"Dead?" Radcliffe's eyes scanned the room, and though Meaghan kept her eyes fixed on Radcliffe's black hair, she could see in her mind Rory's toy animals scattered under the chair, his little coat hung on the peg beneath her shawl.

"He died of ship fever three weeks out of Ireland."

"But you have three beds." Radcliffe shifted around the room with a predatory gait. "You wouldn't, perchance, have hidden—"

"I just had the baby. Sean and I couldn't... couldn't..."

"O'Fallon couldn't keep his rutting in check so he stuck you on this pallet? How tender."

Meaghan jarred the cradle, the disbelief in the dark man's voice striking dread through her. Ceara came awake with a shriek, her earsplitting wails of protest causing Radcliffe to spin around.

One cloaked shoulder knocked Meaghan away, and before she could react, Radcliffe had swept up the babe. "Oh, no," he crooned evilly. "I remember your hell-cat ways. You'll travel much more obligingly, I'm sure, if I'm holding the brat. Especially when you know my fingers will be wrapped around its throat."

Meaghan's heart chilled at the sight of those gloved fingers curling about Ceara's tiny neck. "No! Don't! I'll go wherever you want me to, just—"

"Oh, I've no doubt you will. Get your shawl, and a blanket for the baby, my sweet. We're going to look for all the world like a happy little family going for a sleigh ride, and we wouldn't want the good citizens of Montreal to think me a neglectful father."

Meaghan grabbed her shawl, catching Rory's coat beneath it and holding it in the wool folds as she hurried to the cradle. Her pulse hammering in her chest, she let the little black garment slip to the floor behind the shield of her skirts, nudging it under the cradle bottom with her foot as she pulled out a heavy quilt. Radcliffe wrapped it around the baby, every move of his hands over the infant's fragile body calculated to draw out Meaghan's fear. "Now one last thing," he said. "It would be such a disappointment if poor Sean-o missed our little assignation." Radcliffe slipped an envelope from under his cloak and propped it upon the bright-colored coverlet on the big bed.

Meaghan cringed as she made out Rory's hand flattened on the floor inches from the toe of Radcliffe's boot. Radcliffe turned, his smile twisting the part of his face left unscarred. Meaghan raised her eyes, trying to hide the fear in them.

"If only I could see that purple-eyed whore's face when Sean comes trailing after you, it would all be perfect," Radcliffe gloated as he slid his fingers beneath the baby's blanket. "She thought she would best me, sneaking off to O'Fallon, ruining my plans. But her little ploy won't matter at all. Because I've got you. And I know O'Fallon will come after you, my lovely. Even if he follows me halfway through hell."

Icy bits of snow stung Sean's nostrils, burning in his lungs with the dread that swelled inside him at each pounding of his boots as he ran toward the broken-down building Meaghan had made a home.

God . . . dear God, what had he done? Whirling on her like some avenging angel, flaying her, long after the fight in her had died. He hadn't even listened, hadn't wanted to. He had only flung out his words like some twisted whip, lashing her and then storming from the room before she could explain . . . tell him what had obviously been eating at her happiness these past weeks. He thought of the secrets, the truths Alanna had used with such consummate skill, knowing he would not stop to think, that he would only hurt and wound. And now . . .

The echo of Alanna's crazed laughter in his head chilled his blood more certainly than the wind that whipped against him. It was as if she knew . . . knew something . . .

Sean banged open the outer door, not stopping even to slam it shut as he raced up the steps, flinging open the doorway to the tiny room.

Not so much as an ember glowed on the hearth, no sound breaking a stillness so thick and ominous it pressed down on his chest like a giant stone. "Maggie?" He let the unicorn box fall to the small table and fumbled for a candle, unable to see in the tendrils of dawn barely creeping through the ice-covered windows. The candle wick flared to life, throwing its feeble light across the empty cradle, empty beds.

Empty . . . Sean fought back a rising tide of alarm. Had she taken the babes and run, afraid he would go back to Alanna? Afraid of Alanna's cruelty, her cunning? Afraid of his own cursed pride? Or had something, someone . . .

"Mama?" The tiny, quavering voice made Sean start, then wheel, as a muffled little sob came from the direction of the beds. He dropped to his knees, looking under the sagging mattress to see the cowering form of his son.

"Rory! What—" Taking the child by the elbows, Sean drew him from beneath the bedropes, cuddling the shivering boy in his arms.

"C-cold."

Sean grabbed up the coverlet to wrap around the boy. A piece of paper tangled in the bright cloth crumpling between them. "Rory, where's your Mama? Ceara?"

"Man."

Sean swallowed, trying to stem his panic as he stroked the child's dark hair. "What man? Tell me . . ."

Rory raised his head, his blue eyes wide with terror as his little hand touched Sean's cheek. "Face man."

Face man . . . Sean's gaze locked on the crumpled piece of paper. The image of an oil lamp shattering and flames searing flesh burned in his mind. *Face man* . . . God . . . God, no—

Thirty-Three

Sean hunkered down in the copse of winter-bared maples, peering through narrowed eyes at the dilapidated cottage perched precariously along the deserted bend at the St. Lawrence River. Radcliffe had chosen his lair with the canny brilliance of a wounded panther. Chunks of ice, broken away in the recent warm snap, jutted like jagged teeth at the rim of the shore, as though waiting to tear out the thick posts supporting the sagging wooden structure above them, to swallow any man foolish enough to challenge the river's treacherous expanse.

The short length of pier, linking the hut with the snow-covered riverbank, was gap-toothed as an old crone's smile, its boards splintered and hanging down, frozen into the ice below. Sean stared at the grimy window, feeling Radcliffe's eyes searching the trees, almost hearing the smug hiss of the Englishman's laughter as he waited. God, what twisted pleasure the sonofabitch would take, knowing the agony of indecision that awaited his adversary, the hopelessness of crossing the pier unseen, the deadly menace of the section of river that surrounded it.

Try anything stupid and your woman will beg for death . . . the note had said. And yet, there were no delusions in Sean's mind about what would happen to Meg and the baby even if he walked into Radcliffe's net empty-handed to exchange his life for theirs as the message ordered. Radcliffe wanted them dead. *All* dead. Thank God Meaghan had been able to keep Rory safe.

Sean fingered the butt of the pistol shoved inside his belt. Damn! In the time he had ridden since leaving the child with Father Tyson, he had plotted a dozen ways to defeat Radcliffe

343

and free Meg, but now, staring into the jaws of Radcliffe's unsprung trap, he knew she was at his mercy...

No. Radcliffe and his sire had stolen their last from those Sean O'Fallon loved. There had to be a chance... If he could somehow cross around to the rear of the hut... Sean backed stealthily into the sparse covering the trees offered, making his way to the curve of shore not visible from the cottage's window. Stiff breezes sweeping down from the slope of Mount Royal had left segments of the river free of snow, baring ice, so clear in some places, Sean could see the currents of water beneath it, black, perilous, coursing toward the Atlantic below a tracery of tiny cracks and faults in the hardened surface. One false move, one slip...

Sean clenched his fists. Damn it, he wouldn't fall. He couldn't. But even now his legs felt rubbery from the residue of whiskey still in his veins, and the waves of shock still yanked at his nerves from his encounter with Alanna.

The heel of Sean's boot dug into the slick surface with a crunching sound as he stepped from the snowy bank, each grating of hard leather on ice making him grit his teeth. Every muscle in his body was coiled, taut, ready to try to catch himself if the ice should break and pitch him into the frigid water. His eyes fastened on the dangerous surface before him, seeing its color and consistency change subtly as he neared the hut, the layer thinning, cracks widening.

Hold, damn you, hold. His jaw knotted as he pushed forward. Ten yards from the wooden posts, three, two... A scraping noise from the hut made him jerk his head up.

Crraack! The sound of the ice splitting was like musket fire as he felt the horrible sensation of the surface giving way beneath him. He threw his body forward, making a desperate grab for the splintered rail, clinging to it as tiny spikes of wood drove deep into his palms, searing-cold water pouring into the top of his boot.

Locking one arm around the rail, he struggled to drag himself up.

"No, Sean! Run!" The scream from behind the gapped boards was cut off midway, the sudden silence shattered by a baby's shrieks. Fear bolted down his spine.

"Run, Sean, run!" The high, mocking laugh rasped on the air.

Sean scrambled to his feet, holding the gun in his hand as he ran around the narrow walkway to the door. "Damn it, don't hurt her! Don't—"

He slammed the portal open, then froze, as his gaze swept the room. A long iron poker was buried in the fire that blazed on the crude hearth inches from Ceara's blanket, sunlight slashing through the gaps in the wallboards to glint blue along the knife Radcliffe pressed against Meaghan's throat. The Englishman gave an evil chuckle, tightening his pressure on the hilt until a tiny bead of blood welled along the blade's edge. Sean could see Meaghan's rope-bound hands knot into fists. "Drop the gun, O'Fallon, or I'll slit her throat . . ."

"No, damn it! Don't!"

"Don't what?"

"Don't cut her. The gun's down. Down."

"Sean, no." Meaghan's choked cry tore at him, her wide brown eyes catching his as he held out the pistol, tossing it to the floor. He held up his empty hands, fear twisting in his gut at the strange, glazed look on Radcliffe's scarred face. Insane . . . God, the man was insane . . .

"It's down. Let her go. I'm the one you want dead."

"Dead?" Radcliffe cackled. Sean's scalp prickled at the sound. "Death is too quick. Too easy. I want you to live, a long, long time. Time to suffer like I have. Suffer over what I've done to your woman and child. Suffer . . ." Sean started forward, then checked himself as Radcliffe jerked Meaghan's hair. "Go ahead. Try it," Radcliffe challenged. "Hear her throat gurgling with blood, watch her die."

The muscles in Sean's chest felt ready to snap, as he fought desperately to leash the fury searing like acid through his body. He had to keep a clear head, for Meg, for the baby, and wait for an opening. Rage . . . rage would only feed Radcliffe's madness.

"Let her go." Voice like silken steel, Sean gave the command, his lips stiff with deadly control, his gaze pinning Radcliffe with a level stare.

"No! You've cheated me too many times. This time . . . this time it's going to be different, O'Fallon. You're going to pay."

"You want me to pay? Then quit cowering behind Meaghan like some craven dog. Try to kill me, Radcliffe. Here. Now."

"No . . . no . . . no one is going to die. I told you . . ." Radcliffe's good eye rolled in its socket, white-ringed, horrible. "They're not going to die, but you'll wish they had." The Englishman ran the point of his knife down to Meaghan's breast, pricking at the thin cloth that covered it. Sean's jaw clenched, as he battled the urge to hurl himself at Radcliffe, and the scarred face twisted with a cunning sneer.

"You don't like that, do you, O'Fallon? Me, touching your woman? You couldn't even bear the thought of me with that slut Alanna, when she was begging for me between her thighs. God, how we laughed at you when you thought her dead. But after I was scarred . . . after . . ."

"She laughed at *you* then, didn't she? Ran back to me." Sean flung out the taunt, trying to draw Radcliffe's fury on himself as he saw Radcliffe's hand tighten convulsively on the knife's hilt. "As though I'd take your cast-offs."

"Bitch . . . should have killed her . . ." The scarred hand knotted in Meaghan's hair. A shaft of terror iced through Sean, and for an instant he thought that the crazed man would slash the blade home, but Radcliffe shook his head, as if trying to clear the fog of insanity hazing his mind.

His malevolent gaze rested on Meaghan with the snarling hunger of a famished wolf. "I can't reach her, now. But I have you . . . you . . . don't I . . . have O'Fallon . . . your brat . . ." Sean flinched, as Radcliffe scraped the knife back up to Meaghan's throat. "Now, witch, you do exactly what I say, or I'll kick your brat into the fire. Pick the whelp up. Slow. Real slow."

"No . . ." Sean could hear the shallow gasps of Meaghan's breath beneath the silvery blade as she whispered, "please, don't . . ."

"Pick it up!"

She bent at the knees, the knife skating a little way up her neck as she awkwardly scooped the squirming baby from the floor, trying desperately to pull the infant against the shelter of her body, to get away. With lightning swiftness, Radcliffe whipped the blade from in front of her, snatching the child, and shoving Meaghan to the floor in one fluid movement that sent her crashing into Sean. Sean felt the rotting floorboards bend, saw slits of gray ice in the spaces between them as they threatened to splinter.

With a satanic laugh Radcliffe ripped the blanket away from the infant, her body incredibly tiny and fragile in the grip of his hands.

"No!" Sean caught Meaghan's arms, as she lunged toward the baby.

"Let me go!" Her cries wrenched like a lance inside Sean, her eyes wild as she screamed at Radcliffe. "I'll kill you if you hurt her! I'll—"

"Stop it, Meg!" Sean yanked her against his chest, crushing her against him as she clawed, struggling to get free. "You'll send Ceara right through the floor!"

"That's it, O'Fallon, tame your whore, or I might be tempted..." Radcliffe's eyes flicked from the stone hearth to Ceara.

"No! You don't want to kill her, remember... Meg will do what you want."

"Ah... what I want... Do you know how many hours I've been planning this? Every time I've looked in a mirror... seen some woman cringe at the sight of me. Even the whores..." Radcliffe's lips curled back from his teeth. He kicked some ropes toward them. "Tell your doxy to tie you up. Tight."

"Meaghan." Sean gripped her, holding her inches from him as she turned her ravaged face to his.

"No! I—"

"Maggie, do what he says." He shook her. She grew still, eyes flashing innocence and rage. Sean hated himself for the torment he had caused her in the hours he had been with Alanna, hated himself for the stubborn pride that had given Radcliffe time enough to implement his plan.

"Go on, Maggie." His voice was gentle... more so than with any love words he had ever whispered to her, and Meaghan drew from his strength.

"Yes, do what he says, *Maggie*." Radcliffe cackled.

Her bound hands shaking, she took the coarse hemp in her fingers, winding it around his wrists, managing the knot by pulling the lengths with her teeth.

"Now, tether the other end to that post." Radcliffe jerked his head toward a thick pole supporting the roof. "We want our prisoner to have just enough freedom to make this interesting."

Meaghan knotted the four-foot piece of hemp around the length of wood, as Sean faced Radcliffe, his feet spraddled wide, head thrown back, in the taut stance of a defiant stallion. But now, now there was something else in his cerulean eyes as they bored into hers, an intensity, as though he expected her to see what was in his mind. His gaze flickered to the floor, back to hers, to the floor, but he was not looking at Ceara . . .

"Tighter!" Meaghan started, almost dropping the strand of rope at Radcliffe's bark. She felt Sean's hands tense beneath her fingers, as though in frustration.

"I said tighter, witch!" Radcliffe yanked on the rope, setting the knot. "Want him to have fighting room . . . but not enough . . . not enough to break loose once I—"

"Once you show what a coward you are?" Sean goaded. "Fight me like a man."

Radcliffe's eyes narrowed to slits. "I'm not a man at all, not since your little witch finished with me in Ireland. But then, by the time I'm finished with her, that won't matter. Even you won't be able to look at her without retching."

"You sonofabitch! You touch her—" Sean's muscles knotted, his bonds tearing at wrists still marred from Radcliffe's shackles, and Meaghan could see the thin veneer of his control fraying to a thread. "Put the baby down and come kill me if you dare!"

"Oh, I'll put the baby down," Radcliffe chuckled, walking with the baby to the rotted segment of floor, testing the weak boards with one foot. The wood canted dangerously. He smiled. "Maybe we should see just how much this wood will hold." The Englishman edged Ceara onto the treacherous flooring.

"No!" Meaghan took a running step toward the baby, but Radcliffe grabbed Meaghan by the wrist, slamming her into the wall as he shoved the child far out onto the rotted boards. Terror stabbed through Meaghan as the wood bent, the gaps widening. She reached out, futilely, hopelessly, as the babe began to cry.

"You think your arms are long enough to risk it? Or will your weight send both you and the brat crashing down onto the ice? Ask your lover what it's like down there. The ice splitting, the water . . . Maybe I should just . . ."

"No!" Meaghan clutched Radcliffe's wrist, her teeth bared as he wheeled on her.

"You want your whelp to live? Then you do as I tell you. Sit." Radcliffe's nails dug into Meaghan's wrist as he forced her down onto a lopsided bench beside the hearth. Yanking on the ropes binding her hands, he pulled them up to run her knuckles over her cheek. "Smooth . . . soft . . . remember how it feels against your skin, O'Fallon?" Radcliffe turned. There was a scraping of iron and wood, a hiss of flaming logs crumbling to embers. "We'll see how it feels after . . ."

Sean's face went ashen and Meaghan knew what Radcliffe held, even before he raised the glowing tip of the poker into her line of vision. The sound of Sean's voice—goading, baiting—was threaded with tendrils of panic, but the insults he was flinging at Radcliffe were lost on Meaghan as her chest constricted with terror.

"Fire . . ." She heard Radcliffe hiss like the angels of hell as he skimmed the white-hot point so close to her face that the heat radiating from the iron singed her nostrils. "You know its power well, don't you, my sweet? How it can maim and scar . . . And the pain, greater than any you could imagine . . ."

Meaghan flinched and heard Sean jerk forward as Radcliffe jabbed with the poker, but instead of shoving it against her face, he drove it down, ramming its point into a rot-softened spot in the floor. Sick horror choked her as she watched the board smoulder and blacken, acrid smoke snaking from the wood. His breath slithered hot across her face as he yanked his weapon free, his voice mesmerizing, hypnotic.

"Now, my little peasant whore, I'll teach you and your bastard lover the cost of trifling with those of noble blood . . ." Meaghan shut her eyes as she felt the heat of the poker burn at her lashes, her temple, waiting for the agony of her skin searing.

"Noble blood like mine? That cursed Radcliffe filth that taints my veins as well as yours?" Sean's harsh voice shattered the hellish aura that had engulfed both her and Radcliffe. She heard air hiss between Radcliffe's clenched teeth, saw him wheel.

Sean's teeth gleamed white and feral, the cerulean shards of his eyes spitting contempt, and Meaghan could see in him the primal fury of a wolf protecting its mate, sensed, even in her confusion, that he was parrying, feinting, with verbal weapons he was unsure of, trying to draw Radcliffe's rage onto himself.

"That's right, *brother*," he spat. "I know why you're trying so hard to kill me. It was Alanna's parting gift."

"That witch! She lied!" Radcliffe's face contorted, beads of drool slipping from the corner of his mouth. "You're nothing but some Irish harlot's—"

"No. For once Alanna told the truth. She gave me the box with the unicorns . . ."

"That box was destroyed in the fire! She told me . . . that lying whore! She . . ."

"Made a fool of you again." Sean cut in with a derisive laugh. "Your *noble blood!* I'd as soon open my own veins as know that my body is tainted with the poison of your father."

"Father . . . the swine! Betrayed me for some peasant slut . . . Tried to take it away. But it's mine, O'Fallon! Mine! You'll never take it—" The insane babble chilled Meaghan's soul, as Radcliffe lunged toward Sean. Sean leapt aside, the white-hot poker slashing the side of his coat, but the rope that tethered him to the pole gave him little room to escape Radcliffe's crazed blows. He threw up his bound hands, trying to fend off the vicious arcs of Radcliffe's weapon, leaping and dodging.

Sean's boot caught on a splintered board. She heard it crack, saw him falter, Radcliffe bearing down on him with a glaze of triumph on his face. The poker lashed toward Sean's head. Meaghan hurled herself at Radcliffe, knocking him to the floor, the poker glancing off Sean's shoulder, skidding from the Englishman's hands to clatter to the floor.

Ceara screeched at the noise, and Meaghan wanted to scream with the same unbridled terror as Radcliffe grasped a handful of her skirt, death in his scarred face. He yanked her toward him, slamming his fist into her jaw.

"Bitch! I'll kill you for that!"

"No! Damn you!" Sean roared as she reeled back, a cry of pain escaping her as she struck the floor. She rolled and kicked, her hands curled in claws, fighting Radcliffe like the hell-cat he had named her as he rained blows on her head, her shoulders. Sean swore savagely. He had to reach . . . his eyes fastened on the poker, burning the wood inches from his boot. The ropes . . . He jammed his wrists down onto the red-hot iron, searing the bonds, not feeling his flesh being branded, burning with the coarse hemp that held him. He saw and heard only Meaghan and Radcliffe.

With a mighty yank, Sean tore the ropes free, snatching up the weapon with a scream of rage as he slammed Radcliffe away from Meaghan. The flooring listed dangerously, as Radcliffe struck it, but in an instant, the Englishman gained his feet, circling Sean like a rabid cur, caring only for the kill.

Ceara's wails came sharper, more piercing, tearing Meaghan's gaze from the battle before her to where the baby lay. Cracks wide as three fingers cut into the flannel nightgown covering the child's back, the rough edges grating, widening with each crashing lunge of the two men in death-grips.

"God . . . please no!" Meaghan whispered the words, fear bolting to the tips of her fingers as Ceara's tiny heels beat on the slanting wood, her little arms flailing as she screamed. Praying, pleading, Meaghan edged toward her, the thump of boot heels, the swish of the iron rod slicing air lost on her as she inched across the creaking floor.

She heard the clatter of iron on stone and glimpsed somewhere in the back of her consciousness a glint of silver from a small object four feet away.

"Meaghan, the gun!" Her head snapped up at Sean's cry, the pistol registering in her mind, as she saw Radcliffe dive toward it, but her panic had nothing to do with the weapon. Ceara . . . if he fell on the boards . . . With a desperate leap she threw herself toward him, slamming him back . . . away from the babe. The boards beneath them as they struck the far wall splintered with a horrible crack.

She felt herself falling, falling, Radcliffe's arms and legs striking hers. Blazing pain shot through her shoulder as she hit the ice, freezing water drenching her face, the air bursting in her lungs as the swift current dragged at her skirts. She kicked frantically, unable to use her tied hands as Radcliffe clutched at her, dragging her farther under. Jagged chunks of ice cut her like shards of glass, the frigid river numbing her straining muscles as it fought to suck her beneath its hard crust.

She saw swirling images of Sean's face, of Ceara and Rory, as the fiery-cold water yanked her down in its deadly fist, its smothering wetness blinding her, bursting her lungs. God . . . sweet God, she was going to die . . .

Thirty-Four

Desperately Meaghan gave one last mighty kick upward, her mouth opening reflexively, taking in gulps of water instead of life-giving oxygen. And then she felt hands dragging her up, lifting her. A blast of wind struck her face as it broke the river's surface, the air searing the raw lining of her lungs as she choked in great gasps of its coldness.

"Sean . . ." She clung to his arms as he hauled her close, onto a solid plane of ice.

"Maggie . . ." The agony in his voice as he crushed her to him penetrated the haze of panic that was smothering her. "God, Meg . . ."

Sean hurried his face in her wet hair as she clung to him, her whole body shaking, her clothes already stiffening as the water in them started to freeze. "Have to get you warm." She felt him lay her gently beside him, heard the impatient jerk of his fingers freeing the buttons of his coat, stripping it off.

But screams, hideous shrieks shattered the air.

Sean raised his eyes to the deadly black hole broken in the icy surface, his gaze arrested by another head breaking water. Radcliffe. Twisted features washed blue, the malevolent dark eye wide with horror, voice pleading in gasps as the river fought to claim him. "Help me! O'Fallon!"

Rage and hatred welled inside Sean as Radcliffe's hand stretched toward him, the fingers spread wide, grasping, begging for a mercy the Englishman had never shown. And Sean wanted to strike the hand, to shove it into the hell it deserved. He wanted to . . .

"Damn you!" Sean swore, straining his own hand toward Radcliffe, not knowing why, hating himself. "Grab on! Grab—" The edge of ice crumbled a little as Radcliffe's freezing cold fingers skimmed Sean's, clawing as he fought to get a grip on the. "Hold on!" Sean grated.

"Help me—" The terror clutching Radcliffe jolted from his frigid palm through Sean's, as Sean felt the fingers slip, the river pulling, tugging.

"Hold on, damn you!" Sean screamed as the black water closed over Radcliffe's face. With all his strength Sean fought to regain a grip, the wild eye and scarred features a grisly mask of horror staring through the patch of clear ice as the current pulled Radcliffe under.

"No!" Sean cried, feeling his fingers snap free. He plunged his arm into the water, groping frantically for the solid mass of Radcliffe, but the tortured face was sucked down . . . down . . . disappearing. The savage joy Sean had always thought to feel at the Englishman's death was strangely absent. A hollow, sick feeling gripped his stomach, the sight of the fear-twisted features still branded in his mind.

"Sean . . ." The faint sound of Meaghan's voice snapped him from his horrified fascination, and he turned. The sight of her was more terrifying than even Radcliffe's death. All traces of rose had been driven from her cheeks, the blue cast across her pinched features sending a shaft of fear through him as he stroked back the freezing strands of her hair. Purple blotches from Radcliffe's fists stood out sharply on the delicate line of her jaw, her lips stiff and swollen as they forced his name through chattering teeth. "Sean . . ."

"I'm here, love. Here." He scooped his arms under her, straining against the weight of her water-soaked clothing to lift her against his chest, levering himself to his feet to start carefully toward the pier. The sound of the ice crunching beneath his boots grated in his head with the rasp of her labored breathing as he picked his way across the slippery surface with an instinct born of desperation. Cold . . . God, she was so cold . . . Fighting to leash the tremor of fear in his own voice, he crushed her against him, willing the strength and warmth of his body into hers. "We have to get you to the fire, Meg. Get you warm."

"No . . . Ceara . . . baby . . ."

"She's safe. Mad as hell . . ." His voice caught in his throat, the lump in its center barely allowing words to pass. "But safe."

"Rory?"

Sean swallowed, feeling as if a rope was tightening around his neck, cutting off words and breath. "Fine."

Her dark eyes fluttered closed, then opened. "He was . . . so scared . . . so little. Didn't want to leave him . . ."

"I know. Rest, now. Don't try to talk."

"Have to. Sorry . . . meant to tell you about Alanna . . . wanted to . . . but couldn't . . . Loved you . . . afraid . . ."

"No . . ." His foot touched the shore, snow burying its polished black leather as Meaghan's fingers feathered up to touch his lips, chin. "No . . . you'll never know . . . how much . . . I love you . . ."

"Meg . . ." The ragged cry tore from Sean's throat as he stumbled toward the hut, the coldness of her flesh, nestled so trustingly against him, numbing his skin. He felt her lips move against his beard-roughened jaw.

"Wanted . . . wanted to make you happy . . ."

Fear, guilt, love balled in Sean chest, crushing him until his whole being ached with it. "You have, Meg. You have. I'm going to take care of you . . . You're going to get well and strong . . ."

The tiniest of smiles touched the pale curve of her lips. Her gold-tipped lashes drifted to the crest of her wax-pale cheeks as her hand fell limp.

"Meaghan?" Her name was ripped from Sean's very soul, the rickety boards of the pier wavering before his eyes. Hot tears spilled down his face, splashing her cheeks. "Maggie, I'm sorry . . . I'll be all right . . . I love you, Meg . . . love you . . ."

Meaghan settled the sleeping Ceara into the carved-wood cradle in the hearth corner, then turned to peer out into the walled courtyard below, where Rory frolicked with a passel of apple-cheeked imps in the drifts outside. The last snows of winter iced the eaves of the city, turning it into a fairyland. The coldness sweeping in from the St. Lawrence River brought only squeals of laughter as little ones nipped up mittenfuls of the sun-sparkled whiteness to slip into each other's coat collars.

Watching their antics, Meaghan found it hard to imagine that glittery world as a dangerous trap, to imagine the sweep of icy St. Lawrence visible over the low stone wall as anything but a ballroom for skate-bladed dancers decked in rich Canadian furs.

Yet for all its apparent innocence, Meaghan knew . . . knew the treachery that could lurk beneath . . . and the dead . . .

She tore her eyes away from the silver-sheened river, tying a sky-shaded ribbon round the mass of her freshly washed hair with fingers still unsteady, the ends of the fine silk ribbon brushing the back of her neck, as soft and warm as spring. Warm . . . God, she had never thought she would get warm . . .

The memory of the trip to the city in Radcliffe's sleigh, Sean carrying her up into the cozy rubblestone house he had arranged for in what seemed a lifetime ago, remained even a week later a vague mist of pain and cold, waves of terror rippling out from the hazy reaches of unconsciousness. The first thing she had truly been cognizant of had been the pain, an agony of sensation returning to her numbed limbs that had knifed through her with a fierceness that had set her screaming.

Sean had held her as she thrashed amid mounds of down-soft coverlets, soothing her with the sweetest words while he rubbed her tortured flesh with hands, warm, strong, and sure as the love she bore him, until at last she had slipped into exhausted, nightmare-racked sleep.

He had never left her alone, always staying beside her, curling her in the circle of his arms to wake her gently and comfort her when the horror began. Only later, when he had banished the demons that haunted her, had she been able to see that he was beset by a torment of his own. And each day as the ravages of her near-drowning faded, the coils of tension binding Sean had cut him more savagely.

Meaghan trailed her fingertip over the box sitting on the escritoire beneath the window, feeling the elegant smoothness of the wood, the tiny bumps of inlay. The box. Alanna's parting gift, Sean had told Radcliffe that last day at the river. Orr had it been the woman's curse?

Meaghan shivered at the thought of the ebony-tressed beauty, Alanna's evil striking deeper fear through her veins than even Radcliffe's had as she stared at the garlanded unicorns and dainty carved maids that guarded the unknown secrets.

Secrets of the past that had all but destroyed Sean the child and that had embittered the man. Or were they lies, more lies concocted in Alanna's diabolical mind?

Meaghan let her hand fall away from the silky wood. Sean had entertained her with books from the shelves in the corner of the room, wove legends and myths he knew from far-off lands to distract her during the tedious hours she had lain in bed. But when he had told her the story of a woman named Pandora, the lilting quality in his voice had vanished, and he had stared in brooding silence across the room to where the box sat, knowing as an ancient sage.

He had told Meaghan that every evil known to man had spilled from the Greek woman's box, yet what in Sean's father's past could be more horrible than what Sean already believed to be true?

Meaghan fingered the filigreed key. Ghosts, shadows of the past, still crept on velvet wings around them both.

"Meg." She turned at the soft caress of her name from Sean's lips to find him in the open door, his hair winter-blown, tousled by the wind, his face oddly still. The blue silk of his cravat skimmed the hard line of his jaw, and in his eyes . . .

A stirring of unease curled in Meaghan's stomach. "Sean . . . what . . . what is it?"

She padded to where he stood, slipping her arms beneath his open greatcoat to ease it off, feeling the heat of him through her night rail, the flat muscles of his chest against her face. His arms closed convulsively around her. "It's over, Meg. Really over."

"What?"

"Alanna—she . . ." Sean felt Meaghan tense against him at the name. He turned her gaze up to his, cupping her cheeks in his hands. An aching stab of tenderness pierced through him as he looked down into her face beneath the wide band of silk, her skin brushed again with peachy gold, her eyes, though robbed of some of their starry innocence, warm with a strength and courage that humbled him. "No, love, don't. Alanna can't hurt anyone anymore."

"She . . . she's gone?"

"I went to the place she was staying, to make certain . . . she couldn't hurt you, or Rory. Didn't even know what I was going to do when I found her. Just knew I had to . . . to do something . . . But when I got there . . ." Sean feathered his fingertips beneath Meaghan's eyelids, taking in the silky, fragile feel of her. "That day I left you she trailed me to every whiskey bottle in Montreal. I found proof that *she* murdered Grace and the little ones. She burned them alive, but she gave their deaths no more thought than she would have if she had crushed a flower beneath her heel. It was like . . . like I'd never seen Alanna before. Or maybe, after loving you, I was seeing her for the first time. After I left, she . . . she flew into a rage, breaking things, tearing apart the room. They . . . they took her away."

"Away?"

"To an asylum, Meg. She'd gone mad." The hackles at the back of Sean's neck prickled as he remembered the scene in the room the proprietor had closed off, not knowing what to do with the riches strewn about, afraid of reprisals from whatever powerful people the madwoman was linked to.

Jagged bits of glass had been everywhere, darkened with flecks of dried blood, great jewels winking from the spattered carpet like evil eyes, and the story the people had told had chilled Sean's blood. The story of the pretty red-haired chambermaid who had happened in to bring Alanna's breakfast, and had nearly been murdered by the crazed beauty. It had taken three passing men to pull her away and bind her, and a doctor had spent the better part of an hour stitching up the slashes Alanna had inflicted upon the girl with the knifelike shards.

But he couldn't tell Meaghan about the horrible scene, distress her with the knowledge that one last innocent had fallen under Alanna's malevolent claws. Sean skimmed the thick fringe of Meaghan's lashes with the tips of his thumbs, seeing in her upturned face a watching . . . a waiting. That same aching doubt he had seen a hundred times before. And it hurt him, more deeply than anything he had suffered at Alanna's hands, to see the uncertainty still in those eyes that had shed so many tears because of him.

"So she's gone," Meaghan said, the corners of her lips trembling. Sean bent his head, brushing their petal-softness with his mouth.

"She was gone a long time ago, Maggie. Out of my heart. From that first day I held you on that hillside, felt you beneath me, so brave and defiant, I knew I'd love you. But it hurt." His voice broke, and Meaghan felt a surge of joy at the myriad emotions in his cerulean eyes. Her own stung with the sweetness of his loving, his pain.

"I fought so damn hard," he choked. "But no matter how I tried to run, all I could see was your face when I made love to you, your smile as you held my son."

"I'm sor—" Sean hushed her with a finger on her lips.

"No, Meg. Never sorry. You wiped out the stain of my bastardy, my bitterness . . . You gave me more than love. You gave me live. No more shadows between us . . ."

A ray of sunlight streaming through the window touched the silvered tip of a unicorn's horn, sparkling on the box where it sat. Meaghan took Sean's long, bronzed fingers in hers, laying them gently on the richly inlaid wood. "Only one shadow," she said softly.

"I don't want—"

"Secrets almost destroyed us, Sean. No more . . ."

His Adam's apple bobbed in his throat, the corded muscles of his neck standing out against his skin as he raised his other hand to close around the wood. But when he sank into the huge leather chair beside the fireplace, he reached out to draw Meaghan down with him.

She curled onto the hearth-warmed rug, leaning against his ruggedly muscled thigh, her arms encircling his breech-clad claves. turning the key, he slipped open the top, its release causing the yellowed pages beneath it to crackle. With shaking hands, he picked up the papers, scanning the bold scrawl and the delicate script.

Meaghan watched as the lines carved in Sean's face slowly faded, softened, the grim set of his mouth gentling to wonder. "Meg . . . my mother . . ." his voice trailed silent, as he raised his eyes to hers, taking up her hand to fold her fingers around the crumbling pages. And then they, together, read the lines of ink, so faded they seemed almost whispers, whispers of another age, another life, another love.

Through the words, Meaghan could see the beautiful dark-haired girl in the miniature, Sean's dashing nobleman father, their love so great they hurled away a fortune to hold it, marrying in defiance of the cruel and proud Duke of Radbury. She could feel their joy in the child born of their love, the babe being carried about in front of his father's saddle, being cherished by his mother. And she knew the anguish in Jonathan Radcliffe as he had sailed for England alone to face the enraged duke.

And then the news that must have destroyed Sean's mother, the newspaper clipping regarding the grand society wedding of Lord Jonathan Radcliffe to heiress Letitia Colins.

"He . . . he took another wife?" Meaghan looked up to Sean's face, expecting to see a hardening, a renewal of bitterness at the desertion of his father, but instead she saw only sadness and understanding.

The last page lay in his fingers, the masculine scrawl stained by tears shed a lifetime ago. Sean looked into her eyes. "The duke was going to have us killed, my mother and me, unless my father did his will. Radbury held such power, there was no way my father could have fought—"

"You fought it." Meaghan wished back the words the moment they had left her mouth, not wanting her doubts to destroy the new peace she sensed in Sean, yet not understanding . . .

"My father . . . I think he tried, but . . ." There was a faraway look in Sean's face, as though he were seeing the face of the man who had sired him, and somehow knew. "This last letter says he was coming back to us, begs my mother to understand."

"Then . . . then you're no bastard."

"No. This proves it is mine by rights, the title and the lands." His eyes flicked down to the box, then back to Meaghan's. "We could have it all, Maggie. Everything you could ever want, wealth, position, fine clothes, carriages. Everything I've ever wanted to give you.", She felt the cerulean depths bore into her with an intensity that searched her very soul. "But I can't take it. I'm going to contact this man Strathmore, whom the letter talks about, have the lands I can dispose of divided between the tenants. The monies from the rest can be dispatched for their good. I'll have nothing of the name that murdered my father and turned my mother out into the world alone, to poverty and ridicule."

He paused, and she knew he was watching her, waiting. "The . . . the happiest days of my life were spent in a single room with rags in the windows," she said gently.

"Meg . . ." He stroked back the riot of red-gold curls that framed her cheeks, and the love shining from the soft brown of her eyes knotted in his throat. "I'll make a good life for you in America. I swear it."

"I have everything I ever wanted, right here." She laid her lips against his knee, then tipped her face up. Cerulean eyes were bright with misted tears, and she soothed her fingertips over the planes of the face she loved.

Sean caught her hand in his, pressing his lips deep into the center of her palm. "Maggie . . . this box . . . the letter says my father had it made especially to give my mother when he found her. That he loved . . . loved her more than . . ." Sean's voice caught, ragged edged, and he laid Meaghan's fingers on the smooth wood. "He died before he could find her, but I want you . . ."

The words trailed off, broken, as he held out the box to her, the box that had borne the gift of his parents' love, and she knew what was in his heart.

With hands that trembled she took the box, her fingers striking a tiny steel lever. Tears of joy and love flowed freely down her cheeks as the strains of *Eileen Aroon* tinkled through the room—her father's song, the song of the fiddle.

She lifted tear-bright eyes to Sean's.

"For all you have given me, Maggie," he whispered. Squeals of laughter from the yard outside and the stirrings of Ceara in her cradle blended with the sweetly haunting melody as Sean's lips sought hers. "For all you have given me."